What U People Think?

VEDASHREE KHAMBETE-SHARMA

CORVUS

Published in trade paperback in Great Britain in 2024
by Corvus, an imprint of Atlantic Books Ltd

1 3 5 7 9 8 6 4 2

A CIP catalogue record for this book is available from the British Library.

Trade Paperback ISBN: 978 1 80546 162 3
E-book ISBN: 978 1 80546 163 0

Printed in Great Britain by CPI Group (UK) Ltd, Croydon CR0 4YY

Corvus
An imprint of Atlantic Books Ltd
Ormond House
26–27 Boswell Street
London
WC1N 3JZ

www.atlantic-books.co.uk

MIX
Paper | Supporting
responsible forestry
FSC
www.fsc.org
FSC® C171272

For Aai.

For Aai.

Dear reader,

This book contains footnotes.

If you have been traumatised before by footnotes in academic textbooks, rest assured that these footnotes bear no resemblance to those ones.

If you are not Maharashtrian, read the footnotes for useful insights into Maharashtrian language, customs and eccentricities.

If you *are* Maharashtrian and think you already know everything there is to know about Maharashtrian language, customs and eccentricities, read them for some banging sociocultural commentary.

Or, you know, don't. It's a free country.

'It is always incomprehensible to a man that a woman should ever refuse an offer of marriage. A man always imagines a woman to be ready for any body who asks her.'

—*Jane Austen, Emma*

'Damme sir, it is your duty to get married. You can't always be living for pleasure!'

—*Oscar Wilde, An Ideal Husband*

ONE

Whenhen Marathi-speaking parents are hunting for a suitable boy for their unmarried daughter, they refer to him as a sthal. In the literal sense, a good sthal is a good place. As in, 'Do you know of a good place where I can dump my daughter?' At least that's what it sounds like to me, when my mother asks people if they know of a good sthal. And my mother makes that enquiry daily – to newspapers, to neighbours, to casual acquaintances and classmates she has long lost touch with. One of these days, she is going to accost complete strangers in her bid to find a good place to dump her daughters.

Daughters. That's right. Plural. In this country, that too. Where having one is considered bad luck, having two is overly optimistic, three is reckless and four, like my mother has, is just plain insane. You have to be richer beyond the dreams of avarice to afford dowry for four daughters. No, wait, not *dowry*. These days offering and accepting dowry is illegal,* after all. So it wouldn't be dowry. It would be called devaan-ghevaan – give-and-take. As in, we'll *give* you one chance to dump your daughter in our family and we'll *take* everything you've got in return.

My parents, Aai and Nana, would have to give-and-take four times to get us all off their hands. And you couldn't do that on one man's salary. To do that, you have to have ancestral wealth or a distant relative addled enough to leave you their estate or, failing all that, at least a very negotiable set of personal ethics. Sadly, for my mother, my father ticks none of these boxes. Academically inclined philosophy professors rarely do.

So the responsibility of obtaining suitable husbands for her daughters has fallen upon my mother. And I'll say this for her: she takes it very, very seriously. Which means I should have seen what was coming when I decided to broach the subject of me studying further.

---

*   At its purest, dowry was supposed to be insurance. It was what a bride got from her parents to ensure that, should the marriage fail or the husband die, the woman had something to fall back on. But, soon enough, dowry became just a list of ridiculous demands made by the groom's family, for anything from a gold-plated watch to an entire house, which the bride's family had to provide, or else. It was only in 1961 that the Dowry Prohibition Act made giving as well as receiving dowry illegal, for all Indian citizens. It has since then been amended several times to prevent dowry-related cruelty, dowry deaths and dowry demands leading to domestic violence. Nowadays in India, only about, oh, twenty women, give or take, die in dowry-related deaths. Every. Single. Day.

'Aai,' I said casually, as I helped her chop ladies fingers[*] for lunch. 'I was thinking . . .'

'Take the dal off the stove,' she ordered, as she tightened the lid of the large aluminium pressure cooker one last time.

I obeyed, grabbing the pot of dal with the steel tongs and gingerly lowering the vessel onto the kitchen counter. Aai set the pressure cooker on the stove, adjusted the heat and began kneading the lump of wheat flour dough in the flat aluminium paraat before her. Every now and then, she'd glance warily at the cooker, as if it would explode any minute.[†]

'So I was thinking . . .' I tried again. 'I'd like to do an MA.'

Silence. She continued kneading the dough as if I hadn't said a word. Had she not heard me?

'Aai, I said . . .'

'I heard,' she replied curtly. 'Are you done with the ladies fingers?'

'Almost,' I said. I had expected this behaviour, so I was prepared. 'See, if I do an MA, I can get a job as a lecturer, maybe even in Nana's college. I'd get a salary, we could use the extra money . . .'

More silence. But I refused to be cowed. I had finished my BA last year and, since then, had sat around the house,

---

[*] Why okra is called ladies fingers in India remains a mystery. The vegetable certainly doesn't resemble a woman's digit. Unless you have compromised vision. Due to an LSD overdose.

[†] Because until the 1970s, pressure cookers in India routinely did explode and kill people. This only stopped a decade later when manufacturers put in thingamajigs to prevent that from happening. So while you may think rice is bad for you *now*, remember, there was a time when it was downright lethal.

doing nothing but housework. I could practically hear my twenty-two-year-old brain begging for some kind of stimulation that went beyond rolling polis* by the stove. No, Aai was going to hear me out, silence or no silence.

'And . . . and . . . I mean,' I continued, 'Nana is going to retire in a few years: a monthly salary will come in handy then.' I went on, fully aware of the icy waves of her disapproval heading towards me. 'I've even found a second-hand shop for the books. I just need the money for the fees . . . and . . . and, I could return that money to you and Nana once I start getting my salary.'

She stopped kneading and looked at me, lips pursed, an exasperated look in her eyes. 'We don't have the money for it,' she began, but I was ready for this line of refusal.

'Aga, but you must've saved some for my wedding, na?' I said plaintively. 'I can use some of that. I spoke to Nana, he says it's the rational thing to . . .'

The piercing whistle of the pressure cooker cut me short.

Aai shot it a beady look, daring it to so much as shudder. It fell silent.

She didn't.

'Oh, you spoke to your father, ka?' She perched her flour-covered hands on her waist and my spirits sank. This was her battle pose. I had seen Nana flee to the park when she took

---

* One might say 'poli' and 'chapati' are the same thing. It all depends on which part of Maharashtra one calls home. Ila, born in Mumbai and belonging to a community from the coastal region of the state, calls it poli. But had she hailed from any of the landlocked districts of the state, she would have called it chapati. Because there, the term 'poli' is conferred only upon that queen of delicacies, the puran poli.

4

this pose in the middle of one of their arguments. 'And what does *he* know about marrying off daughters? Spends all his time thinking about what dead men thought. Like that ever got anything done!'

She returned to the dough, pounding it with extra vigour.

I had indeed spoken to my father about it. Nana had seen my point. But now, considering how vehemently Aai seemed to be against it, I wondered if he would support me in this fight. And if he did, whether it would make much of a difference. No, I needed to make Aai see the sense in what I was proposing.

'What is so wrong with what I am saying?' I asked, trying to keep my voice level. 'Prachi from my class in college got a job at BPT. Anagha is working as a clerk in State Bank. They're both giving their entire salary to their parents and . . .'

'Am I Prachi's mother? Anagha's? No, na? Then what do I care what they do?'

'But what is the problem if I get a job, Aai?' My voice was rising but I couldn't help it. She was being so unreasonable.

'The problem?' She spun around and glared at me. 'The problem is you don't seem to understand the situation we are in. Your father's salary just about covers our monthly expenses. What little we save, you want to blow it all on studying *more*?' Her voice, already shrill, now reached an alarming pitch. 'It's going to be difficult enough to find someone for you with your complexion, and now you want to go and get an MA? Who will marry you then?'

And there it was. My complexion, as she called it. The millstone around Aai's neck. The subject of all her prayers.

My sisters had all taken after her, see – fair, rosy-skinned beauties, perfect little flowers of Konkanastha Brahmin womanhood. Me, I had inherited, from God knows which ancestor, skin several shades darker. But we didn't call it dark in this house, oh no, of course not. Aai was staunch in her denial: I was 'wheatish'. Nothing some gram flour mixed with cream and raw turmeric wouldn't fix. Never mind that it had done no such thing in the past twenty years. I hated the smell of the wretched stuff by now.

I slammed shut the villi* on which I was chopping the ladies fingers, and stormed into the living room. She followed, waving her flour-covered hands.

'Men want wives whom they can feel superior to,' she announced. 'They don't want a girl who is more educated than them, let alone one that works! If the wife brings home money, what use is the husband, tell me? If you don't believe me, ask Juee.' She turned to my elder sister, who was sitting cross-legged on a chattai on the floor, correcting the homework of the children she tutored every afternoon. 'Juee! Tell her. Tell her what that fellow at the marriage bureau said yesterday.'

Juee looked at me apologetically. With her alabaster skin, dark brown hair and light brown eyes, she was Aai's golden

---

* A villi is a kitchen instrument in the same way that the Colosseum is a historical monument – the label technically fits, if you ignore all the blood involved. What a villi actually is, is this: a viciously sharp, crescent blade attached to a wooden board. On one end of the blade is an evil, serrated disc. Marathi women through the ages have sat on the wooden board, casually chopping vegetables into wafer-thin slices on the edge of the blade or nonchalantly grating fresh coconut on the sharp disc. Experienced Marathi women, that is. Novices have cut themselves to varying degrees. Ergo, the blood.

child. Since the day she had turned eighteen, five years before, Aai had been absolutely sure men would line up for Juee's hand, not only because she was objectively beautiful, but also because she seemed to have all the qualities men love in a wife. Juee was obedient, graceful, patient and an excellent cook. In other words, nothing like me. I should have hated her with all my heart, but she also happened to be . . . caring and humble and, well, just deeply likeable. Besides, she actually liked me. So, now, as she turned to me with an embarrassed expression on her face, I knew that it was only Aai's direct command that was making her say what she was about to.

'He said . . . that the families who came to the bureau to find a match for their sons usually want a girl who *is* educated,' she said, not looking directly at me, 'but a graduate is enough for them. They . . . they seem to think that a woman who is too educated or has a job can't . . . wouldn't be interested in or . . . or be able to run a house.'

'It's 1976!' I snapped. 'A woman is running this whole country right now! What world are these fools living in?'

'The real world,' Aai shot back. 'Something you know nothing of. Aga, forget interest or ability, you should first have time, no, to run the house? Married life* isn't easy – there are a hundred little things you have to keep track of. Nobody can handle all that along with the responsibilities of a proper job!'

---

* Tellingly enough, married life in Marathi is referred to as saunsaar, literally meaning 'the world'. That your life as a married woman will become your entire world is not so much implied as hammered in using iron nails and a sledgehammer.

'You're wrong!' My fingers clenched into fists. 'I know about the real world! I know you need money in it, that's why I want a job, so that . . .'

'If she gets to have a job, I also want one, huh!' My younger sister Latika sat up from her reclining position on the divan that stood along one wall of the living room, her mouth turned down in its habitual petulant pout.

People often think Latika is immature. But that's not entirely true. She is also spoilt and foolish. Not for her the claustrophobic shackles of rational thought. An impulse is enough. She is eighteen and believes this makes her behaviour both adorable and excusable, which just goes to show the extent of her self-delusion.

Now, with a dreamy-eyed expression, she sighed. 'I want to be an air hostess. Fly all over the world, meet interesting people, visit exciting places . . .'

Of course. Why wouldn't Air India take someone who failed geography three years in a row, as long as they had a burning desire to 'visit exciting places'. But I didn't say that out loud. Latika is Aai's pet, and I was in enough hot water with her as it was.

Aai gave me a look as if to say, 'Now look what you've done', then shook her head in exasperation and marched back into the kitchen, just as the doorbell rang.

Latika lay back down again, against the pillows, unperturbed by any desire to answer the door. Juee looked like she was about to get up from her seat on the floor, but I gestured to her to not bother.

I opened the door and let Nana, our father, in.

He took off his chappals by the door, handed a cloth bag full of vegetables to Juee and settled into his wooden easy chair, stretching out with a small sigh against the striped nylon fabric that formed its back and seat. With his fake leather hand-pouch* resting on his stomach, he wiped his sweat-soaked grey hair with his handkerchief and gave me a tired smile.

When I didn't return the smile, his own dimmed.

'What happened?' he asked gently. Apart from Juee, Nana was the only person in the family who showed me any modicum of affection.

'Aai said no,' I said tonelessly. 'No MA, no job.'

'I'll talk to her.' He reached out and patted my hand.

'That can wait,' Aai said, coming out of the kitchen with a glass of water in her hands. '*I* have to talk to *you* before that.' She handed him the glass, then pulled up a small stool and sat next to him.

Nana was looking enquiringly at the rest of us. 'Can I have some tea first?' he asked wearily.

Nana always seemed weary around Aai.

'Yes, of course.' She was about to get up when Juee offered to get the tea, and bustled into the kitchen, the cloth bag of vegetables in tow. She was back in a trice with a cup

---

*   Long before the messenger bag and the backpack fought for supremacy as the accessory of choice for Indian men, there was the hand pouch: a small flat pouch stuffed with all the things the discerning seventies man needed on the go. That's where his house keys went, along with a ballpoint pen, his train permit, a handkerchief and maybe even a small comb. The hand pouch nestled cosily in his armpit as he made his way to and from his office, holding on for dear life to a handle in a train compartment or in a public transport bus. It set him apart as a man of taste, of refinement – and one who could always be depended on for the loan of a ballpoint pen.

in her hand. Tea was made three times a day in our home. Once in the morning, for breakfast. Once in the afternoon around four. And once in the evening, with an extra cup for Nana to have when he returned from work. Thrice a day, I'd be assailed with the sweet aroma of cardamom, left longing for what I couldn't have. See, I was banned from drinking tea in our home: Aai had decreed that tea darkens the complexion and mine 'didn't need any more of that'.

Now, I watched Nana take a sip and close his eyes in bliss. Then he turned to Aai and said. 'Is there anything to munch on, with this?'

'There's a poli left over from morning, if you want,' she replied.

'Will do. Just put some toop* on it and bring.'

Aai disappeared into the kitchen. Quick as lightning, Nana held out the cup to me and gestured frantically. I snatched it from him with a grin, took a long sip and handed the cup back to him, just in time.

Aai came back from the kitchen with a toop-smeared poli, steaming on a plate. She must've warmed it quickly on the tava before bringing it out. 'So what I was saying was . . .' she began, taking her seat on the stool once again.

'Where's Malu?' Nana asked loudly, taking a sip of his tea.

---

* Toop – clarified butter – is an integral part of the Konkanastha Brahmin household. So much so that tradition dictates that any visiting son-in-law be given a tiny bowl of melted toop to drink before his meal. This is called aaposhnee and is meant to help the rest of the meal go down well. You are not allowed to protest or say things like 'I actually don't like ghee much' or 'Isn't that too fatty?' Because as far as Konkanasthas are concerned, there is no such thing as too much toop.

He was referring to my youngest sister, Malati, born a full three years after Latika, thanks to my parents' last-ditch attempt at having a boy. I don't think they had thought things through when they conceived her because by the time Malu came into the world, Aai's attention was already divided between three daughters, all under the age of ten. Malu pretty much grew up being left to her own devices and, even today, neither demands nor is given much attention by my parents. So Nana asking about her right now, while Aai was trying to talk to him about something else, was clearly his way of deliberately annoying Aai.

Except Malu, who had been in the bedroom during this conversation, didn't know that. On hearing her name, she came out into the living room, a questioning look on her face. 'Yes, Nana?' she asked. 'You called?'

'Oh,' Nana replied, a little thrown. 'Uh . . . how was school?'

'It's a Saturday,' Malu said, puzzled.

'Never mind, then.'

Malu returned to the bedroom looking so nonplussed she was practically minus.

'Done?' Aai asked crossly. 'Now . . . I wanted to talk about tomorrow.'

'Why, what's tomorrow?' he asked me, the ghost of a mischievous smile on his face.

'Sunday?' I shrugged.

'Ah.' He took a bite of the poli. 'And that warrants a discussion, is it?'

'It's the Kelkar boy's wedding tomorrow, as you well know.' Aai pursed her lips. 'And now don't ask "Kelkar who?"' Kelkar, from the floor below, whom you sit with on the katta after dinner, whose cigarette you take puffs from and think I don't know, whose son I told you would be a good match for Ila, but did you listen? No. It's *that* son's wedding tomorrow, and we are invited and we are going and that is final!'

She placed her hands on her waist and threw Nana a challenging look, while I shook my head in disbelief. Me, marry Arun Kelkar? Ha, ha, ha. We'd been in the same class through ten years of school. Arun had been the class duffer. How he'd scraped through his matric exam, when he was forever playing under-arm cricket in the quadrangle below our building, was beyond me. That was his only passion, cricket. Imagine me, having to take an interest in that god-forsaken game for the rest of my life. What next, develop a sudden enduring love for kadve vaal?*

Nana finished his tea in one long sip and handed Aai the cup. 'Okay,' he said, getting up from his easy chair and going to the window where the clothes were drying. He pulled his striped cotton panchaa† from the washing line and began walking towards the bathroom for a bath.

Aai seemed to have expected some kind of revolt from him because she stood up and looked around expectantly.

---

*   Ila is in a minority in hating vaal, because the Maharashtrian dish called vaalachi usal, made from vaal – field beans – is considered a delicacy on the Konkan coast. Which just goes to show that hunger truly is the best sauce, because nothing else but crippling hunger could have made an entire community love such a pedestrian – to put it mildly – dish.

†   A panchaa is to a towel what a meringue is to a buttercream frosted pastry – roughly the same ingredients, but vastly different densities.

12

'And . . . and we better get there early too!' she called out, as the bathroom door shut. Only I heard her add under her breath: 'Before all the good boys are taken.'

TWO

And to think some of us were looking forward to this nonsense event.

By some of us, of course, I mean Aai and Latika. My mother seemed to have made it her life's mission to snag a groom for one of us at Arun's wedding. And Latika had fussed so much about her clothes it had been as if she were the bride, not the hapless girl who had fallen for Arun's dim-witted charms.

All that getting dressed up, the careful selection of who will wear what, Latika bawling because she had to wear a sari instead of bell bottoms – bell bottoms! At a Maharashtrian wedding! She may as well have asked to go nude! – Aai scolding first her, then the rest of us for some reason, and for what? This staid, boring affair. I don't know what we had expected, frankly. Maharashtrian weddings – at least, those in our community – are all the same. Every single time. And this one was no different.

14

The muhurta was, as usual, at the ungodly hour of 8.32 in the morning. On a Sunday. In Dombivli. And we, well, we lived on the other side of the city, in Parle. Which meant waking up at an even more ungodly hour, bathing, having breakfast in case we missed the breakfast they were serving at the wedding, getting dressed up, leaving the house, returning to the house because Nana forgot his wallet, leaving the house again, waiting for the BEST bus while listening to Aai complain the entire time that we always did this, it wasn't her fault, why could we never be on time anywhere, getting into the bus, getting off at Parle station, getting into a train bound for Dadar, getting off at Dadar station, waiting for the Kalyan local, boarding the train, watching Aai yell at Latika and Malati for fidgeting with their clothes and jewellery, getting off at Dombivli station, then walking for fifteen minutes to the wedding hall, which Nana had *sworn* was 'just next to the station' and sweating right through the armpits of my blouse in the process.

All this, when it wasn't even my wedding! Someone in the building gets married and I am the one put through this torture.

There is clearly no justice in the Universe.

The good thing was, I had someone to rant to. Chitra and I were neighbours and had gone to the same school and the same college. Her mother – or rather step-mother, I should say – Lele Kaku, and Aai, were friends as well. But theirs was a strange kind of friendship. They were very warm and affectionate with each other, but Aai was always a little irked when good things happened for Lele Kaku. Like last month, when Lele Kaka bought a new Lambretta scooter, Aai was effusive in her praise of the thing, but in the privacy of our

15

home she had huffed that the colour was too gaudy. I never told Chitra about my mother's mean-spirited comments, which is possibly why we were still friends.

Like so many of our neighbours, Chitra and her family had been invited to Arun's wedding and now, as we sat at the back of the hall eating the bland upma and tea they invariably served for breakfast at these things, I told her about my argument with Aai the previous evening.

'Can you imagine?' I asked her, taking a sip of my tea. 'I'm actually suggesting something that will ease the burden on them, and she just refuses!'

'But she is okay with Juee taking tuitions at home?' Chitra asked, her forehead wrinkling.

'Exactly! *That* she is okay with. But me go out and work? No, no, no!'

'But do you *have* to go out to work? Couldn't you tutor children too? You could teach history! You were such a scholar in that subject!'

'I don't think I'm cut out for teaching school children.' I took another sip. 'I don't have Juee's patience.'

'But wouldn't it be better than doing nothing, like you are now?'

'I don't know, Chitra.' I made a face. 'To tell you the truth, one of the reasons I want to work is it will get me out of the house. Give me some time away from Aai and her incessant nagging. But no. That's too much to ask of her. Somehow it will make me totally ineligible for marriage! As if I want to get married in the first place!'

'Don't you?' Chitra asked, a small puzzled frown on her face.

'Why should I?' I demanded. 'Have some man I barely

know come eat kande pohe* and gape at me, deciding if I am fair enough to be his wife? Then have my parents pay him godknowswhat to take me off their hands? And then cook and clean for him for the rest of my life, only to have him complain about too little salt or too much spice in my cooking? Why would anyone want to go through any of that?'

Chitra burst out laughing. 'It doesn't have to be as bad as all that,' she said, shaking her head in amusement. 'I wouldn't mind it so much, if it were me.' Her expression turned wistful. 'If it meant I could have my own house, where someone cares about me.'

I put a hand on her shoulder. Chitra's step-mother had always been unkind to her, behind her father's back. How Lele Kaka didn't notice that his daughter was doing all the housework, all the time, while his wife and her sons lorded it over her, was beyond me. Maybe he did and left well enough alone. I decided to change the subject.

'This colour is lovely,' I told her, admiring her sari. It was light lavender with small golden buttis embroidered all over, and had a dark green border. 'It looks really nice on you.'

'Thanks.' She smiled. 'Kaku also has one in a similar colour, no? How come you didn't wear that? In fact, I've never seen you wear it . . .'

---

*   The official snack of the horse show that is called 'going to see the girl'. It's what's served when a boy and his family come to 'see' a girl and decide if she is pretty enough, bright enough, obedient enough and yes, fair enough to be considered for matrimony. Kande pohe is usually served with tea, sprinkled with liberal helpings of 'Our Sheelu has embroidered that cushion' and 'Sheelu is very fond of cooking, she herself has made these pohe.'

I rolled my eyes and looked down at my own maroon sari. 'Because dusky girls shouldn't wear light colours, it makes them look darker!' I spoke in the slightly nasal, sing-song tone Aai unwittingly used to dispense these pearls of wisdom. 'We should only wear dark colours.' I pointed to my maroon sari and spoke in my normal voice. 'Wearing maroon makes me feel as if I have died.* But what does Aai care?'

'Remind her it's the colour widows would have to wear in the nineteenth century.' Chitra grinned, taking a sip of her tea. 'You know, after they shaved their heads and all.† That'll put her off it.'

'If only that worked.' I grinned wryly. 'Knowing her she'll be all' – I changed my voice to the nasal tone again – '"To become a widow, first someone has to marry you. And who will want to do that if you look dusky?"'

We both laughed at that, the sound carrying to the front of the hall.

A horde of guests sat there, facing the podium where the wedding rites were taking place. A few of them turned around at the sound of our laughter. One, a young man in his mid-twenties, smiled and nodded amiably at Chitra. The

---

*   'Maroon jaane' in Marathi means actually dying.

†   True story. In the nineteenth century, Brahmin widows did have to have their heads shaved. You know, so they wouldn't tempt other men with their . . . hair. Because straight men, through the ages, have proven that they can withstand any temptation except . . . women's hair. And alcohol. And sporting events. And declaring wars on neighbouring states. And . . . some other stuff, but basically just hair. Oh, and those women also went through some pretty terrible physical and sexual abuse, but hey, we don't talk about that stuff, sshhh.

other two – a young woman around my age and another man, perhaps in his late twenties – only glared. The young woman had a sneer on her face. The man's expression was unreadable.

I saw Chitra smiling back and asked, 'Do you know those people?'

'Aga, they are Arun's friends from college,' she said, gesturing at Arun, who was currently on the podium, having his feet washed by his soon to be mother-in-law, because traditions are fun like that. 'He introduced us earlier. We got here really early.'

'Aren't I always saying we should get to these places early?' Aai was suddenly there, glaring at me as if it was my fault we hadn't reached the place when the hall was being swept and swabbed. Then her gaze moved to Chitra and softened.

Aai approved of me being friends with Chitra. Not because Chitra was a good girl, a good friend, although of course she was. No, it was because Aai had decided that Chitra, with her round face and upturned nose, was plain. Fair, certainly, but plain.

Next to her, my sharp jawline (acceptable, but what man looks at jaws?), high cheekbones (from Aai's side of the family, of course) and almond-shaped eyes (pity they were dark) could almost pass for pretty, in the right light. Or so Aai claimed.

It was a vile, vile thing to think, and you wouldn't have imagined Aai capable of such thoughts as she looked kindly at Chitra and asked, 'So, who are they?'

'Uh . . . Arun's friends?' Chitra looked confused. I didn't blame her. She had just answered that question a moment ago.

'Yes, yes, you already said that.' Aai waved her hand dismissively. 'I mean, where are they from? What do they do? What do their parents do?'

Oh, no. For a short happy moment, I had forgotten what Aai was like at weddings. For her, a wedding wasn't just a wedding. It was a chance to scope out the right man for Juee, find out all about his antecedents and wrangle a meeting with his family to see where things went. (They hadn't gone anywhere so far, things always coming to a standstill once the family in question realised we had no dowry to give Juee.) But Aai was clearly not about to give up. The woman was obsessed.

'Well, u-uh . . .' Chitra stammered, looking in the direction of the three people under discussion. 'The one on the right' – she nodded towards the friendly looking young man – 'is Sadanand Pingley, the girl next to him is his sister Kalyani and the one next to her is Aniruddha Darshetkar.' She looked at Aai's eager face apologetically. 'That's all I remember, Kaku.'

But Aai was smiling thoughtfully. 'Pingley . . . Darshetkar . . . They sound like our kind of people,' she muttered, hurrying away.

Our kind of people indeed. I knew what that was code for. She had heard their surnames and surmised that they belonged to the same community we did – they were Konkanastha Brahmins. Lovers of kadve vaal, alucha fatfataa* and spending as little money as humanly possible. So now it

---

* A vegetable preparation of taro leaves that looks marginally less disgusting than it sounds, but tastes rather nice actually.

didn't matter if either of them was an axe-murderer or, worse, a non-vegetarian – they would do for Aai's daughters.

We watched her go and find Juee, who had been happily chatting with her friends* from the building, and whisper something in her ear. Juee looked embarrassed and said something I couldn't make out, but Aai was looking stern and shaking her head. A moment later, Juee was being practically pulled through the crowd towards where the Pingleys and their friend was sitting.

I hurriedly put down my half-eaten upma and leapt up from my seat. If Aai was going to push Juee into an awkward social situation, the least I could do was make sure she wasn't in it alone.

'I'll have to go,' I told Chitra, and hurried towards my mother and sister.

I reached them just in time to hear my mother say, '. . . live in the same building as Arun. I've seen him since he was a child. The number of windows that boy broke with his cricket ball, ha ha ha, never mind. This is my daughter, Juee,' she said, thrusting my elder sister to the front. 'She is also your age I thought you might enjoy each other's company, instead of being stuck with old people like us, ha ha ha . . .'

They all looked a little stunned at Aai's verbal barrage. Sadanand Pingley was the first to recover. He was boyishly

---

*   Marathi weddings double up as occasions for guests to meet and chat with friends and relations they haven't seen in years. The prevalent feeling is that if the bride and groom want to get married, that's their business. They get gifts for their trouble, right? They can't then demand the complete attention of every wedding guest through the *whole* ceremony as well. There's a limit to entitlement, you know.

handsome, of average height, with large eyes and an easy smile.

He smiled at Juee now and asked, 'Hello . . . so . . . are you studying?'

Juee had barely opened her mouth to speak when Aai butted in.

'No, no, she finished her BA two years ago. Now we're looking for a nice boy to get her married. It won't be long now, with a beautiful face like hers, no?' She looked fondly at Juee, who looked deeply mortified.

'Aai, Lele Kaku was looking for you,' I said loudly. 'Something about the rukhwat.'*

Aai spun around and spotted me. She pursed her lips in annoyance, before turning back to the other four and saying sweetly, 'I'll just go and see what she wants,' before giving me a look that said she'd deal with me later.

'And you are—?' Kalyani Pingley asked, with a disdainful look. A fair, full-figured girl, she was wearing a magenta paithani sari and a haughty sneer on an otherwise pretty face. Her hair was styled in a movie-star bouffant and she wore chunky gold jewellery – a chandra haar around her neck, thick gold kangans on her wrists and large gold earrings. In comparison, the bride herself, who was wearing a simple

---

* The rukhwat is an exhibition of all the gifts the bride has been given by her parents, to take to her new home. Till the mid-eighties at least, this included everything from tea-sets and dinner-sets to transistor radios and pressure cookers. The higher-priced the rukhwat, the more impressed the guests. The rukhwat also displayed crochet tablecloths, embroidered cushion-covers and other specimens of the bride's artistic skills, but nobody gave a damn about those.

yellow silk sari and light gold jewellery, seemed practically underdressed.

'This is my younger sister, Ila,' Juee replied.

Kalyani's eyes travelled from her to me in disbelief. I noticed, but only because I was used to this behaviour from people by now: that little double take, as they tried to wrap their heads around the fact that the creamy-skinned beauty was related to the dark girl next to her.

'You are all Arun's friends from school?' Juee continued, oblivious to all this.

'College,' Sadanand corrected her. 'We were in Poddar together.'

'Oh! That's near Ruia, isn't it? I wanted to go to Ruia!' Juee exclaimed. 'But Aai thought it was too far for me to travel alone, so I went to Parle College instead.'

'Really? I have a cousin who was studying there!' Sadanand beamed. 'Do you know a Kaustubh Ranade?'

They were chatting amiably with each other now, completely lost to the fact that they were leaving the rest of us out of the conversation. I had no idea what to say to these people, but I had watched Aai and Nana ask polite questions to slight acquaintances, so I knew the drill.

'So . . . what do you do?' I asked the other two pleasantly.

'I run a charitable foundation,' Kalyani said, in a bored voice. 'My mother had started it before our parents passed away and since Sada has to manage our father's departmental store, I have to take care of all that now. It's very dull.'

I was torn. On one hand, I felt sympathetic: Sadanand and Kalyani were in their early twenties, and losing their parents at such a young age must've been hard; on the other hand, the offhand way in which Kalyani dismissed her charity work made me want to flick her nose.

But I kept my thoughts to myself before turning with an enquiring smile to the other fellow, the one Chitra had called Aniruddha Darshetkar.

'And you?'

'I take care of my father's cargo business,' he said quietly.

'Always so modest!' Kalyani chirped. 'He has single-handedly run the place since his parents passed away. By the way, cargo business means his company exports things to other countries.' She smirked. 'In case you didn't know what it meant.'

'Thanks for explaining,' I said, with a smirk of my own. 'You needn't have bothered, though. I know all kinds of words. Like "condescending", for instance.' Then I smiled sweetly, and was rewarded by a stunned look on her face.

The sarcasm wasn't lost on Aniruddha. He gave me an appraising look, which I met head-on, with a straight face. So young and managing a business all by himself? He must be quite capable, even if his face did suggest that he'd rather be serving a life sentence in prison somewhere than be there.

For the first time, I really looked at him. Sadanand was good-looking but Aniruddha was *handsome*. Every feature was a tick-mark on Aai's list of traditionally perfect attributes: light eyes, fair complexion, curly brown hair. He was also a head taller than his friend, and the height, the chiselled jawline and the perennially serious expression gave him a gravitas his friend lacked.

'That's very impressive, managing a whole business,' I said to him, just as Kalyani yawned pointedly at the men.

She could have been one of the strands of marigold hanging from the walls of the stage, for all the attention they paid her. Sadanand was still immersed in the list of common acquaintances he had with Juee, and Aniruddha simply looked uninterested in everything.

Kalyani pouted for a moment, then her eye caught Aai, who was looking at the rukhwat with Lele Kaku, peering at the items on display with a calculating look in her eyes.

'Look at that tea-set,' Aai was saying, her voice carrying all the way to us. 'It looks so expensive! How much do you think it cost? They must've given some solid dowry with the girl!'

I didn't know where to look. Trust Aai to have no volume control in a place like this.

Kalyani gave a small mocking laugh and turned to Aniruddha. 'This place is so noisy, na,' she said, looking pointedly at me. 'How can people be so loud?'

Aniruddha said nothing, merely looked in Aai's direction as if he were mentally giving her marks and placing big red crosses on things he didn't like.

There were lots of crosses, judging from his expression.

'Let's go stand outside for some time.' Kalyani looked up at him, batting her eyelashes. 'I want some fresh air.'

And before he could respond, she had pulled him away in the direction of the exit.

I marvelled at her sheer gall. She hadn't even bothered to excuse herself. That was basic etiquette: making at least the smallest noise of apology before leaving a group to flounce off on your own. But they had simply left, with no acknowledgment that I was even there. Mannerless nitwits.

Well, I didn't need to stay there like a doormat. Juee

seemed to be managing very well on her own anyway, so I told her I was going to find Chitra and left.

Chitra had moved to one of the chairs placed in rows at the front of the hall, for guests to sit. Her step-mother and brothers were sitting in the row in front of her. None of them was paying her the slightest attention, let alone talking to her. I slid into the empty chair next to her and she grinned at me. She had already filled her fists full of akshata* and she poured some into mine saying. 'It's almost time.'

A moment later, the bhatjis began chanting the sacred hymns and we turned to the podium. The bride and the groom were facing each other, relatives holding an antarpat† between them. Some random aunts had decided to sing the mangalashtak and they were murdering the tune with enthusiasm.

I don't know why this happens in Maharashtrian weddings, but it always does. There's always at least one middle-aged lady who treats the wedding ceremony as a one-woman talent show. *Hah*, she thinks, *a captive audience at last.* And so she rewrites the mangalashtak to showcase her creativity, weaves in the bride and groom's names or some such thing, then proceeds to sing the whole thing at a

---

* Coloured grains of rice hurled at the couple getting married. Enough akshata is found on the floor of Maharashtrian wedding halls after a wedding to feed a family of five. This is not counting the fistfuls picked up by any children present, which they then fling mercilessly at each other. Of such violent joys are childhood memories forged.

† A white cloth drawn with sacred symbols, which allows the happy couple to play one last game of hide-and-seek before resigning themselves to a lifelong relationship with whatever is on the other side of the cloth.

deafening volume. Knowing in her heart of hearts that the audience dare not, will not, *can* not protest – or escape.

We were much too near the front: as if the auditory assault wasn't bad enough, people would soon crowd the area, trying to aim the akshata right at the happy couple. If we got in their way, all that thrown akshata would fall into our hair and inside our clothes for sure. And once inside, those little coloured grains of rice would prick like anything. I tapped Chitra's shoulder and pointed to an empty-ish place a few rows behind. The mangalashtak would go on for some time: the aunts were really stretching each syllable in the hymn to breaking point. If we hurried, we could manage to be in a place with a good view before the akshata-pelting began.

Pushing and shoving as demurely as we could, we ended up on the spot, all the while the aunts screaming, 'Laxmi-heeee Kaoooo-stubha Paaari-jataka-surahaaaa, Dhan-van-tareeee-shchandramaaaaaa!'

Despite the volume, however, I could still hear some sotto-voce muttering from the people standing in front of me. I could sympathise. Those women were really putting the tune through the wringer. Then one of the men turned his head slightly and I realised it was Sadanand Pingley. Next to him were Aniruddha and Kalyani, who had obviously had their fill of all the fresh air Dombivli could provide that morning.

'Where did you two disappear to?' Sadanand was asking.

'Outside, to get some air,' Kalyani drawled.

'By yourselves? Leaving Juee's sister behind?'

'Oh, *Juee*, is it? Didn't you just meet her? And you're already so concerned for her?'

'It's pointless talking to you.' Sadanand shook his head

and turned to his friend. 'But I expected better from *you*, Aniruddha!'

'Why?' Aniruddha asked. 'You found a beautiful girl to talk to, so I have to entertain the plain one?' He shook his head and added in English. 'Not fair at all.'

I froze. Chitra turned to me, surprise clearly etched on her face. I rolled my eyes dismissively, but it had felt like a blow to the stomach, those words. How many times had I heard Aai despair to neighbours and relatives about the colour of my skin? How many times had I heard her worry aloud about who would want to marry me? How many times had she aired her deepest fear: that nobody would want me without a hefty dowry, because I wasn't milky fair? I had lost count. I had always assumed she was right, but a part of me had wondered if it would be as bad as that. And now, here was the proof. Plain? Hah. I knew what that meant. I wasn't fair enough. No, that's not what he had said. He had said: Not fair *at all*. So that meant I wasn't pretty enough for him to even consider having a full conversation with me? Even *that* was such an insufferable obligation? To afford me the courtesy of small talk?

I felt the hurt melt into anger as the women on the podium screeched. 'Gan-gaaa! Seeeeen-dhooo Saras-wateecha Yamu-naaaaa! Godaaaa-vareeee Narma-daaaa!'

I took a deep breath to steady myself. To hell with Aniruddha Darshetkar and his kind. I didn't need some man to give his expert opinion on my looks. He didn't get to decide my worth. Only I would do that, and if Aai wasn't going to shell out the money for my MA then . . . then . . . then I'd go and get some other job. Lots of places would happily hire a graduate. I'd apply to the lot of them. Aniruddha Darshetkar could keep his stupid opinions and his sackfuls of money, and stuff his precious cargo business up his nose – it probably had better manners than he did. Besides, I would never run into these clowns again. It didn't matter how they behaved. And – I grinned as the realisation sunk in – it didn't matter how I behaved either.

I smiled to myself as the aunties on the stage finished with, 'Shubha Mangala Saaavdhaaan!' – and gleefully chucked a fistful of rice grains straight at the back of Aniruddha and Kalyani's heads.

THREE

I will say this about Maharashtrian weddings – they are mercifully short. Anything that boring ought to be, really. But that doesn't mean that you're away and scot-free once the last of the akshata has been swept off the floor. No, there is a veritable line-up of post-wedding rituals that the family must indulge in, some starting the very next day.

The day after Arun's wedding, for instance, the Kelkars had a Satyanarayan pooja at home and all the neighbours were invited.

So there we were, the Bendres, doing what we did best: Aai helping Kelkar Kaku in the kitchen, while Nana chatted with Malvade Kaka, who lived on the floor above us, about . . . whatever it is 40-something-year-old men talk about. And Juee and me, sitting together like spare parts nobody had any use for. Oh, and let's not forget Latika, sulking next to us, because Aai had forced her to come instead of staying at home with an unexplained illness that had sprung up the moment Aai told her we had to go next door for a pooja.

'I should be at home with Malu,' she grumbled. Malati was at home studying for her ninth standard half-term tests. 'I really am unwell, you know!'

'Of course, of course.' I exchanged smiles with Juee as I took a bite of the sweet sheera that was the prasad.* 'And what is the name of your illness? *Cine Blitz*-itis?'

Latika's eyes grew wide. 'You . . . how did you know? Have you told Aai? Say you haven't told her!'

She was right to panic. How she had smuggled the magazine into the house I don't know, but I had found it while dusting under the cupboard in the bedroom. If Aai had caught her with that film gossip rag, God alone knows what she would've done. Panic herself, I suppose. Aai let her innocent darling read a magazine that just last year had carried pictures of that starlet running naked on Juhu beach? Perish the thought.

'I haven't told her,' I reassured Latika. 'But what are you doing with that thing, anyway?'

'You wouldn't understand,' Latika said, wearing an expression of dramatic sorrow.

I glanced at Juee, who seemed about to say something

---

* The primary agenda of visiting a Hindu temple or religious cere-mony is to have a glimpse of the God or Goddess you are visiting. This is called 'taking darshan'. It involves a namaskar – nodding, bowing or prostrating yourself before the deity – depending on your level of piety – with your palms brought together at chest level. For your troubles, you are rewarded with teertha-prasad – a liquid and a solid food item, usually sweet.

encouraging, and shook my head slightly. 'You're absolutely right,' I told Latika airily. 'Best not to tell us.'

Five seconds later, she burst out with: 'It's Rajesh Khanna! I'm in love with him!'

I smacked my forehead with my hand and Juee gave an embarrassed smile.

'You can laugh if you like.' Latika's head was held high. 'But he has a fever! I'm worried! I wanted to hold a hanky dipped in cold water over his forehead to help him feel better.'

'How?' I was utterly confused. I had a sudden mental vision of Latika storming into the film star's home and accosting him with a wet handkerchief.

Something similar must've occurred to Juee, because with a concerned look she reached out and felt Latika's forehead with the back of her palm asking, 'Wait, do *you* have a fever or something?' Then she turned to me and whispered. 'She is sounding hysterical.'

'I was going to hold the hanky on his picture in *Cine Blitz*!' Latika snapped, brushing away Juee's hand.

'Because . . . that will bring the actual Rajesh Khanna's fever . . . down . . . somehow?' I made a face. 'See, this is what happens when you daydream about film stars during science period.'

'Love can make even the impossible possible!' she said with a scornful sniff. 'But you wouldn't understand.'

I leaned closer to Juee and said in a stage whisper, 'You may be right. She is definitely sounding hysterical.'

Latika sprang up from her chair in a huff and glared at us. 'I'm going home!' she said. And then, with an expression of maddening superiority: 'Make fun of me all you want! You'll never know what it's like to be in love, till you actually fall in love!'

I nodded understandingly, which seemed to irritate her even more – which was exactly why I had done it. Then she turned on her heel and flounced out of the room. Or tried to flounce out, because a moment later she had crashed into someone who had just walked in at the door. Someone with a bunch of heavy, spiral-bound photo albums in their hands, which had now fallen to the floor.

As Latika squealed an embarrassed apology, I rushed to help the man pick up the fallen albums. And looked straight into a pair of laughing brown eyes.

'Sorry, sorry, I didn't see you only,' Latika said, flapping her hands in what she probably thought was an endearing fashion.

'No harm done,' the man said, not taking his eyes off me. 'This is the Kelkars' house, isn't it?'

'Yes, I'll just call them,' I said, fighting the instinct to smooth my hair as I turned towards the kitchen. 'Kaku! Someone to see you!'

'So . . . you aren't Kelkars?' the man asked. 'Should've guessed.'

'Why?' I asked, puzzled. 'What is so unKelkar-like about us?'

'Well, I can't speak for all Kelkars everywhere, of course' – the man shrugged, and then gave a roguish smile – 'but you ladies look far too beautiful to be one of *these* Kelkars.'

Latika gave a surprised gasp, then broke into nervous giggles. I considered the man. He was on the taller side, with wavy hair, long sideburns and a smart moustache. In his short coral kurta, with flared brown pants, he looked like an artist. I found the word 'dashing' trying to worm its way into my mind.

'We could be Arun's cousins, you know,' I said, looking serious. 'And we could be quite offended by what you just said.'

'Even better,' he said, smile firmly in place. 'That would mean I'd absolutely *have* to make amends for my behaviour. Take you out for cold drinks to say sorry. Maybe tomorrow?'

I arched my eyebrows at him, before looking in Nana's direction. He seemed deep in conversation with Malvade Kaka – he had certainly not seen his daughters talking to a perfect stranger.

But before I could respond to this ridiculous proposal, Kelkar Kaku came bustling out of the kitchen. The man handed her the photo albums.

'Vivekrao* sent me,' he told her. 'He said there was some balance amount remaining . . .'

'Just wait, I'll have to ask.' Kelkar Kaku hauled the pile of albums inside with a cry of 'Aho!'†

'Who are you?' Latika asked, an eager look on her face.

'Just a lowly photographer,' he answered, with a smile. 'in search of a muse.' This last bit he said looking right at me.

---

* The suffix 'rao' is an honorific for men, much like 'bai' is an honorific for women.

† 'You', in Marathi, but formal. It's supposed to be a marker of a wife's respect for her husband that she doesn't address him by his first name. Although, in many cases, the tone used to yell 'Aho!' completely belies that respect. For example, in the sentence. 'Aho! I had told you to call the plumber, no? How you forgot like that? Where is your attention?'

34

It was such a . . . stupid line, I had to look away to hide my smirk.

'A photographer!' Latika trilled. 'Waah!'

'So, you do weddings mostly, is it?' Juee asked, glancing at me through the corner of her eye. I hadn't noticed my elder sister approach. Had the sight of her two younger sisters talking to a handsome stranger awakened her protective instinct?

'Any event my boss doesn't want to go for.' He smiled disarmingly. 'Weddings, prize-distribution functions, lectures . . .'

'And do you offend people in *all* those places, or . . . ?' I asked, crossing my arms.

'Oh, no, only in a few *special* cases,' he replied. Then, running his hands through his hair he said. 'I am Jayant, by the way, Jayant Waknis.'

'I'm Latika Bendre,' my younger sister announced, boldly holding out her hand to shake his. 'I'm eighteen,' she added, making it sound like an achievement.

'Is it?' He gave her an impressed look and shook her hand, before turning to me and holding out his hand. 'And you are . . . ?'

I smiled and replied, 'I am Latika's older sister. And this is Juee,' I said, indicating her. 'She is the eldest.'

'Nice to meet you, Juee.' Jayant bowed a little. 'And you, Latika's sister—?'

Latika rolled her eyes. 'Tell him your name, Ila!' she said with her hands on her hips. 'Stop acting so strange!'

Jayant looked at me with an amused expression, which changed when he saw Kelkar Kaka coming our way.

'You are Vivek's boy, is it?' he asked Jayant, removing

a few notes from his wallet. 'You've taken good pictures, I saw some right now. But how come they're ready so soon? I was told it would take at least a week to develop all the rolls.'

'Oh, I worked through the night,' Jayant replied. 'It's a wedding, after all. People are very eager to see their pictures soon. Making you all wait for that . . . it didn't feel right.'

Kelkar Kaka patted Jayant's back companionably and slipped a rupee note in the breast pocket of his kurta. 'I have friends,' he told him. 'I'll be sure to mention you to them.'

Jayant inclined his head respectfully as Kelkar Kaka left. Then he beamed at us, his gaze staying on me for a fraction of a second more than strictly necessary. 'We'll meet again,' he said, before he swept out through the door.

'Oh!' Latika sighed, looking at his departing back. 'That is the most handsome man I have ever seen in real life!'

'Even more than Rajesh Khanna?' Juee asked, nudging me in the ribs.

But I didn't respond. Because, possibly for the first time in her life, Latika had said something I had to agree with. Not that I was going to own up to it. No, I left her to her own devices, allowing her to discreetly escape back home to moon over Rajesh Khanna – or, more probably, the man we had just met.

Ten minutes later, Juee and I communicated via complex hand gestures to Nana that our piety with regards to Lord Satyanarayan had been adequately expressed and we were ready to return home. He waved us to go, which we assumed meant that he still had matters of vital importance to discuss with Malvade Kaka. And by that I mean, most probably, the Indian cricket team, their current line-up and how badly they would fare against West Indies if Gavaskar sprained his ankle.

We left him to it and were almost out of the door, when a pleasant male voice exclaimed, 'Oh, are you leaving already?'

Sadanand Pingley was beaming at us as he walked down the common corridor towards the Kelkar home. His sister and his surly friend were right behind him. We smiled at him but before we could say a word, Arun came out of his home and bore down on the little group with a cry of 'Sada! You made it!' This was the same Arun, by the way, who had disappeared inside the house the moment the pooja was done, leaving his wife to do all the smiling and nodding at us. Which she had, as shyly and sweetly as befits a new bride. But still, there is such a thing as being a good host, which as far as Arun Kelkar was concerned, just seemed to be a collection of nonsense syllables.

Now, he thumped Sadanand on the back in that way some boys do, which makes you wonder if they secretly despise their friends. Then turning to Aniruddha, he shook the man's hand saying. 'Good, *good*! Sada dragged you here!'

'Dragged is the perfect word.' Sadanand grinned. 'You would have thought I was asking him to come to a funeral, not a pooja.'

'Dada!' Kalyani hit her brother on the shoulder with mock admonishment. 'You are really too much! All he said was he'd rather stay home and read.'

'I had some work to do as well,' Aniruddha added gravely, looking at Arun. 'Some of us aren't here on vacation.'

But Sadanand waved his words away. 'Nonsense!' he declared. 'How can you even think of staying cooped up indoors instead of getting out and meeting people?' He turned to us. 'How are you both? How are your parents?'

I was about to answer when Juee – a little pink in the face – assured him that we were all fine, and delighted to meet them all again.

I smiled to myself, making a mental note to tease her about this later.

'Oh, it's so nice to hear that!' Kalyani said, taking Juee's hands in her own. 'It's such fun to *finally* have some female company, you know! I always get dragged to Mumbai with Dada and I get so awfully bored by myself!'

'Nobody forces you,' Sadanand told her. 'You're perfectly welcome to stay home the next time.'

She ignored him and smiled at Juee. 'Will you come to our house tomorrow? Please?' She made a pleading face. 'I will be *so* bored if you don't.'

Juee seemed a little taken aback at this charm offensive, but she rallied and told Kalyani she'd ask Aai for permission.

I was a little insulted, honestly. I mean, I was standing right there – Kalyani could've invited both of us. She was probably still annoyed about all that akshata I had pelted at her hairdo. Eh. I regretted nothing. Besides, a little part of me was actually relieved – imagine spending time with Kalyani Pingley, that too voluntarily. I'd rather eat a bitter gourd raw. I shuddered at the mere idea.

'Are you alright?' Aniruddha asked, giving me a quizzical look.

'Who? Me? Yes, absolutely, why?'

'Only . . . you looked like you were shivering.'

'The weather *has* been a little chilly,' Sadanand said.

'It's the rain,' Juee told him. 'Comes and goes as it pleases . . .'

'It's Shravan, after all,' Sadanand said. 'As Balkavi[*] has said, 'Shravanmaasi harshmaanasi hirval daate chohikade—'

'—kshanaat yete sarasara shirve, kshanaat phiruni oon padey!' Juee finished, a delighted smile on her face. 'You like poetry?'

'I have read only a little,' Sadanand admitted, with a bashful expression. 'But what little I've read, I've loved.'

I watched them talk about the poems they liked and smiled to myself. For a brief moment I thought of asking the others if they read any poetry, just to include them in the conversation, but then I thought the better of it. Kalyani and Aniruddha had been rude to me before, and I had no motivation whatsoever to be polite to them now. So I looked blankly at their faces instead, only to find Aniruddha looking right back at me.

'Do you read poetry as well?' he asked.

'A little,' I said carefully. Why was he talking to me? 'I like Pu. La.'s[†] poems. They're funny.'

'Such as?'

'There's that one about living in Pune . . .'

---

[*] Balkavi was the pen-name of Marathi poet Tryambak Bapuji Thombre, whose poem 'Shraavanmaas' is a lyrical ode to monsoon and one that perfectly captures the romance of the rains in Maharashtra. It is a far cry from that other famous Marathi song about the rains – 'Dhagala Laagli Kala' – which, thanks to its double-meaning lyrics, is by far more popular, especially among youngsters.

[†] Purshottam Laxman Deshpande, or Pu. La. as he is popularly known, wrote everything from plays to screenplays and was, apart from his literary endeavours, an accomplished actor, orator and singer. Known for his hilarious insights into Maharashtrian life, he is called Maharashtra's most beloved personality.

'We live in Pune,' Kalyani said, beaming with pride.

'Oh, then you won't like it,' I told her, trying not to smile.

'Why?' She frowned. 'What does it say?'

'Just something about how people from Pune love to talk a lot and don't like to listen much,' I said. 'He basically says that talking is like a religion in Pune. Whereas listening is an act of charity.'

'That's nonsense!' she scoffed. 'Why would anyone write that? People from Pune aren't chatterboxes! We are actually very cultured. We don't go just chattering away for no reason. What does he mean to imply? That we like the sound of our own voices? That we just catch people in the middle of the road and lecture them? Imagine! These poets also, na, they just write anything for the sake of writing!' She made a disparaging sound. 'Rubbish, really. People from Pune talk a lot, it seems – hah!'

I waited for a moment, after she had finished blustering. Then, 'No, of course not, the very idea,' I said dryly.

Sadanand snickered and I thought I saw a shadow of a smile on Aniruddha's face, but it vanished before I could be sure of what I'd seen.

'Pu. La. is very good,' he admitted. 'Have you read any Grace?'

Wait, this blank-faced blackboard of a man had heard of Grace? I was so taken aback, it took me a moment to reply, which was all the opening Kalyani needed.

'*Everyone* doesn't read English poetry like you, Aniruddha!' she sang, fluttering her eyelashes at him, before shooting me a pointed look. I had to admire the way she had found a way to flatter him, while simultaneously making me look like a village yokel.

'*I* do sometimes,' I told her cheerfully. 'But . . . Grace isn't English.'

'She *sounds* English.' Kalyani thrust her chin out at me.

'Grace isn't a woman.' Aniruddha corrected her, and it took everything I had not to laugh at the way Kalyani's expression deflated.

'It's the pen name of the poet Manik Sitaram Godghate—' Aniruddha continued, but she tossed her head and interrupted him.

'Then why does he call himself Grace?' she asked disdainfully. 'Couldn't he pick a male pen name?'

'Grace actually refers to—' I began, but this time Arun interrupted me.

'Are we going to stand here the whole day discussing dreary poetry, of all things?' He glared at me, as if I had broached the subject. 'Come in, come in, all of you . . .' He began corralling Sadanand and Kalyani towards the open doorway, as if they were wayward sheep.

'We were just leaving actually,' I said.

'Okay, bye,' Arun said, without a backward glance at us, and I fought the urge to give him a smart rap on the back of his head. In the playground one time, when I was eight and he was eleven, I had whacked him for calling me a kalundri.*

---

* Marathi insults don't mess about with political correctness. They go straight for the jugular. If you can't talk properly, you are a bobadkanda – a stammering onion. If you like eating food a lot, you are a khaadadmau – a greedy cat. And if you, like Ila, happen to not resemble a walking-talking vat of milk, you are a kalundri – a black female mouse.

41

Sent him crying home to his mother. I could do it again, if he continued to behave like this.

'Bye, then.' Juee smiled at Sadanand, who smiled back.

'Come tomorrow, okay? Please!' Kalyani thrust a piece of paper in Juee's hand. 'This is our phone number and address. Call me and tell me what your mother says! We'll send our car to pick you up.'

FOUR

I don't know why Juee didn't just say yes, right to Kalyani's face. I mean, I know *why* – it's because she is sweet and well-behaved and wouldn't dream of doing anything without Aai-Nana's explicit permission. But surely she could've predicted Aai's reaction? An invitation to spend time at Sadanand's house, with him and his sister and, most importantly, without any other eligible young women in sight? Oh, and not just any old house either. The address Kalyani had given Juee said Hindu Colony. If the Pingleys had a chauffeur-driven car and a home in Hindu Colony, arguably the poshest part of Dadar, it was unlikely to be a modest affair.

It's a wonder Aai didn't carry her there in her own arms and throw her straight at Sadanand.

Although, I *was* surprised that Aai told her Kalyani didn't need to send a car. Ordinarily, a private car coming to pick up her daughter at the gate of the society* would've given Aai the perfect opportunity to preen in front of the neighbours, particularly Lele Kaku. But she made Juee call Kalyani from Kelkar Kaka's phone (he was the only one on our floor with a telephone) and say that she'd come to their home on her own.

I thought maybe Aai didn't want to jinx the whole thing – you know, attract someone's evil eye by showing off her good fortune too early. But I was wrong.

Barely twenty minutes after Juee had left home to catch a train to Dadar, from where she would walk to Kalyani and Sadanand's home, it began to rain buckets. As Malati and I (Latika was reading another contraband magazine behind that day's newspaper) rushed about, trying to bring in the clothes that had been hung outside the windows to dry, I saw Aai smile broadly to herself.

'Thank goodness Jueetai has carried an umbrella,' Malati said, as she walked to Aai, her arms full of slightly damp clothes.

'She hasn't,' Aai replied airily, from the divan in the living room where she was sitting.

---

*   A cooperative housing society is a group of residential buildings, filled with people who take every available opportunity to not cooperate with each other. On anything. From monthly parking charges to decoration costs for various festivals, no issue is too small for a disagreement. Indeed, quarterly society meetings often become battlegrounds where grudges are aired and vendettas lovingly allowed to flourish, over questions of national importance such as flat 15B's potted plants leaking water all over our new car or how the dog from 10A needs to do his business outside society premises.

'But I saw her take one,' I said, frowning, as I dropped a pile of clothes on the divan.

'I made her put it back.' Aai smiled.

'What? Why?'

'Because I thought it might rain.' Aai picked up a petticoat from the pile and began folding it.

'That makes no sense.' I stared at her.

She looked at me as if I were a five-year-old who had been asked the answer to two-plus-two and answered nineteen.

'Of course it does,' she said. 'Juee will be caught in the rain. By the time she reaches Sadanand's house, she will be drenched. They will have no option but to give her a change of clothes, something warm to drink, let her recover. This will take time – much longer than if she had just gone over for a visit. Then, if it's raining – for that matter, even if it isn't – Sadanand will offer to drop her home. Meaning even more time in each other's company. After spending that much time with Juee, do you honestly think any man is capable of not wanting to marry her?'

She went back to folding a towel with a self-satisfied expression on her face.

I was open-mouthed. Till then, I had known Aai was capable of going to any lengths to get rid of us, but I now realised that that knowledge had been purely theoretical. Watching her actually put her plans into practice was a disorienting experience. She hadn't even stopped to consider if Juee might want this match, if she actually liked Sadanand. It was another matter that – at least in my opinion – Juee did seem to like him a lot. To Aai, that seemed as irrelevant as Lalita's existence was to Rajesh Khanna.

I decided to bring this up with Nana when he got home

from work. But, just an hour later, Arun's wife, Sudha, knocked on our door, her round face looking worried. 'Kaku, Jueetai has telephoned . . . her voice seems hoarse,' she said, her eyes wide. 'I hope she is well?'

I glared at my mother before following her to Kelkars'. When she put the receiver to her ear, I put my ear close to hers.

'Hello? Juee?' she said.

'Hello? Aai? Don't worry, I am okay . . . um . . . mostly okay . . .'

'What happened?'

'I . . . it's nothing serious . . . When I was getting out at Dadar station, it was raining very heavily and I slipped in a muddy patch and sprained my ankle . . .'

'Oh, no, you poor thing! Where are you?'

'Some people helped me get to Kalyani's house. I'm here now . . .'

'Thank God! Are you okay? You can walk properly, right?'

'Yes, yes . . . well, no, not totally. Kalyani called a doctor and uh . . . by the time he got here, I had a . . . slight temperature. Nothing to worry about. But he says I should stay here for a day or so at least. Hopefully my ankle will be a bit better by tomorrow and then I can come home.'

'Absolutely not,' Aai replied in a business-like way. 'You will do no such thing. Stay there till you are fully okay!'

'But I . . . why to trouble them so much?'

'Nonsense! You are their guest. You are unwell. You are staying. Give the phone to that girl . . . Kalpana, is it? I will talk to her.'

Which Juee refused to do, obviously. Assuring Aai that she would explain things to Kalyani herself, she hung up the phone.

As we returned home, Aai was practically bubbling with joy. I, on the other hand, could feel faint pangs of worry in my stomach. I knew my older sister. She hated causing any worry to Aai and Nana. I had a strong suspicion that she was underplaying how unwell she was, and it made me even more annoyed than I had been before.

'Satisfied now?' I asked her as we entered our home. 'You could've let her have an umbrella, but no! Now she is down with a fever, at the mercy of people we barely know . . .'

'You make them sound like dacoits.' Aai rolled her eyes. 'They seemed like perfectly nice young people to me.'

'Aai, that Sadanand Pingley could have a vestigial tail for all you'd care. It just doesn't matter to you because all you can think of is how you can tie Juee around their necks!'

'Okay, I admit it, I want to see my daughter married into a well-to-do home!' Aai threw up her hands emphatically. 'What mother doesn't? And besides, I don't see your father lifting a finger to make any of this happen. Someone has to care about your futures!'

'And giving your daughter a limp is the way to do that, is it?' I demanded. 'Setting her up for pneumonia is your way of showing you *care*?'

'Rein in your tongue,' Aai snapped. 'Pneumonia! As if! She will be alright in a few days and if she spends those few days in the company of a good-looking boy from a decent family—'

'—and his snooty sister—'

'—I don't think the world will come to an end! So stop bickering and go down and get me some coriander.'

The abrupt change of subject ought to have given me whiplash, but that was Aai for you. If she didn't want to discuss something, she merely moved on to a subject she considered more important. Which, in this case, was the kitchen's lack of coriander, apparently. Well, I had different priorities.

'I'm going, but to check on Juee,' I said, striding towards the steel almirah I shared with Juee and Latika. 'She'll need some clothes if she's going to stay there for "a few days".'

I reached the Pingley home at just after five in the evening. Laxmi Sadan was a stately two-storeyed structure, built in a pre-Independence architectural style, with towering trees on both sides.

As I climbed up the neat wooden staircase, I surveyed the hem of my sari. It was speckled with mud – but that was nothing compared to the state of my ankles. It had rained non-stop through my bus ride from home to Parle station, and continued to pour when I had got off the train at Dadar. Taking a taxi would've been an unforgiveable indulgence, had one even agreed to go the 'walkable distance', as Nana would've called it. So, I had hitched up my sari at the waist, balanced my bag and my umbrella and walked, my rubber chappals slapping at my heels, covering my bare calves, my ankles and the edge of my sari in brown muddy flecks.

It didn't matter. I'd just wash my feet the first chance I got and it would be okay. Oh, and preferably change my sari – this one was damp already and the cold breeze was making goosebumps erupt all over my arms.

When I reached the door with a brass number 4 above it, I unhitched my sari, shook out my umbrella so I didn't wet their floor and rang the doorbell. A few moments later, the door opened.

Aniruddha Darshetkar stared at me, his eyes widening in surprise.

Now what in the world was he doing there?

'I...I thought this was...uh...Sadanand and Kalyani's house?' I stammered.

'It is. They're inside.' He cleared his throat and looked away abruptly, moving out of the doorway so I could go in. 'I am just visiting.'

'Oh,' I said, stepping inside gingerly. No floor mat on the floor? Who doesn't keep a floor mat at the door in the rainy season? I tiptoed, trying not to leave my muddy footprints on the clean tiles.

'Are you okay?' Aniruddha threw me a curious look as I balanced shakily on my tiptoes.

'Yes. Uh...where can I wash my feet...before I go inside?'

'Of course.' He pointed towards the bathroom and I hurried in that direction.

It turned out to be twice the size of the one we had at home. With smooth white tiles and a money plant in the windowsill. A plant! In the bathroom! I marvelled at the extent of this fanciness.

As I poured a tumbler full of water over my feet, I heard Kalyani's shrill voice. 'Who?' I heard her exclaim. '*Here?* Whatever for?'

I sighed. I *had* tried to telephone them before just showing up at their door, but the line had crackled and sputtered and the call hadn't gone through. What was I supposed to have done? Wait for Mahanagar Telephone Nigam to get its act together, while my sister lay in bed with a fever?

I came out of the bathroom, forcing a polite smile on my

face. 'Sorry I came without calling first,' I said to Kalyani. 'I just thought I'd bring some clothes for Juee to change into, and check on her.'

Kalyani looked me up and down, the beginnings of a sneer on her lips. Her eyes stayed a long moment on the muddy edge of my sari. 'How nice,' she said, with a patently false smile. 'Juee is resting at the moment. Do you want to wait till she wakes up, or—?'

'Of course she wants to wait! You can't possibly expect her to leave!' Sadanand's voice rang out down the corridor. He walked towards us, an amiable smile on his face. 'I'm sure your sister will appreciate you coming.' Indicating a maroon paisley-print sofa near the wall, he said, 'Please sit. Will you have some tea?'

I smiled and nodded, thinking to myself how different the brother was from his sister.

'Prabha has gone to the market.' Kalyani sniffed. 'We can have tea when she returns. We weren't expecting . . . company, you see.'

I opened my mouth to apologise again for not calling before, but Sadanand was already shaking his head. 'Don't be ridiculous,' he told his sister. 'Surely we can manage tea for our guest on our own?' He strode into the kitchen without waiting for an answer and I heard the sound of water pouring into a vessel. Sadanand was making tea? This was . . . unprecedented, in my limited experience. Nana never stepped into the kitchen, except to fetch himself a glass of water sometimes. My male cousins, too, would be hard-pressed to even find the tea things in their own houses, let alone actually making a cup of tea for guests.

I had found Sadanand likeable enough till this point, but

this tea-making business was rapidly making him rise in my esteem. As I took a seat on the sofa, I found myself secretly supporting Aai's one-woman campaign: Juee could do a lot worse than this man.

He came out of the kitchen ten minutes later, carrying a tray with four steaming floral cups resting on matching saucers. The first sip was heaven. An entire cup of piping-hot tea, without Aai's disapproving scowl somewhere on the horizon, seemed like the very limit of pleasure at the moment. Sadanand had made it with crushed ginger, and the heat of it spread through my damp body like fire. I could actually feel it warming my stomach.

'This is excellent tea.' I sighed. 'Perfect for a cold, rainy day.'

'Would you like some more?' Sadanand asked, holding the tray down so Aniruddha and Kalyani could also help themselves. 'I've made plenty.'

'Yes, and get us some biscuits too,' Aniruddha replied.

I waited for Sadanand to protest at his friend casually ordering him about like that, but he simply nodded and went back to the kitchen. I drank my tea and minded my own business. If he wanted to let Aniruddha walk all over him in his own house, that was his choice.

A few moments later, he returned with a plate full of the strangest biscuits I'd ever seen. Back home, we'd have brown Parle glucose biscuits with our tea (or turmeric milk, in my unfortunate case); unless Nana had run into a khari-seller on his way, in which case we had the delicious, light-as-air maska khari. These biscuits, on the other hand, were thick, dense, creamy white and speckled with green and yellow pieces of . . . something. I took one off the plate and bit into it.

It was buttery, dissolving into sugary powder in my mouth, the green and yellow bits harder than the rest of the biscuit, which nevertheless made for an interesting change.

'Where are these biscuits from?' I asked Sadanand. 'They're quite delicious.'

'You've never had Karachi Bakery biscuits before?' Kalyani asked, an astounded look on her face, which was pretty unjustified in my opinion. These weren't exactly Marie biscuits, were they, that *everyone* would've had them at some time or another?

'No, nobody from my family has ever been to Pakistan,' I replied.

Kalyani kept her cup on her saucer and giggled. 'Karachi Bakery biscuits don't come from *Karachi*!' she squealed.

Oh, how I wanted to wipe that superior smirk from her face! It was clear she was enjoying this, possibly more than strictly necessary, given her Grace fiasco yesterday.

'I bought them in Delhi,' Aniruddha said quietly. 'The last time I was there for a meeting.'

'Please, take some more.' Sadanand held out the plate to me with a smile, but I shook my head politely and downed the rest of my tea.

'May I see Juee now?' I asked, placing the cup and saucer on a small wooden teapoy* next to my chair. 'If she's woken up, I mean?'

---

* The coffee table is a comparatively recent addition to the Indian living room. Before its arrival, we had the teapoy, a three-legged stool that derives its name from a mispronunciation of the Indian words for 'three legs'. Given the nation's obsession with tea, it is somehow a more fitting item of décor.

'Of course!' Sadanand put down his half-finished tea and led the way.

Juee was in a richly furnished bedroom, lying on an old mahogany four-poster bed under a thick cotton dulai. A barred window on the wall next to the bed overlooked a quiet, leafy cul-de-sac. When we entered, she was looking out of the window, her face wan. The moment she saw me, though, her face brightened and a surprised smile appeared on her lips. 'Ila! Aga . . . but how—?'

'I brought some clothes for you.' I sat on the edge of her bed and felt her forehead. It was hot. 'I thought you'd be more comfortable in your own things . . .'

She was wearing a maxi,* probably one of Kalyani's, and seemed a little conscious of it, to be honest. We wore saris at home, usually, as did Aai. The idea that you needed a separate kind of clothing to sleep in, seemed very . . . like something rich people did in movies. But I suppose Kalyani was rich enough to afford maxis.

'How are you feeling now?' Sadanand asked softly from the doorway. He had not come into the room.

---

* A quintessentially Indian word for the nightgown, the maxi liberated Indian women from the confines of the sari at bedtime. As opposed to the sari, which required a blouse and a petticoat worn underneath, the maxi needed no such crutches. It was a garment complete in itself and as Ila rightly notes, a definite indicator of class, as seen on generations of Bollywood actresses portraying rich heiresses in Hindi movies, all of whom inexplicably wore ruffled pink maxis to bed. Even today, the maxi speaks volumes about the class of the person who wears it, especially if said person is wearing it with a dupatta thrown over it, as she haggles with the vegetable vendor.

'Better.' Juee beamed, the colour rising on her fair cheeks. 'Honestly, I think I am fine now . . .'

'You feel warm,' I told her. 'Your fever doesn't seem to have gone.'

'It comes and goes,' she said, with a tired sigh. 'I think it'll get better once I go home.'

'Absolutely not!' Sadanand stepped into the room, a mock-stern expression on his face. 'The doctor says you must rest here till your ankle gets better and the fever goes.'

'I don't want to trouble you all unnecessarily . . .' she said pleadingly.

'It's no trouble at all.' His voice was gentle. 'Please, stay as long as you need to.'

They were looking at each other shyly. I might as well have been a decorative cushion on the bed for all the attention they paid me in that moment.

I hid my smile.

'Well,' I said archly, as I got up from the bed, 'I see you have *everything* you need over here. I'll come back tomorrow to check on you.'

'You're . . . you're going?' Juee sounded so forlorn, I sat back down.

'Well . . . yes, but I'll come tomorrow morning again.'

'Couldn't you just . . . stay here?' Sadanand asked.

I didn't know what to say. It was bad enough that Aai's stupid machinations had forced Juee to stay uninvited at the Pingleys. Adding myself to the guest list felt like a colossal imposition.

'I . . . no, how can I?' I looked at Juee for help, but she was looking hopefully at me.

'You must,' Sadanand said firmly. 'You can sleep in this

54

room with Juee, Kalyani can take my room and I will sleep in the living room.'

'No, I couldn't possibly . . .' I imagined Kalyani's face when her brother broke this news to her. 'It's too much trouble for you . . .'

'Like I told your sister' – Sadanand smiled at me and then at Juee – 'it is no trouble at all.'

FIVE

'How is she now?' Sadanand asked, as I came out of the bedroom.

I had spent all evening taking care of Juee, after calling Aai and telling her of the change in plans. She was more than glad to have me stay, as long as it meant Juee stayed as well. So I had stayed, pressing Juee's aching legs, placing a handkerchief drenched in cool water on her warm forehead from time to time, and coaxing her to eat. The fever had taken away her appetite and spoiled her sense of taste, but she had agreed to have a biscuit with some tea, before falling into a fitful sleep a few minutes before.

I was glad I'd come. Juee would never have allowed Kalyani to massage her legs, no matter how much pain she was in. Nor would she have slept with her head in Kalyani's lap, like she had in mine. Some things, you need a sister for.

Now, as I slipped out of the room to make mau bhaat for Juee – I would sprinkle some salt and add a spoonful of ghee to make the rice gruel more palatable for her – I saw worry etched on Sadanand's boyish face and gave him a reassuring smile.

'She is asleep,' I told him. 'I thought I'd take the chance to make some dinner for her.'

'Prabha, our cook, can help you with anything you need,' Sadanand said, leading the way to the kitchen.

In the living room, we passed Aniruddha, who had been asked to stay the night. I was a little surprised that he had agreed to – after all, he would have to sleep on a sofa, like Sadanand, and surely he would have a problem with that, considering how rich and fancy he seemed, with his Delhi biscuits and business trips. But he had not made a word of complaint and now seemed to be quietly occupied at the writing desk, the silence around him punctuated only by the soft scratching of his fountain pen on the paper.

Kalyani was sitting on the sofa next to the desk, watching him . . . *write a letter*? The woman clearly had nothing to do all day. My disapproval must've come out in a sigh or something because I saw Aniruddha glance at me for a long moment, before quickly looking away.

The rain I had faced on my way there had reduced my sari to a crumpled mess and hours of sitting in a warm, humid room meant my hair was probably dishevelled as well. Not quite the picture of feminine beauty then. *Not fair at all.* I sniffed, refusing to even look in his direction, the judgmental fool.

In the kitchen, Sadanand introduced me to Prabha, who turned out to be a reed-thin woman in her thirties. She had a no-nonsense air about her and when I asked her if she could make mau bhaat, she nodded.

'I'll see if we have some metkoot* as well,' she told me briskly. 'It'll be good for her.'

'Please tell me if we don't,' Sadanand told her. 'I'll ask if the neighbours have some.'

I smiled inwardly at his concern, as we returned to the living room. There, I couldn't help but look around with carefully concealed admiration. Earlier, with my mind filled with concern for Juee, I hadn't quite noticed the beauty of the room. Oh, I had realised that it was spacious – more so than any room I'd ever been in. But now, I could appreciate the details. The elegant art deco light fixture on the ceiling. The tasteful print on the curtains. And, oh! An entire wall lined with glass-fronted cabinets full of books. The titles were a mix of Marathi and English literature. I saw books by N. S. Inamdar and Shivaji Sawant rubbing shoulders with the collected works of P. G. Wodehouse and James Hadley Chase.

My gaze landed on the newspapers stacked neatly on the teapoy and I pulled one off the top, sitting myself down on a sofa chair – as far away from Aniruddha's desk as the room allowed – to read it.

Sadanand picked up a magazine from the teapoy and sank down on the sofa opposite me. I rifled idly through the pages of the newspaper, till I reached the Vacancies page. There were job openings by the dozen. Most of them didn't

---

* A quintessentially Maharashtrian accompaniment to soft, sticky rice, metkoot is made from roasted and powdered lentils, cereals and spices. Generations of Marathi kids have grown up eating this ultimate comfort food, and its ability to be easily digested makes it a very nourishing option for the ill.

even require a master's degree, as they were for graduates. I sat up straight in the chair, staring at them. Hmmm. *I* was a graduate. Could I get one of these jobs? It wouldn't matter that Aai wasn't letting me pursue an MA – I could still work. All I had to do was apply to any of these places.

A dozen possible futures swam before my eyes. *I could be a clerk at an accounting firm. No, they need someone with a commerce degree and I have a BA. At a bank, then? Maybe as a typist? But I would have to learn typing for that. Perhaps I could. There has to be a typing course somewhere near our house, where I could enrol. I could dip into my savings for the fees. Or borrow from Nana perhaps . . .*

My thoughts were interrupted by the sounds of Kalyani's cooing conversation with Aniruddha. I tried to ignore it, but the woman seemed incapable of operating under a certain volume.

'Your handwriting is so neat!' she exclaimed. 'Dada's looks like scratches and squiggles. I keep telling him he should have been a doctor, he writes so untidily!'

No response.

'Is this a very important letter?' she tried again.

'Yes.'

'Who is it for?' She craned her neck, trying to see who it was addressed to.

'Kishore.' Aniruddha's voice was deep and steady. 'My meetings in Bombay have changed some things for us.'

'But not your plan to bring Gauri here, I hope!' Kalyani got up from the sofa and leaned coquettishly against the desk. It moved a little, shifting the paper on which Aniruddha was writing. He stopped writing and gave an impatient sigh, and she stopped leaning against the table immediately.

'No, she will be here in a few weeks,' he replied, continuing his letter.

'Oh, good!' Kalyani clapped her hands. 'I want to take her to see a play this time, or maybe a movie—'

'No.'

'But why?' Kalyani looked affronted.

'She's too young to go to the movies without supervision.'

'*I'll* be there with her!'

'That's not saying much,' Sadanand declared.

Kalyani glared at him but fell silent for a few moments. Then, she asked. 'Ila . . . it is Ila, isn't it?'

'Yes,' I replied, looking up from the newspaper.

'Do you want me to lend you some clothes to change into? Yours must be wet. We wouldn't want *you* to catch a cold as well, would we?'

Her smile was almost a sneer. For a split second, I imagined myself through her eyes – dark-skinned and damp with sweat, a messy plait dangling over the shoulder, sari hem splattered with dirty water. Unwelcome and unwanted, an object of charity to her.

'I'm fine, thank you,' I replied evenly. 'I've brought some clothes. I'll change before bedtime.'

'Bai-bai,' she said pointedly. 'Didn't you come . . . *well-prepared*?'

'It's the rains,' I told her, refusing to let her implication annoy me. 'Better to be safe than sorry, na?'

She gave me a long look, then changed her tack. 'So . . . now that Arun is married,' she came and sat on the sofa next to Sadanand, 'people must be asking your parents about all of you girls as well, right? About when you'll be married, I mean.'

'I don't see why,' I said lightly. 'It's not like we're related to Arun.'

'Still,' she moved again, this time sitting down on the matching sofa chair next to me, 'one wedding in a building and suddenly everyone wakes up and starts noticing all the other unmarried people in the building.' She turned to Sadanand and said. 'Yes, na, Dada?'

Sadanand shrugged noncommittally and Kalyani turned back to me.

'Your parents *must* be worried. You mother practically said so at Arun's wedding.' Again, that mocking smile. 'But I don't blame her. What with there being four of you to marry . . .'

'Three,' I corrected her.

'Oh? Don't you have two younger sisters?'

'I do.' I turned my attention back to the newspaper. 'It's just . . . *I* have no plans to get married.'

The sound of Aniruddha's pen on the paper stopped, leaving the room in sudden silence for a moment.

'Really?' Sadanand asked, lowering his magazine. 'That's very modern of you.'

'Oh, come on!' Kalyani rolled her eyes. 'She doesn't really *mean* it.'

'Yes, I do,' I said and as I said it, I realised it was completely true. 'I don't see any reason to get married.'

'So you'll just . . . just . . .' Kalyani couldn't seem to find the words to finish the sentence.

'I'll just . . . get a job and take care of my parents in their old age.'

'Very admirable.' Sadanand grinned.

'Admirable?' Kalyani asked derisively, turning to me.

'It's ridiculous. You can't tell me that's what your parents want for you.'

'It's what *I* want for me,' I replied, with a small smile.

'Hear, hear!' Sadanand said. 'Women's rights and all that.'

'Really, Dada, what do women's rights have to do with getting married?' Kalyani snapped. 'Are you saying women lose their rights once they marry? What rights do they lose? Simply absurd things you say.' She brushed back a stray wisp of hair and looked him squarely in the eye. 'And you don't really support this way of thinking, either. If tomorrow *I* said I didn't want to get married, that I just wanted to stay with you my whole life, would you be okay with that?' Without pausing for an answer, she continued. 'I don't think so. And why just you? Ask Aniruddha.' She turned to him. 'Would you want Gauri to stay unmarried her whole life and take care of you? No, na?'

Without looking up from his letter Aniruddha replied. 'Absolutely not.'

'Even if *she* wanted to?' I asked, looking at him.

'What she wants doesn't come into the picture,' he said, looking at me. 'She is not mature enough to make that decision.'

'I see . . .' I said, folding the newspaper slowly. 'I don't know how old your sister is but when she is eighteen, she will be considered legally mature enough to get married, but *you* won't consider her mature enough to *decide* if she wants to get married?' I nodded in an expression of exaggerated understanding. 'Ye-es, that sounds logical.'

'So, in your opinion, she should have the freedom to decide if and when she will get married?' he asked, with a blank expression. 'And if she decides to get married at . . . let's say, forty, or later, when she can't have children—'

'Then that will be her choice,' I supplied.

'That will be a travesty,' he corrected me. 'There is a time for everything in life and if one doesn't marry at the right age, then . . .'

'What? Will the sky collapse?' My tone was light, but my eyes narrowed. 'Anyway, I should think any decent brother would have no problem supporting his unmarried sister, if she decided not to marry.'

'That is . . . not the issue, at all.' He bristled. 'I just want my sister to be happy . . . have her own life, her own family . . .'

'But if she thinks she can be happy staying unmarried, you would deny her that?' I arched my eyebrows. 'Seems contradictory. Besides, whoever said marriage is a guarantee of happiness, anyway?'

'Well, if you're going to question the very institution of marriage . . .' It was his turn to narrow his eyes.

'But you have to admit,' I said, 'there is no guarantee. You could end up married to a wife-beater, to a habitual cheater, a gambler . . .'

'All men are not like that.' Aniruddha shook his head in exasperation.

'Aha, but how do we women know what a man is like, *before* getting married to him? It's not as if men wear signboards announcing all their bad qualities.'

'Sorry, but neither do women,' Sadanand interjected mildly. 'A woman can also have bad habits, bad qualities. But when there is mutual respect and understanding between

63

two people, then they can get over their own drawbacks and work together towards a happy marriage.'

'I admire the way you think the best of people.' I gave him an amused smile. 'You and Juee have that in common.'

'Oh, good, then it can't be a bad quality.' He laughed.

'Not at all, it's a fine quality,' I said. 'I just think you give people more credit than they deserve.'

'Oh, so you don't like people in general?' Kalyani's tone was of exaggerated understanding, as she played with her braid. 'I thought it was only men.'

'I have nothing against men.' I shook my head and held up my hands. 'I just wish they treated us women like human beings.'

'Oh, come on!' Kalyani shook her head dismissively. 'You speak as if we were being yoked to ploughs and made to till fields!'

'We are being yoked to the kitchen and made to raise children,' I replied.

A moment of silence followed my words. Then:

'Some women find fulfilment in caring for their families.' Aniruddha frowned. 'They consider it their life's work.'

'And that is admirable.' I nodded. 'But the fact is, *that* is all the work a woman is allowed to do. If we want a job, it must come second to our household duties. Why? Are our dreams and aspirations not as important as a man's?'

'Nobody is saying that,' Sadanand said hastily.

'No, nobody is saying it,' I agreed. 'They are saying, "Marry right after college and have kids." They are saying, "Men don't like wives who are too smart." They are saying, "A working woman won't pay enough attention at home." *That*'s what they are saying.'

Again, there was a silence. Kalyani was staring at me like I was a dangerous animal. Sadanand was avoiding my eye. Only Aniruddha looked directly at me. His gaze was cold.

Thankfully, just then, I heard Juee's voice feebly calling out my name from the next room. I excused myself and rushed to see her.

'What is it?' I asked, feeling her forehead. It wasn't warm anymore. 'Is it your legs? Are they aching again?'

'No . . .' She shook her head. 'I just . . . is there anything to eat?'

I smiled in relief. If Juee wanted food, she was on the mend.

I was about to go to the kitchen to ask Prabha if the mau bhaat was ready, when I heard Kalyani's voice from the living room.

'Oh, please, Dada,' she said, and I could practically hear her scowl. 'Juee is sweet enough, but the other one is a nightmare! Honestly, who speaks like that in front of the people whose house you're staying at? Uninvited too!'

A murmur from Sadanand.

'So what if she hears me?' Kalyani demanded. 'She should know how mannerless she sounded just now! Getting into an argument with Aniruddha like that—? As if she knows everything—? More than *him* she knows—? Good she doesn't want to get married. Who will want to marry a girl like that anyway?'

I turned around to see if Juee had heard Kalyani. The shock on her face was evident. I shook my head airily to make it seem like a small thing, then I noisily pulled open the bedroom door and stepped into the living room.

Giving Kalyani a broad smile, I headed to the kitchen

to fetch Juee the mau bhaat. It didn't matter what Kalyani thought of me. Juee was getting better. And that meant that very soon I could be free of Kalyani Pingley, and the know-it-all who was the object of her attentions.

SIX

'But what did you say?' Juee asked the next morning, sitting up in bed and eating her moog dal khichdi. 'Why did Kalyani say all that about you?'

I rolled my eyes in response. I had successfully dodged this question the evening before as Juee had been too weak to grill me. She had fallen asleep after having her rice, but I had stayed in the room till the others had retired to bed.

I had no intention of reliving Kalyani Pingley's words now – I could still hear the outrage in her voice when she questioned how I could possibly know more about anything than the great and mighty Aniruddha. As if he were some sage, some treasure-house of wisdom and we should all fall at his feet. *All men are not like that*, it seems. Hah. The nerve of the man. Aniruddha? More like Anir-uddhat.*

---

* Uddhat in Marathi means insolent, but the meaning differs with context. For example, to be considered uddhat, a boy must insult his elders or be openly rude to complete strangers. For a girl, it's much

I grinned at my pun and Juee's forehead creased.

'What's so funny?' she asked.

'Nothing,' I replied. 'I'll tell you what's *interesting*, though. How much Sadanand is . . . um . . . *concerned* . . . about you.' I waggled my eyebrows at her meaningfully.

'Nonsense.' She looked away, a half-smile on her lips. 'He's just being a good host. I'm his guest, after all . . .'

'Ah, but I think he's hoping you'll be a *lot* more than just a guest . . .'

'Oh, be quiet!' Juee laughed.

'And I think maybe you wouldn't *mind* being a lot more than his guest . . .'

She threw a pillow at me, which I caught deftly. The only reason we were being quite so relaxed and open was because the Pingleys and their friend were all out. Sadanand had gone to drop the doctor back to his clinic after he had declared Juee well enough to go home. Sadanand's smile had been muted when the doctor had given Juee the clean chit, and I could tell he had hoped she would stay for longer.

His sister had had no such concerns. After professing her tremendous relief and announcing how worried she had been for her 'dear friend', Kalyani had informed us that she absolutely had to step out of the house to buy a new sari. You know, instead of spending any more time with her 'dear friend'. And I assumed the thought of spending all morning alone with Juee and her *not fair at all* sister had horrified Aniruddha to his core, because at Kalyani's insistence he

---

easier. All you have to do to be considered uddhat is not smile as much as you're expected to. Mission accomplished.

had accompanied her. Leaving Juee and me alone to discuss current events to do with a certain Mr Pingley.

'But seriously, Juee,' I said, my tone sober. 'Don't pretend you don't like him. I see how shy you get around him.'

'I can't help it,' she said, hiding her face in her hands. 'When he looks at me . . . it's all I can do not to grin like a buffoon.'

'Oh, but you *do* grin like a buffoon,' I told her with a sage nod. 'He grins like a bigger buffoon, though, so it's okay.'

'You . . . you really think he . . . likes me?' Juee looked up, her eyes wide with hope.

'Please, it's so obvious! He keeps coming and checking on you, he's forever looking for ways to make you more comfortable, and the way his face fell when the doctor said you could go home—? The man is clearly in love.'

'I don't know . . .' Juee sighed. 'You really think so?'

'I do. In fact' – I smiled broadly – 'I think if he had it his way, *he* would be your doctor.'

'What?' Juee's face was blank.

I cleared my throat and sang a verse from a song I had heard recently, from the musical play *Swarsamradni*.

> *Come as a doctor, treat me in private,*
> *Give me a kiss like sugar syrup, a bandage-like embrace,*
> *My love, charmer of my heart,*
> *I grow restless when we are apart.*

Juee's eyes grew round and a blush spread across her cheeks. 'Ey! Stop saying these things!' she said, pinching my arm, but I was relentless.

'I'm only singing—ow!' I said, massaging my arm and

laughing at the outrage on her face. '*You* are the one think-ing it.'

Juee reached out to slap my arm, but stopped with her arm mid-air, a look of shock on her face. I turned around and my laughter caught in my throat.

Oh, no. Kalyani was standing at the door and, behind her, Aniruddha's expression was stunned. How much had they heard?

'When did you come?' I asked, scrambling off the bed. 'We didn't even hear the main door open.'

'Oh, but *we* heard.' Kalyani had an odd smile on her face. 'Didn't we, Aniruddha? What an . . . interesting choice of song, Ila.'

'Oh . . . uh . . . I was just . . .' *Oh, God*, I prayed, *please let them not have heard anything before the song.*

'Have you seen *Swarsamradni*?' Aniruddha asked. He sounded genuinely curious.

'Ha, ha, no,' I said, wringing my hands. 'I haven't been that lucky. I just heard it on the radio and it sounded—'

'—so *romantic*.' Kalyani grinned. 'A song about love. And lovers. And yearning. I have to say, I was surprised to find *you* singing it.'

I must have looked puzzled, because it was an extremely bizarre thing to say to someone you barely knew.

'Since you don't mean to marry, I mean,' Kalyani clarified. 'Why would you be interested in romantic songs, na, otherwise? Unless of course, you *do* mean to marry and everything you said last night . . . well, you didn't actually mean any of it, as I said. Not that romance necessarily has to mean marriage, for you modern types.' She gave me a smug smile.

Oh, God, the pettiness of this woman. Mentally, I took a deep breath. It was okay. I didn't have to put up with her for much longer.

We were going to leave as soon as Aai came to pick us up. She had insisted, over the phone, for some reason, despite Sadanand offering his car to drop us. I was just waiting for her to be there soon so we could be on our Kalyani-less way.

'No, no,' I replied lightly. 'I'm not *that* modern, if that is the right word. And I meant what I said – I don't actually plan to marry. But that doesn't mean I can't appreciate good music, just because it has to do with love, right? I mean, I don't actually plan to study linguistics, adopt a flower-seller and teach her how to talk Marathi like a posh person, but that hasn't stopped me from watching *Tee Phularani.*'

I saw one corner of Aniruddha's mouth turn upwards, ever so slightly.

'That's the play *Swarsamradni* is based on, right?' I asked him, arms crossed. I might not know *everything*, like Kalyani insisted the mighty Aniruddha did, but I knew *some* things.

'You could say that,' he said slowly. 'Except *Tee Phularani* itself was an adaptation of George Bernard Shaw's *Pygmalion.*'

Damnation. Did he absolutely *have* to be such a know-it-all?

Kalyani's face, which had looked sour while I was speaking, now broke into such a huge smile one could almost think someone had come and told her that the powers-that-be had decreed every day of the year to be Diwali from now on.

'How do you do that?' she asked, looking at Aniruddha with shining eyes. 'How do you know so much about . . . oh, about *everything*?'

He looked away without replying, an embarrassed

expression on his face. As if he wasn't secretly thrilled to bits at this effusion of admiration.

I was struggling to keep a straight face at Kalyani's little performance. If she threw herself at him any harder, he was going to get a bruise.

Fortunately, the doorbell rang just then and I was saved the necessity of holding in my grin: 'Perhaps that's Aai,' I said to Juee with a wide smile, a facial expression I had not recently used in association with my mother.

We followed Kalyani to the living room, Aniruddha bringing up the rear, just behind me.

As Kalyani opened the door, we saw Sadanand in the doorway and, behind him, Aai, accompanied by Latika.

I thought I heard Aniruddha sigh.

'Juee!' Aai yelled from the doorway. 'How are you, my girl?'

'I'm fine,' Juee said, a little sheepishly. Aai's volume rivalled Kalyani's but this wasn't her own home that she could just become a human loudspeaker whenever she felt like it.

'Such a lovely area Hindu Colony is,' Aai said, bustling in behind Sadanand. 'But so confusing! All these lanes! We would've just kept roaming around in circles had we not run into Sadanandrao.'

'Your house is nice and big,' Latika said to Sadanand, flopping down on the sofa next to Aai, like she owned it. 'It must've cost a lot!'

'Latika!' I hissed. Honestly, this girl! No tact, no politeness, no brain.

'I wouldn't know,' Sadanand said with a genial smile, settling on a chair. 'Our parents bought it a long time ago.'

'Well, it was an excellent investment,' Aai announced, looking around with interest. 'Are you planning to settle here after you get married?'

'Aai!' I exclaimed, looking at Juee's mortified face. 'That's quite a personal question.'

'I'm only asking!' she said to him, ignoring me completely. 'You must have given the subject some thought, na? I mean, you seem like you're of marriageable age. What are you, twenty-four? Twenty-five?'

'Twenty-six,' Sadanand replied. 'And, honestly, I've never thought about marriage before now. I suppose' – he glanced at Juee – 'I just didn't meet a girl who'd make me think of all that.'

'Well, don't waste more time,' Aai advised. 'Getting married at the right age is extremely important, you know. There is a right time for everything.'

'Not everyone agrees with that, though,' Kalyani piped up, shooting me a meaningful look.

'Anyone with sense will agree.' Aai shrugged. 'And why would you consider the opinions of senseless people, na?'

Kalyani did a terrible job of hiding her smile. Oh, how it must've tickled her to hear my own mother call me senseless, to see her uphold the old-fashioned opinions of that precious gift to mankind, Aniruddha Darshetkar. Little did she know that my mother was now at a point where she would probably be open to disowning me, if it meant her other three girls would get married to decent boys.

'We should leave,' I said brightly. 'It'll take us time to reach home otherwise.'

'No, please sit,' Sadanand appealed. 'We haven't even

offered you any tea.' He looked pointedly at Kalyani, who got up with a huff and headed to the kitchen, possibly to instruct Prabha to make some tea for Aai and Latika.

'Juee, look in on the Kelkars in the evening, if you're feeling up to it,' Aai said. 'Arun's wife was asking after you yesterday, when they came for dinner.'

She has a name, I thought. *You can stop referring to her as 'Arun's wife'*. Aloud I asked. 'Arun and Sudha came for dinner yesterday? What for?'

'Look, it is traditional to invite a newly married couple to your house for a meal,' Aai explained. 'Arun, his wife, his sister and Kelkar Kaka-Kaku all came.'

'Aai made puran polis.' Latika gave me a teasing look. 'You missed it!'

'I haven't had homemade puran polis in so long,' Sadanand said wistfully.

'Juee makes *excellent* puran polis!' Aai beamed. 'You must come over for a meal, once she is better. She can make them for you.'

'I'd . . . love to,' Sadanand said, looking from Aai to Juee, who looked at her lap shyly.

I sighed. Was subtlety just a word to my mother? She couldn't be any more obvious if she dangled some mundaavlya* in front of Sadanand's face and winked.

I saw Aniruddha watching the entire scene with a look of quiet disapproval on his face. He must've felt my gaze

---

* Strings of pearls or flowers tied around the foreheads of Maharashtrian brides and grooms, which dangle on both sides of their faces. Because subtlety *is* just a word when it comes to Maharashtrian weddings.

because he turned to look at me. For a moment our eyes met, then he looked away, seemingly in confusion.

'You can also come, if you like,' Aai told him, as an afterthought.

'Thank you, but I don't like sweets,' he replied.

Aai looked affronted. 'What? No *sweets*? *No* sweets? I have never heard of such a thing!'

Aniruddha shrugged.

'Is it a health issue?' she asked, frowning.

'No. I just don't like sweets.'

'What about paakatlya purya?'

'No.'

'Chirote?'

'No.'

'Shankarpaali?'

'No.'

'Sudharas then?'

'No.'

'But that's just . . .' Aai began, only to be interrupted, thankfully, by Latika.

'So . . . are *you* going to invite Arun and his wife for lunch or something?' my sister asked Sadanand, eyes wide, smile broad. 'You should, you know. It's traditional.'

'It's not traditional for friends to do that,' I told her. Really, did Latika have any idea how presumptuous she sounded? 'It's only the done thing for relatives or neighbours, right, Aai?'

'Hmm, but it would be a nice gesture,' Sadanand said, leaning forward in his chair and looking thoughtful. 'Yes. Yes, I think we *should* invite Arun over. Na, Aniruddha?'

Aniruddha made a non-committal sound. 'If you want to,' he said. 'It's your house.'

'Then it's settled.' Sadanand grinned and slapped his thigh, as Kalyani emerged from the kitchen, followed by Prabha carrying a tray laden with tea things.

'What's settled?' Kalyani asked, perching on the arm of the sofa next to Aniruddha.

'We're having Arun and his family over for lunch,' Sadanand told her.

'Ooh, good, can we come too?' Latika asked, clapping her hands together in excitement.

I waited for Aai to say something, but other than a fond smile in Latika's direction, there was no response. Of course.

'Latika, you can't just invite yourself over to someone's house—' I began.

'*You* can,' Kalyani muttered, in what she must have thought was a quiet manner.

'—for a meal,' I finished lamely. Clearly, she was never going to let this go.

Sadanand, who hadn't heard his sister, opened his arms in a magnanimous gesture and announced. 'Of course, you all must come! Shall we say sometime next week? I'll invite some other friends also. Let's make it a grand lunch!'

SEVEN

The day after we returned from the Pingleys' house was a Saturday. Nana had returned home early from college. As I took his things, I noticed an inland letter* in his hands.

'Who's that from?' I asked, pointing at the blue folded paper.

'Yamuna Atya's son,' he replied, checking the back of the inland for the sender's name and address.

'What does *he* want?' Aai, who had just come out into the living room with Nana's tea, asked the question with one hand on her hip. Her voice was cold.

---

* Like many other countries, before email zoomed into our lives, India communicated through its postal service. An inland letter was a sheet of blue, pre-stamped, pre-gummed paper on which you could write a nice, long letter, then seal it on three sides and send it anywhere across India for just a few paise, confident in the knowledge that it would reach its recipient – eventually – without its contents being exposed to prying eyes.

'How can I tell without reading?' Nana settled into his armchair and slit open the letter with his thumbnail.

'Dear Mama,' he read. 'Saa. Na. Vi. Vi.* It is with a heavy heart . . . inform you that our respected mater . . . passed on from this world . . . Oh, no.' Nana frowned and gave a deep sigh.

Yamuna Atya† was my father's sister. We had never met her in our lives because of some family feud that Nana avoided talking about and Aai refused to mention because she said it raised her blood pressure. Now, it seemed, this aunt was no more.

'In her last hours, our . . . mother expressed her considerable regret at . . . the way things ended between our two families.' Nana squinted at the tiny, spidery handwriting that filled the page. 'Father, as you must recall, was . . . a man of very . . . fixed ideas . . .'

'Hah!' Aai exclaimed. 'Understatement.'

'When an idea took root in his mind, it was impossible to change it,' Nana continued, holding the letter a little away,

---

*   Short for Saashtang Namaskar Vinanti Vishesh. A saashtang namaskar is when you prostrate yourself before someone to show your respect. Vinanti is a request. Vishesh is anything special. The whole thing is a deeply respectful greeting, usually to someone elder. What? Did you think no acronyms existed before someone invented YOLO? Lol, friend, lol.

†   The English simply have aunts. Maharashtrians are rather better organised when it comes to female relatives. Is she your father's sister? Then she is your Atya. Is she your mother's sister or friend? Maushi. Mother's brother's wife? Mami. Father's brother's or friend's wife? Kaku. Elderly neighbour who is of no relation to you? Friend's mom? Random woman who is older than you and whose name you don't know? Once, twice, three times a Kaku.

so he could read it better. 'So after the unpleasant incident, of which you are well aware, took place, it was likewise impossible for him to look favourably upon the persons involved, till the day he died. This tragic occurrence occurred last year. He had forbidden Aai from keeping in touch with her relations in his lifetime and, as his wife, she would not dream of defying her husband.' Nana continued: 'Since his passing, however, my mother has felt the urge many a time to write to you. But remorse and a profound sense of shame held her back. However, on her deathbed she bid me to repair the rift between our families. This letter is an attempt to do so.'

He scanned the rest of the letter in silence for a few seconds. Then he turned to Aai slowly and said, 'He wants to come and stay with us for some time. He is in town on some business for his employer.' Nana looked at her. 'Wants to stay for a few days till his work is over. Says what is past is past and that he is very eager to meet us and his cousins.'

'Is it? Us and his cousins?' Aai demanded, handing him the teacup and planting both hands firmly on her hips. 'And did he happen to mention how eager he is to see the house he will inherit after you die?'

She was referring to the fact that Nana's father, our grandfather, had left behind a complicated will. According to this will, we were free to live in the house we were currently living in, till Nana passed away. But after that, the house would pass to Yamuna Atya and her heirs. Which meant that if Nana died, we wouldn't just have to vacate this house we were living in, we'd essentially have no place to live at all.

I glanced around. It was a nice little house, really – well, to *my* mind at least. One bedroom, one kitchen, one living room with a small balcony on one end. The balcony overlooked the quadrangle below, which stood in the centre of our little society surrounded on three sides by buildings, outlined by ixora bushes. Right in the heart of the quiet little suburb known as Vile Parle East. Or just Parle, as we called it. A neighbourhood of peaceful lanes lined with tall, shady trees and small housing societies, with the odd bungalow here and there. Where people carried on with their hard-working lives and chased simple joys, coming together for festivals and weddings as a tightly knit community. With the faraway chugging of the trains at Parle railway station punc-tuating the stillness of the afternoons and, now and then, a tantalising whiff of biscuits from the famous Parle biscuit factory dancing on the breeze. We had all been born here. We had grown up here. We had all gone to the same school down the road, as had all our friends. We had played hopscotch in that quadrangle below. Everything we knew and loved was here. But if we wanted to continue living here after Nana was gone, then we would have to pay Yamuna Atya and her son rent – which we wouldn't have money for; or beg them to let us live here for free – which was unlikely, unless Aai grew a new personality overnight.

'He didn't.' Nana shook his head. 'But seeing as he will inherit it anyway, do you think refusing to let him stay here now is an option?'

'Obviously not,' Aai snapped. 'We wouldn't want him to hold it against us and throw me and the girls out on the street after you go up there' – she pointed heavenwards – 'would we?'

'Cheer up,' Nana said, with a crooked smile. 'Perhaps the girls will all be married by then.'

'Oh . . . so only I will be destitute?' Aai's nostrils flared.

'How nice. And why should I think the girls will be married by then? How will that happen if their father takes no interest? By magic?'

I left them to bicker and went into the bedroom, where Juee was embroidering a cushion cover. She really was quite good at it.

'They started again, huh?' she asked, as I sat down on the floor next to her. She was making small flowers by knotting the thread in some nefarious way I didn't understand.

'Yes.' I nodded. 'Really makes you wonder what they saw in one another, back in the day.'

'Oh, you know,' Juee said, head bent on her sewing. 'You've seen their old photos.'

'They were both good-looking, yes,' I said, running my fingers over the silky skeins of the embroidery threads. 'You're telling me that's all?'

'Aai once told me that the moment Nana stepped into her home to see her, she decided he was the man she would marry.'

'Without even talking to him once?' I rolled my eyes. 'That explains it.'

'Maybe when you know . . .' Juee said, a dreamy look in her eyes, 'you just know.'

I eyed her critically. 'Hmm . . .' I said, stroking my chin dramatically. 'The patient's symptoms seem to be getting serious.'

'What?' She looked up from her needlework, confused.

'Looks like the *doctor* will have to be called . . .' I waggled my eyebrows at her and gave her a knowing smile.

She smacked her forehead with her hand and burst out laughing. 'Ila, sometimes, na, you really . . .'

But I never got to hear the next part of that sentence because Aai chose that moment to walk in and nod at me.

'Come,' she said. 'Help me make puran polis.'

'What? Now? Why?' I demanded.

'Because I'm telling you to,' Aai replied, making furious gestures towards the kitchen. 'Come, come, don't waste time now.'

I got up with a sigh and followed her to the kitchen. The hulk of the puran[*] yantra – the puran-making machine – was lying on the kitchen counter already. I tucked my sari padar at the waist and pulled it to me, as Aai ladled the sticky puran mixture into it.

As I turned the handle of the yantra, making its blades rotate and mash the puran, I threw a sidelong glance at Aai. She looked resolute, her lips pursed in grim concentration as she watched my hands to make sure I wasn't slacking or doing something wrong.

'So . . . these puran polis are for Sadanand?' I asked.

'Not just him,' came the cryptic reply.

'But mostly for him, right? And you are going to tell him Juee made them?'

'Why?' she asked, looking at me. 'Is that a problem?'

'No.' I said. 'Juee makes good puran polis anyway . . . you didn't ask her to make these because she is still a little weak, right?'

----

[*] A mixture made of cooked chana dal fried in spices, and cooled. That this humble mixture can transform into the culinary marvel that is the puran poli only goes to prove something philosophical, which the author cannot quite pinpoint at this moment due to a sudden and urgent craving for puran polis.

'Exactly.' She returned her gaze to my hands, rubbing my back in a fond sort of way. 'I'm so glad you understand.'

I wish you understood, I thought to myself. *That as happy as I am for Juee, I know marriage can never make me happy. Not if I have to lure a man into matrimony with the promise of sweets, like some kind of halwai-hunter combination. And certainly not while the man in question gapes at the shade of my skin and thinks he could've done better.* But I kept my thoughts to myself.

A couple of hours later, the kitchen filled with the sweet smell of roasting puran polis. Latika tiptoed in for a peek. Aai fondly fed her a morsel of a poli, hot off the tavaa, dousing it in toop beforehand.

'Mmmmm,' Latika said, shutting her eyes in a paroxysm of delight.

Aai and I exchanged a look before laughing. 'Arre! See this!' Aai slapped her forehead and shook her head. 'I almost forgot.' She walked out of the hot kitchen and, a moment later, we heard the heavy iron almirah in the bedroom open. Another moment and she was back, holding a thin cardboard box in her hands. She handed it to me with the air of someone giving a small child a prize.

It was a light pink box, with 'Fair & Lovely' written on it in purple lettering. In one corner were two pictures of the same girl: in one she looked dusky; in the other, fair.

'It's brand new, just came out last year,' Aai gushed excitedly. 'The Jadhavs from the first floor? Their Prerna swears by this! So I got you also a pack.'

I sighed. Prerna Jadhav had luminous skin the colour of rosewood, perfect pearl-white teeth and the brightest, most intelligent eyes I'd ever seen. Her posture was ramrod straight, her hair long, lush and raven-black. She looked like

83

some kind of tribal* Goddess to me. But, of course, she swore by this . . . this atrocity.

I would swear too, if someone suggested that I needed to be fair to be lovely.

'Go, keep it with your things,' Aai told me. 'Apply it every day, okay?'

I was bubbling with irritation as I turned on my heel and strode away, only to hear Latika complain behind my back: 'Why does *she* get a new cream? I also want one!'

That settled it. This family was going to drive me crazy. Aai's idea of being fond towards Latika was to feed her puran poli that *I* had made, and me—? I was to be given this abomination of a face cream. Was she so convinced that I was worthless without it? Without fair skin? Without a husband? And Nana . . . he had pitched a tent on the path of least resistance for so long, very soon he'd start getting his mail there.

I had to get out of this place somehow. Marriage was clearly not going to be the way out. It was high time I found a different path.

---

*   Mainstream Hindu Gods and Goddesses are all somehow depicted as being fair. There are a few notable exceptions, of course: Krishna, Ram and Kali come to mind. But so entrenched is the bias against dark skin that Ram, and more notably Krishna and Kali – whose names *literally* mean the Dark One – are nevertheless usually shown to have blue skin instead of dark brown or black. On the other hand, the deities worshipped by the tribal, aboriginal and far-flung rural communities of India often have their likenesses carved from dark rock or sandstone and, perhaps for that reason, embrace much more readily darkness in appearance and power alike.

I flung open the fadtaal* and buried the hated cream under the piles of clothes at the back. From the bottom shelf, I pulled out some lined paper and my fountain pen. I fetched my purse and pulled out the job listings I had cut out from the newspaper at Sadanand's place, with his permission. Settling down on the floor, with the newspaper cuttings by my side, I picked up an old book lying nearby and held it in my lap for support. Placing the notepaper over it, I uncapped the fountain pen and wrote:

'Respected sir, this is with regard to the advertisement for the vacancy in your esteemed company, for the position of . . .'

---

* A closet or cupboard in Marathi, but given the phonetics of the word, you'd be entirely forgiven in thinking it was some kind of ravaging demon.

EIGHT

Sometimes you work yourself into a frenzy imagining the worst possible scenario for something that's about to happen, but what actually happens ends up being not that bad.

The past few days have been the exact opposite of that experience.

Because when Nana announced that we were going to be hosting some long-lost cousin of ours for a few days, none of us had imagined that the cousin in question would be anything like Vishnu Chhatre.

He arrived on Tuesday evening with a bulging hold-all and an expression that was simultaneously ingratiating and apologetic. He appeared to be in his early thirties, with thinning hair, a pencil-thin moustache and slightly protruding eyes. And he was dressed in a shirt and . . . a dhotar! To what century did this man belong? As soon as he entered, he bowed low and touched Nana and Aai's feet.

Then, he gave a speech. That's right. A fully prepared speech. Peppered with words like 'familial responsibility', 'filial estrangement' and 'domestic sanctity'. He sounded like he had eaten a dictionary for lunch. Juee had to elbow me in the ribs because clearly my face reflected both amusement and bafflement.

'Some people aren't good at first impressions,' she had whispered. 'Don't be mean.'

Well, as it turned out, Vishnu was great at first impressions – in the sense that every subsequent impression only made him seem worse. Take dinner that night.

'What a lovely house, Mami,' he said to Aai in his slightly nasal voice, looking around the room as if taking measurements for curtains. 'And this meal!' He looked at his plate as if it was filled with gold nuggets. 'Reminds us of our teerthroop Aai.'

We were all sitting cross-legged on the floor in a circle, our dinner plates before us. Sitting across from Vishnu, I tried to catch Juee's eye. To the best of our knowledge, he was an only child, so his use of the first person plural was bizarre, to say the least. Was he using it as a 'royal we'? Gods above.

'Was Yamuna Atya a good cook?' Juee ignored me completely as she asked this question.

'Not really.' Vishnu beamed. 'But everything she made, she made with such love.'

I turned from Juee to Aai, to see how she had taken this backhanded compliment to her cooking. I could see from the faint frown on her face that it had landed on her like a swarm of flies.

'So what is it that you do?' Latika asked, in her usual abrupt fashion.

'I am the head priest of the Bhagwati temple in Wai,' he said, chest all puffed up. 'You must have heard of it?'

Wai, would we have heard of it? I vaguely knew that the place was somewhere close to Panchgani, but I saw a glimmer of recognition on Aai and Nana's faces, so apparently they had heard of the temple.

'Bhagwati temple . . . you mean the one made in Hemadpanti style?' Nana asked. Turning to us he explained. 'Hemadpant was—'

'—Is it anywhere near the temple built by Ramdas Swami?' Aai interrupted.

'Yes and no,' Vishnu said, shovelling varan-bhaat into his mouth. 'Yes, it is made in the Hemadpanti style, and no, it's not near the other temple.'

'You know about Hemadpant?' Nana peered at Vishnu over his glasses, his eyebrows arched in surprise.

'Naw,' Vishnu mumbled with his mouth full. 'But' – he swallowed – 'Kaveribai Bhagwat, whose family built the temple back in 1305, she told us the history.' A satisfied smile crept over his face. 'We are a little . . . special to her, you see.'

'How come?' I asked, in spite of myself.

'Well, see, it is like this.' Vishnu crammed a huge portion of rice into his mouth. 'When the previous head priest died childless, Kaveribai handpicked us to fill the position. She is a very gracious lady. Comes from a long line of noblemen – very old family, the Bhagwats, very connected. Naturally, we are always eager to hear anything she feels like sharing about the family's history. And what a history it is! We find ourselves quite unable to resist gasping at the exploits of her ancestors. And pointing out how it was a black day in Indian history when the princely states were dissolved.'

I struggled to keep my face straight as I met Nana's eyes. His face was expressionless, but he was betrayed by the twinkle in his eye – the kind he got when he was about to pull Aai's leg.

'Kaveribai and her daughter value our company highly because of all this, you see,' Vishnu continued, wolfing down the varan-bhaat on his plate. 'Kaveribai's daughter is also like her – elegant, cultured, the very model of womanhood. We never fail to bring this to their notice and, needless to say, they fully agree. Yes, we like to think Kaveribai has no cause to regret appointing us as the head priest of such a prestigious temple.'

'That sounds like a very respectable way to make a living,' Nana said solemnly. I spotted the double meaning in that sentence instantly. 'So . . . it is on her business that you're here?'

'Well, partly,' Vishnu said, and a gleefully shy expression came upon his face. 'Kaveribai's daughter had ordered a piece of jewellery from a store here in Mumbai and Kaveribai told us we were the only man she trusted to see that it would be made properly. Goldsmiths, you see. Liars and cheats, the lot of them. We must make sure they use pure gold and not fleece Kaveribai in the bargain. Only then will we bring it safe and sound back to Wai. So we were coming here for that anyway . . .' He looked down at his plate and added, 'And she also told us, "Vishnubhat,* find

---

* The suffix 'bhat' is used to address priests, in the same way the prefix 'pandit' is in Hindi. Drop an extra 'a' in there and 'bhat' becomes 'bhaat', a cook. Make the 't' sound softer in the end of 'bhaat' and it means cooked rice. What is the relevance of all this here? Who can tell?

yourself a good wife while you're there, you're twenty-eight already."'

And then, to my horror, he looked directly at Juee.

That was two days ago. Since then, Vishnubhat – as I insist on calling him now, because, really, he asked for it – has been looking at Juee with the single-minded creepiness of ... well ... a single-minded creep. I get it, my sister *is* beautiful, but to come into her own home and leer at her so obviously takes a special kind of man. And Vishnubhat genuinely believes he is special. Special enough to warrant our undivided attention when he 'treats us' to a post-dinner analysis of the finer points of the Bhagavad Gita. Special enough to tell Malu not to take it too hard if she didn't get good marks because 'female minds are not designed for the rigors of studying'. Special enough to tell a flabbergasted Latika that 'western clothing corrupts young minds and invites trouble for girls'. Special enough to point out to me when my tikli* fell off my forehead that, 'according to the shaastras, an empty forehead is a misfortune destined only for widows. No young woman should wish for one.' The words 'Who the hell asked you?' sprang to my lips but I bit them down at a glance from Juee. This idiot was going to get this house after Nana – no sense in antagonising him, for small-small things like having a spectacularly annoying personality.

---

* Marathi word for bindi. And for the small, red, circular firecrackers you put into toy guns and shoot at people. Why are the two things called by the same name? One has to assume it's because both things achieve the same effect.

90

I decided to ignore him and managed successfully to do just that. Now, as I sat on the floor writing more job applications (because, I mean, I have good marks and everything, but I would be foolish to pin all my hopes on one application, right?), I hoped he wouldn't come snooping and discover what I was doing. Imagine! The man thinks women aren't clever enough to study. His brain would probably explode if he found out that I was actually trying to go make some money using my brain.

I stopped writing and considered this. In other circumstances, I would actually love to see that happen: Vishnubhat, shell-shocked as he discovers one of his cousins would step out of the four walls of the house and actually get a job. Oh, the horror! He would probably sprinkle gaumutra – cow urine – all over himself and shudder from head to toe going, 'Shiva-shiva-shiva!'

The mental image of him doing this made me snicker and look around to see what he was actually doing. To my surprise, I found him in deep discussion with Aai. Both of them had put their heads together and were whispering in low voices. I scowled. Since when was Aai such great friends with this buffoon? She had an arch smile on her face, and he looked like a man who had just been given a prize. A consolation prize, but a good one at that.

He caught me looking at him and gave me a knowing smile. I looked away quickly. I had no idea what those two were talking about, but I was beginning to get a feeling that it couldn't be anything good.

'Ila!' Aai called out to me and I looked up reluctantly. 'You were saying you wanted to go to that lecture series, no?'

'Yes.' I blinked. 'It's tomorrow and don't worry, it's going to be very educational, it's about—'

'Enough.' Aai held up a hand. 'You already told me all this yesterday. You can go.'

'Really? Oh, good!' I beamed. 'Juee also wanted to come along, so I won't be alone . . .'

'You won't be alone anyway,' Aai said. 'Latika is also coming, with Arun's wife.'

I made a face. 'Why? Latika has never been interested in history.'

'Then we should be happy that she is showing interest in it now, no?' Aai scolded. Then her voice softened and she said in a tone that was casual – too casual – the words that chilled my heart: 'Oh, and take Vishnu along, will you? He's getting bored sitting at home.'

NINE

The Lokmanya Seva Sangh hall on Tilak Mandir Road was a hub of cultural activities in Parle East. It was a short walk from our home, so we ought to have easily reached the lecture well before time. But between Sudha Kelkar suddenly getting a headache and bowing out, Latika dithering about whether to come for the lecture or not, then eventually deciding to, and Vishnubhat being quite possibly the world's slowest walker, by the time we had reached the Lokmanya Seva Sangh hall on foot, it was too late to get any good seats.

The Sangh routinely organised kirtans and lectures on a number of spiritual or educational subjects and, since these were for the good of the public, entry was usually free. The lecture series we were attending was by Shivshahir Babasaheb Purandare: Maharashtra's, and perhaps the country's, greatest living expert on Shivaji Maharaj.* So it was hardly a surprise to find the hall on the first floor packed with people. Even the looking gallery on the mezzanine floor, which ran on three sides and overlooked the main hall, was full of people standing and waiting patiently for the lecture to begin.

Cotton satranjees had been spread on the floor of the hall itself for the audience to sit on, and Juee ushered Latika and me towards one that seemed to have a modicum of space left. Vishnubhat remained standing. I'm assuming he thought it improper to sit so close to females of any stripe – you know, in case our feeble mental prowess spread by touching or something.

'It's so hot here,' Latika complained, and Juee and I shushed her.

On the dais, under a huge frieze depicting scenes from the life of Lokmanya Tilak, we saw Babasaheb Purandare turn to face the audience. And the lecture began. For the next fifteen minutes, I listened with rapt attention as Babasaheb recounted the socio-political background of Maharashtra early on in the seventeenth century, at the time of Shivaji's birth: how most of present-day Maharashtra was then under the rule of Adilshah of Bijapur and Nizamshah of Ahmednagar. How the troops of both these sultans would inflict

---

* How do a people, bullied and terrorised, helpless and petrified, go on to become the single largest threat to the British East India Company? The answer is Chhatrapati Shivaji Maharaj. The son of a lesser noble at the court of Adilshah of Bijapur, Shivaji Maharaj radicalised the people of Maharashtra and formed his own kingdom. This was the foundation of what was to become the formidable Maratha Empire, which at the height of its power dominated most of the Indian subcontinent.

94

brutalities upon the common people. How crops were burned, women abducted, villages razed. How fear had percolated the life of commoners at the time. He was an excellent storyteller, making the people, the events, come alive in my mind. I felt transported to that era, when he described how Shivaji Raje was incensed by the atrocities committed by Bijapur soldiers and how the experience cemented his decision to break free from the tyrannical rule of the sultanates and establish a new kind of self-rule in Maharashtra – Hindavi Swarajya.

As Babasaheb began describing the sixteen-year-old Shivaji's legendary vow of acquiring freedom, taken at the feet of his family deity, Tuljabhavani, I felt something very different happen at my own feet: I had been sitting on the outer edge of the thick cotton mat with my knees bent together on one side, to take up as little space as possible, and some clumsy fool of a man had tripped over my feet and collided with the standing onlookers in front of him. He turned to see what had made him fall and his eyebrows rose in recognition. So did mine.

It was Jayant Waknis, the photographer we had met at the Satyanarayan pooja in Arun's home.

He crouched next to me with that jaunty smile of his. 'Why, if it isn't the beautiful Bendre sisters,' he whispered, adjusting the camera slung around his neck. 'What are you doing here?'

'Learning about the life and times of Shivaji Maharaj, of course.' Latika, who was sitting next to me replied to him, a delighted smile on her face.

'Why?' I asked archly. 'What did you come here to do? Gardening?'

He chuckled. 'No such luck.' He nodded towards Babasaheb. 'I'm supposed to be taking pictures of him. A newspaper wants to carry a report on this series.'

'Good for you,' I said in a low voice. 'Getting to meet such interesting people in your line of work.'

'It's a decent way to make a living,' he said nonchalantly. 'Beats accountancy.'

'Ah, so your motives for being here are purely financial then?' I teased.

'They were, till about a moment ago.'

Our eyes met. His brown ones were filled with amusement and, with his easy smile, they gave him the look of a man with nothing to hide. I looked away and smiled, just as Juee noticed Jayant's presence. She nodded at him with a polite smile, which he returned before standing up and moving away.

I watched him walk towards the front and aim his camera at Babasaheb.

'The lecture is going on about six feet to the right of where you're looking, you know,' Juee whispered to me behind Latika's back, and I could see that she was trying to hide a smile.

I pinched her arm discreetly and saw her wince and grin at the same time.

Two hours later, our minds buzzing with the exemplary portraits of valour painted by Babasaheb, we rose from our seats to find Vishnubhat missing. As we scanned the hall, hoping to spot him, Juee spotted someone very different, but equally irritating.

'Kalyani!' She waved. 'Over here! Kalyani!'

Kalyani Pingley turned in our direction at the sound of her name. For a moment she looked taken aback to find us there, but the next instant her face had a wide smile and she was coming towards us, her brother and his friend following behind. At the sight of Juee, I saw an equally wide smile spread on Sadanand's face, while Aniruddha looked predictably serious.

'Juee! What a lovely surprise!' Kalyani said, holding Juee by the shoulders as if they were long-lost sisters. 'How are you feeling now?'

'I'm good, I'm good.' Juee beamed at her. 'You remember my sisters.' Kalyani gave Latika and me a stiff nod as Juee continued: 'It's so nice to see you here. I didn't know you were interested in history.'

'Of course I am!' Kalyani said effusively. 'I absolutely love it, don't I, Dada?'

'First I'm hearing of it.' Sadanand grinned at Juee, who smiled back shyly.

'Don't listen to him,' Kalyani told us. 'When Aniruddha told us Babarao . . .'

'Babasaheb,' Aniruddha corrected.

'Punekar . . .'

'Purandare,' Sadanand muttered.

'That only, that only,' she said in a huff. 'When he told me this great man was giving a lecture series on Shivaji Maharaj, I told Dada we must come!'

Of course. If darling Aniruddha had wanted to go to a lecture series called The Design and Fabrication of Post-Independence Drainage Systems, Kalyani would be right there by his side, pretending that sewage was the most fascinating topic in the world. I smirked at the thought and almost didn't reply when Aniruddha looked right at me and asked, 'You are also interested in history, is it?'

'Yes,' I said staunchly. 'Nana used to tell us stories of Shivaji Maharaj when we were little. I found him fascinating.'

'Really.' His look was a little condescending.

'I thought his views on women and religion were pretty progressive, for the time,' I said, my chin out. 'I mean, he stopped his own mother from voluntarily going sati,* he didn't enforce conversions, he allowed the Kalyan subhedar's daughter-in-law to go back to her home, when she could've rightfully been considered the spoils of war—'

'Those are lovely earrings,' Kalyani cooed, holding the small golden hoop in Juee's earlobe in her fingers. She seemed completely oblivious to the fact that she was interrupting me. 'Are they real?'

'I don't know,' Juee replied, a little thrown at the sudden change in topic.

Kalyani snuck a quick glance at me. Ah. So she *wasn't* completely oblivious then. Just rude. Aniruddha, however, hadn't noticed. His gaze stayed on me as he asked, 'Then you must have visited his forts?'

'Sadly, no.' I gave a rueful smile. 'Nana promised to take us to Sinhagad fort, but . . .' – I pondered how to say 'we

---

* It was *said* that the historical practice of sati – sacrificing yourself by sitting atop your husband's burning funeral pyre – was the ultimate proof of a wife's loyalty to her husband. It was *said* that it prevented the physical and sometimes sexual abuse of widows by doing away with the key ingredient – the widows. Nobody s*aid* that a buy-one-get-one-free deal on death meant someone had fewer mouths to feed and the dead widow's jewellery to keep. Nobody *says* these things. Ahem, ahem.

couldn't afford it' without sounding embarrassed so I settled for – 'we never ended up going.'

'That's a shame.' He looked genuinely sympathetic. 'Sinhagad is worth seeing. Pratapgad also, especially the—' He froze mid-sentence, looking over my shoulder, and a moment later we heard Jayant's voice say, 'There you all are, I was wondering . . .' He stopped short as he reached us and his affable smile dropped when he saw Aniruddha, whose face seemed to have turned to stone.

For a few seconds, an awkward silence fell upon the group. Then Sadanand put out his hand and introduced himself.

Jayant shook his hand, but his manner was nowhere as warm as before.

'Jayant is a photographer, you know,' Latika said, fluttering her eyelashes in a way that made it seem she had a tic. 'He took all those lovely pictures of Arun's wedding.'

'Oh, how nice,' Sadanand said politely.

'You should invite him for the lunch you're giving for Arun and Sudha!' Latika exclaimed, wide-eyed with excitement. 'Maybe he can take pictures of all of us!'

I saw Aniruddha give her a sharp look, as Juee said, aghast, 'Latika, you can't just invite other people to someone's house like that!'

'Why, have you invited a lot of people?' Latika pouted at Sadanand. 'Is there no room for just one more? Especially someone we all think so highly of?'

'No, nothing like that.' Sadanand smiled at her and then turned to Jayant: 'It's just a small lunch, but you're more than welcome to join us.' And with that, he gave Jayant his address and the date and time of the lunch.

Jayant was just thanking him for the invitation, when a puffing and panting Vishnubhat found us.

'Your Mumbai is far too humid, buva. And such a crowd! We had to go and stand outside to get some air!' He fanned himself furiously with a small towel, and that's when his eye fell on Aniruddha. 'One minute,' he said, wonderstruck. 'Aren't you Kaveribai Bhagwat's nephew? She showed us a photo of you! May we say how honoured we are to finally meet you in person, sir?'

Aniruddha gave him a curt nod and said in a cold voice, 'We'll leave now.' And without waiting for Sadanand and Kalyani to join him, he turned on his heel and walked rapidly away. The other two said their goodbyes hurriedly and, exchanging a puzzled look, all but ran after their friend.

I looked at Juee, whose face mirrored my confusion. What on earth had just happened? We were about to ask Jayant exactly that when Vishnubhat looked Jayant up and down and enquired, 'And who is this gentleman?'

We introduced him to Jayant, and I prayed that he wouldn't make a fool of himself before the photographer. Vishnubhat seemed a little cowed in fact, and I thought I understood why. First of all, standing next to the taller and it had to be said, infinitely better-looking Jayant, Vishnubhat suffered in comparison. The camera around Jayant's neck further placed him as a professional in a vastly more excit-ing field than a priest. But I had badly underestimated our cousin's self-confidence. He began to ask polite but pointed questions about Jayant: did he live nearby? Oh, on rent, is it? How unfortunate. But ... surely a photographer made enough to own his own house? Hadn't property rates in Mumbai dropped recently? No? Oh, dear.

Jayant batted these queries away with polite amusement, but I was annoyed on his behalf and abruptly interrupted Vishnubhat, saying, 'Shall we leave now? It's a long walk home.'

'Of course, of course.' Vishnubhat puffed himself up. 'We can't make Mama-Mami wait. They will worry. Of course, they know you are with us, so you will be safe, but these days . . .'

'Will you mind if I walk with you?' Jayant asked us. 'I am going in the same direction.'

Before Vishnubhat could object, Juee, Latika and I gave him our hearty consent and the five of us began to walk home.

I glared at Juee, who took the hint and picked up her pace, dragging Latika behind her with one hand. Then, she turned around and called out, 'Vishnu Dada! Can you come lead the way? I wouldn't want us to get lost in these lanes!'*

Vishnubhat, unable to turn down her request, especially after he had promised her parents that he'd protect her, hurried to walk by her side.

Jayant and I dropped our speed by an unspoken agreement and soon we had put a small distance between us and the other three. The street lamps had come on by now and the road before us was bathed in pools of amber light. The heat of the day was gone and a pleasant chill in the air suggested that it would rain later tonight. It was quiet, but from every

---

* The lanes of Vile Parle East are notoriously confusing. They all look alike, are lined with buildings and bungalows that also all look alike, and have absolutely zero landmarks most of the time. Only people who live in Vile Parle can navigate these lanes without a map, which makes Juee's request to Vishnu both redundant and mischievous.

building we passed came the muffled sounds of the evening: a pressure cooker whistle as dinner was prepared, a baby fussing as it was put to bed, a distant conversation that ended in quiet laughter. The silence between us was ripe. Any moment now, words would fall.

'How do you know Aniruddha Darshetkar?' Jayant asked.

'Oh. He's Arun's friend,' I replied, blinking in confusion. I don't know what I had expected, but that question wasn't it. 'We met at Arun's wedding. Didn't you see him there?'

'I must've missed him. So you don't know him personally as such?'

'No. Why?'

'Nothing, nothing, I just asked.'

'You can speak freely. I don't particularly like him or anything.'

'No? How come?'

'I think he thinks too much of himself. And not quite enough of others.'

'That's true. He's been like that ever since he was a boy.'

My eyebrows rose. 'You knew him when he was a boy?'

'We were very close friends, growing up.'

'But he didn't say a word to you just now! How come?'

'That is a long story.'

'We have a long way to walk,' I said, with a small smile.

'Fine. If you must know, my father worked for Aniruddha's father. I used to go over to their home every day to play. Aniruddha was the kind of person who always liked to have his own way, in everything. It used to annoy me sometimes, but I always let it go. After all, I did not have his wealth or his position, and my family owed everything to Aniruddha's father – Appa Darshetkar, people would call him.' He sighed. 'That man loved me like his own son. I was never made to feel that I didn't belong there, you know. Appa never treated me and Aniruddha any different. When he would go out of town for business trips, if he bought Aniruddha a toy, he would buy me one as well. We were like brothers, in his eyes. I certainly thought of Aniruddha as my brother. I thought he felt the same way about me. But when the time came, I found out just how wrong I was.' Jayant's face hardened. 'My father died, just as I entered college. Without me even asking, Appa said he would pay for my college education. But the year I was due to graduate, he passed away. That year's fee hadn't been paid, so I went to Aniruddha. Told him that Appa had said he'd pay for my education . . .' A bitter laugh. 'Aniruddha said Appa's promises died with Appa. He told me he didn't have the money to waste on a servant's son, that too a servant who was no longer in service. Told me to clear off and said if I showed my face there again, he'd call the police.'

'What?' I nearly shouted.

'What happened? Everything alright back there?' Vishnubhat called out from ahead.

'Uh, yes, yes, I tripped . . . there was a hole . . .' I lied wildly. 'I'm okay.' In a lower voice I said to Jayant, 'But that's unbelievable! How can he be so cruel? So . . . so heartless? And you were his childhood friend?'

Jayant nodded. 'To tell you the truth, I always suspected he was a little jealous of me. Appa always treated me like a son and I think that upset Aniruddha. I suppose he didn't like having to compete for Appa's attention, and that too with, as he put it, a servant's son. Must've felt it below his dignity. He always took his position in life so seriously, you know. Anyway, I cut all connections with that family that day and never went back. To this day, I haven't got my graduate degree.' He gave me a sad smile. 'But I can say this – that whatever I am today, I have become on my own. I took up a job as a photographer's assistant. I say assistant . . . I was little more than a servant. I'd clean his studio for him, cook for him, hold his lights and tripods when he was shooting outdoors. In exchange, he gave me a little money and taught me photography. So now, I use that skill to fill my . . . Oh, no . . . have I made you cry?'

I blinked quickly to settle my brimming eyes and gave a small laugh. 'No, no, nothing like that,' I said, dabbing the corner of my eye. 'Speck of dust or something . . .'

'I hope so,' he said gently. 'I would hate to make such a pretty girl weep.'

The slightest flutter happened in my chest at those words. Pretty. He had called me pretty. Not 'pretty, but dusky'. Just pretty. I looked at him when I was sure he wouldn't see. His expression was stoic, making him look all the more handsome. To have been betrayed like that, insulted, cheated even, by his once best friend? A man who had everything and yet behaved in such a miserly, mean-spirited manner?

I felt a deep resentment rise in me. My instinct about Aniruddha Darshetkar had been correct after all. Not only was he unreasonably proud of himself, his wealth, his station in life, that pride was entirely unjustified by his behaviour to those who did not have his privileges. That he should prosper, while a hardworking, pleasant-mannered man like Jayant should have a life of scraps, seemed utterly unfair to me.

After walking for some time in silence, Jayant asked, 'So . . . this Vishnu . . . he is related to you?'

'Our Atya's son.'

'How does he know Kaveribai Bhagwat? Is your family related to her?'

'No, no, he's the priest in some temple founded by Kaveribai's family,' I said dismissively. 'I didn't even know of her till he mentioned her.'

'Oh, so you don't know she has a daughter?'

'Vishnu mentioned her, in passing.'

'Ashalata Bhagwat will inherit all of Kaveribai's estate one day. And guess who she is supposed to marry?'

I held up my hands in a questioning gesture.

'Aniruddha Darshetkar himself.'

I smiled savagely at the thought of Kalyani's face the day she would discover this.

'Kaveribai and Aniruddha's mother, Mai, were very close friends and when both women had children, they decided to get them married when they grew up.'

'What's Ashalata like?' I asked.

'Much like her mother – proud, snobbish and rude.'

Seems exactly right for Aniruddhat, I thought gleefully. *A wife just as insufferable as he is. The perfect match.*

Who would be a perfect match for Jayant, I chose not to dwell on. We walked the rest of the way in silence, the backs of our hands brushing one another's in the dark.

TEN

The next morning, when I told Juee what I had learned from Jayant, her reaction was predictable: she was horrified at first, like she is when she hears of anything distressing or unjust. But then, her better nature took over and she shook her head.

'There must have been some misunderstanding,' she told me. 'How could Aniruddha behave in such a way? No, no, he is better than that.'

'Is there *anyone* you think badly of?' I asked in wonder. 'And what misunderstanding? What do you think happened? Jayant asked for money and Aniruddha thought he was asking for an elephant and politely declined?'

'We don't know exactly what happened, Ila.' Juee still looked doubtful. 'We weren't there. All kinds of misinterpretation can happen between two people. We have to give them both credit.'

'Why are you so hell-bent on giving Aniruddha credit?' I asked incredulously.

'Because . . . well . . .' Juee clicked her tongue in an exasperated gesture. 'Because if he is truly a bad person, then I just can't understand how Sadanand can be friends with him! You know what Sadanand is like – so good, so decent – I don't think he can be *that* mistaken about someone's character as to be good friends with a person capable of doing what you say Aniruddha has.'

I didn't respond. What Juee said had some truth in it. Sadanand's friendship spoke in Aniruddha's favour, if only because Sadanand didn't seem the type to stay friends with someone so . . . dishonourable, was the only word that came to the mind. And yet . . .

'Maybe Aniruddha has just never shown that side of himself to Sadanand,' I said slowly. 'That's the only explanation.'

We left it there, mostly because by the time our conversation was over, Latika and Malati were up and it would've been extremely stupid of us to mention anything about this matter in their presence. Latika, in particular, was the type in whose mouth sesame wouldn't get wet.[*]

As it was, we had our hands full. First we had to help Aai with breakfast, and then decide who was wearing what,

---

[*]   Marathi saying meaning someone incapable of keeping a secret. Presumably it implies that a person like that is always blabbing and hence always has their mouth open, which would leave any random sesame seeds in their mouth dry because of the continuous gush of wind. They say a picture is worth a thousand words, but if a phrase ever painted a graphic picture, it would be this one.

because today was the day we were descending on the Pingley home for lunch.

The term 'we' seems woefully inadequate, considering the sheer size of our group. Apart from Juee and me, there were Nana, Aai, Malati and Latika. And Vishnubhat, who had not let a small thing like the lack of an invitation stand in the way of barging into a total stranger's house.

'See, the thing is, Mami,' he had said to Aai, 'we are very close to Kaveribai. Practically family. And Aniruddharao is actually her family. Now, since *he* is Sadanandrao's friend, that practically makes us also Sadanandrao's friend only, no?'

After murdering logic in such a gruesome manner, he had turned to me with zero remorse and said with an oily smile: 'Besides, we couldn't stay away from you . . . all . . . for so long. Your absence would be . . . felt.'

I resisted the urge to tell him that what he would actually feel was the back of my hand if he continued talking nonsense. He had become extremely . . . sticky . . . these last couple of days. First there was the way he had insinuated himself into attending the lecture with us. Since returning from there, he had refused to leave my side. Whenever I looked up, there he was, with his sugary smile and his leery eyes. And Aai, who had found him so annoying when he first landed with us, now looked at him fondly and turned a blind eye to this rubbish behaviour of his.

Still, how bad can it be? I asked myself as I ironed the navy blue, ikat-print cotton sari I had chosen to wear. *There will be lots of people there he can irritate.* I could always slip away and meet more interesting . . . persons.

Person, really.

As I pleated the sari, I glanced at Juee, who was already

ready. She had pinned a red rose in her hair behind her ear. With her light pink sari and Aai's tiny pearl kudis in her ears, she looked the very picture of feminine innocence.

My usual silver studs were in my ears but I had just chosen a side parting for my braid when a thought occurred to me: 'Juee, can I borrow your kajal?' I asked.

'Of course,' she replied, pressing the small, flat, green container of Jai kajal into my hand, just as Latika marched into the room and began rummaging in Aai's cupboard.

'Where are your gold earrings?' she asked Juee. 'I want to wear them today.'

'Then ask for them nicely, you brat,' I chided. 'They are *hers*.'

At that moment Aai walked in. Shooting me a gleeful smile, Latika turned to her and pouted. 'Aai! See, na, all I said was I wanted to wear Jueetai's gold earrings and Ila is being so mean to me!'

'You should have heard how she was speaking, Aai . . .' I began, but, as usual, Aai was shaking her head already.

'Let her be,' she said. 'She's young. And besides, I don't think Juee minds lending her the earrings, do you, bala?'

Juee shook her head slowly but I could see the struggle inside her. Being the eldest of four sisters meant her things were usually handed down to the rest of us, when we were children. But these days, we shared nearly everything. The gold earrings had been made specifically for Juee, for her wedding. They were the one possession she shouldn't have had to share. But who would explain that to Aai?

As Aai opened the locker in the cupboard and handed Latika the earrings, my younger sister flashed me a triumphant grin. She put them on and twirled before the mirror, looking very pleased with herself. She had managed to convince Aai to allow her to wear her bell bottoms. With them, she was wearing a polka-dotted shirt, knotted daringly at the waist so a sliver of skin showed above the waistband.

'Aai, don't I look just like Dimple Kapadia from *Bobby*?' she asked, grinning from ear to ear.

Juee sighed, and I was about to reply when Nana's shocked voice was heard from the doorway: 'This is what you're wearing?'

'It's fashion, Nana!' Latika replied. 'All the young people are wearing this!'

'And what are we?' I demanded. 'Grandmothers?'

'Mrinalini!' Nana admonished. 'Are you going to let her come like this? What will people think?'

'Aho, let it be, we are already late,' Aai said, pulling out her purse from the cupboard. 'There's no time for her to change.' And as Nana left the room with a resigned expression, I heard her mutter, '*Now* he thinks of what people will think! Four unmarried daughters at home – what will people think of *that*, huh?' And with that, she shepherded Latika out of the room.

I placed a hand on Juee's shoulder.

She turned to me with a bright, brittle smile. 'You look nice,' she said. 'All dressed up.'

'It's just kajal,' I told her. 'Why would I get all dressed up?'

'Oh, you have no reason to dress up, is it?' she asked teasingly. 'Absolutely nobody you want to impress?'

I *had* been hoping Jayant would be there, but to say I was trying to impress him was too much. I only wanted him around so I could have someone to talk to while Juee and

Sadanand played who-grins-more-like-a-buffoon with each other. Still, the kajal made my eyes look striking, and even Aai gave me an approving sort of look when we left, so I didn't say anything much about it.

We reached the Pingley home about an hour later. Sadanand greeted us all enthusiastically, took Vishnubhat's presence in his stride and asked if he could introduce Juee to some of his friends. Since Aai had probably prayed to the Parleshwar Ganpati for this very moment, she happily allowed it.

I looked at Vishnubhat to see how he was taking this – his leering at Juee in the first few days of his arrival had made me think he was working up the nerve to ask for her hand in marriage.* But not only did our cousin look perfectly content, he nudged me and whispered: 'Stay close to us, Ila. We have experience with parties like this.' He puffed his chest out like a confident rooster. 'Kaveribai hosts many a soiree and invites some very distinguished people. She has graced us with an invitation to one or two of those, so we know exactly how to conduct ourselves in a setting such as this.'

I was about to appeal to Aai for help, when I saw her steer Nana in the direction of Kelkar Kaka-Kaku, who were waving to them from the other side of the room. Latika had already disappeared, taking Malati with her, and I could see absolutely nobody else I knew there. No sign of Jayant.

Disappointment rose in my chest. I wore a nice sari, kajal,

---

*   As disturbing as it sounds, marrying your maternal uncle's daughter is considered perfectly normal among Maharashtrians. Want to *really* scandalize a Maharashtrian, especially in the 1970s? Go marry someone from a different caste and watch people lose their shit.

and for what? To stand there and listen to Vishnubhat recount some dinner at Kaveribai's house where he had been invited to hold forth on some random part of some Upanishad?

Thankfully, just then, like a friendly oasis in the middle of a horrible desert, Chitra emerged from the crowd of strange faces and walked towards us.

'What are you doing here?' I asked her, delighted.

'Sadanand asked Kelkar Kaka to invite us on his behalf.' Chitra gestured to her parents, who were just coming out of the kitchen with plates laden with food. It seemed this was a buffet lunch. How very not middle-class.

'That was nice of him,' I said, ignoring Vishnubhat's exaggerated clearing of his throat.

'Yes! He is rather nice, isn't he?' Chitra beamed.

'Namaskar!' Vishnubhat interrupted loudly, and I saw a few people turn and look in our direction. What was with my family's lack of volume control?

'Namaskar,' Chitra said politely. 'I am Chitra Lele, we live on the floor below Ila. And you?'

'We are Vishnupant Chhatre,' Vishnubhat declared. 'Head priest at the Bhagwati temple of Wai.'

'Oh! I've heard of that temple!' Chitra smiled. 'And you. You're Ila's cousin, aren't you?'

'Well.' Vishnubhat looked bashful. 'For now.'

Chitra gave me a questioning look, which I dismissed with a shake of my head. This twerp was getting too bold for my taste now.

'Vishnu *Dada*,' I said, emphasising the last word to remind him that I saw him strictly as a brother. 'Could you fetch us some water? The kitchen looks crowded and I don't want to go so close to so many strangers.'

'Of course, of course.' Vishnubhat hurried towards the kitchen and I gestured to Chitra to move into one of the bedrooms. It was the same room Juee had convalesced in and, to my delight, miraculously there were no people there.

'Hopefully he won't find us for some time,' I told her, settling on a chair.

Chitra looked around, an impressed look on her face. 'Nice house, na?' she asked. 'Very tasteful furniture. His wife will be a very lucky girl.'

'His wife will be Juee, if my mother has anything to do with it,' I whispered to her and she laughed.

'Does Juee like him?' She looked out through the open door of the bedroom, to the living room where we could see Juee standing with Sadanand and a few of his friends, quietly listening to their conversation. Every other moment, Sadanand turned to look at her, a bashful smile on his face. 'He certainly seems to like her.'

'I think so too,' I told her. 'And the feeling is mutual, I believe.'

'Then what is she waiting for?' Chitra wondered. 'Tell her to get a move on.'

'And do what?' I teased. 'Ask him to propose?'

'Don't be silly.' Chitra swatted my arm. 'But she needs to let him know that she would be open to a proposal. Talk to him about how she dreams of getting married, of having children . . .'

'And he'll just take the hint?' I asked, bewildered.

'He's a man, Ila.'

'Yes, exactly my point.' I gestured at Arun, who was in the same group as Sadanand and Juee, telling some long-winded story, while Sudha stood next to him looking bored.

'Look at this specimen. Look at the expression on Sudha's face. Isn't that hint enough? But no, he wouldn't take it if it dressed up as Helen* and did a little dance for him.'

'To be fair, he *might* take it then,' Chitra said, and we both burst out laughing.

'Hello.'

I stopped abruptly as Aniruddha loomed into view, like a sudden cliff on a misty day. He was ridiculously tall, really. My last conversation with Jayant rushed to my mind. This was a man who had cruelly, sadistically even, refused to help a close friend in need, and left him to the mercy of the world. And all when it would have been so easy for him to do just the opposite.

'Oh. Hello,' I said curtly.

'Have you had lunch?'†

'No . . . we . . .' A little bewildered at this unprovoked interest, I looked at Chitra, who was watching saucer-eyed. 'We were about to.'

'I was about to as well,' he said gravely. Then he extended an arm in the direction of the kitchen and asked, 'Shall we?'

---

* Helen Ann Richardson, known on-screen simply as Helen, is an Indian dancer and actress of Burmese origin. She is well-known for her supporting roles and raunchy cabaret-esque dances in Hindi movies. At the height of her career, her dance numbers were so popular that people would throng movie theatres just to watch them. The rest of the movie could go hang, as long as there was Helen, in her spangly, skimpy outfits, shaking what the more sedate actresses of the time would never dare to.

† Most Marathi boys have very little game. Which is why perhaps Maharashtrian culture is the only one where 'Jevlis ka?' aka 'Have you eaten?' counts as a pick-up line.

No, thank you. I don't feel like eating. I hate food. All of these would have been acceptable replies – if only a single one had occurred to me at that instant. But Aniruddha's question was asked in such a tone of voice as to make refusing seem out of the question.

I found myself nodding, and Chitra and I followed Aniruddha to the kitchen. But before we could reach it, we found our path obstructed by Vishnubhat, holding two glasses of water.

'Namaskar, namaskar, alabhya labh, alabhya labh!'* Vishnubhat grinned excitedly at Aniruddha as he tried to fold his hands in greeting, then realised he was holding a glass in each, and ended up bringing them together and bobbing them up and down, sloshing water over his shirt. 'We met the other day at the lecture, but we couldn't speak much then!'

'You are—?' Aniruddha asked bluntly.

'We are Vishnu Chhatre,' my cousin said, standing a little straighter and still ending up a head shorter than Aniruddha. 'Head priest at the Bhagwati temple and close family friend of your respected aunt, Kaveribai Bhagwat. She has told us so much about you, we feel like we know you already, heh heh heh.'

'We? We who?' Aniruddha asked with a frown.

Before Vishnubhat could respond, I pushed Chitra forward and said, 'Vishnu Dada, Chitra is very interested in the Gita, aren't you, Chitra?'

---

* A phrase meaning 'a rare profit', which is used to describe a happening that is unexpected and delightful in its occurrence. Like being an Indian girl and suddenly being allowed to marry whom you like, no questions asked.

Chitra looked at me as if I had just suggested that she was interested in taming lions. 'I am?' she asked and then, at a nudge from me, said: 'I am! Yes. The Gita. Of course.'

'She was hoping you could tell her about . . . whatever you were telling us about the other night,' I said. 'Things in the Gita.'

'Of course, it would be our pleasure.' Vishnubhat bowed low and I took that opportunity to move to the kitchen, Aniruddha close behind me. I would make it up to Chitra later. One conversation with Vishnubhat, and she would understand.

Of course, I had only dodged Vishnubhat and sacrificed Chitra to that cause to stop my cousin from talking rubbish in front of Aniruddha and embarrassing my family by association. Unfortunately, that meant I was now stuck with Aniruddha in the kitchen. Alone.

'So . . . how are you liking all this?' He handed me a steel plate from a pile and pointed to some bowls and spoons kept on one side.

'A buffet lunch is . . . unusual,' I told him truthfully. 'But seems like fun.'

In our house, if guests were invited for lunch, they would sit cross-legged on the floor in a row on a satranjee, and all of us except Nana would serve and fetch till they were done. Nana would eat with the guests and the rest of us would eat last. It was supposed to be the hospitable thing to do. But this serve-yourself-and-move-along style seemed so much . . . fairer.

'Sadanand's idea of fun is usually unusual,' Aniruddha said, with a small smile.

'Prabha must've been slaving for hours to cook this

spread,' I muttered, as I peeped into the huge pots filled with a variety of foods I had never seen before.

'They got a caterer to cook and provide the plates and everything,' Aniruddha said, and my eyebrows shot up.

Caterers? So fancy! Hosting a lunch at our home meant Juee and me helping Aai all morning with the cooking. If Juee married into a home where she didn't have to slave before a stove for guests, it would be absolutely amazing. I smiled at the thought as Aniruddha ladled a large helping of a green, creamy-looking bhaaji on his plate.

'For you?' he asked, gesturing to my plate.

I hesitated. 'What is it?' I asked, trying not to look suspicious. It looked like spinach. I am not a fan of spinach.

Aniruddha placed the ladle in the vessel, dipped a forefinger in the bhaaji on his plate and tasted it, a thoughtful expression on his face. 'I have no idea,' he said, cocking his head to one side. 'But it's quite tasty.'

I took a small helping and two polis from a plate next to the pot. Aniruddha moved in front quietly, helping himself to more dishes. I noticed he completely ignored the sweet dish, which was kheer.

When our plates were full, he led me out into the living room, but didn't stop there. We went past one bedroom, through the other and ended up on a small balcony, just wide enough for two or three people to stand in.

Great, I thought. *Now I'm really stuck here with this hateful man.* I started to eat my food in silence, trying to get it over with as soon as possible.

'You look different today,' Aniruddha said softly, not looking at me.

I didn't respond.

'Have you done something with your eyes?' he asked.

'Kajal,' I replied curtly, and continued eating.

'Ah.'

Silence.

'Are you liking the food?'* he asked.

'Yes.'

More silence.

'You are very quiet today,' he remarked.

'Just following your example,' I said archly.

'My . . . ?' He gave me a searching look. 'Why is that?'

'Well, I assume you stay quiet because small talk is too *small* for you. And the only things you consider worth mentioning have to be big and dazzling for your listeners in some way. And because people know this, they wait with bated breath to hear what you have to say when you *do* speak,' I said, picking up some bhaaji with a piece of poli and putting it into my mouth. 'I thought I'd like to have that effect on people as well.'

'I don't think there is any truth in anything you just said.' He smiled.

'Okay.'

Even more silence.

'I don't think small talk is . . . small,' he said finally. 'Although if that is the only flaw you find in my character, I suppose I should be thankful.'

'Why?' I raised my eyebrows. 'Do you have a long list of flaws that you keep hidden from people?'

I hadn't expected him to actually take the question

---

*   No. Game. Whatsoever.

seriously, let alone give me an answer, but he paused to think.

'Not a long list, no,' he said, utterly unaware of how big-headed that sounded. 'But I don't forgive easily. If someone crosses me, they have a black mark against them in my mind forever.'

'How interesting,' I said, thinking of his past behaviour with Jayant. 'And do *you* expect to be forgiven if you offend or hurt someone?'

'Depends on the size of the offence.' He looked at me intently. 'Why do you ask? Have I offended or hurt you in some way?'

I just laughed. Could a person have so little self-awareness? Or did he imagine people just had thick skin and couldn't possibly be hurt by anything he said?

'I wasn't thinking of myself,' I said lightly.

'Oh? You mean I have hurt someone else?' This time he looked genuinely surprised.

'Well' – it was my turn to shrug – 'you left pretty abruptly the other day at the lecture, when we introduced you to Jayant Waknis. He might even be entitled to feel it was . . . rude.'

I watched his face intently as I said it and saw his jaw clench.

'I assure you, that . . . man's feelings are not on my list of priorities,' he said, and I could almost hear his teeth grinding. 'Excuse me.'

He turned to leave and found Kalyani standing in the doorway. Her eyebrows rose as she first saw Aniruddha's stern face, then, at the other end of the small balcony, me. Her eyes narrowed and she stepped aside quietly to let him pass.

'The food is really rather good,' I told her, taking another morsel of poli-bhaaji.

'The credit goes to you,' she said, with a smirk. 'After all, if it wasn't for your family, this lunch would never have happened.' Then she took a step closer and said with a sneer: 'A word of advice? Stay away from that Jayant Waknis. You might think he's interesting because he's a photographer, but you don't know his background. His father used to work for Aniruddha's father in some small, measly job. And Aniruddha *hates* him. I don't know why exactly, but Dada says even the mention of his name annoys him. So there!'

'If you don't know the exact reason why Aniruddha hates him, then how can you be so sure he deserves it?' I asked her calmly.

She didn't need to answer, of course – Aniruddha's bad opinion was all it would take to seal someone's character in her mind.

'Oh, sorry!' She gave me an entirely unapologetic look and took a step back. 'I was only trying to help.'

'As always.' I gave her my fakest smile, and was rewarded with a little toss of her head as she turned on her heel and marched off the balcony.

I stood there for a few more minutes. The cul-de-sac that the balcony overlooked faced another building, but the view was blocked by a majestic copper pod in full bloom. I eyed its yellow flowers, trying to keep my disappointment down. I hadn't realised how much I had looked forward to meeting Jayant here. It would've been fun to hear his merry laugh and join him in mocking the likes of Kalyani Pingley. Annoying girl. Who had asked her for her opinion on Jayant? Not that it *was* her opinion in the first place. She was simply parroting Aniruddha's beliefs. I clicked my tongue in exasperation and decided I'd had enough lunch.

As I stepped out of the bedroom, plate in hand, I saw Aai sitting across the room, on a sofa with Kelkar Kaku. But I could still hear her clearly, thanks to her usual loudspeaker volume.

'. . . consider it almost certain!' she announced. 'I won't even mind if he asks Juee directly – these are modern times, after all!' She gave a happy giggle as she slapped Kelkar Kaku's hand in glee. 'Juee Pingley! Sounds so nice, na?'

I looked around for Nana in panic. Someone had to rein in my mother before she made an even bigger fool of herself, and it would be a cold day in hell before she would ever listen to *me*.

To my dismay, I saw Nana standing in the corner, his attention diverted elsewhere: Latika and Malati were having an argument, apparently about who was more handsome – Rajesh Khanna or Amitabh Bachchan.

Latika's shirt was hitched significantly higher than it had been when we left home – she must've pulled it up sneakily, when none of us were around. Totally oblivious to the stares of the crowd, she tossed her head and announced, 'You're talking rubbish, Malu! Stop being such a baby!' To which my youngest sister responded in tones of great indignation, saying, 'I'm not a baby, I'm fourteen years old! I also know things! And I *know* for certain that Amitabh Bachchan is any day better than Rajesh Khanna! He totally stole the show in *Namak Haraam* – your Rajesh Khanna was completely over-shadowed . . .'

Nana was standing next to them but instead of reprimanding them, he was simply glancing from daughter to daughter like an interested onlooker at a table-tennis match. But his face betrayed him: no matter how much he pursed his lips, anyone could see that he was vastly amused at this silliness.

Not to be outdone, Vishnubhat chose that moment to examine a vase on a side table and tell Chitra in what he probably thought was a low voice (it wasn't): 'This must cost two hundred rupees at least! We know about these things, you see, because at Kaveribai Bhagwat's palatial home . . .'

I couldn't watch anymore. I closed my eyes and shook my head. It was all too much. Nana had worried about what people would think of Latika's outfit. Aai had worried what people would think of her daughters being unmarried. Had neither or them stopped to worry about what people might think of their behaviour here today? Or did my entire family have some sort of bet going on to see who could embarrass us most in public?

Looking around, my eyes found Juee's. She was standing in another corner of the room, with Sadanand and his friends. She smiled at me, then went back to listening intently to something Sudha was saying, while Sadanand stood smiling at her in his trademark besotted buffoon way.

I sighed in relief. Good. At least *he* hadn't noticed any of my family's tomfoolery.

Then, my gaze travelled further and I saw Aniruddha and Kalyani standing by a window. Kalyani's mouth was turned down as she watched my mother; Aniruddha's arms were crossed and his lips were in a thin, tight line.

At that moment, he seemed to sense my gaze. His eyes met mine for a moment, and then he looked away.

ELEVEN

I had thought I couldn't be any more embarrassed than I had been at Sadanand's lunch. But as I discovered the following Sunday, I was mistaken.

Latika didn't have college, Malati didn't have school. It was Nana's day off from work, though Aai had dispatched him to the market for vegetables.

I was enjoying a relaxed morning, when Aai called out to me: 'Aga, listen.' Aai's voice sounded so loving, at first I assumed she was talking to Juee or Latika. 'Ila? I'm talking to you, bala.'

Bala? Aai was using a term of endearment used for babies and children? For me? I was so taken aback, I entirely forgot to notice the smell.

'Uh, what, Aai?' I asked, with all the naivete of a new-born rabbit. A particularly dim one, at that.

'Me and the girls are going to Shetye Kaku's house for

some time. I want you to stay here and give Vishnu some company, okay?'

'Can't Malu or Latika stay back?' The very idea of spending any sort of time alone with Vishnubhat was deeply nauseating, especially given the level of attention he was paying me these days. 'I'd much rather come with you than—'

'Must you argue every time?' Aai snapped, then took a deep breath to steady herself. Summoning a smile out of thin air she said, 'Just do what you're told. You may find the experience . . . to your liking. Alright?'

I made a face behind Aai's back. Spending time with Vishnubhat would be to my liking? It ranked right up there with that time there had been a lice outbreak in school and Aai had made me pull lice out of Latika's tangled hair with my bare hands because the lice comb was 'too sharp for her delicate scalp'.

I shuddered with disgust as I watched her march out of the living room, giving a meaningful nod to Vishnubhat – who seemed to have been waiting in the doorway.

Wait a minute. Oh, no. It couldn't be. Could it? I now knew what I should've smelled before. A big fat rat. Aai's loving words had caught me unawares and now I'd fallen into this trap. It was an ambush!

The main door slammed shut as my mother and sisters left and I practically fell flat on the floor in my rush to leave the room. But a moment later, I found my way blocked by Vishnubhat himself, who was now wearing an expression that was part coy, part confident.

Well, he must've thought he looked confident, anyway. I thought he looked like a rodent eyeing a ripe piece of garbage.

'Will you wait a moment?' he asked in formal Marathi, and I was forced to stop. 'We wanted to talk to you.'

'I was just going to the kitchen to make some tea,' I lied. 'Can we talk afterwards?'

'We would prefer to do so now,' he said firmly, gesturing at the satranjee where I had been sitting moments before. 'Customarily in these cases, the custom is to approach the forebears of the young lady in question,' he said, giving me a broad leer as he sat down before me. 'But as we have observed you to be a young lady of a . . . *modern* disposition, we thought it would perhaps be wiser to converse with you regarding this matter as well.'

So many flowery words! Who spoke Marathi like this, outside books? I fought the impulse to massage my temples. And what did he mean 'as well'? So this – whatever this was – was happening with Aai and Nana's blessing then? Surely not!

'As we mentioned earlier, Kaveribai believes it is well past time that we married,' Vishnubhat said. 'One of our reasons for coming here, apart, of course, from mending relations with your honourable father, was to procure a wife.'

Procure, I thought. *Like a part of industrial machinery.*

'Our design initially was for your elder sister. Naturally. But Mami tells us she is spoken for. However, we are sure you would make a virtuous wife as well. You are educated, which isn't an entirely bad thing, but Mami tells us you can also run a household. And, of course, Mami was kind enough to let us sample the puran polis you made the other day. They were quite exemplary. So the decision was easy for us to make. We have already spoken to Mami about this and she is delighted. She has promised us she can convince Mama to give his permission. We think we should have the wedding next month. We are sure you would also want to have it as soon as possible.'

He beamed at me in such a self-satisfied manner I wanted to throw something at him.

See, when Maharashtrians make a proposal of marriage, it is called maagnee ghaalne. Maagnee is demand. So, literally, a proposal of marriage is a demand. And it is always and exclusively made to the girl. You go to a girl's family and you demand the girl. As if you were a dacoit pointing a gun at some hapless wayfarer. Like this complete ape was doing right now. And grinning like a joker, while he was doing it too!

Well, time to wipe that grin off.

'What wedding?' I asked, standing up. 'Whose wedding? Are you implying that you want to marry me?' I glared down at him. 'Why are you so sure that *I* want to marry *you*?'

That did the trick alright. The man's mouth fell open.

'But . . . but . . .' he spluttered. 'Why wouldn't you? We are a good match! Respectable, respected in our circles! We have our own house, a good, steady income, the support of a wealthy patron! Any girl would be lucky to marry us, especially someone like . . .' He faltered and I took the opening.

'Someone like me?' I crossed my arms and narrowed my eyes. 'And what's that supposed to mean?'

He got up and held his hands out in a reassuring gesture, all the while smiling his usual condescending smile. 'We don't want to be blunt . . .'

'No, no, I insist! *Please* be blunt.'

'Very well.' He looked at me with contempt. 'Someone

with three unmarried sisters, no dowry to speak of and who . . . well . . . can only generously be described as "wheatish".'

So *this* was the real reason Aai was 'delighted' with this match. She had found a good sthal to dump her bad coin. Her dusky-skinned burden. What did it matter who took me off her hands? Even this pompous, nonsense factory of a man would do.

Look at him, with that self-satisfied grin that doesn't quite hide the touch of nastiness inside. I imagined reaching out with one hand, palm outstretched, and landing a good, tight slap right across that flabby cheek. Would he cry? Would that plaster-of-Paris skin turn red? My hands itched with the impulse but I controlled myself.

He took my silence for second thoughts, the half-wit. 'Look, we understand,' he said, in a placating tone. 'It must sound overwhelming. Leaving your loving mother and sisters behind, coming to live in a neighbourhood filled with dignitaries like Kaveribai, being wife to someone whom she holds in such esteem!' He shook his head, a little, self-satisfied smile on his lips. 'But we assure you, you *will* grow accustomed to it and even enjoy it one day, like we do!'

I took a deep breath and looked him right in the eye. *Aai can be delighted all she wants. If she likes him so much, she can marry him herself.*

'You're right,' I said. 'I *am* educated. So I can write this down for you, if you like, so you don't forget. My. Answer. Is. No.'

I marched out of the house, fists clenched. My first wedding proposal and it had to come from this . . . this . . . donkey! The gall of the man! Making it seem like he was doing me a favour by marrying me! First of all, he assumes that I'm simply dying to marry him! Has he ever looked in a mirror? Oh, he probably has and loves what he sees. Where does he get this confidence from? Where do men get their confidence from, in general? How to they grow up thinking they deserve anything they happen to want? I suppose it must come from the hordes of doting relatives telling them they alone are the important ones in their family. The kuldeepak. The family lamp which will keep the family name shining bright for generations to come. Never mind that those generations will be born of women, whose names will be forgotten. Ugh!

I stomped down the stairs, imagining Vishnubhat's face on every single one of them. I was heading to Chitra's house on the first floor, my plan to ask her to come with me for a small walk. All I wanted was some time in the fresh air, away from Aai and Vishnubhat and their machinations, just ranting to my friend about this travesty. But, unfortunately, the Limaye home was two doors down from Shetye Kaku's, and the Shetyes didn't believe in shutting their main door. Godknowswhy, but their door is perpetually open. And so, as I strode past, I heard Aai's voice call out my name. The next instant the woman herself rushed out of the door.

'Aga? What are you doing down here?' she demanded.

'Going to Chitra's house.'

'What? Didn't Vishnurao talk to you?'

'Vishnu*rao*?' I glared at her. 'Yes, Vishnu*rao* spoke to me.'

'And?'

'And what?'

'And what did you say?' Aai hissed, throwing a glance behind her back where the Shetye door was still open.

'I said no!' I snapped. 'Like any girl in her right mind would!'

Aai grabbed my arm and dragged me to the staircase, out of earshot. 'Don't be *stupid*!' She scowled, wagging a finger before my face. 'He is a respectable man, he doesn't even want a dowry, he doesn't mind your complexion . . .'

'Oh, of course! That's all that matters, isn't it? Someone's ready to marry your dark daughter for free, so what if he is a total clown?' I asked sarcastically.

'Wheatish, not dark,' she corrected me. 'And of course it isn't all that matters. You'll get the house also once you're married, you silly girl!'

'And love? Respect? Intellectual compatibility?' I demanded. 'Or are those not important?'

'Haven't you heard? Ati parichayat avadnya.'* Aai wagged her finger before my face again. 'After twenty years of marriage, all this love, respect, intellectual whatever, they all fade. But a roof over your head? That lasts a lifetime!'

'Speak for yourself,' I muttered, but Aai heard.

'Talk more and one slap you'll get under your ear!' she snapped, just as someone's footsteps were heard, climbing up the stairs from the floor below.

It was Nana, arms laden with cloth bags full of vegetables, standing a few steps below us. 'What's all this?' he asked mildly, the sweat shining on his forehead.

'Aho, see, na!' Aai's tone was complaining. 'Vishnu has asked Ila to marry him and she turned him down!'

---

* A Sanskrit phrase meaning, 'Knowing a person too well reduces their worth in your eyes.'

'Is this true?' Nana looked at me over the frame of his spectacles.

'Yes.' I raised my chin defiantly. 'I can't marry him, Nana.'

'I'll just see how you don't marry him!' Aai frowned, hands on her hips. 'You think good boys are just lying by the side of the road, or what? And who are you, to say no to a perfectly good proposal? The queen of England?'

I ignored her and looked straight at Nana. 'Please don't make me marry him,' I said quietly. 'I will never be happy with him.'

'Just go back up and say yes,' Aai said, 'or I swear to you . . . I will . . . I won't touch food or water till you do! Do you want your mother to starve because of your stubbornness? Do you?'

Suddenly, I felt like I couldn't breathe. This was my *life* we were talking about, and Aai was making it all about her. This is how she expected me to make a decision that would affect my whole life, my happiness, my future? With her threat hanging over my head like a sword? I couldn't let her win this one. I wouldn't.

Taking a deep breath, I clenched my fists and said nothing.

'Aho, say something to her!' Aai clicked her tongue. 'Don't just stand there!'

'Ila, this is a big problem,' Nana said seriously. 'I have just bought a whole bunch of things from the market. And your Aai says she will not eat till you agree to marry Vishnu. So we are going to have a lot of surplus. Why don't you go and ask the neighbours if they want to take whatever is extra? Because' – and here, he looked straight at Aai, and his tone hardened – 'while I am alive, there is simply no possibility of you marrying that idiot.'

I ran forward and gave Nana a grateful look, before rushing down the stairs in my relief. Behind me, I could hear an argument erupt between Nana and Aai, but I didn't care. I didn't have to marry Vishnubhat with his entitlement and his smarmy ways.

I was so, so relieved, but something else was mixed with that feeling. In that moment, when Aai had threatened to starve herself to force my hand, an understanding had dawned on me: that till I married someone, anyone, this was what my life would look like. Full of tiresome arguments, angry threats and emotional blackmail. She wouldn't let up till I did what she wanted, no matter what toll it took on me. She was so convinced that she knew what was best for me, so confident that whatever she was doing was for my happiness, she wouldn't stop to ask if I wanted it at all.

There is a small katta on the ground floor of the building. I sat there, looking out at a group of young boys playing cricket, running between wickets and calling out to one another to field better. It had always been like this here, on Sunday mornings.

I had heard how married women missed their maaher – their parents' house. How they would long for it and visit often, to cure their homesickness. Would I ever be homesick for this place? I doubted it. Even if I did, I wouldn't want to return here for anything.

To feel homesick, though, I first had to leave home. And there was no doubt in my mind after today that I absolutely needed to. I couldn't bear more of this. I had to get a job, somehow, anyhow and just . . . get out of here.

If only I had received a single response to all those applications I had sent! That was a puzzle: I didn't have bad qualifications, and some or other office should've snapped me up by now. And if they didn't want to, didn't these places usually send a letter saying, 'Sorry, you're not good enough for us'? But not one of them had extended me even that courtesy.

I sighed. The world just seemed full of Aniruddhats.

TWELVE

The second and final part of Babasaheb Purandare's lecture series was to happen on Wednesday evening.

I was looking forward to see Sadanand and Juee do their little courtship dance again, and I urged Juee to call up Kalyani and remind her to come with her brother, preferably forgetting their snobbish friend somewhere along the way.

By mutual agreement, we had decided not to speak of Vishnubhat and his ridiculous proposal, although the more time passed, the more I found myself finding it funny. Me, marry Vishnubhat? Hah. The man made Arun Kelkar seem like some prince from a fairy tale.

'But what if Sadanand picks up the phone?' Juee asked, a tentative frown on her face, which implausibly made her look even prettier.

'Then you can stop pretending you want to speak to his sister and ask him when he proposes to propose!' I replied calmly.

'Ila!' She clicked her tongue in exasperation. 'You also, na!'

'Yes, I also, na,' I said, looking in the mirror and pinning up a stray strand of hair, 'feel you two are taking far too long to get to it!'

'Oh, be quiet,' Juee said, and slid off the bed she had been sitting on.

At that moment, Malati came into the room, an open notebook in hand. 'Tai,' she said to Juee. 'Will you help me with this sum?'

'I'll help you, come,' I offered, as Juee gave me a grateful smile and went next door to borrow the Kelkars' phone.

'Perhaps I should wait for Jueetai,' Malati said, looking at me doubtfully.

'Why? You think I can't handle ninth standard maths?' I asked, narrowing my eyes.

'Yes.' She nodded with a mock-stoic expression on her face.

'Oh, ho ho ho,' I said, taken aback. 'Just listen to yourself, you cheeky little thing! Come here and tell me what this sum is!'

Malati explained the problem to me and I was just summoning whatever maths knowledge I had retained after school to help her arrive at the solution, when Juee returned. One look at her face and I knew something was wrong.

'Malu, go out for some time, na,' I said.

'I knew it!' She shook her head in a resigned manner. 'I knew you wouldn't be able to solve it! I should've just asked Jueetai—'

'Fine, fine,' I said, exasperated. 'Just give me ten minutes and we'll try again, okay?'

Malati rolled her eyes and went out into the living room, as I raised a questioning eyebrow at Juee.

She looked pale. 'They . . . they're not coming for the lecture,' she said, in a shaken voice.

'Oh,' I said. 'Not to worry, we can make up another excuse to . . .'

'They're not coming because . . . because' – she seemed to be steeling herself – 'they're going back to Pune.'

'What? For how long?'

'She didn't say.'

'But . . . but . . .' My forehead creased. 'Why?'

'She didn't say.'

'Juee . . . what *did* she say?'

'She said . . .' Juee's eyes were brimming, but her face was composed. Like a marble statue. 'She said she couldn't wait to be back in Pune, so she could see Aniruddha's sister, Gauri. She said Gauri is like a sister to her. That Gauri is very sweet, very talented and she has grown up into a beautiful young woman. She said she knew Sadanand was also very eager to meet her again – so eager, that Kalyani suspected that Sadanand had feelings for her.'

I blinked rapidly, trying to make sense of what I had just heard. 'No . . .' I shook my head, slowly. 'No, Juee, that can't be true. Kalyani is lying. Sadanand would never . . .'

'Why would she lie, Ila?' Juee sniffed. 'What would she gain from lying to me?'

'I saw how Sadanand was looking at you at that lunch.' I held her hands in mine. 'That was not the face of a man who was thinking of someone else.'

'You are saying this?' she asked, with a bitter laugh.

135

'You, who think so little of men? Who calls them opaque, duplicitous creatures?'

'They may be.' I squeezed her hands gently. 'But Sadanand doesn't seem to be the type, Juee, he really doesn't.'

'The type to do what?' Aai stood at the door of the bedroom, wiping her hands on a dish towel.

Juee and I exchanged glances. Then, in halting tones, Juee explained what had happened.

Aai stood stock still for a moment. Then, in one stride, she crossed the room and held Juee to her chest. 'My poor child!' she wailed. 'My poor, poor child! How could he do this to you?'

Juee, who had been close to tears thus far, was now forced to leave her own troubles aside and tend to Aai. I watched as daughter comforted mother, who was now cursing the unfairness of destiny, the cruel Gods, the evil eye of the neighbours and the fickleness of young men, all at the top of her voice.

I could understand. One failed proposal, thanks to me, she may have been able to live with. A second one was too much for her to bear.

'You luckless thing!' she cried, cupping Juee's face in her hands. 'Such a beautiful face and yet, such a broken fate!'

Juee pulled herself away gently and went into the kitchen. Kelkar Kaku's voice could be heard through the living room window, asking what the trouble was. She must've heard Aai's lamentations – they were certainly loud enough.

Aai hurried to the front door to share her misfortunes with her neighbour and I decided to step out of the house for some time. Knowing my mother, she would gather all her building friends and curse Sadanand with the direst fate for

136

what he had done. Then she would curse her own fate, ask God why he had singled her out for such a punishment, ask all those present what Juee had done to deserve such cruelty and then explode into tears.

I did not want to be there for the outpouring of sympathy that would then happen, because, sure as sunrise, at that point in the evening some well-meaning auntie or other would look at me, my complexion, sigh and then turn to Aai saying, 'Don't worry, Mrinalini. God only gives us the hardships he thinks we can cope with.' And then I would have to fight back the impulse to throw a bucket at her.

'Juee,' I said, walking into the kitchen. 'You want to come downstairs for a walk? Maybe have a chat . . . if you feel like it.'

She had been staring out of the kitchen window, tears streaming slowly from her eyes. At the sound of my voice, she wiped her cheeks and turned to me. 'No, I . . . I'm okay,' she said tonelessly. 'I just . . . I will be alright.'

I nodded. If she wanted to be by herself for some time, I would let her. I just wished she would talk. If not now, later. This . . . everything she was going through right then, it didn't seem fair that she should go through it all alone. But that was Juee for you. Never one to burden others with the weight of her own troubles. Even if her very heart was slowly breaking into two.

Sadanand hadn't struck me as a heartless man, yet, if what Kalyani had said was true, he was just that. Only a heartless man could lead someone on like that and then leave them, without even a word of goodbye. How could he do that to Juee? Someone like her, so good-natured and kind? It seemed wildly out of character for him. Or had I misjudged him?

I still wasn't convinced that Kalyani had told Juee the full story, but whether she had lied or told the truth, the fact was that my sweet, wonderful sister was heartbroken now. And I could do nothing for her.

I sniffed and turned away, before Juee could see my eyes brim.

Slipping on my chappals, I walked slowly down the stairs. I needed to think about something else for a while. Maybe Chitra was free. We could go to the park nearby and talk.*

I knocked on her door and Chitra herself opened it.

'D'you want to . . . uh . . . go to the park?' I blinked, a little thrown by what I was seeing

Chitra was beaming. I had never seen her smiling like this. She was positively radiant with joy. She nodded enthusiastically, put on her sandals and shut the door behind her.

As we walked towards the park, I told Chitra about the Pingleys' sudden decision to leave. She was as indignant on Juee's behalf as I was and agreed with me that, despite what Kalyani claimed, Sadanand was besotted with Juee and wouldn't drop her overnight for someone else, no matter how beautiful and talented that other girl was.

'See? I had told you, no?' she said. 'Juee should have made her interest in him clear. Men need to be led into these things sometimes. Otherwise, they lose their way.'

She smiled as she said that.

We settled down on an empty park bench – it was the

---

*   Because the only places in Mumbai you can talk privately to some-
     one are public spaces. Parks. Beaches. Train platforms. Try talking
     privately to someone in a one-room flat. See how far you get.

middle of a working day, and there were hardly any people about.

'Alright,' I said, giving her a critical look. 'Tell me whatever it is that's making you so giddy. You haven't stopped smiling since you opened the door!'

She laughed – an open, carefree laugh, the kind I'd rarely seen from her. 'Aga, what to tell?' she said, shaking her head fondly. 'I can hardly believe it myself!'

'What is it? What has happened?!?'

'I . . .' She dropped her gaze for a moment, then looked straight at me. 'I've had a marriage proposal. From . . . from . . . your cousin.'

I stared blankly at her for a moment. My cousin? *My* cousin. My *cousin*? No. She couldn't possibly mean . . .

'Vishnubhat asked you to marry him?' My laugh was incredulous, but she didn't join in. 'That is . . . baap re . . . that is . . . crazy!'

'Why?' she asked quietly. 'Because I'm not good-looking, like Juee?'

'Mad or what?' I exclaimed. 'It's crazy because he is . . . he's ridiculous, Chitra!'

'Stop it,' she said seriously. 'I've said yes.'

'You . . . ?' I sprang to my feet in a most unladylike way. 'What are you saying? Have you met him? Have you spoken to him? Have you lost your mind?'

'Sit down and stop being so dramatic, will you?' She shook her head, like an exasperated mother at an unruly toddler. 'He is a respectable man from a decent family. He makes a good amount of money. He has his own house. He has no siblings, so there is no question of any problems on *that* front. His parents are no longer alive, so I don't have to nurse anybody. It makes complete sense to accept his proposal. Tell me if you think anything I just said is wrong.'

'It's . . . not . . .' I struggled to find words. The very idea of my friend being married to that . . . that joker! I had to show her what he really was. I decided to try a different tack. 'You *do* know that he initially planned to propose to Juee?'

'Yes, he told me,' she replied calmly. 'But seeing that Juee seemed to be reserved for Sadanand . . .'

'Not the point. And please don't make her sound like a train berth,' I said, a tiny flare of irritation sparking in me. 'So then, did he also tell you that less than a week ago he asked *me* to marry him?'

'He did,' she said staunchly, but she looked away as she said it.

Why was she avoiding my gaze like this? What was happening? I tried to stick to my point, but it was becoming increasingly difficult to focus on my argument because my irritation was slowly transforming into annoyance.

'And you think it is acceptable to . . . well, accept someone who is so fickle?' I demanded.

'What do you expect the poor man to do, Ila?' Chitra threw up her hands. 'Just . . . never marry because *you* rejected him?'

'I didn't say that!'

'Then just say what you want to!'

'Fine! I think he is a smarmy, pretentious, self-important fool, and you are far too good for him! Happy?'

'No, I'm not.' Chitra said it quietly, and her voice sounded so sad that I felt like all the air had been knocked out of me. 'I'm not happy, Ila. I haven't been happy for a long, long time. And I'm tired of not being happy.'

'But that doesn't mean you . . .'

140

'You know how you say you're sick of your mother hounding you girls to get married? At least she *wants* you married. My step-mother hasn't lifted a finger in that department. When Baba brings up the subject, she says "Why hurry? There is time." She's told him that they can't waste money on my dowry. My guess is she wants me to stay at home and continue to do all the chores, like a family retainer, just without any wages. That is the future she has planned for me, Ila.' Chitra sighed and I reached out and held her hand. She gave me a half-smile and continued. 'I'm not . . . beautiful, I know that. And I'm not rich. If I don't want to spend my old age at the mercy of my step-brothers, I must . . . I have to get married.'

'Or you could get a job,' I suggested.

'Hah! Me? A job?' She let out a disbelieving laugh. 'Working in an office with all those men? I wouldn't know the first thing about it. And I don't want to. I've told you before – I want my own home to run, my way, peacefully. And if a husband is the price I have to pay for it, so be it.' She smiled. 'Your cousin, he's not a bad person. Not really. He has his own . . . peculiarities, but those can be managed. Give him a little attention, a little importance, and you can make him do whatever you want.'

'And . . . what about love?' I asked, although I thought I could guess her answer.

'That is a luxury not all of us can afford,' she said, squeezing my hand.

I took both her hands in mine without a word. Chitra's expression was firm, it gleamed through the sorrow, as if she was determined to make this marriage a success, at least for her.

I still thought it was a ridiculous idea, her marrying Vishnubhat. But if it got her away from her slave-driving step-mother, perhaps it made sense. At least I could see now that I didn't have to worry about Chitra. My cousin probably had no idea what he was getting into, but my friend certainly did.

'So,' I said, with a weak smile. 'Tell me everything. What did he say?'

THIRTEEN

The next few days passed predictably. By which I mean they were liberally punctuated by Aai's sighs, sniffs and moans. She would clutch Juee in a hug whenever she was overcome by emotion – which happened so often you would think my sister had been diagnosed with some incurable illness. At other times, she would settle for patting her sadly on the back or running a motherly hand over her head. I lost count of how many times Aai cursed Sadanand for breaking her daughter's heart, using epithets I had never heard before.

The effect this had on Juee was difficult to describe. She appeared to bear it all stoically. But at night, when the lights were turned off and we were lying on our mattresses, she would turn on her side, face away from me and I could see the silhouette of her shoulders shake as she wept quietly.

I was amazed that she didn't snap and just ask Aai to shut up with her anti-Sadanand litany.

And perhaps she would have, had our Mama-Mami not come to visit.

Padmakar Mama was Aai's elder brother and Ujwala Mami was his wife. They had no children of their own and they would come down from Pune to visit us often, showering all the love they couldn't give their own children on us four sisters.

Mama was an outdoorsy sort, but despite their contrasting natures he somehow got along excellently with Nana, who was fond of joking that Mama was the only Godbole* whose words actually sounded sweet. Like Mama, 'Ujoo' Mami was affectionate and patient, and above all an excellent listener, so naturally Aai doted on her.

No sooner had they arrived, than Aai pulled Ujoo Mami into the kitchen and began pouring out all her recent troubles to her.

'. . . without so much as a goodbye, Vahini!'† Aai wiped the corner of her eyes with the edge of her padar and placed a cup of freshly made tea on our small kitchen table before Ujoo Mami. 'My poor girl! Jilted! Who would look at her and think she deserved it?'

'Nobody deserves that, Vansa.'‡ Mami placed a sympathetic hand on Aai's back.

---

*   The surname 'Godbole' literally means sweet-talker so Nana's joke is at the expense of Mrs. Bendre née Godbole.

†   A form of address for your brother's or brother-in-law's wife, especially if she is older than you.

‡   An old-fashioned way of addressing your husband's sister. It was commonly used, but not anymore.

'God is truly testing me, I tell you.' Aai shook her head, her face a picture of misery. 'One daughter, jilted! The other one? Turns down a perfectly good proposal, for no reason!'

Ujoo Mami gave me a questioning look.

'He was a nitwit,' I said, by way of explanation. 'And *related* to us. By blood. Which is just plain wrong, if you ask me.'

Ujoo Mami turned her questioning gaze to Aai.

'Yamuna Vansa's son.' Aai sniffed, before glaring at me. 'There is nothing wrong with him, hunh. This one has just sprouted horns, na – that's why she thinks he is beneath her.'

'When heifers sprout horns, they are put to work,' I replied tartly. 'Here, I'm ready to work and you're not letting me!'

With an exasperated shake of her head, Aai put two cups of tea on a tray. 'There is no point in talking to you only,' she said, as she carried the tray out to Mama and Nana.

'You are thinking of getting a job, is it?' Ujoo Mami asked, taking a sip of her tea.

'I want to,' I said, eyeing her cup. 'But chance would be a fine thing.'

'And what about you, Juee?' Mami asked Juee, who had just come into the kitchen and was rifling through the steel containers filled with snacks. 'What are you going to do now?'

'I don't know,' Juee said. Her eyes were downcast as she toyed with a dabba she had pulled down from a shelf. 'I have tuitions to take, so I guess . . .'

'*I* think you should forget about Sadanand,' announced Latika, traipsing into the room. She opened the dabba in

145

Juee's hands and peeped inside. Then she pulled out a fistful of chivda* and in a swift motion popped it into her mouth. Her face took on a thoughtful expression as she chewed. 'He's not the only man out there! You should cheer up and find someone new! Someone dreamy and dashing and exciting!'

'Like who? Rajesh Khanna?' I teased, then added in mock-horror, 'or that Aniruddha Darshetkar?'

'Sheee! No, no! Who would want to marry Aniruddha Darshetkar?' Latika squealed.

'He is quite handsome,' Juee said thoughtfully. 'And very rich, Aai was saying.'

'Yes.' I nodded. 'He is also arrogant, thinks too much of himself and not quite enough of others, considers himself superior to the rest of us mortals and . . .'

'Who is this boy?' Ujoo Mami asked.

'He is not important.' I made a dismissive gesture.

'Absolutely!' Latika nodded vehemently. 'Besides, he is *nothing* compared to—'

'—Rajesh Khanna?' I deadpanned.

'No, okay?' Latika snapped, then, looking beatific, she sighed. 'I was talking about Jayant Waknis!'

---

* How to make chivda? Let me count the ways. This staple Maharashtrian snack comes in as many variants as there are dialects of Marathi. With rice flakes, with puffed rice, with corn flakes or millet, with dried fruit, grated coconut, fried peanuts . . . like Mumbai itself, chivda accepts any and all ingredients and remains all the more delicious for it. So it is really no wonder that there is an entire lane devoted to chivda in the city. For over seventy years, the roughly thirty shops in Chivda Galli in Lalbaug have sold all kinds of chivda and have a monthly turnover that runs to hundreds of thousands of rupees. Are you rethinking your career choice now? You should be.

146

I studied the tabletop, avoiding Juee's small smile. But Ujoo Mami caught it and asked, 'Oh? And who is this Jayant Waknis?'

'Oh, Mami!' Latika clutched her hands to her chest like she was a first-time actor in a college dramatics competition. 'He is a photographer! And so handsome! Like a movie star! And he knows so many interesting and important people, you know! Sudha and I ran into him the other day and he was telling us that he has even met Amitabh Bachchan in person, for a photo shoot! Isn't that exciting? I told him Amitabh Bachchan was okay, but Rajesh Khanna was best and he laughed and laughed! Said I was a very smart girl who was definitely going places!'

'How about you start by going to the market?' I asked. 'Aai was saying we are out of kadi patta.'

Latika made a face at me and stormed out of the kitchen as we all laughed.

'So . . . Jayant Waknis, is it?' Mami asked Juee, in a playful voice. 'He certainly sounds dashing.'

'Oh, no, no, Mami,' Juee said, with another small smile. 'You are directing your teasing at entirely the wrong person. After all, *I* am not the one he has long, soulful conversations with.' Then she looked directly at me and grinned.

'Aga, Juee! Did you not find the biscuits?' Aai's voice rang out. 'I said the third dabba on the second shelf!'

Juee rushed out with the biscuit pack, leaving Ujoo Mami to give me the full force of her attention. 'So?' she asked. 'Tell me more, go on!'

'Aga, there is nothing to tell,' I said, looking away. 'We have met a few times and spoken, that's all. Juee is just—'

'So you don't like him or anything?'

'He is a likeable chap, but that doesn't mean—'

'And handsome also?' She nudged me with her elbow.

'Yes, you could say that.' I grinned at the meaningful way she was looking at me. 'But nothing has happened.'

'And he's a photographer.' She took a long sip of her tea. 'Not a very . . . stable profession, I should think.'

'How does that matter?' I asked idly. 'Like I said, nothing has—'

'I believe you,' she said, holding up a hand. 'But you're like a daughter to me so it's my duty to tell you all this. A man not being rich, that's okay. Money doesn't guarantee happiness in a marriage. But stability – that's a whole different thing. If a man's job is unstable – today he has money, tomorrow there is no money, that sort of thing – then his home life can't be stable. And you can't have happiness without stability, Ila, remember that.'

'Okay, okay!' I held up my hands defensively. 'If I ever marry, it will be to someone who has a job at the Sachivalaya,* okay? Full government pension and everything!'

'Wait, did you say "if" you marry?' Mami frowned, just as Aai came back with the empty teacups. She deposited them on the counter, then pulled out a stool next to Ujoo Mami and continued as if there had been no break in their conversation.

'And on top of everything, now Lele's daughter is

---

*   Till the late 1970s, the headquarters of the Maharashtra State Government was called the Sachivalaya. The name was changed to Mantralaya in the early 1980s, because, well, is a government even a government if it doesn't change the name of at least one long-standing institution to suit its political agenda? Shakespeare can keep his 'a rose by any other name' bullshit to himself. Else they'll rename him Shankar Pyaare and see how he likes it.

marrying the boy Ila refused to marry!' she said, shaking her head. 'So I will have to go and nod and smile at their wedding, knowing fully well that one day that girl will throw us all out of this house!'

'Don't be silly, Aai, Chitra isn't—' I tried.

'Chitra Lele is Sharayu Lele's daughter!' Aai said, with an air of finality. 'Step-daughter, but still. You mark my words. When the time comes, she will be just as ruthless as the woman who raised her!'

I didn't see the point in arguing with her. To Aai, the entire world was in some kind of conspiracy against her and telling her otherwise simply meant she would assume that you too were plotting against her.

I quietly walked out of the kitchen, into the living room, just in time to hear Nana say, 'It's settled then!'

'What's settled?' I asked.

'Juee will go and stay with Mama-Mami for a few weeks,' Nana declared.

I looked at Juee, who shrugged. It wasn't a bad idea. A change of scene would probably be good for her.

I said as much to Nana when I found him standing in the balcony as he usually did after dinner.

'Seneca once wrote in a letter to his mother that grief is not to be intruded upon, while it's fresh,' he said. 'Because even well-meaning consolations tend to scrape its already raw surface.' He glanced at Juee, who was visible through the open door that connected the balcony to the living room. She was sitting on the divan, staring blankly at the opposite wall. 'She'll come out of it quicker if she's away.' Nana smiled. 'And when she does, her heartbreak will give her all the glamour of a tragic heroine. Our very own Meena Kumari.'

I gave an exasperated sigh. For one moment, Nana had shown empathy, but now he was back to his usual joking self. Did he not realise that Juee was actually suffering?

'You really are too much sometimes, Nana,' I muttered.

'Don't worry, I haven't forgotten about you,' he said, a mischievous twinkle in his eyes. 'I gather you're next in line for a doomed romance? With a certain photographer, if I'm not mistaken?'

'You are very much mistaken!' I glared at him and he laughed.

'Pity, pity.' He shook his head dramatically. 'Your mother would've loved the chance to prove for once and for all that God really isn't on her side.'

And before I could protest, he went back inside, laughing to himself.

A few days later, Juee informed her students that she would be unavailable for a few weeks because of a health condition, offered to reimburse the tuition fees they had already paid, packed her bag and left for Pune with Mama-Mami.

Before she left, I took her aside and told her to see if she could try to run into Sadanand in Pune. Visit his shop, perhaps. See, I was pretty sure that Sadanand hadn't left Mumbai on a sudden whim. He definitely seemed to have feelings for Juee and perhaps seeing her in person would make him rethink his decision. Maybe he'd even explain the reasons behind it. I told Juee all this and she nodded, but I had my doubts that she would actually do anything about it.

Hoping that she would take my advice, I bid her goodbye as she left for the train station with Mama-Mami.

I missed Juee almost from the hour that she left, but in the succeeding days my pining got worse. With Nana at work the whole day, and Juee away, I had nobody to talk to anymore. Aai had decided to speak as little as possible with me after what she considered my great betrayal: turning down the golden opportunity to be out of her hair forever. That left Malati, who had nothing interesting to say, and Latika, who had too many things to say, each more nonsensical than the last. Ordinarily, I would've taken succour in Chitra's company, but now that was also not a possibility.

The invitation had come the very evening Juee left: Chitra was getting married in a week's time. Apparently, that was the only good muhurta to be found in the next two months, according to the couple's kundalis, and Vishnubhat simply refused to wait that long to be united with his bride-to-be.

'Gudghyala baashing baandhun tayaar,' Nana said when he heard, and he was right. Vishnubhat did seem overeager, like a bridegroom who ties his bridal headdress to his knee instead of his forehead in his rush to get married. He had barely waited a week after proposing to me to make his advances to Chitra. From what she had told me in the park, they had met at the Parleshwar temple after I had broken his heart (his words), and she had comforted him and lent a patient ear to his outpourings of grief. This had happened three more times, and that was all it had taken for him to directly propose marriage.

I wasn't exactly complaining – the man had already overstayed his welcome with us by a long shot and if his wedding meant he would finally leave, that was something to be thankful for. But losing Chitra as well, and so soon after Juee's departure – that would be difficult for me. Not that she was the same Chitra as before. Our conversation that day in the park had changed something between us. Where once we were frank and honest with each other, now I found us being carefully civil. Once, I would've been invited to go shopping with her and her family for her trousseau, to come and gush over her jewellery, or help her get ready on her wedding day. But none of this happened. It seemed like her loyalties had changed from me, to her husband-to-be.

It hadn't struck me when I had expressed my opinion of him so vocally to her, but it made sense. She had, after all, decided to spend her whole life with the man. She couldn't possibly have taken it well, hearing a dear friend call him names. Names that he deserved, true, but all the same, it couldn't have been easy for her to hear. So here I was. Demoted from the closest of friends to the politest of acquaintances. I suppose there comes a day in every girl's life, when she has to play second fiddle to a beloved playmate's spouse. Even if he is a prize idiot.

We were told the wedding was going to be a small affair. Lele Kaka had made it sound like this was because of how little time they'd had to make all the arrangements, but I suspected it was because Lele Kaku had decided to spare every expense in the wedding of her step-daughter.

Juee would miss Chitra's wedding, but that wasn't necessarily a bad thing, I felt. Juee could probably do without seeing someone else experience the joy she had so recently imagined for herself, and which had been taken out of her reach so suddenly.

Aai, of course, had a totally different take on the matter.

'It's good Juee isn't here for the wedding,' she had said thoughtfully, while reading the wedding patrika. 'She would've completely upstaged the bride.'

I didn't say anything to this crass comment. Anything I said could and would be used against me in any future arguments. So I kept mum and focused on picking out a nice sari to wear for the wedding. One that would, under no circumstances, take the spotlight away from my friend on her big day.

Aai, on the other side, chose her good silk sari. When I asked why, she informed me that she and Nana were to stand in for Vishnubhat's dead parents, and since Vishnubhat had no sisters of his own, Latika and Malati would be his karavalis.* They would all be an integral part of the wedding, performing all the rites and rituals with him.

That left me, all by myself, looking around the hall on the day of the wedding, practically bored out of my senses. I could see that not all families from the building had been invited. This, despite the fact that the wedding was happening in the room that passed for our building's community hall. From my seat at the front of the hall, I could see the proceedings on the stage clearly. It was time for the kaanpili† and Chitra's step-brother was wringing Vishnubhat's ear with all his might. Vishnubhat was trying to smile through his grimace of pain and, I was pleased to see, failing. *Cousin dearest*, I said to him in my mind, *you cause my friend any sorrow, and I promise*

---

* Sort of like bridesmaids, karavalis are usually sisters of the bride and the groom, and stand around holding various sacred, symbolic objects during a wedding ceremony.

† The ritual of kaanpili is where the bride's brother wrings the groom's ear and tells him, 'Hey, if you hurt my sister, if you cause her any pain of any kind, I will hunt you down . . . and kick your ass.' So now you know where Ross in *Friends* got it from.

you – the agony you are in now will seem like a vacation, compared to what I'll do to you.

The flash of a camera made me look to my left, where I saw Jayant Waknis.

He gave me a polite nod, but didn't approach me, instead continuing to take pictures of the wedding ceremony.

I was surprised to say the least. First of all, I'd had no idea that he was going to be there, and secondly, given his past behaviour, I had expected him to at least come and talk to me, if nothing more.

I wasn't the only one surprised. Latika came and deposited herself on the empty chair next to me and complained in her most petulant voice: 'What has happened to this Jayant? Why is he acting so differently?'

'Because his wedding is fixed, no!' said Sudha Kelkar's voice from the row behind us. 'How can he act like a free bird now?'

Latika and I both turned around to face her.

'To whom?' we asked in unison.

'He is engaged to Lele Kaku's niece, Damayanti. But don't tell anyone, haan? Saasubai* told me not to blab!' She suddenly looked a little guilty.

'We won't tell a soul,' I whispered in a conspiratorial tone. 'But this is all so sudden!'

'Yes, apparently they just met a few weeks ago and the girl is absolutely hell-bent upon marrying him,' Sudha whispered back. 'Jayantrao asked for her father's permission and he said yes also. Lele Kaku was telling Saasubai that the girl's father

---

*   Mother-in-law.

never denies her anything. She's the only child, na. She's used to getting what she wants. No matter how expensive it is. Saasubai was telling me her father is quite rich.'

'That must be her then,' I said, noticing Jayant smiling at a young woman of roughly my age, who was smiling back shyly.

'No, no, what rubbish!' Latika's voice was full of disdain as she peered at the girl. 'She is nowhere near beautiful enough for a man like Jayant to marry!'

'No, that's her.' Sudha nodded. 'Saasubai pointed her out to me earlier.'

'But how can Jayant want to marry her? Look at her nose!' Latika made a face.

'Aga, they say, na, love is blind!' Sudha quipped and they both laughed.

I didn't join in. The girl looked . . . fine enough, I guess. Who was I to judge, honestly? And who was Latika to comment on her nose, as if she herself was Sharmila Tagore or something! Or Sudha, piping up with that nasty remark. Love is blind? Really? Certainly explained her own choice of husband – Arun was hardly an oil painting.

Now, as I watched Jayant scan the audience, camera in hand, and Damayanti give him the buffoon-smile that is the hallmark of the recently-in-love, I marvelled at the man's luck. First he is let down by his dear friend. Cast out and forced to fend for himself in a world that couldn't care less. And then, all of a sudden, he wins the love of an heiress and is all set to marry her. Amazing how fortunes can change.

In a way, I was glad this had happened. Not that I was in love with him or anything, but I *had* started taking a little more pleasure than required at the thought of him. Not of us two together, in some clichéd scene of domestic felicity, but just . . . the mental image of him smiling his rakish smile.

Well, say goodbye to all that now, my girl, I told myself. *Damayanti Whatsherface is going to make an honest man of him. And where you are headed in life, there is no place for a man, honest or otherwise.*

I turned my attention from the happy couple off the stage, to the one on the stage. Chitra sat on a paat, looking solemn in her traditional green sari, her face framed by the pearls of her mundaavlya. She was wearing roses in her hair, what I guessed was some of Vishnu's mother's gold jewellery and a quietly contented expression. Next to her sat Vishnubhat, in a pristine white dhotar-kurta and a stiff ceremonial cap, carefully writing Chitra's new name in a copper taaman filled with rice grains. *God knows what he will call her*, I thought bitterly, wondering not for the first time at this bizarre tradition of casually changing a woman's first name after marriage. Imagine! Having no say in what you are called! Just because some man decides he likes the sound of some other woman's name rather than yours! I glared at my cousin. *Don't change it*, I said to him in my head. *Prove that you are capable of one sensible action at least.* He looked up, almost as if he had heard me, then announced in a loud voice. 'Padmini!'

There was a murmur of appreciation from the other guests. Padmini. Of course. Another name of Goddess Laxmi, Lord Vishnu's wife. It must've thrilled Vishnubhat no end, to make his wife's name match his so perfectly. I wondered if I should point out that the most famous Padmini in history was the beautiful queen of Mewar, who had to kill herself because her husband couldn't protect her from another man. But I held my tongue.

When I met them on the stage later, I simply said, 'Congratulations.' I hugged Chitra and waited as Aai, Nana, Latika and Malati positioned themselves around the new couple, so we could get a photograph together.

Through sheer bad luck, I ended up next to the groom.

'We just want to say,' he whispered to me, 'that we bear you no ill-will about . . . what happened. And that we are grateful things turned out the way they did, because we feel truly blessed for the blessing that is our Padmini.'

Don't ask me how I kept my face straight and my mouth shut during this, as I don't know. But I did, and even managed a stiff smile as Jayant aimed the camera at us and called out, 'Ready . . . ? Smile, please!'

FOURTEEN

The month or so after Chitra left was brutal. Without her or Juee around, the only thing that was capable of distracting me from my life was the Ganpati celebration in the society.

We had stopped keeping a Ganpati idol in our home after my grandfather passed away, so we paid our respects each year to our society's community Ganpati. A few weeks before Ganesh Chaturthi, the society's Sarvajanik Ganpati mandal, headed by Malvade Kaka, went around collecting contributions from each family in the society. Very soon, a tall sturdy mandap began to take shape in the quadrangle.

On Ganesh Chaturthi, a respectably-sized Ganesh idol was installed at one end of the mandap and for the next few days, our lives filled with the smell of incense and flowers and the sound of aartis twice a day.

Malu, never the most devout among us, began stopping

on her way back home from school to take the God's darshan. Aai believed that her youngest daughter was praying to the God of Wisdom so He would help her in her studies. But I knew better.

'Admit it,' I told Malu. 'You're just in it for the prasad.'

'Aiyya, Ilatai, how can you *say* such a thing?' she said, looking completely affronted, a charade I didn't believe for a moment. I should know – I had devoured more than my share of prasad at the society Ganpati when I was in school. But that was then.

Now, with Juee gone, Aai had enlisted me in the task of making modaks* to offer Ganpati. They had turned out . . . acceptable.

But like all good things, one fine day it was time for Ganpati to leave. To the accompaniment of bhajans and cymbals, surrounded by eager children playing lezhim† in almost perfect coordination, the Lord left the mandap and

---

*   Filled with a sweet filling of fresh coconut, jaggery and even roasted poppy seeds, a modak is a rice flour dumpling steamed to perfection and best enjoyed with a generous drizzle of pure, homemade ghee. Making good modaks is merely tricky; making good-*looking* modaks is a Herculean task, designed to test your agility, fine motor movements and culinary skill. Not for nothing is it considered a sport, with prizes given out for the best modaks made.

†   A lezhim is a thick wooden cudgel, with heavy cymbals attached to one side, which is used in a dance that should actually be considered more of a military drill or a martial art, because of the sheer damage it can cause. It speaks volumes for how tough Maharashtrians are, that the act of swirling the lezhim about, right and left, up and down while you bend, stand, crouch and advance, keeping perfect time with the music while making sure you don't put someone's eye out, is called 'playing' lezhim in Marathi.

began his long journey home, in a small cargo truck headed to Juhu beach.

Life fell back into its routine and, free from all distractions, I was forced to accept the fact that I had not received a single reply to the – by now – dozens of job applications I had sent.

Were Vishnubhat and his ilk right after all? Was I simply not bright enough to get a job?

If I believed that, I would have to believe something far worse: that the only course now open to me was to do what Chitra did. What Aai wanted. Accept whichever man deigned to overlook my complexion and my lack of dowry and get married to him quickly, bent low under the weight of this magnanimity. Spending every waking moment cooking, cleaning, clearing up after him, without a word of complaint, in case he started to mention his great sacrifice. Or worse, being reminded by his family that he had so many proposals from fair, good-looking, well-off girls, but he chose *you*, so be grateful and do as you're told. Or perhaps the worst of all: to wake up one day and find out that your blessed husband regrets not taking a dowry and has now decided to harass you till your family coughs up whatever he asks for.

'Woman burned by in-laws for dowry' was the headline in today's paper. See? I wasn't exaggerating. These things happen. I turned the page, hoping to read something more cheerful. Hema Malini had been nominated for the Best Actress Filmfare. Good for her. I turned the page again – and there they were. The job listings. I recognised a few from my applications. Mostly from government bodies and banks. Clearly the posts they had advertised were still open. Just not for me. I skimmed the rest, looking for other places to apply to but a small part of me asked, *What's the use in applying to these? You'll just get rejected again. No, sorry, not even rejected – you simply won't hear from them. It'll just be a waste of postal stamps.*

'Give me that!' Latika yelled, as she snatched the newspaper from me.

'I'll give you a slap!' I snapped. 'And since when do you read the paper?'

Latika didn't answer, but rifled impatiently through the newspaper till she found what she was looking for. With a whoop, she rushed to the kitchen yelling, 'Aai! Aai! They're hiring!'

I frowned. What the hell was this monkey up to now?

'Absolutely not!' I heard Aai's voice from the kitchen. It had all the finality of a mill gong.

'But why not?' Latika returned to the living room, stamping her feet, and threw herself on the divan. 'What's so wrong with it?'

Wait, Aai was denying Latika something? My eyebrows rose so much they must've reached my hairline.

Aai stood at the door of the living room, wiping her hands on a dish towel. 'You're not becoming an air hostess and that is final!' she said.

'But whyyyy?' Latika whined. 'It's Air India, Aai! It is so prestigious and . . . and . . . posh! And . . . have you even *seen* the Air India girls? So elegant! So . . . so stylish!' Latika's eyes had glazed over with imagined visions of the national airline's air hostesses. 'Don't you want me to travel to exotic foreign countries and earn a lot of money?'

'I want you to get married and settle down,' Aai replied calmly.

161

'Who says I can't do both?' Latika sprang to her feet and put her hands on her hips in a way that was so reminiscent of Aai, I had to laugh.

'Stop laughing!' she snapped immediately. 'That Godrej man's wife also used to be an Air India air hostess! That's how they met! Maybe I will also find a rich, handsome man once I become an air hostess—'

'You know it's not all just dressing in fancy saris and travelling, right, Latika?' I asked. 'I mean, you also have to *work*.'

'I can work!'

'Oh? You can serve food and clean up after people and smile and be polite, is it?'

'Of course I can!'

'Really? Never seen you do it before,' I teased, as the doorbell rang.

I opened the door to find the postman nodding at me genially. He handed me a beige postcard, which was, strangely enough, addressed to me.

Before I could see who it was from, Aai had snatched it from my hands. I looked at her in surprise, but she just read the sender's name and handed it back to me. I frowned. Why was she suddenly so curious about who was sending me mail? Did she think I was having an affair with someone? And did she think that person was daft enough to send me love letters by post? That too on a postcard, which anyone could read?

I glanced at the sender's name. It said Sau. Padmini Chhatre.

As I flipped the postcard around to the side where Chitra had written, I heard Latika whine: 'Aai! Say yes, na!'

162

'It's not safe, ga rani.' Aai's voice was gentle as she pulled Latika into a hug to console her. 'Planes can be hijacked. You know, a few weeks ago an Air India plane was hijacked from Delhi airport and flown to Pakistan? Some years ago same thing happened with an Indian Airlines plane . . .'

'Just two planes . . .' Latika scowled.

'That's two more than I am comfortable with, so enough of this nonsense!' Aai glared at her.

'Tch!' Latika pulled away from Aai and stormed into the bedroom. 'You never let me do anything I want!'

'I hope you're happy,' Aai said to me. 'It's all your fault, you know, talking all that drivel about getting a job. That's what's put this ridiculous notion in her head!'

Without looking at my incredulous expression, she sniffed and went back to the kitchen. I sighed. How were Latika's delusional ambitions my fault? I swear, if Aai could find a way to blame all of Kalyug* on me, she would. With a shake of my head, I began reading.

Dear Ila, Chitra had written. *How are you? I know it has been only a few weeks since I left Mumbai, but it has seemed like a lifetime. Wai is a lovely place – quiet, quaint and peaceful. Our home is right next to the Bhagwati temple and my morning chores are done to the gentle sound of temple bells. The house is comfortable – much bigger than our Mumbai flat and rather too big for just the*

---

* The last and worst of the four ages of the world mentioned in Hindu mythology. It's the one where sin and evil will rise till an apocalypse wipes out all life. It also happens to be the age we're currently living in. So get a move on with your reading list – we don't have a lot of time.

two of us. Having a home to call my own has brought me so much joy, I cannot begin to put it into words. I doubt I would do a good job describing the feeling, even if I could. We have a small garden behind the home, which I wish you could see. It gets a lot of sun, so I've planted roses – hopefully, they will bloom well. I was also introduced to Kaveribai Bhagwat and her daughter and they have both been most kind and welcoming.

If there is anything at all in my life that is less than perfect, it is how much I miss my life in Mumbai. It happens in the strangest ways. My ears crane to hear familiar noises – the rattle of a local train, the low roar of a BEST bus, the boys playing cricket down in the quadrangle. My eyes miss familiar sights – Naik Kaku haggling with the fisherwoman, your mother hanging out the washing on the lines outside your balcony. And your face, my friend. I miss it so much. Because while life is peaceful in every other way, I have no one to talk to but your cousin. I miss our shared confidences and jokes, the gossip in the building and your witty remarks. Not my family, not even my father, but you. To me, you are home, Ila. And so I ask you – please, won't you come and visit me? Your cousin will be happy to pay for your ST ticket and pick you up from the bus depot at Wai. Come for a few days – the weather has just turned here, and the evenings are pleasantly cool. Send a reply soon and reply with a yes to

Your friend,
Padmini

I tapped the postcard on my hand as I considered her request. A few days in Wai didn't sound so bad. Even if I'd once again be under the same roof as Vishnubhat, it would give me a chance to see Chitra again, see how she was getting on. Besides, it would be a break from the self-flagellation I went through every time I opened the newspaper to the Vacancies page.

Aai, as usual, had an entirely different take on the matter. 'Ohhh!' she said, one hand on her hip, when I asked her permission to go and stay with Chitra. 'First you don't want anything to do with Vishnu, and now you want to go and stay in his house? Nice! Very nice!'

'I'm not going there to see *him*!' I said, exasperated. 'I'm going because Chitra is homesick!'

'You do know that she is calling you there to rub your face in her good fortune?'

'She married Vishnu, Aai! What good fortune?'

'On second thoughts,' Aai narrowed her eyes, 'you *should* go. Go, go. Go see how happy your friend is, living the life that *could* have been yours if you hadn't been so stubborn! Maybe then you'll accept that you don't know better than your own mother!'

I let out a frustrated sigh. Legend has it that when Hanuman went to rescue Sita from the Ashok Vatika, he got hungry and asked for her permission to eat fruit from the trees. Sita told him only to eat the fallen fruit. So Hanuman shook the trees till all their fruit fell down, and ate it all. There's a phrase in Marathi based on this: Padtya phalaachi adnya ghene. Taking orders about falling fruit. It means taking the bare minimum instruction, even if grudgingly given, as an order to do something you want to do.

Well, if Hanuman could do it, so could I.

I went to pack my bag.

Two days later, carrying my holdall in one hand and clasping my purse in the other, I stepped off the State Transport

165

bus at the Wai bus depot. Rolling my shoulders, I tried to get rid of the stiffness. It had been close to seven hours since I'd left Mumbai, jostling and bumping in the window seat of the bus, which had all the shock-absorbing prowess of a wet biscuit. I squinted in the afternoon sunshine, trying to spot Vishnubhat and was rewarded by a figure waving wildly in my direction.

'There you are!' Vishnubhat beamed as he approached me. 'We were beginning to worry. How was your journey?'

He led the way out of the gate, without offering to take my bag.* Outside stood a horse-drawn taangaa, the driver digging into his ear industriously as he waited for us to get in. Once we settled inside, he clicked his tongue and the horse began trotting down the road.

'How are Mama-Mami?' Vishnubhat asked jovially.

I assured him I had left them in good health.

'Good, good.' He nodded. 'And the girls? They are well?'

'Yes.'

'Good, good, that is good,' he said again. 'Our mandali will be very pleased to see you.'

'Your . . . what?' I frowned.

'Mandali . . . wife, as you would say.'

---

* In seventeenth-century Maharashtra, there lived a milkmaid called Hira, who would come to Raigad fort from her village every morning to sell milk. One day, she couldn't get out before the gates of the fort were locked at sundown. Her newborn baby was alone at home, in her village outside the fort. So Hira climbed down the steep drop on one side of Raigad fort, in total darkness, just to be with her baby. Most Maharashtrian men seem to think that if a woman can manage *that* feat, then lifting her own bags and opening her own doors shouldn't be too much trouble.

166

Mandali? Seriously? I blinked rapidly to keep from rolling my eyes. Who in ever-loving heaven referred to their wife as a committee? Not for the first time, I wondered what Chitra had seen in this halfwit.

'I'm looking forward to seeing her too,' I said, forcing a thin smile.

We travelled in silence for a while, the clip-clop of the horse's hooves the only sound to be heard. I saw several towering spires as the horse-cart moved through the streets of the town.

'There are a lot of temples here,' I observed.

'Over a hundred.' Vishnubhat nodded proudly. 'Not for nothing is Wai called Dakshin Kashi! In fact, the Dholya Ganpati temple . . .'

I let his voice drone on, not really listening. Wai didn't seem to be a very big town from what I was seeing. Not exactly a village, although many of the homes seemed built in the style of village houses: walls of black stone or red brick; wooden doors; floors plastered with dried cow dung. And roads paved with flat broad stones. I saw women carrying pots and pails of brass and steel, the water in them sloshing about as they went their way. Does Chitra have to fetch water from the river like these women? I wondered. What a far cry from the piped water we were all used to in Mumbai! In the name of marriage, had my friend just exchanged one set of domestic chores for another, more arduous list of tasks?

But my doubts were put to rest as the horse-cart pulled up outside a neat, old-fashioned home with a red clay tile roof, that stood next to an imposing black stone temple.

Chitra didn't look remotely weary as she stood outside the door, waiting to greet us. Beaming from ear to ear, she took me by the hand and asked, 'The bus ride wasn't too rough, was it? Come, have some water.'

She took my holdall, thrust it into Vishnubhat's hands and, without waiting to hear his surprised exclamation, pulled me into the house.

The front room was a long rectangle, with big windows letting in the light, and paved with polished black stone that felt icy cold to my travel-weary feet as I slipped off my chappals at the front door.

'Come, sit, I'll get water.' Chitra smiled, pointing to a wooden swing at one end of the room. She disappeared inside the house and returned moments later with a copper tambya-bhanda* set. She poured some water into the small glass and handed it to me.

I took a sip and tried not to make a face. Water from a well has a unique taste, and it is certainly an acquired one. It can be refreshing, especially if you're having it after hours in the sun. But years of living in the city and drinking tap water meant I merely found it incapable of quenching my thirst.

Chitra must've guessed because she smirked. 'I've got used to it by now,' she said, then added briskly, 'You must be famished. Shall I serve lunch?' And without waiting for an answer, she called out. 'Aho! Show your cousin where she can freshen up!'

Vishnubhat emerged from somewhere inside the house, where he must've gone to stow my bag. With a benign smile, he gestured me to follow him. In the small corridor that led

---

*   A tambya is a pot shaped like a kalash, used to store and serve water. It was called tambya, presumably because it was often made of copper or taamba.

to the other rooms, I blinked to adjust my eyes to the sudden dimness. Outside, the afternoon sun had been bright, almost too bright, but inside the house, its light was allowed only in pockets. It streamed in through the grilles of the small windows in every wall and was grudgingly given admission through a few patches in the roof, where some of the clay tiles had been replaced with transparent glass. I felt transported to another century, where electricity would have been ignored as an unholy rumour.

Vishnubhat led me down a short, narrow corridor. The front room had been the largest. Immediately behind it on one side was the kitchen. On the other was a bedroom. A narrow wooden staircase next to the bedroom led presumably to the maadi.* The corridor ended almost as soon as it had begun and opened out into another rectangular space at the back of the house. At one end of this open space was a well. Next to it was an area partially enclosed by a low wall. I guessed this was the nhaanee – the village equivalent of a bathroom and scullery rolled into one. There was a brass bucket filled with water, along with another copper tambya.

Vishnubhat hung a cotton panchaa on the wall-hook and excused himself. I poured the chilled water on my feet and washed my face, goosebumps erupting on my skin. Chitra was right. I was famished, and now I felt tired as well.

Lunch was simple but delicious. Chitra had made vang-yacha bharit, some aamti and served us piping-hot bhakris, straight from the stove. Vishnubhat politely urged me to try

---

* The attic-like space on top of the main house used for storing things you don't need for the moment, like old furniture, odds and ends, or visiting relatives.

some sweet lemon pickle and we finished the meal with some watery buttermilk, which Chitra had seasoned with salt, sugar and powdered cumin.

I could barely suppress my yawn as I washed my hands afterwards and Chitra must've noticed, because she laughed.

'Lie down for some time if you want,' she said, gesturing towards the only bedroom. 'I'll wake you up when it's time for tea.'

Giving her arm a grateful squeeze, I retired to the bedroom, where a mattress had been made up for me, and let the fatigue of the journey claim its dues.

FIFTEEN

The next few days passed by peacefully. Vishnubhat would bathe and leave early in the morning to attend to his duties in the Bhagwati temple. Till he returned for lunch and a short nap, Chitra and I would have the house to ourselves. We'd talk and laugh while I helped her with her chores – drawing water from the well, watering the plants, cooking our meals. In the evening, sometimes we'd go and sit on the Krishna river ghats outside the temple, enjoying the cool breeze blowing from the river.

Vishnubhat was his usual pompous self, but Chitra seemed genuinely content when I asked her if she was happy. 'It's such a . . . such a . . .' She had paused, then brightened. '*Relief*, I suppose that's the word, yes, relief. To know that I am the lady of the house . . . that feeling of ownership? That too with nobody to question or criticise me all day long? Oh, Ila! I can't tell you how wonderful it feels.'

I was glad. A part of me had worried that after moving

there she would regret marrying my cousin, and by then, of course, it would be too late. But from what I saw of them, she seemed to take his silliness in her stride and he seemed to consider himself truly lucky to be married to her. Their marriage was so much calmer than Aai and Nana's.

For Chitra's sake, I hoped it would stay that way: that she wouldn't find the sameness of everyday life here boring.

Then, one evening, I got a glimpse of what passed for unboring in the lives of my friend and her husband. I was sitting in the front room, reading the newspaper, when Vishnubhat rushed into the house panting, his face red with exertion and quite out of breath.

'What happened?' I asked, taken aback by his appearance.

'She . . . called . . . dinner . . .' he gasped, holding on to his side as if he had a stitch.

'Who? What? Do you want water?'

He waved me away as if I were a fly.

'Padmini!' he yelled, and Chitra came rushing out of the kitchen, wiping her hands on her padar, looking alarmed. 'She has . . . called us all . . . Kaveribai . . . for dinner . . . tonight!'

'Agabai, tonight?' Chitra put a hand on her heart as if thrown by this information. 'All of us, you say?'

'Yes, yes . . .' Vishnubhat's nod was vehement. 'There is very little time . . . you must get ready!'

'Of course, of course.' Chitra was nodding as if he had asked her to prepare for war, not a meal. 'Come, come, Ila. We must get ready!'

I was watching this whole scene play out like an audience member at a badly acted play. But I went indoors with her, and watched as she pulled out her best sari and urged me to do the same.

172

My head swimming with a dozen unspoken comments, I surveyed my holdall with misgivings. I had brought three saris in total for what I had thought would be a quiet stay with my friend. How dressed up would I need to be to roam around the town? To go to the temple? Now, as I watched Chitra ponder whether her wedding sari would be too much or too simple for the occasion, I didn't know whether to laugh or guffaw. What did it matter what we wore? Surely it was just a meal at someone's house? How fancy could it possibly be?

My first inkling that I had maybe underestimated the occasion came when we stood on the threshold of Kaveribai Bhagwat's house. For starters, it wasn't a house. It was a wada.* Bhagwat Wada, it was called, and it was a twenty-minute walk from Vishnubhat's house.

We entered from majestic iron gates onto a long driveway, which led to the main building: an imposing double-storey sprawl with white walls. Two cars were parked on one side of the building. A tulshi plant in a stone vrindavan shaped like a lotus stood before the entrance door, which was a heavy teakwood affair with polished brass rivets. Once we stepped inside, the entranceway opened into a square chowk open to the skies, which were presently a riot of pink and purple as dusk set in. Each side of the chowk seemed to be lined with windows.

---

* A large mansion with a central courtyard is called a wada in Maharashtra. Most wadas today are either historical relics or have been converted to luxury hotels. Which essentially goes to prove that whatever era you choose, you need be loaded to live in one of these places.

How many rooms does this place have? I wondered, as I took it all in.

A genial man in a kurta-pajama nodded at Vishnubhat and led us to the first floor via a well-maintained wooden staircase, before depositing us outside a room with rich-looking curtains at each of its five windows. It seemed to be some sort of small darbar-hall – the low teak divans with bolsters, and the carved wooden pillars behind them certainly gave that impression – not to mention the lady sitting at the far end of the hall on an ornate chair.

Kaveribai Bhagwat seemed to be in her fifties, with greying hair parted in the middle and tied in a severe bun. She wore a purple Narayanpet sari – a silk one! For dinner! – and a string of pearls with matching earrings and pearl bangles. Her mouth was turned down and her gaze looked disapproving.

Next to her, leaning back on one of the bolsters, sat a young woman of about my age. Her face was pale enough that Aai would've wept tears of jealousy if she'd been there, but there were dark circles under her eyes, and her skin had an unhealthy cast. *This must be Kaveribai's daughter*, I decided, *the one Jayant mentioned*. What had he said her name was? Asha-something. Ashalata, yes! She too wore a Narayanpet, a dark orange one, but her jewellery consisted of a simple gold chain with a navratna pendant, and small gold studs. An older woman, in her forties, was wrapping a cosy shawl around her shoulders as we entered. Once convinced that her charge was properly covered, the woman stepped back a respectful distance and stood, silent.

Vishnubhat opened his mouth to greet them but Kaveribai's voice was like a whipcrack as she snapped, 'You are two minutes late, Vishnubhat! I expected better of you!'

My cousin looked like a deflated tyre, but then a crafty expression appeared on his face and he answered: 'Our apologies, Kaveribai, but you know ladies. One cannot hurry them when they are getting ready, heh, heh, heh.'

It was a flagrant lie, of course: Chitra and I had got ourselves ready in record time. I glared at Vishnubhat, who refused to make eye-contact with me, and then turned to Chitra hoping she'd say something, but my friend merely looked embarrassed.

'You must be Padminibai's friend from Mumbai. What's your name?' Kaveribai frowned at me.

'Ila Bendre,' I replied. 'Thank you for inviting me to dinner.'

As I said this, a movement caught my eye. Next to Kaveribai's chair was a wooden pillar, partially hidden by a curtain. Two men had been standing there this whole while, looking out of the window – at the sun setting over the Sahyadris, I presumed. One of them now walked out from behind the curtain – and I could not believe my eyes.

It was Aniruddhat godforsaken Darshetkar!

He was looking at me like he had just seen a ghost. He cleared his throat. 'Hello,' he said.

'You . . . hello.' I blinked. 'What are you doing here?' And then I felt like a fool because of course he had every right to be there – hadn't Vishnubhat said he was Kaveribai's nephew or something?

'You know each other?' Kaveribai asked, her gaze travelling from Aniruddha to me and back.

'My sis— . . . uh . . . his fri— . . . erm . . .' More stupid behaviour! What was wrong with me?

'We met at a mutual friend's wedding,' Aniruddha replied gravely.

'Take a lesson from this mutual friend then,' Kaveribai told him pointedly. 'And get married yourself. It's high time.'

Aniruddha didn't say anything, but someone else did.

'How are you finding Wai so far?'

The other man at the window now walked out from behind the pillar. I liked the look of him immediately. He had a broad, open face, not handsome, but there was a sincerity about him which made me feel instinctively friendly towards him.

'My cousin, Kishore,' Aniruddha said, nodding in the man's direction.

'It's a welcome change from Mumbai.' I smiled at Kishore, who beamed back.

'I don't know how anyone can bear to live in Mumbai,' Kaveribai declared. 'Houses like chicken coops, so much dirt, so much noise! And the crowd!' She shuddered with distaste. 'What is so good in these cities that you can't find in towns and villages, I would like to know!'

'Good hospitals, clean water, jobs,' I said without thinking, and as the yellow lights in the brackets above us flickered, I added, 'And reliable electricity.'

The look Kaveribai gave me could have etched a message on a marble wall. It wouldn't have been a pleasant message, either. But it was nothing compared to the look Vishnubhat was giving me – his expression suggested I had questioned the very existence of God while standing in the middle of a temple.

'Heh, heh, heh, what are you saying, Ila?' he asked, managing the delicate tightrope act between laughing awkwardly

176

and glaring at me in mute rage. 'Of course the city is no comparison for the countryside! Such peace and quiet! The lap of nature! That's why our saubhagyawati* was so eager to leave the hustle-bustle of Mumbai and move to Wai. Isn't it?' He nudged Chitra, who smiled enthusiastically.

Kaveribai seemed a little mollified but again she fixed her gaze on me and said, 'I suppose with your attachment to Mumbai, your parents must be looking for a sthal for you from there only?'

There goes that word again, I thought. 'They are busy looking for a boy for my elder sister, actually,' I replied, not wanting to explain to this lady how and why I didn't want to get married at all.

I noticed Aniruddha look away.

'Our Mama has four daughters in total,' Vishnubhat blurted. 'Ila has two younger sisters as well.'

Kaveribai pursed her lips and shook her head slowly. 'Tch, tch, tch,' she said mournfully. 'Four daughters! That is a heavy burden indeed.'

I did such a stupendous job of not rolling my eyes at that, I almost gave myself a pat on the back.

Just then an attendant entered the room, and with a respectful bow announced that dinner was ready.

The dining room had western seating, with a long

---

*   Antiquated word for married woman. Literally means 'the fortunate one'. Because she is married, as opposed to independent. No known equivalent for men exists, obviously. Because having someone to cook your meals, run your home and raise your children doesn't make you fortunate. Getting to do all these things for someone else, does.

rosewood table that sat fourteen. The chandelier overhead cast a beautiful yellow light, which was very welcome given that darkness had begun falling outside. The table had been set for seven. Kaveribai sat at the head of the table, with her daughter to her right and Kishore to her left. Next to Ashalata sat Chitra, who was flanked on her other side by Vishnubhat. Aniruddha sat next to Kishore and I had to take the remaining seat next to Aniruddha.

God alone knew what I would talk to him about. But, as it turned out, I didn't have to even make an effort.

'How is your family?' he asked me, as silent bearers served us food from porcelain serving plates that looked imported. 'I hope they are all in good health?'

I thanked him for his concern, then added, 'Juee is actually in Pune right now, at my uncle's.'

He paused before taking a bite of his food, then said, 'The weather in Pune is quite fine at the moment. I'm sure she will enjoy it.'

I tried not to purse my lips. As if my sister was in Pune for the weather.

'When you were talking about how cities are better than towns,' he said, after a moment's pause, 'were you referring to only Mumbai, or does Pune qualify as well?'

'Whatever I know of Pune is based on what I have heard,' I replied. 'Never been there myself, so I can't really say.'

He nodded thoughtfully and went back to his food. A moment later: 'So, have you seen the sights in Wai yet?' he asked.

'Not really. I wasn't aware there's much to see. Apart from temples, I mean.'

'For someone interested in history, like you? I'd say

178

there's quite a bit. Nana Phadnavis's wada, for one. Did you know Afzal Khan stopped here on the way to Pratapgad, where he was going to meet Shivaji Maharaj?'

'I vaguely remember reading that somewhere.'

'Wai was also the hometown of Manikarnika Tambe, better known, of course, as—'

'—the Rani of Jhansi,' I finished, nodding my head. 'How are Sadanand and Kalyani? You all left so abruptly, we didn't get a chance to say a proper goodbye.'

He looked away and cleared his throat, then replied, 'Yes, some urgent business came up that I had to be in Pune for, so we left.'

So Sadanand had left Mumbai simply because this man had work to attend to? Did he not have a mind of his own? No free will, whatsoever? I was so busy wondering about what that meant for Juee, I almost didn't hear Kaveribai addressing me.

'So . . . Vishnu was saying your father is a lecturer?' she asked, looking at me in a calculating sort of way.

'He teaches philosophy,' I replied.

She nodded thoughtfully. 'So all of you must've gone to college then.'

'My youngest sister hasn't yet given her matric exams, but the one older than her is in college right now, and my eldest sister and I have done our BA, yes.'

'Hmm,' she said, plucking a morsel from her plate, a note of disapproval in her voice. 'I wonder if college education is really a help for girls. Women of my generation generally never went to college and we didn't suffer for it. And why just us?' She nodded at her daughter, who was listlessly picking at her plate. 'Ashalata has never gone to college either, because her health didn't allow it. But I don't see how she is any the worse for it.'

'Perhaps . . .' I began, and then hesitated. I wanted to tell her that having boatloads of money and a mansion meant Ashalata probably didn't need a job to support herself and her family. And she'd be marrying Aniruddhat, to boot, who was equally rich from the sounds of it. The rest of us weren't so lucky.

I took a deep breath. I didn't want to shoot off my mouth again. Not because I was afraid of offending Kaveribai, but because I was Chitra's guest and any rudeness on my part would reflect badly on her. Having framed my words carefully in my mind, I said, 'I cannot speak for you or your daughter, of course, but higher education has nothing but benefits for girls, I feel. The world is changing, it is full of possibilities that didn't exist a generation ago. And education makes girls aware of these possibilities, and capable of exploring them. They don't need to be at the mercy of their husband's income – they can get a job, earn money and help him support the family. Surely that can only be good news, given the standard of living of most families in the country?'

I wanted to add that with education, a girl could also have the financial independence to leave a useless or abusive husband, but I kept my mouth shut.

'Well, I can see a college education certainly gives girls the boldness to air their opinions before people,' Kaveribai said, eyebrows raised. 'Tell me, are you allowed to speak so freely before your elders at home?'

'Oh, yes,' I replied airily. 'Nana is a big fan of Voltaire. And like he says, I may not agree with what you say, but I will defend to the death your right to say it.'

'Let's hope it doesn't come to *that*,' Aniruddha said, in an undertone.

I narrowed my eyes at him. Humour? At my expense? Really? Aniruddhat, indeed.

Kaveribai turned her attention to him. 'So, then, Aniruddha,' she asked. 'How is Gauri doing? Does she also feel like she must go to college?'

'She is considering it,' he said, with a quick glance in my direction. 'We'll see.'

I gave him a sidelong glance. He had a small, proud smile on his face. How was he fine with the idea of his sister going to college and at the same time willing to marry a girl who was just matric-pass? The man was a jumble of contradictions. Or maybe it was simpler than that. Maybe he was just a hypocrite.

Given how he had treated Jayant, it wasn't difficult to reach that conclusion.

SIXTEEN

After that evening, we were frequently invited to dine at Kaveribai's home. I suppose she got tired of seeing the same faces every day and we provided some novelty that hadn't worn off yet. The meals were usually delicious, but having to put up with Kaveribai took the sheen off them, to be honest. On one occasion she lectured Vishnubhat on the proper maintenance of the small garden behind their house. On another, she told Chitra that she must start having children soon. 'These things should be done while you are still young, then your body can snap back into shape in no time,' Kaveribai said, while Chitra looked at her lap in embarrassment. 'Have two-three children now, then you will have someone to take care of you in your old age. Say what, Vishnubhat?'

And as my cousin laughed ingratiatingly and thanked her for taking an interest in their lives, I wondered if there was any subject under the sun Kaveribai didn't consider herself an authority on. I found out soon enough.

One afternoon, while we were having lunch at the wada, I noticed Kaveribai staring at me with a calculating expression on her face. For a moment I thought I'd got some food stuck to my cheek or something, but the next second, I was proven wrong.

'You know, I had a cousin who was dark-skinned, poor thing,' Kaveribai said, in a tone of voice that suggested she was talking about someone with a terminal illness. 'Didn't get any good sthals for a long time. Then a vaidya gave her a lep to apply. It had sandalwood and some medicinal herbs. She used it religiously for six months and it was like a miracle! Got married into a nice, rich family after that.'

I felt my jaw clench as I looked at the plate of food before me.

'You should tell your mother to take you to a vaidya,' Kaveribai continued, graciously. 'These things can be cured, you know.'

I shouldn't have been surprised, really. It was hardly the first time some allegedly well-meaning person had suggested nonsense tips to lighten my skin. But, so far, most of them had been relatives and usually they had had the grace to not say it to my face. Kaveribai was obviously in a league of her own. Of course she felt totally entitled to spout this garbage to me. She wasn't a woman who would let mere decorum stand in the way of saying whatever the hell she liked. Still, it was irritating me all the same, and I was about to retort angrily when Aniruddha cut in.

'This puran poli is really excellent, Maushi,' he said, glancing at me calmly from across the table. 'I wonder . . .

183

could your cook write down the recipe so I can pass it to mine?'

I stared at him as Kaveribai launched into a long and tedious monologue about how it was a family recipe handed down from generation to generation since the time of the first Sardar Bhagwat. So now he liked puran polis, is it? After declaring that he hated sweets, all sweets, suddenly he liked puran polis. Just to save his future mother-in-law from my riposte. What a gentleman. I crushed my own poli between my fingers and chewed angrily.

Kishore, who was sitting next to me, gave me a sympathetic smile. 'Don't mind my aunt,' he whispered. 'God has given her so much, she never hesitates to share it – particularly when it comes to advice.'

I snickered at that. 'She is certainly generous with her opinions,' I agreed.

'But to her credit, her generosity doesn't end there. I believe she helped your cousin a lot?'

'Yes, I'm told she gave Vishnu the house he currently lives in, along with his position as head priest.' Chitra had told me that.

'Is it comfortable to live in, the house? It looks like, from the outside.'

'It is, it is,' I said. 'I must get Chitra to ask you to tea sometime, then you can see for yourself.' I paused. Had I overstepped? After all, Kishore was barely an acquaintance. As a single woman, inviting an acquaintance home for tea, that too on behalf of a married friend . . . I hoped he wouldn't construe my friendliness for something else. From what I had seen so far, men were fully capable of interpreting the merest politeness as an overture, especially from a single woman.

It didn't take much for a man to believe that a woman was besotted with him. I certainly had no intention of giving Kishore any such impression. Luckily, he didn't seem to read too much into the invitation.

'That would be nice,' he said genially. 'I'm actually planning on building my own house in Pune, and I'm quite fond of the style of architecture in the homes around here. It would be useful to see one up close.'

'You want to live in a house like *that*?' I asked, puzzled. 'You're cousins with Aniruddha, na? I assumed his family was rolling in money.'

'It's a big family tree.' Kishore shrugged. 'And not all branches are equally fortunate. Till a few years ago, my parents had trouble making ends meet. I've always gotten along with Aniruddha. When Appa – that's Aniruddha's father – when he died, and Aniruddha took over the estate, he made me his estate manager, so I could earn a decent living.'

'That was . . . kind of him,' I said, glancing at Aniruddha, who, to my surprise, was looking intently at us.

'Oh, he is *very* kind with people he considers his friends.'

'Really.' I couldn't keep the disbelief out of my voice. Didn't I know at least one person whom Aniruddha had considered his friend and then promptly reduced to living like a vagrant?

'You find that surprising, is it?' Kishore asked, mistaking my tone entirely. 'But it's true. Why just recently . . .'

But at that moment, Kaveribai called out to Kishore and prevented me from discovering a possibly exaggerated account of Aniruddha's kindness. What had he done? I wondered, resuming my meal. *Not* act like the rest of the world should be lying prostrate at his feet? Let someone express their opinions without sneering at them? Smile as if he wasn't paying tax for the exercise?

The days passed slowly. The pace of life in Wai was much slower than in Mumbai but, after a few days of feeling disoriented, I had grown used to it. While I spent most of my time with Chitra at home, sometimes I stepped out on my own. Wai was a small town and there really wasn't much to see, but I did visit Nana Phadnavis's wada in nearby Menawali, with Chitra. Aside from that, one of my favourite spots was along the ghats outside the Bhagwati temple. These led directly to the banks of the Krishna river, and made for a soothing place to sit and think.

I had bought a postcard from the post office and brought it there with me, intending to write to Juee. The ghats were paved with sandstone and the black stone temple looked striking against this beige background. It was a fine, sunny day, all blue skies and wispy clouds. A gentle breeze blew across the river. Down by the water, some women were washing clothes, the *dhup-dhup* of the wet fabric slapping against the stones of the ghat. Now and then, a bell would toll in the temple, a deep sonorous sound that broke the silence of the surroundings, filling it with a peaceful resonance.

I sat cross-legged on the chauthara of an old banyan tree at the edge of the ghat. *My dear Juee*, I began and then stopped. What should I say? Should I tell her how happy Chitra seemed in her new life? How Vishnubhat had been chased by a buffalo yesterday? How annoying Kaveribai was? Or how I had been forced to socialise with Aniruddha Darshetkar, through no fault of my own? Perhaps a little of everything? I wasn't sure if I should ask about Sadanand, whether she'd had a chance to meet him. Whether she had stopped crying at night. My pen was poised, the postcard was blank and ready, when a shadow fell on it.

'Namaskar,' Kishore said, with a cheerful smile. 'Looks like I'm not the only one who felt like seeing the Goddess today.'

'Oh, how nice to see you here,' I said. 'I was just writing a letter.'

'Oh, then I shall not disturb you.'

'No, no, I hadn't started yet.'

He gestured at the space next to me and I shuffled along a little to make more room. He sat down a respectable distance away from me.

'It is so peaceful here, isn't it?' he said, looking at the river. The breeze was leaving gentle ripples on the water.

'It is,' I agreed. 'Makes me wish we had some place like this in the city.'

'Don't you have a whole sea in Mumbai?' he teased.

'We do. It's just . . . the beaches are more crowded than here.' I turned to him sternly. 'But don't tell your aunt I said that!'

He laughed. 'Goddess-swear,' he said, nodding at the temple. 'Besides, we're probably leaving in a day or two, so I wouldn't have time to tell her even if I wanted to.'

'You're leaving? Work beckons, I assume?'

'Well, work beckons Aniruddha, and when he goes, I must too.'

I made no effort to suppress my smile.

'What?' Kishore asked.

'Oh, nothing. It's just . . . the other day you were telling me how kind and considerate your cousin is, but now you say whenever he decides to leave, you *have to* go too. Doesn't seem to leave much room for what *you* want.'

'No, no, you misunderstand me,' he said earnestly. 'He seems serious and formidable but—'

'Oh, you mean overbearing and high-handed?' I asked playfully.

'No, no, it's not like that.' He grinned. 'I mean, yes, he acts a little domineeringly from time to time, but he always has his friends' best interests at heart, I can assure you. If he hadn't offered me this job, I'd have been a . . . a slacker, a loafer, a burden to my parents!'

'That can't possibly be true.'

'It's true. I was well on my way towards being a complete good-for-nothing till Aniruddha stepped in.' Kishore looked serious. 'And you may say he helped me because I'm family. But he treats his friends like that too, believe me. I think he . . . he feels very protective towards people he cares about. And I know for a fact that he can go to great lengths to make sure they come to no harm.'

'That's . . . not the same as controlling people's lives, I suppose,' I said carefully. 'Although that is what he ends up doing, from what I've observed.'

Kishore thought for a moment. 'You're not entirely wrong,' he conceded. 'But sometimes, people need someone to help them make the right decisions. Not everybody is a clear thinker. Sometimes people allow their emotions or their optimism to steer them into dangerous situations. Situations that are bound to backfire on them, you know. At times like these, it's good to have someone like Aniruddha take over and guide you to safer shores.' He paused, as if remembering something. 'Just the other day, in fact . . . I heard how he helped a friend of his. The man was apparently considering a sthal that Aniruddha didn't approve of. Too mercenary, I think he called them. Very money-minded and just . . . inappropriate, you know? So Aniruddha convinced him to leave town and forget about that business altogether.'

I felt uneasy. A suspicion suddenly grabbed my mind like a bird of prey landing on a rabbit.

'Was the girl . . . did she also not meet with his approval?' I asked.

'No, I don't think that was the issue. It was the family from what I heard. Not our kind of people, he said.'

'What was the friend's name?' I asked, my heart thudding in my chest, every inch of my being pleading with the Universe that the answer be something I didn't already know.

There was a pause and then the blood rushed through my ears as Kishore replied: 'Sadanand Pingley.'

SEVENTEEN

Our kind of people. The words swirled around in my mind, like a storm gathering momentum, sharp grey winds slashing through the skies. I don't remember the rest of the conversation with Kishore, don't remember the short walk back to Chitra's house. All I remember is Chitra's face, anxiously asking, 'Are you feeling well, Ila? Your face . . . will you have some tea or something?' My voice shaking a little, I told her I needed to lie down for some time, which was not true, but meant that I could shut the bedroom door and pace without being thought a madwoman.

Our kind of people.

My family . . . Aniruddha didn't think they were 'our kind of people'. And so he had swept Sadanand away, leaving my sister, my wonderful, sweet Juee, heartbroken and alone. I remembered how her shoulders shook while she cried quietly at night. She had chosen to suffer alone, not burden any of her family with the weight of her broken dreams. She didn't make a sound, not one word of complaint, but decided to bear it quietly and sweetly, like she did everything. Considerate? Kishore was deranged if he thought Aniruddha Darshetkar understood even a syllable of the word.

I found I was wringing my hands as I paced. Money-minded? Yes, I suppose it must seem like a cardinal sin to be money-minded, especially for someone who had buckets of money. It's so easy to judge someone for wanting what you already have more than enough of. Mercenary? And whose fault was that? I know I mocked Aai for trying to get us all off her hands, but she didn't make the rules. She hadn't decided that an unmarried girl was a burden. She had no courage to question the idea, yes, but she hadn't created it. She was just trying to play a game with a less-than-ideal hand. But who had made the rules of this game? Who had decided that a highly educated girl wasn't marriage material? Who had decided that a bride isn't enough, without dowry to sweeten the deal? Who had decided that a dusky – no, to hell with that! a *dark* – girl (there! I said it!) didn't deserve love, only sympathy? WHO?

Angry tears sprang to my eyes.

Juee hadn't done anything wrong. She had been good, kind, obedient, her whole life. She had always toed the line, never back-answered her parents, and when she had fallen in love, it had been with a man her family would fully approve of. A man her mother had practically thrown her at. She had done absolutely nothing wrong and she had still had her heart broken, still been plunged into misery.

All because Aniruddha Darshetkar felt her family wasn't 'our kind of people'.

What did those words mean to him? I wondered. I suppose it was about money, wasn't it? My family wasn't as rich as Sadanand's. We couldn't possibly hope to match his social status. And that meant that no matter how lovely, how sweet Juee was, she could never be good enough for Sadanand. I sniffed. I could've expected this kind of thinking from Kalyani, but I suppose Aniruddha was cut from the same cloth.

A visceral hatred for him boiled within me – hot, acrid, almost solid.

I sank down on the mattress, wiping my eyes with the corner of my padar. I couldn't go out with my eyes red and puffy. It would just invite questions from Chitra and Vishnu that I was in no mood to answer, and certainly not truthfully.

But, as it turned out, I needn't have worried. Because when I finally opened the door of the bedroom around dinner time, I saw Vishnu and Chitra talking excitedly in the kitchen.

'You will never believe what has happened!' Chitra beamed.

'Kaveribai has received tickets to *Swarsamradni* and she has most graciously invited us to accompany her!' Vishnubhat looked so excited you would've thought he had been invited to meet the prime minister herself in Delhi. 'Such generosity! Such munificence! We told her at once that only personages of high breeding can be so obliging to those lesser than them.'

'How nice.' I sniffed and masked my disgust at his words with a small smile.

'Isn't it?' He grinned. 'It is precisely these kinds of prestigious invitations that our position allows us to provide for our Padmini. Indeed' – he gave me a sly glance – 'it takes incredible good fortune for a young woman to make this kind of advantageous marriage that opens such doors for her, don't you think?'

I ignored his implication and replied instead: 'I didn't know there was a theatre in Wai for plays.'

'Not in Wai, in Pune!' Vishnubhat squealed. 'We will travel there in Kaveribai's car, attend the play in the evening, spend the night at Kaveri Baisaheb's house in Kasba Peth and then return the following day!'

'In her car?' I asked, puzzled. 'But we couldn't all possibly fit in it.' I was thinking of the driver and of Ashalata, whom her mother would hardly go without.

'No, no.' Vishnubhat shook his head impatiently. 'There will be two cars. In one Kaveribai, Ashalatabai and Aniruddharao, and in the other us, Padmini, you and Kishorerao.'

I blinked. The idea of spending an entire day with Aniruddha Darshetkar made my stomach roil. No. No, it was too much to ask, on the heels of what I had heard today. 'Um . . . you both go, Dada,' I told him with a wan smile. 'I'm . . . I'm not feeling too well, actually . . .'

'Nonsense!' Vishnubhat snapped. 'You cannot turn down an invitation from Kaveribai—'

'Are you sure, Ila?' Chitra asked plaintively. 'It's a really good play.'

'—do you not know how much the tickets must've cost?' her husband continued. 'How hard they are to come by?'

'I have no intention of insulting anyone by refusing,' I assured him, as sincerely as I could. 'I just don't want my health to get worse tomorrow and spoil everyone else's trip.'

Vishnubhat considered this. The idea of his own cousin spoiling the exalted Kaveribai Bhagwat's day in any way must've terrified him, because he quickly nodded. 'So be it,' he said. 'What about your meals?'

'I'll make her lunch and dinner before we go,' Chitra interrupted. 'You can heat them up and eat, na?' she asked me.

'I can make my own dinner, you needn't bother,' I told her, but she held out a hand to silence me.

'You're not well, na?' she said in a voice that brooked no argument. 'Then you rest. I'll take care of it.'

And take care of it she did. The next morning, at breakfast, I found my meals and Chitra, both ready to the nines. She was wearing a new pink sari and a jasmine gajra in her hair, as she instructed me on the intricacies of her stove.

'I've drawn your bath water from the well already.' She pointed to a large brass vessel on the kitchen counter. 'When you're ready, heat it on the stove and . . .'

'I'll manage, ga. Don't worry,' I said fondly. 'You enjoy yourself, okay?'

'You're sure you don't want to come along?'

'I'm really not feeling up to it, honestly,' I said and I meant it. *Swarsamradni* would've been a wonderful treat, but my rage had still not calmed down and there was no telling what I'd say to Aniruddha if I was forced to spend the day with him.

'Okay, you rest.' She squeezed my arm lightly. 'Feel better quickly.'

I gave her a reassuring nod, and then, a few minutes later, bid her and Vishnubhat goodbye.

By the time I had bathed and dressed, I was feeling a

little more composed than before. The day stretched before me. Perhaps I would read one of the novels Chitra had brought with her from Mumbai. I would take it with me to the Bhagwati temple ghat and read under the shade of the banyan till the river breeze and the temple bells quieted the unease within me. But first . . . and now a daring thought occurred to me. Why not make myself a cup of tea? Yes, a second cup in the morning and then maybe another one in the afternoon, and again in the evening. Oh, the bliss! There was no Aai to stop me today. No Vishnubhat to emphasise snidely how much my stay was costing him in terms of tea leaves, sugar and milk.

No sooner had the idea occurred, than I hastened to bring it to fruition. A few minutes later, with my freshly brewed* cup of tea, I settled on the swing in the front room and took the first delicious sip. Shafts of sunlight were streaming in through the grilles in the windows, illuminating the black stone floor. A small black ant crawled along one wall, oblivious to its own tininess.

I had brought Vishnubhat's portable Murphy radio with me so I could listen to some music while I enjoyed my tea. I fiddled with the knob till I caught the faint, scratchy sounds

---

* Connoisseurs and sticklers for the English language might point out that while coffee is brewed, tea is steeped. They may find it useful to know that while tea in England is indeed steeped – or allowed to soak in hot water till it releases its flavours – in India, it is boiled to an inch of its life, drowned in milk and lashed with all kinds of spices till it bears no resemblance to the English drink. Do the English find Indian masala chai an abomination? Perhaps. But you don't get to colonise a country, force its people to grow tea for you and then have *opinions* on how they should drink it, so there.

of a song, then settled down and took another sip, savouring the taste of ginger and lemongrass, which I had plucked from the small garden at the back of the house. *Where does he get the nerve?* I asked myself. Where did Aniruddha Darshetkar find that kind of entitlement that made him think he could pass judgements on people, take decisions for them, change their lives? What did he know of Juee, of our family, outside of what he had seen the few times we had met? How could he just—

The sound of the iron knocker on the front door brought me out of my reverie. When I opened the door, the postman gave me a quizzical look.

'Vishnubhat and his wife are out,' I explained. 'I'm his cousin.'

His expression cleared and he handed me an inland letter addressed to me, care of Vishnu Chhatre. I shut the door and returned to the swing, letter in hand. It was from Juee.

Dear Ila, she wrote. *I called Nana from Mama-Mami's home and he told me you were at Chitra and Vishnu's place. I thought I'd write to you since it's been so long since we spoke. How are you? How is Chitra settling into her married life? How is Vishnu doing? Hope all of you are in good health.*

It has been a while since I've been here in Pune and it's so different from Mumbai! There are many lovely places to see. Mami and I visited Shaniwaar Wada, which must have been very grand once upon a time; Peshwe Park which is a zoo; and we even climbed Parvati! Exactly 103 steps, Ila, all the way up the hill! Mama is going to take us to Mastani's mahal which is actually a museum. He said it's worth seeing and Mami said shame on him, he just wanted to ogle the dead beauty but it was all said in fun.

How we laughed! They are so relaxed and free with each other, Ila, not at all like Aai and Nana. I hope one day I too have a marriage like that.

But I don't think it will be with Sadanand anymore. I have accepted that. A few days after coming here, I looked up Sadanand's shop number and called him. He wasn't at the shop, but the manager gave me his home number so I called there. Nobody picked up. I thought maybe they all were out, so I tried again the next day. This time, Kalyani answered the phone. She didn't seem thrilled to hear from me, honestly. But I told her I was alone in Pune, I didn't know anyone my own age and it would be nice if she could show me around. She said she was too busy! Can you believe that? After the way she was with us in Mumbai, I really was not prepared for such coldness from her. But I persisted, said we should meet at least once, to which she very grudgingly agreed. She came over to Mama-Mami's house one afternoon and she was so . . . distant! It was like we had met a totally different person in Mumbai. She looked like she couldn't wait to leave, barely sat for twenty minutes, had a cup of tea and bolted. I was so confused. In Mumbai she had acted as if we were great friends, and now this? I didn't know what to make of it, really. When I asked about Sadanand, she said he was very busy these days. Didn't even have time to go to the shop, had left things on the manager there because – the ink had smudged in this bit, as if a tear had dropped on it *– apparently, he is spending a lot of time with Gauri Darshetkar. You know, Aniruddha's sister. Kalyani says he has taken quite a shine to her. She is supposedly very beautiful, sweet-natured and considering who her brother is, extremely wealthy. Kalyani kept saying how they are well-matched – Sadanand and Gauri – and then she turned to me and asked, 'Don't you think so, Juee?'* Here, Juee's handwriting looked very shaky and my heart went out to her. *I just nodded, I didn't know what to say. She left soon after that and I haven't heard from her since. I don't think I ever will.*

I suppose it wasn't meant to be, Ila. I've decided to accept that and go on with my life. If Sadanand marries Gauri, I wish them well, from the bottom of my heart. They do sound well-suited to each other – another smudge, this one bigger than the one before – *I will return to Mumbai in a day or two, so I will be there when you come back. Do pass my best wishes to Chitra and Vishnu.*

Your sister,
Juee

I folded the letter and put it down on the swing. My tea had gone cold, but it didn't matter. I didn't even feel like drinking it anymore. I had always thought Kalyani Pingley was a sow but . . . of all the callous, cruel ways to treat someone. Disgust and anger filled me. I wanted to grab that girl by the hair and ask why she felt the need to treat my sister so badly! And then, like an eclipse, another, darker thought took over. Had this been Aniruddha's plan all along then? Did he want Sadanand for his sister? Is that why he had manufactured reasons to separate his friend from Juee? All he would have to do was tell Kalyani he wanted Sadanand to marry Gauri. Besotted fool that she was, she would have agreed even if the man had said he wanted to sell her brother in the cattle market. Between the two of them, they would've made short work of Sadanand's feelings.

The enormity of the conspiracy sat on my mind like an anvil. Could people . . . did people . . . stoop to such lengths in the pursuit of the right sthal? A new song began playing on the radio just then, a song completely at odds with my state of mind. Manik Varma sang Ga. Di. Ma's words.[*]

> *My braid undone, my hair loose*
> *My eyes brimming because dust blew*
> *The kajal flowing down my cheek*
> *Tomorrow in Gokul, all of this*
> *Will be taken the wrong way*
> *Don't make the swing sway . . .*
> *My indigo love,*
> *Don't make the swing sway . . .*

Even Manikbai's honeyed voice couldn't stop the bile from rising to my throat. I needed water. Preferably a bucketful in which to drown Kalyani, but for the present a glass would do for my parched throat.

As I got up to go to the kitchen, the knocker on the front door sounded again.

When I opened the door, there stood the last man I had wanted to see, the absolute worst possible person who could've caught me at this moment: Aniruddha Darshetkar himself.

---

[*] The story goes that someone once complained to famous Marathi poet G. D. Madgulkar that the letter ळ in the Marathi language is completely pointless and has no use whatsoever. In response, Ga.Di. Ma, as he is known, penned 'Ghananeela Ladiwala', a 10-line poem capturing an interaction between Radha and Krishna, in which the letter ळ is used a whopping 13 times. The poem was later recorded as a song for the Marathi film *Umaj Padel Tar*. Moral of the story? Don't fuck with poets.

EIGHTEEN

I frowned. *What is he doing here?* He ought to have been halfway to Pune by now.

He was fidgeting, which was surprising in itself: I had never seen him anything but calm and collected. So, watching him act as if he didn't know what to do with his hands was . . . strange, to put it mildly. I adjusted my expression to a marginally more polite one.

'Namaskar,' I said curtly.

'May I come in?' he asked, after a moment's hesitation, and I stood aside to let him enter the house.

He stood in the middle of the room, looking unsure whether to sit – and possibly where to sit, too. There was the swing, of course, but since I hadn't expected company, there were no chairs in this room. Still, Aniruddha Darshetkar, unsure about something? This man looked utterly self-possessed wherever you put him. I could very well imagine him standing with quiet confidence in the middle of a circus tent, looking disdainfully at the lion, till the poor thing tamed itself out of sheer embarrassment. Why did he look so nervous here, then?

'I'll get a chair for you,' I said, turning to go, but he called out almost instantly.

'No, no, it's fine.' He wiped his forehead with a handkerchief. His temples were wet with perspiration. In Wai? It was practically a hill-station! Had he run all the way here? What was going on?

'Water then,' I said, and went to the kitchen to fetch a glass of water.

'Thank you,' he said in English, as I offered it to him. He gulped down half the water in a single swig.

'I thought you were—' I started.

'Are you un—' he began. 'I heard you were unwell,' he continued, worry etched on his face. 'I came to see if . . . you needed someone to take you to . . . a doctor.'

'No, I'm just tired,' I told him, puzzled. Why was *he* suddenly so concerned with *my* health?

'Are . . . are you sure? You look a little red in the face.'

'I'm fine,' I said.

'Good, good.' He nodded and looked away. All of a sudden, he began pacing the room. Then, abruptly, he stopped and turned to face me. There was a pleading look on his face. 'This is difficult for me to say,' he began, 'but I have to say it. Um. For the past several weeks, I have come to realise that . . . I seem to have fallen in love with you.'

My eyebrows rose but I couldn't find a single word to say.

Aniruddha Darshetkar was in love? And not in any abstract sense, with say, the philosophy of narcissism, ha ha, but with *me*, of all people? Was this some kind of elaborate joke?

I watched his face intently, but the earnest expression didn't crack.

Instead, he took a deep breath and stood straighter. 'I find myself thinking of you all the time. On several occasions, I had to stop myself from coming to see you here. But I wanted so badly to spend more time with you that I . . . I arranged for tickets for us all to a play I knew you wanted to watch . . .'

'*You* got the tickets?' I asked, struggling to control my anger.

'I did,' he replied impatiently. 'I know . . . I know it sounds desperate, but I am!' He shook his head, as if exasperated. 'Believe me, I did not plan for this to happen. I had no intention . . . I . . . this is a nightmare!' He looked at the floor, running a hand through his hair.

Well, yes, I wanted to say, *considering I want to slap your snobbish face for what you did to my sister, yes, I would most definitely say this isn't ideal, you pompous blockhead.*

Aloud, I asked sarcastically: 'Oh, is it?'

He gave me a look of sheer disbelief. 'Of course it is!' he said scornfully. 'Men like me . . . I don't . . . men like me fall in love with girls like you only in movies.'

Waah, I thought to myself. *He really* does *think very highly of himself.*

Unlike Latika, I hadn't spent hours daydreaming about what it would be like when a man confessed his love for me, but between Vishnubhat and this prince among men, it really didn't have a lot to recommend itself.

'Surely you can see why?' he said, taking a step towards me. 'Your family's financial position isn't anywhere close to mine. Neither do you move in the same social circles I do. People from such different backgrounds as ours . . . just think, what would people say? And . . . I have to bear in mind what kind of a family I would be marrying into. The character, the personalities, the culture of the people involved. And your family' – he shook his head with an incredulous nod – 'leaves a lot to be desired, in that department.'

I crossed my arms and struggled to keep my composure.

He seemed to take that as encouragement (which just goes to show that I had been right: men wouldn't recognise a hint even if it gave them a shave every morning): 'But whatever objections my mind presented in that regard . . . if ignoring those objections means I could . . . spend a lifetime with you as my wife, then those objections are nothing. Nothing at all.' He sighed. 'That's why I have come here today. Instead of going on an excursion *I* organised, lying to my aunt and cousin about why I couldn't come – looking and acting like a madman! – to ask you to marry me and put me out of my misery.'

He looked straight into my eyes, looking utterly confident in my response.

I didn't respond immediately. From the road outside, I could hear people going about their day – the tring of a bicycle bell, a dog barking in the distance, a child shouting to his playmates. Inside, Manik Varma continued to sing:

> *This evening, both of us,*
> *All would seem suspicious.*
> *See, the moon dawns behind the tree*
> *And on the banks of Kalindi*
> *The little cowherds play –*
> *Don't make the swing sway . . .*
> *My indigo love,*
> *Don't make the swing sway . . .*

If ever a marriage proposal had sounded like a demand, this one did. Aniruddha had not asked for my hand, but demanded it. As if it was his right or something. As if he was entitled to me by virtue of simply being himself.

I took a deep breath to steady myself. It would be terrible for Chitra if the people in the next house heard me ranting at this man. 'Thank you for your interest,' I said, through clenched teeth. 'But I think it would be best for both of us if I said no.'

He actually blinked a few times, as if trying to understand what had just happened. 'You're . . . what?'

'The answer is no.'

Now he looked confused, taken aback even, as if he hadn't expected things to go quite this way. This made me even angrier.

'Don't,' I said, my voice heavy with scorn, 'don't act like this comes as a surprise. It shouldn't. Not when you have just acted as if I should be grateful that someone like *you* wants to marry *me*! Did it never strike you that I may not want to marry someone like *you*?'

'Someone like me?' His eyes narrowed. 'And by that you mean . . . ?'

'Someone who considers the rest of the world inferior to him! Someone who has such a high opinion of himself that he is unwilling to even say two straight words to people whom he doesn't consider rich enough, or beautiful enough, or . . . or fair enough!'

He looked startled, almost as if I had physically slapped him.

'Don't pretend you haven't done anything to make me react like this!' I held up a hand to silence him. 'I heard what you said about me at Arun's wedding! I heard you say I wasn't fair enough to talk to! And as if that weren't enough, all those things you just said under the guise of a *proposal*' – I spat the word – 'would've been enough for any normal girl to turn you down. But that isn't even—'

'The things I said?' His voice rose and I could see the confusion turn to outrage. 'Me saying I loved you, that I wanted to marry you, you find that *so* offensive that—'

'Oh, is that what you were doing?' I asked, my own voice rising. 'I thought you were listing all the reasons why marrying me would be beneath you! This wasn't a marriage proposal, it was a never-ending insult. To me *and* my family! No character? No culture? Let me ask you – is *that* how a man of character and culture talks about someone's family? What self-respecting girl would listen to someone abuse her whole family, then agree to marry such a man? That too, when she knows that this man' – I felt my voice crack at the edges – 'has single-handedly engineered her sister's heartbreak?'

His eyes widened as what I had just said sunk in. He opened his mouth to say something, but no words came out.

I had no such problems.

'Admit it,' I said, taking a step towards him, my breath coming fast and shallow. 'Did you or did you not tell Sadanand to leave Mumbai? Did you, or did you not, keep him away from Juee? Knowing that he loved her! Knowing that she loved him! Didn't you? DIDN'T YOU?'

We were almost face to face now, closer than propriety allowed really, but I didn't care. My hands were clenched into tight fists and it was taking every bit of self-control I possessed not to slap his face at that moment.

'I didn't—' He seemed torn, gazing into my eyes one moment, then at his feet the next. 'I saw nothing in her behaviour that suggested that she felt anything but friendship for—'

'Because you are such an expert in these things?' I snapped. 'Did it ever cross your mind that a girl can just be *shy*? That no matter how deeply she feels for someone, she is bound by propriety to not display it, in case she is considered too bold, too crass, too unladylike?'

'I—'

'Of course it didn't! Why should it? *Your* judgment must always be accurate. *Your* opinion is all that matters, isn't it? I should've known what kind of man you are, what you are capable of,' I hissed, bitter tears forming in my eyes. 'What would you care if two people in love are plunged into misery? As long as you get your way, the rest of the world can go to hell, right? You don't care about anyone but yourself. You couldn't even treat your own childhood friend right!' I shook my head. 'What you did to Jayant, how you treated him—'

'Jayant?' His voice rose, sharp with disdain. 'Waknis. Right. Of course. Your *friend*.'

'So what if he is?' I stuck my chin out. 'He deserves *good* friends. Or do you think *everyone* needs to treat him like garbage and renege on their father's promises?'

Anger flashed in his eyes for a moment, then he turned away from me. When he spoke again, his voice had gone dangerously quiet. 'What Jayant deserves is between him and his maker,' he said quietly, then turned around to face me again. His expression was cold. 'But let me not waste any more of your time today. You have made your position clear. I'll take my leave. Sorry for interrupting your morning.'

He strode out of the door, slamming it shut behind him. Leaving me standing there, chest heaving with emotion, eyes brimming with angry tears.

NINETEEN

The morning's encounter had taken away my appetite, so I skipped lunch. The day passed slowly, leaving me to the ferment of my thoughts. Reading brought no pleasure and I put aside the book I had started reading when I realised that I was reading the same line over and over again, without the meaning really registering.

Aniruddha's words sounded in my ears again and again. *Men like me fall in love with girls like you only in movies.* What an aggravating man! Who did he think he was? What could've possessed him to propose to me? And to imagine I'd accept! After knowing what he had done to Juee! Perhaps he thought I'd never find out, the condescending ass. Oh, the nerve of the man! Suddenly, I felt like the walls of the house were closing in on me. I found my breath laboured, sweat beading my brow. I needed to get out of the house, into the fresh air, and clear my head a little.

I locked the house with the key Chitra had left for me and headed for the Bhagwati temple.

Cool air greeted me inside the dark stone structure. Outside, sounds of life carried on, but inside all was quiet, the hush punctuated only by the whispers of the devotees, which echoed softly against the high ceiling. The door to the inner sanctum was open and I joined my hands and bowed to the Goddess inside.

Some assistant priest had draped the idol in a dark green sari, probably an offering from some believer whose wish the Goddess had granted. The idol was carved in roughly hewn stone, black like the temple, with staring eyes of black and white beads that seemed to lock you in their terrifying gaze, hard and unblinking. The figure looked only vaguely humanoid and somehow, I felt, that made it all the more holy.

Because privately, I have always felt that if there are Gods, then they have existed since before civilisation, and have no business looking like they shave every weekend. Likewise, for Goddesses: I deeply mistrust those paintings of Saraswati and Laxmi you get on calendars – fair, young, lithe women with hair and make-up that look like it has taken hours in a beauty parlour to achieve. Faces frozen in a gentle smile, as if that is the only expression they were allowed to have. How . . . tame they look.

If a Goddess had any power at all, then why would she bother looking like she smiled in photographs for a living? A Goddess should look wild and free. She should look like she was birthed by the wind and the rain, as dangerous as the ocean, as feral as a forest, as hard as the rock she was carved from.

This one did and I bowed to her, praying for peace. For who can grant calm better than She who can stare down a storm?

Kaveribai had told us the story a few days before – of how the first Sardar Bhagwat, ancestor to Kaveribai's husband, had come to the foothills of Wai after being separated from his hunting party in a storm. As he curled up under a tree, lost and tired, he had fallen into a fever-dream and a Goddess had appeared to him. She had said that he would live through the storm and escape unscathed through the others he would face in life. All he had to do was build a temple in her name. And he had.

So here I was, praying to her for peace. And somehow, in the stillness of the temple, sitting cross-legged on the cold floor, I felt like I almost found it.

'Sister, it is time for the Goddess to sleep,' someone said, and I looked up to see one of the younger priests gesturing towards the inner sanctum. Another priest had covered the idol with a cloth and was now closing the sanctum's doors.

I nodded and stood up with a sigh. If Bhagwati wanted a nap, maybe Krishna would do the rest.

I found my way to the banyan tree, and sat in its shade on the chauthara, leaning against the trunk of the tree for comfort. The breeze on the river was balmy but pleasantly so. There were no women on the banks today – they had probably finished their washing in the morning. Hardly any people about, really. Just a few birds crying at a distance. I breathed deeply, feeling the tightness in my chest receding. I felt my eyelids droop, fatigue claiming my limbs, sleep snaking its way through my body.

A twig snapped nearby.

My eyes flew open. Aniruddha Darshetkar. *Now* what did he want? I sat up straight.

'Sorry to bother you again,' he said curtly. 'I'm leaving for Pune early tomorrow and I wanted to give you this before I leave.' He thrust an envelope into my hands. 'I'd be obliged if you read it.'

And without a backwards glance, he left.

I opened the envelope to find sheets of lined notepaper covered with writing. A letter? For me? What could he possibly have left to say to me that he hadn't this morning? Did he miss out on an insult or two that he absolutely *had* to convey before he left?

I began to read.

To:

Miss Ila Bendre

I hope this letter finds you recovered from the tortures of this morning. But do not worry. This is not a continuance of that episode. In fact, it will be best if you forget all that happened then, as I intend to do. No, this letter is a response to your accusations against me. Ordinarily, I would have let them pass, but I will not have my character questioned and malice attributed to me where none exists.

Your first allegation is that I separated your sister from my friend, knowing full well the depth of their feelings for each other. This is categorically false. I knew Sadanand was falling in love with your sister. I have known him for years and I have seen him infatuated several times, with women not half as pretty as your sister. But not like this. I would have been happy for him, in principle, if I thought your sister returned even a fraction of his

211

sentiment. Whenever they met, she talked to him, yes, and seemed to enjoy the conversation even. But other than that, nothing in the way she behaved suggested that she had any feelings towards him, save those of friendship. However, if you insist that she is in fact in love with him, I will accept that on the basis of the fact that your sister might have confided her feelings in you. I obviously am not privy to her innermost feelings. I can only make my deductions based on my own observations and what I observed was a polite, well-mannered girl: not one in love.

More importantly, even if she had returned his feelings with equal fervour, I still would have had reservations about the match. Sadanand looks at me more like an older brother than a friend, and in the absence of his parents, I consider it my responsibility to stop him from making foolish decisions. Marrying into your family would have been an exceptionally foolish decision for him. Not because your family doesn't belong to the same social circle as his — that is a problem, yes, but not a large one. For Sadanand. His family background is not quite the same as mine and his marrying your sister would have raised eyebrows, but people would have attributed it to the wild emotions of young love and forgotten about it in a few days. No, the trouble with him marrying your sister is the rest of your family: your mother and her obvious designs to snag a wealthy son-in-law; your sister Latika's complete lack of decorum; and your father turning a blind eye to all this.

Let me also say I have seen nothing in your behaviour or your elder sister's to invite any sort of criticism. I couldn't point out a single social misstep on the part of either of you, which, given your family's unacceptable behaviour in public, is certainly to be lauded. And that, unfortunately, is the issue.

A marriage isn't something that happens between two people alone; it is a decision that ties families together. And I admit, I was

212

not in favour of Sadanand being tied to a family like yours. You may as well ask how, if that is the case, I was so willing to subject myself to it – I know I have asked myself this very question several times. I can only say that while I was willing to make that decision for myself, I did not want to be responsible for the consequences of Sada making the same choice.

I stopped reading and let out a breath. Of all the presumptuous, entitled behaviour in the world! Had he taken it upon himself to orchestrate the love lives of everyone he knew? That stupid, pompous know-it-all! I shook my head and continued reading.

Now, for the second, more serious allegation. You implied that I had refused to help Jayant, that I had broken my father's promise. I don't know what he told you, but allow me to correct the record. Jayant and I were childhood friends. As boys, we were close, despite Jayant's disturbing obsession with my family home and his tendency to filch things he liked. That's right. Small things often went missing around him but because he was never caught in the act, my mother insisted we give him the benefit of the doubt. I did, till my mother's silver letter-opener, the only thing she had to remember my grandfather by, went missing just hours after I'd seen Jayant admiring it. We never remained as close after that.

Still, my father was very fond of him – Jayant, even at that age, knew how to endear himself to others and usually did. When Jayant started college, my father offered to pay his fees. Jayant's father Bhaljee Kaka had been our accountant all his life and my father felt responsible for Jayant's education after he died. Appa himself passed away just before Jayant entered his final year of college. But he had informed me on his death-bed that I was to pay Jayant's final year

213

fees and after he had got his degree, give him a job. I intended to do just that.

I never got the chance to. Jayant was rusticated from college after being caught selling exam question papers. I offered to use our family connections to get him admitted to a different college despite this, but he refused. Said he wasn't interested in studying anymore, or in getting a job for that matter. He wanted to start his own business. Said I could give him the amount I was going to pay in fees, plus a little extra, so that he could stand on his own feet. Said it's what Appa would've wanted. I agreed.

But, three months later, he was back, asking for more money. He said he had been duped of the money I had given him — but three different people told me, for a fact, that he had lost the whole amount gambling. I refused to pay him. We had an argument in which he accused me of sullying Appa's good name, told me I wasn't fit to call myself his son, told me Appa would have rather died than go back on his word like this. Then he left, and I prayed I would never see him again. But life is not that kind.

A few months after that, in August last year, my younger sister Gauri came to me saying she had fallen in love and wanted to get married. When I asked to whom, she said to Jayant. Apparently, he had met her secretly over the previous few weeks and had convinced her that he was head over heels in love with her. Gauri had grown up around Jayant. She had no reason not to trust him. She didn't know what he was. And she was sixteen — legally, she could get married if she wanted to, as this was when the legal age for girls to marry hadn't yet been raised to eighteen. If Gauri married, she would inherit two lakh rupees, which Appa had left to her in his will. When I said no, she sulked and told me that she regretted telling me. You see, Jayant had told her not to inform me just yet — they had planned to run away to Goa the next day, get married there and then 'surprise' me over a trunk call. It was only Gauri's affection for me that made her tell me the whole plan, so confident was she that I wouldn't deny her anything that gave her happiness. Needless to say, I put a stop to the whole thing.

I don't have to tell you what would have happened if Jayant had been successful in his plan. Sadly, we live in a world where a girl's reputation is more fragile than a man's. The slightest whiff of scandal can tarnish it and the girl is then doomed to be subjected to people's snide comments for a lifetime. I shudder to think what may have happened if Gauri hadn't come to me first. Wealth can only cushion you so much from the wrath of a world that feels it has the moral upper hand. It wouldn't have saved Gauri had she eloped with Jayant. It did help me remove him from her life – I paid him a generous amount of money to keep his mouth shut about the matter and never see Gauri again. She was heartbroken, of course, but a heart can heal. A reputation hardly ever does.

No doubt Jayant's version of the story is different and paints me and mine in a most unflattering light. That you believed his story is not your fault. The details of this whole affair have been kept strictly under wraps by anyone in the know, at my request. However, should you doubt the truth of what I have just written (given your general opinion of me as a despicable man in every way, I find that very likely), you can ask Kishore. He witnessed the entire unfortunate episode and assisted me in tracking Jayant down and bringing him to task. And he doesn't seem to inspire the same distaste in your eyes that I do.

Sincerely,
Aniruddha Darshetkar

P.S. You also mentioned something about me not deigning to talk to people who aren't rich or fair-complexioned. Where and why you *got that idea is really beyond me. I understand you have resolved to not find a single redeemable quality in me, but surely you have no cause to attribute to me a prejudice so base as that?*

How long I sat there, numb, clutching the letter in my hands, I don't know. It couldn't have been more than a few minutes, but my racing mind made it feel like hours. Could it all be true? What he said about Juee and Sadanand might be, but his tone made it seem like he was shrugging off all blame for it. *Oh, I didn't know any better, that's why I interfered for no reason and ruined the happiness of two people I know.* Please. Where was the apology? I wondered. There wasn't one. There was a justification of his actions, but nowhere did he seem to feel any remorse.

Then I recalled what he had said about Aai and Nana and Latika. Shame rose within me in a foul column. I couldn't pretend there wasn't some truth there. The way Aai had boasted at Sadanand's house, and the way Latika and Malati had quarrelled so loudly that day too. And Nana! Just standing there, grinning at the way they were making a spectacle of themselves! Why hadn't he intervened? I remembered seeing smirks on people's faces at Aai and Latika's behaviour, and I realised now that their foolishness had tainted Juee and me as well. We would forever be judged for their follies.

I felt bad for Juee. What kind of a man would my sweet sister now have to settle for? Juee wasn't like me. She genuinely wanted to get married. Have children. A happy little family. And she deserved it. She deserved a man who loved her, not only because she was beautiful, but because she was so good at heart. Someone who saw beyond her pretty face,

216

who didn't judge her for her lack of dowry, who treated her as a partner in both his household and his life.

Till yesterday, I had wanted none of that. Because, well, if I was being honest with myself, I had given up whatever slim hope I may have once had of receiving a marriage proposal worth accepting. The fact was, I was dark. It may not have mattered if I had been born to another family. There were enough wheatish-skinned and dusky people in the country. But I hadn't been born in any of their families. I had been born into a family of milky-white, light-eyed Konkanastha Bramhins, amongst whom I stood out like a smudge on a whitewashed wall. I had seen the confusion in people's eyes when I stood beside my sisters. I had seen the sympathetic pats Aai got from various relatives when the topic of my marriage came up. I had seen it and known what it meant right from the time I was ten. Forget the fact that I was able-bodied and healthy and had a level head on my shoulders. No, she has dusky skin. So she must marry the first idiot willing to take her without money to sweeten the deal.

And yet.

Aniruddha Darshetkar had wanted to marry me. Yes, he had described the experience of being in love with me as 'a nightmare', but still. He wanted me to be his wife. I read the post-script again. He sounded deeply indignant in that. Had I misread it, when he told Sadanand I was plain? No, I remembered his words clearly. He had said: 'Not fair at all.' But could that have meant—? A slow, painful realisation crept up on me, like a particularly wily scorpion. Had he been referring, not to my complexion, but to the situation? I took a deep breath. After all, if he had such a problem with me being dusky, why on earth would he propose to me? I covered my eyes with one palm. Oh, no. Did he actually have the higher ground here? Had I . . . misjudged him? Oh, God.

I scanned the letter in my hands again. I seemed to have made a habit of misjudging people. What Aniruddha had said about Jayant . . . I must confess, it left me feeling sick to the stomach. Gauri had been little more than a child. How easily a child's affections are won! To prey upon a girl's innocence like that . . . I couldn't believe Jayant was capable of such a thing! I still remembered that evening we had walked side by side. What he had said about Aniruddha then . . . it was striking me just now, after all these days, how inappropriate it was of him to tell me all that. It was personal, after all, and we barely knew each other. And me! How had I believed him right away? Had I lost all my sense that evening?

And then, a small traitorous voice inside me said: *It was because he is good-looking and he smiled at you and flattered you.* I swallowed. Was that true? Did it come down to something that stupid? Was I so starved for praise and affection that a few kind words from a handsome stranger made me forget all reason and jump to false conclusions about a man I had no real reason to despise? I mean, yes, Aniruddha was haughty and a snob, but an eye-roll was an adequate response for that, not the kind of single-minded hatred I had allowed to grow within me. Whereas Jayant was . . . the kind of man of whom cautionary tales are made. And I had laughed with him and allowed him to tell me how pretty I was!

My skin crawled at the memory.

Aniruddha was right. I could very well imagine his poor sister's fate if she hadn't been retrieved from Jayant's clutches. If I were him, I'd thank the Gods every single day for making her see reason.

A crow squawked harshly from a tree nearby, rousing me from my thoughts. I had been sitting there for a while. Suddenly, I felt ravenous. I got up and headed back to Chitra's house, my mind clamouring with thoughts.

TWENTY

Chitra and Vishnubhat returned late next morning, her full of the songs from the play, him full of praise for – who else – the gracious Kaveribai and her daughter. I could barely get in a word edgewise while he waxed eloquent about their grand lodgings in her stately home at Kasba Peth.

'We could practically see Shaniwar Wada* from one of the windows!' he squealed. 'Well, the stone gates anyway, but still!'

'Sounds like you had a lovely time,' I said, wondering how to find my opening.

---

* The grand fort palace built as the residence for the Peshwas was largely built out of wood and stone, and ended up mostly burned in a fire in 1828. The landscaped gardens and surviving masonry and architecture are preserved as a tourist attraction these days.

'We did. You really missed a marvellous trip, Ila.' Chitra beamed, and I smiled in relief.

'Speaking of missing things,' I said. 'I would like to return to Mumbai. I'm really missing home.'

'Oh,' she said. 'But you've barely been with us a few days . . .'

'It's been two weeks, Chitra.'

'Really? It didn't seem that long, did it?'

'No, it didn't,' I agreed. 'But I think it's best if I go back now. Malu's exams will be coming up and Juee is not around to tutor her. I should be there to help.' I turned to Vishnubhat. 'You will arrange for a bus ticket for tomorrow? Early morning, if possible.'

'That soon?' Chitra's voice was plaintive. 'Navratri* starts in a few days – I thought you'd at least stay till it's over. The celebration at the Mahalaxmi temple here is really worth seeing . . .'

'I'm sure it is. Maybe I'll see it next year.'

'Did something happen while we were away?' My friend peered at me, as if trying to read in my face what my words weren't revealing.

---

*   It's amazing how the nine-day Navratri festival – dedicated to worshipping the Goddess in her myriad forms – is celebrated so differently in different parts of India. The state of Gujarat celebrates Goddess Amba through dance and music; West Bengal reveres the Goddesses Durga and Kali through food and pageantry; the Northern states, by worshipping young girls who symbolise the maiden form of the Goddess. And in stark contrast to these, in Maharashtra, many people also choose to fast and walk barefoot everywhere for nine days. And just when you thought only God works in mysterious ways.

'No, no,' I lied, easily. 'Nothing like that. I just suddenly felt homesick. I feel like I have to see Aai-Nana as soon as possible.'

'Of course, of course.' Vishnubhat nodded sagely. 'It's difficult for young women to stay away from loved ones. We understand. Everyone isn't as stoic in this respect as our Padmini.'

True to his word, my cousin got me a ticket for the early morning bus. Handing it to me after dinner and waving away my thanks he said, with his usual oily smile, 'We hope you enjoyed your stay with us, Ila. We know your presence has made our Padmini happy. Just like our marriage to her has made us happy. Happier than we had ever imagined. Why, we cannot think of a single person we would rather be married to! Even if they regretted their decision to not marry us.'

I was saved from the necessity of making a reply by Chitra, who called out to me just then to hand me the packet of ghavan and chutney that she had prepared for me to take along on the journey.

The next morning, Vishnubhat dropped me at the bus depot in the same taangaa that had come to pick me up – presumably, he had told the driver the night before to be ready in the morning.

Grumbling about the cold, Vishnubhat wrapped his ghongadee* tightly around himself as he said a quick goodbye

---

* A handwoven blanket, often brown or black, the ghongadee's warmth is rivalled only by the itchiness of its coarse woollen fibres. It's used as everything, from a floor mat or bedding to a shawl. Its users are varied, too – from generations of Maharashtrian shepherds, outside the bus headed for Mumbai. Ten minutes later, with my holdall under the seat and my purse clutched to my chest, I was on my way back home.

What a different journey it was to the one that had brought me to Wai! Then, all I could think of was . . . I strained to remember what had bothered me back then. It suddenly seemed a long time ago. So much had happened and I hadn't really had a chance to sit down and think about it all with a clear mind.

Aniruddha Darshetkar had asked to marry me. Me! If someone would have suggested the idea to me back in Mumbai I would've laughed in their face. Or made a face myself. The very thought was crazy. And even crazier – I had turned him down. I had turned down someone who – in Aai's eyes at least – would've been the ideal sthal to dump me on. Fair as a datura flower, with his own business, his own house, an acceptable surname and, as an added bonus, easy on the eye too. The kind of man, in fact, that she would have been certain would reject me.

I wondered how she would react if she learned that *I* had turned *him* down, that too because he didn't consider *her* and the rest of the family good enough.

Can a woman explode with indignation? I think science would receive the answer to that question if Aai ever found out. I amused myself for a while imagining the scenario in

---

to dacoits kidnapping women in black and white Marathi movies, to noted activist Jyotiba Phule, who was never seen without one. The humble ghongadee is hardy, simple and designed for hard work. Much like the state it hails from.

great detail. Oh, how much drama would transpire in the Bendre home if that happened!

Still, I had to admit that a small part of me, a very tiny, miniscule part of me, was maliciously pleased. That a man like Aniruddha had put aside his asinine reservations and actually proposed marriage to me. It was a slap in the face for all of Aai's fears, a blow to the assumption that only fair, dutiful girls deserved a man's admiration. Such a pity that this validation had to come from that . . . that . . . aggravating man!

By the time the bus reached the depot in Mumbai, I had reached two conclusions. One: I could allow myself to feel a little flattered at the proposal, but it could in no way derail my plans to get a job. Aniruddha Darshetkar was one man. An outlier of sorts. I could not expect such behaviour from the rest of the male race. What if the next man to overlook my complexion and propose marriage still expected me to be all chool ani mool? Bound to the hearth and the children? Ugh. And two: there was no way on earth that I was going to tell my family about any of this.

I reached home around lunchtime and was welcomed with a look of surprise on Aai's face when she opened the door.

'Agabai, what are you doing here?' she asked, as I entered the house. 'You didn't inform us you were coming.'

'Okay, should I go back?' I asked sarcastically, and was rewarded with a thump on the back.

'It's not enough that I have to get this from your father or what, that you also have to start?' Aai shook her head, annoyed. 'Have you eaten? Should I make something?'

'Yes, what's for lunch?'

224

I washed in the bathroom and returned to the living room to find Latika rifling through my holdall.

'What did you get for me?' she asked, like she was six years old.

'Dhapaate,'* I said, biting back my exasperation. 'You want some?'

'Yes! Where are they?' She bent over the bag, digging deeper.

'Here they are!' I whacked her back with both my palms outstretched. 'How do you like them?'

'Aaaaaai!' Latika wailed, shooting me a poisonous look. 'See, na, Ila is hitting me!'

'Leave her alone!' Aai yelled from the kitchen.

'Aaah!' Latika rubbed her back furiously. 'How hard you hit! Now just wait. I won't tell you only what has been happening here!'

'Okay, don't,' I said lightly, lying down on the divan and putting my feet up.

'You won't believe when you find out,' Latika continued, malicious joy on her face. 'You all thought you were so clever, but I always knew! And I had *told* you then itself . . . but you didn't listen!'

'Latika, I'm still not listening,' I said, closing my eyes, letting the fatigue of the journey spread through my limbs.

She crept close to me and whispered with glee: 'Jayant is not marrying Damayanti!'

---

*   Another word for thalipeeth, which is a flatbread made from multi-grain flour, best enjoyed with a dollop of homemade butter. It is also the plural of 'dhapaata', which is basically a whack on the back with a flat palm.

My eyes sprang open. 'What did you say?'

'Jayant Waknis is not marrying Damayanti Whatever-hersurnameis.'

'Why? How come? Where did you hear this?'

'Sudha told me.' Latika sat on the divan next to me, a superior smile on her face. 'Isn't it great news?'

She babbled on about how she always knew Jayant wasn't destined for someone as ordinary as Damayanti, but I wasn't listening. My mind had flown to what Aniruddha had told me about Jayant. Damayanti's father had been rich. Is that why Jayant had pursued her? I needed to talk to someone. Suddenly, I wished Juee was here.

'Aai!' I called out. 'When is Juee coming back?'

'In ten-fifteen minutes or so,' was the reply.

'Wait . . . she's here . . . she's in Mumbai already?'

'Yes, she arrived last evening,' Latika replied, stretching like a cat.

'So, where is she?'

'Gone down to get something for Aai.'

'Onions,' came a voice from the door, and I looked up to see Juee standing there, a cloth bag in her hands.

I laughed and ran to the door to take the bag from her. Over lunch – polis hot from the tavaa, cucumber koshimbir and a potato and drumstick curry – we exchanged accounts of our trips. I imitated Vishnubhat's fawning over Kaveribai, which had Latika, Juee and Malu in fits of laughter but earned me a glare from Aai. And Juee told us about the people in Pune she had encountered, with their outrageous notices.

'They are so strange and rude!' Juee said, shaking her head in amazement. 'I saw a notice outside the gate of one

226

house which said, "This is not Sadashiv Peth. If your vehicle blocks our gate, we will puncture your tires."'

'What?' Latika's face was a mixture of amusement and horror.

'And another one said, "This is not a post office. Please don't ask us for directions and waste our time."'

'Baap re baap!' Malu giggled helplessly.

'And not just homes, shops are just as bad,' Juee continued. 'First of all, they all stay shut in the afternoons—'

'What? Why?' I asked.

'The shopkeepers have lunch and then take a nap till four,' Juee said, with a straight face.

'No!'

'Yes, godswear.' Juee touched her fingers to her throat. 'And outside one, a photo studio I think, they had put up a notice saying, "If you think your picture looks bad, complain to your father, not us!"'

Later that night, as we lay side by side on our mattresses, I told Juee what I had learned about Jayant. Unsurprisingly, my sister was appalled. To someone who essentially sees only the good in people, the idea that someone could manipulate an innocent girl to get his hands on her money is absolutely revolting. But to my surprise, she didn't defend him like she had defended Aniruddha once. Instead, there was a thoughtful pause and then she said: 'You know, Damayanti's father recently faced some losses in his business. I heard Lele Kaku telling Aai the other day. It seems he is in a lot of debt. They might have to mortgage their house.' She turned to me. 'Do you think that's why Jayant called off his engagement to Damayanti?'

I certainly did now. It did seem as if the only reason he had pursued the girl was for her fortune. And that meant he was just as mercenary as Aniruddha had painted him. I tried to remember what they had looked like at Chitra's wedding. Damayanti's adoring glances at Jayant. Had he seemed as besotted? Or had that been an act? I found myself awash with relief for Damayanti. Her father might have lost his wealth, but it seemed that had saved her from a bigger misfortune: being married to a rogue.

TWENTY-ONE

The next day being a Sunday, I got to regale Nana with my observations from my stay at Vishnubhat and Chitra's home. We were all gathered for breakfast, which was mokal bhajani doused with generous amounts of toop.

'And the poor girl is genuinely happy, being married to that senseless lump?' Nana enquired, taking a sip of his tea to wash down the bhajani.

'Seems to be,' I replied, which was a mistake.

'See?' Aai pounced on my words immediately. 'I told you! Happiness in a marriage is a matter of choice. If you are determined to be happy, then you will be happy with just about anyone!'

'Waah, waah.' Nana closed his eyes and made an appreciative gesture. 'I am very flattered, I must say.'

'Haan, bas, you just sit there and make fun of me!' Aai glared at him. 'But ask you to go find some husbands for your daughters and suddenly you will have fifteen other things to do!'

'You know, Mrinalini,' Nana said, eyes twinkling, 'Aristotle says that patience is bitter but its fruit is sweet.'

'May he burn on a cremation ground, your Aristotle!' Aai snapped, and then in the same breath asked: 'Do you want a second helping?'

'No, no, that was quite enough.' Nana got up from the chair and picked up the day's newspaper from the table. 'Now I must go to the washroom—'

'Nana, Nana! Wait!' Latika said, with a wide-eyed smile. 'I have something to ask you!'

Nana raised his eyebrows.

'So Sudha, na . . . Arun's wife . . .' Latika said, looking up at him hopefully, 'actually, Arun's whole family, they are going to Goa . . . Kelkar Kaka-Kaku, all of them, because Sudha had this dream . . .'

'Is it possible, bala' – Nana shifted uneasily on his feet – 'for you to get to the point any quicker?'

'Yes. So. A few nights ago Sudha dreamed of a red-eyed woman, very scary-looking and angry. This woman told Sudha to give her her husband, meaning Sudha's husband, Arun.'

'Agabai!' Aai clutched her heart. 'Really?'

'That's what Sudha told me,' Latika said in a hushed voice, clearly enjoying the rapt attention of her audience. 'She woke up very scared, naturally, and Kelkar Kaku went with her to this priest they know, and that man said that she had been visited in her dreams by Shantadurga Kunkalikarin – she is Kelkar Kaka's family Goddess, you know! The priest said that they had to go and make an offering to the Goddess's temple in Goa, or else Arun's life was in danger!'

We all gasped in unison. All, that is, except Nana, who just looked uncomfortable.

230

'So, anyway, they are all going to Goa for a few days and Sudha has invited me to come along,' Latika finished, with a winsome smile. 'Kelkar Kaka-Kaku have agreed but I need your permission. Please? Please say I can go?'

'Well—' Nana began, but couldn't get any further.

'It's not fair!' Latika said immediately. 'Juee went to Pune and Ila went to Wai and Malu got to go on her school picnic—'

'We went to the Vasai fort!' Malu protested. 'That's not even out of Mumbai!'

'You went, no? Then don't complain!' Latika snapped, before turning her attention back to Nana. 'It's not fair! Why do *they* get to do all the fun things and *I* have to sit here and be bored all day! All day! Just sit at home doing nothing!'

'You *could* help around the house,' I suggested but was ignored, as expected.

'Goa must be lovely this time of the year.' Aai sighed. 'Pity *we* all can't afford to go.'

'Tell you what, first you get a dream that means my life is in danger and we'll all go to Goa, alright?' Nana said waspishly.

'Shee re Ram! Don't be disrespectful about these things,' Aai chided. 'And your life in danger would be my worst nightmare because, in case you forgot, when you die, we are all going to be forced to—'

'Aga, Aai! Let it go!' Latika yelled. 'Nana! Say, na! Can I go? Please? Please?'

Nana, who had begun to look increasingly fidgety, shook his head in exasperation. 'Fine, fine! Go!' He scowled and rushed to the washroom, newspaper in hand.

Latika squealed and hugged Aai before rushing out of the door, presumably to break the good news to Sudha.

But, as Juee and I helped Aai clear away the breakfast things, I felt a strange uneasiness in my heart. How cavalierly Nana had agreed to send Latika to Goa! As if he couldn't be bothered with her. It was the same attitude that had given Aniruddha such a low opinion of my family. Not that I cared what *he* thought, but Nana's borderline indifference was . . . well, it didn't reflect well either on us or him.

I waited for him to return from the washroom, then went to him as he sat in the armchair reading a thick book with yellowing pages. 'Nana?' I said. 'I wanted to say something to you.'

'You don't want to go off somewhere too, do you?' he asked, without looking up from the book. 'Because you've only just returned and . . . it's good to have you back.' He looked up and smiled.

'No, it's not that,' I said, settling down on the floor next to the chair. 'I . . . I don't think Latika should be allowed to go to Goa.'

'I never took you to be the jealous type.' He frowned at me in a teasing way.

'I'm not!' I retorted. 'It's just . . . Latika is . . . you know how Latika is. Sending her so far away on her own, who knows what she'll do there?'

'She's not going to be alone,' Nana said, dismissively. 'Kelkar is a decent man, he'll keep an eye on her. And this trip is practically a pilgrimage! What trouble could she possibly get into?'

'I don't know,' I said, rubbing my neck absently. 'Latika . . . isn't exactly the most responsible person . . .'

'No, she is young and foolish.' Nana smiled to himself. 'But to say the one is to imply the other. Besides,' he added,

232

a mock-serious expression on his face, 'you are always going on about girls needing independence, na? But you're saying Latika doesn't deserve it. That's a bit hypocritical, bala, isn't it? What is sauce for the goose must be sauce for the silly goose, too.'

I didn't have a reply to that. Yes, I was all for girls getting more independence. But Latika was immature and stupid and extremely likely to misuse that independence. The yardstick for her and me couldn't possibly be the same, could it? Didn't Nana see that? Or was this too a joke for him, like everything else?

'Latika is a frog in a puddle, Ila,' Nana said, taking my silence to mean he had convinced me. 'Let her go and see the ocean and realise how small she is.' He returned to his book. 'Anyway, if I don't allow her to go, she'll just stay here and eat all our heads the entire time!'

And that was that.

Over the next few days, Latika was insufferable. She teased Malu with visions of Goa, and boasted to Juee and me how her trip would be so much better than ours. One morning, I saw Juee's favourite new Punjabi dress* peeping out from Latika's half-packed bag.

---

*   The traditional dress of women from the Punjab region of India consists of a loose-fitting pant or salwar, coupled with a long tunic or kurta. A wide, long scarf called a dupatta completes the ensemble. These days, the outfit is popularly called a salwar suit, salwar kameez or salwar kurta. But till the early nineties at least, in Marathi households it was commonly referred to as a Punjabi dress. After all, you may not have heard the phrase 'calling a spade a spade' but that doesn't mean you can't be the living embodiment of it.

'Did you give this to Latika?' I asked, holding it out to Juee.

'No.' Juee sounded mystified.

'Latika!' I yelled. 'Did you take this without asking Juee first?'

'What are you yelling ab—?' Latika strolled into the room, took one look at the dress I was holding and without missing a beat said, '—Oh. *That*. Yes, I took it. So?'

'You shouldn't have done that,' Juee said reproachfully. 'What if I wanted to wear it? You could've asked.'

At which point, Latika rolled her eyes and said, 'But what's the harm if I take it? I'll need nice things to wear in Goa. You don't need pretty clothes right now anyway. It's not like Sadanand is coming back to town!'

Juee was so taken aback, she couldn't find a reply to make. I had no such problem, and five minutes later Aai came running into the bedroom to find Latika wailing that I had hurt her feelings.

'What did you say?' Aai demanded, as she hugged her favourite daughter and ran a soothing hand down her back.

'Oh, I called her a spoiled, selfish and immature girl,' I said conversationally, 'who deserves to have sense slapped into her.' I crossed my arms. 'And I offered to do it, if you and Nana were too busy.'

Before Aai could express her outrage, Latika yelled from behind Aai's arms: 'You're just jealous that *I* get to go to *Goa*!'

'No, I'm disgusted,' I told her much more calmly than I felt. 'There's a difference.'

And with that, I turned on my heel and walked out of the house.

234

I had no idea where I was going. I had even forgotten to carry my money-purse. All I knew was I had to get out of there. I had thought coming back to Mumbai would still the troubled feelings in my heart, but they had just been pushed back by the feelings I had left Mumbai to escape. Nothing had changed: Aai's attitude towards Latika, Nana's attitude towards his family . . . and it would only be a matter of days before Aai started hounding Juee for marriage and it would be like Juee's heartbreak hadn't happened. I would go back to looking at job listings and put my self-respect through the wringer.

I suddenly remembered the Bhagwati temple in Wai. How peaceful it had felt to sit there. Perhaps I could go to the Parleshwar temple. Maybe He would soothe me like She had.

I took a sudden sharp right turn and collided with a man coming out from the travel agent's office on the corner. 'Sorry, I . . .' I looked up and stopped.

'Well, lucky me.' Jayant Waknis smiled. 'And how is the beauty of the Bendre clan this morning?'

'Fine,' I said curtly.

He looked as handsome as ever, but I saw him differently somehow. His smile didn't seem so charming anymore; his words not quite as honeyed.

'What are you doing out so early on a Sunday?' he asked.

'Oh . . . just going to Parleshwar.'

'Praying? Waah. For whom? Don't tell me someone has snagged you already? The young men of Vile Parle will go into collective mourning!'

'No such thing,' I said lightly. 'I just hadn't been to the temple in a while, so thought I'd go. I've been away.'

'Oh?'

235

'Visiting my friend in Wai. And,' I added, a perverse mood striking me, 'do you know whom I met there?'

'No idea. Who in the world lives in Wai, anyway?'

'He doesn't live there, but he was visiting.' I studied his face. 'Aniruddha Darshetkar.'

His smile faltered. 'Ah, *him*,' he said, looking away. 'And was he as obnoxious as you remember him?'

'Not at all. He was very well-mannered and considerate.'

'Really?' he jeered. 'Quite a change for him.'

'In fact, now that I have got to know him a little more, spent some time with him, I believe he isn't all that bad at all,' I said sweetly. 'A little . . . restrained, perhaps. But not obnoxious, no. Just goes to show we mustn't be hasty to judge people, isn't it? There's no telling what we might find out about them, as time passes.' I looked at him pointedly, wondering if he would take the hint.

'I suppose.' He gave an awkward laugh and refused to meet my eyes. 'Anyway, I must run. I have to go out of town for a project, so I'll take your leave.'

And with a hurried goodbye, he rushed away. Leaving me to resume my journey to Parleshwar and, if at all possible, find some modicum of peace.

TWENTY-TWO

The Kelkars had been advised to pay their respects to the Goddess as soon as possible, so they left on the morning of Ashtami, the eighth day of Navratri. On that day, my community worships a life-sized idol of Mahalaxmi, whose face is made from rice flour. Unlike her usual depictions – sitting cross-legged on a lotus flower – this Mahalaxmi idol stands tall.

This is a nod to the restless nature of the Goddess of wealth – today she will stay in your home and bless you with prosperity, but tomorrow, just as easily, she can leave.

Ordinarily, the Kelkars would have accompanied us to Lokmanya Seva Sangh hall on Ashtami evening, but this year we went without them. We made our way to the hall in the early evening. Clouds of camphor smoke greeted us as we entered, making my eyes water. The Goddess stood at one end of the hall, decked in silks and finery. Sixteen threads, sixteen flowers and sixteen leaves adorned her, and sixteen lamps made of kneaded dough burned at her feet. A group of married women roamed before her, holding ghagars – brass water pots – which they blew into repeatedly. They would continue to do this till midnight, without eating, without drinking, without rest.

'See, Malu?' Aai whispered. 'The Goddess has possessed them. They say if you have a question, you can ask one of them and the Goddess will speak through her and give you the answer.'

Malu looked a little nervous at the prospect and I didn't blame her. Between the smoke, the all-pervading smell of camphor and the rhythmic *hhoo-hhoo* of the women blowing into the ghagars, the entire atmosphere seemed mystic, even downright uncanny. It was the kind of setting that made you think that anything was possible.

We paid our respects to the Goddess, Aai placing an offering of a piece of fine cloth, a coconut and some rice grains at Her feet. Nana placed a rupee and twenty-five paise – an auspicious amount – on the cloth. Then we bowed our heads in unison and were about to leave, when Aai seemed to change her mind.

She approached one of the women with the ghagars. Applying some vermillion and turmeric on the woman's forehead, she murmured something to her. The woman's breaths came louder. Without pausing the periodic blowing into the brass vessel in her hands, she made some reply that we couldn't hear. Aai nodded, then bent down to touch the woman's feet. The woman placed a hand on her head and blessed her.

Aai returned to us and, with the air of someone who

had done absolutely nothing extraordinary that day, said, 'Come, come, let's go home.'

'What was all that about?' I asked, as we reached home.

'Never you mind,' Aai replied.

'Aga, what do you think it'll be about?' Nana said, with a laugh. 'She must've been asking when all of you will be married. What else?'

'Aai?' Juee asked. 'Is that what you asked?'

'That is between me and the Goddess,' Aai replied, happily for once – then she frowned. 'Malu! Aga, what have you done to that dress?'

Malu checked her long silk frock and gasped. There was a tear at the sleeve.

'How can you be so careless, ga!' Aai shook her head with irritation.

'It's a small tear, Aai, never mind,' Juee said cheerfully. 'Malu, take it off. I'll stitch it up in no time.'

She got out the sewing box as Nana picked up a book and settled into his armchair. Aai, Malu and I changed out of our clothes in the bedroom and Malu handed her dress to Juee to repair. Aai brought a basket of peas from the kitchen and she and I settled down on the floor to shell them.

'Aai, this green thread is nearly finished,' Juee said. 'Is there any more? This much won't be enough.'

'Look in my cupboard, on the second shelf, on the left side,' Aai replied, busy with the peas. 'There are some threads there. See if you find a green one.'

Juee left the room to fetch the thread and returned a few moments later, a puzzled expression on her face and some envelopes in her hands. 'Ila,' she said, holding them out to me. 'These all seem to be addressed to you.'

Aai looked up from the peas and her eyes widened in shock but, before she could move, I reached out and grabbed the envelopes from Juee. She was right – they were all addressed to Ms. Ila Bendre. And each of them, every single one, was torn open.

I pulled out a paper from one of them. It was a letter, printed on an SBI letterhead, dated 20 August.

Dear Ms Bendre, it said, *thank you for your application. Please visit our offices at the address given below on August 27 with your certificates, for an aptitude test.*

My breath caught in my chest. I opened another letter.

Dear Ms. Bendre, thank you for your application and resumé. We are pleased to offer you the post of Junior Clerk, pending a written test and personal interview at our office on September 4 at 11.00 a.m. sharp.

The printed letters looked blurry to me and I realised my eyes were brimming. I opened a third.

Please come for an interview on September 11.

A fourth.

Please come with your certificates on September 29.

One by one, I read all of them. Barring one or two, they had all called me for an interview on dates that had already past. And I hadn't seen hide nor hair of them till this moment.

'You hid them,' I said to Aai, my voice blank. 'They all replied. And you hid them from me.'

'I don't know what you are talking about.' Aai sniffed.

'Don't . . . lie,' I said, through gritted teeth.

'How dare you?' Aai demanded in a shrill voice. 'Have you gone mad?'

Nana lowered his book and looked at us inquiringly. 'What is going on?'

'I had sent some job applications.' I was trying hard to keep a lid on my temper, but the rage inside me was a surging inferno. If I kept talking, it was going to erupt. 'A lot of them had replied, asking me to come for interviews, but Aai hid those letters from me!'

'Mrinalini?' Nana sounded troubled.

'Yes, fine, I hid them!' Aai snapped at him. 'So what? What did you want me to do? Let her get a job? Do you want people to think we are shameless? That we support our family on our daughter's earnings! Not to mention, if she gets a job she'll become totally unmarriageable! As it is, she is—'

'—she is *what*?' I demanded, getting to my feet. 'Say, na, Aai! She is WHAT? Dark? Ugly? A millstone around your neck? WHAT AM I?'

'Ila, aga—' Nana began, but Aai interrupted.

'What you are is stubborn and selfish.' She glared at me. 'Hadn't I told you not to get a job? You still went ahead and applied! In our time, we didn't dare to disobey our parents, but your generation doesn't have any respect! All you think of is what *you* want, what *you* think is right . . . it's all about *you*! All I asked is for you to get married so that—'

'—so that you could wash your hands of me?' I said, my eyes stinging. 'That's all you want, na, Aai? Just get all of us

241

married off to whatever buffoon walks in off the street! What does it matter if we want something else? What does it matter if the man isn't right for us? What does it matter as long as we are out of this house and your life?'

'Don't be dramatic.' Aai went back to shelling the peas. 'What I did, it was for your good only. Everything I do is for you girls. But do you appreciate that? No!'

'Our *good*?' I nearly laughed. 'Throwing Juee at Sadanand, what *good* came of that? Letting Latika do whatever she likes is for her *good*? And forcing me to get married, instead of taking up a job as I want to, is for *my good*?'

'Ila, calm down,' Nana said.

'And you!' I turned on him. 'Instead of talking sense to her, you let her do this to us!'

'Don't you dare talk to your father in that tone!' Aai's voice was like a whiplash, but I ignored it.

'Why can't you see?' I looked from her to him, my voice cracking. My lungs felt like they were being held in a vice. 'Me getting a job means I can live life on my own terms! I'm tired, Aai! I'm tired of being told I'm not good enough as I am! Yes, I'm not as fair as Juee or Latika or Malu but that can't be all you see when you look at me! And that is ALL you see! That is all you have EVER seen!' Angry tears spilled down my cheeks and I wiped them away furiously. 'I will not let a man treat me like a consolation prize! I will write to these companies again and again!' I brandished the crumpled envelopes in my hands. 'And I will beg them to give me another chance! I WILL get a job, Aai! And when I do, I will be out of this house for good! I won't be your responsibility anymore – isn't that what you've always wanted?'

Without waiting for Aai to reply, I barged out of the

242

house, ignoring Juee's voice that anxiously called my name behind me.

I stayed out almost till dinnertime. I didn't know where to go so I wandered around the lanes of Vile Parle, walking away my anger. I hadn't realised the lengths to which Aai was capable of going, just to stop me from getting a job. Her plan had almost worked, hadn't it? I had begun to doubt my own capability. A few more weeks of thinking I was good for nothing and perhaps my self-esteem would have been at sea-level. All she would have had to do then was bring me a man who said two kind words to me.

I've already proven I can fall blindly for those.

I sniffed back the tears. No. I wouldn't let it come to that this time. I would write the letters again, explain what had happened. They'd understand, I'm sure they would. All I needed was one company to give me a job. One company that paid me a wage that let me move into a working women's hostel, away from Aai and her obsessions with fair skin and marriage. Where I could just . . . be. It would be a hard life, perhaps, but at least I wouldn't have to be someone else while I lived it.

I walked to the post office and bought fresh stamps and envelopes, before returning home.

The house was quiet. Malu stared at me warily, as if expecting me to explode again any second. Juee rubbed my back in quiet sympathy. But Aai? Aai ignored me entirely. She just got the dinner ready as if nothing had happened. Nana was immersed in his book again, pretending all was well. This is what we did in this family. And I couldn't take another day of putting up with it.

I took a deep breath and walked into the kitchen. Aai and Juee were bringing the dinner things into the living room, where we would all sit cross-legged on the floor in a circle and eat. But my appetite was gone. I couldn't bear to look at the food. So I got out the tea vessel. Placed it on the stove. Poured water into it. Then I lit the stove. As the water heated, I peeled cardamom pods and dropped the seeds into the iron mortar. Aai, who had come in to fetch drinking water, frowned at me but didn't say anything. I crushed the carda-mom seeds with the heavy iron pestle till they turned into a coarse powder. I poured it into the simmering water, added sugar, and waited. As the water began to boil, I gave Aai a defiant look and added a big heaped spoon of tea powder. The kitchen filled with the scent of cardamom tea. I added milk till the tea went from brown to orange, allowed it to boil some more, then strained it into a cup.

Aai shook her head in exasperation – then brought her hands together in a namaskar. But instead of holding her palms at the chest-level, she raised them to her forehead and then let them go all at once, in a gesture that clearly said she was done with me.

I ignored her, picked up my cup and walked out onto the balcony. In the living room, I passed Nana. He looked as if he was about to say something, but wisely decided against it.

I turned on the yellow light bulb in the balcony. Sitting on the floor in that light, my back against the wall, with Malu's wooden exam board in my lap for support, I began writing the letters. Every now and then, I took a sip of the tea.

It was strong, fragrant and sweet, just the way I liked it.

*

An hour later, I had written to every single company that had asked me to come for an interview, requesting them to reschedule if the position hadn't already been filled. I sealed the envelopes and addressed them. Then I took them to the post box down the road. As I dropped them one after the other under the red flap, I was struck by a thought. It would take another week or so for the letters to arrive and the replies to be returned. I had no wish to be around Aai for that long. The way things stood, sooner or later, we would have words again and I'd had enough of trying to argue or reason with her. I needed some place to escape to; some place where I could lie low for a few days.

And, fortunately, there was one such place where I knew I would always be welcome. But it would cost me. I would have to dip into the prize money I had got from my college for coming first in history.

I walked to the store around the corner where we got our monthly groceries, and asked the shopkeeper if I could make a trunk call to a Pune number, and pay him later. He looked a little surprised to see me out so late, but he waved me towards his telephone and went back to serving his customers. I dialled the number and waited.

'Hello? Mami?' I said, when the call connected. 'Would it be alright if I came and stayed with you and Mama for a few days?'

As it turned out, it was more than alright. Mama-Mami were planning a short trip to Matheran, and Ujoo Mami wondered if I'd like to go with them. I gratefully accepted the invitation and she said Mama would convince Aai-Nana, if I could get them to call him.

With the Kelkars away in Goa, this meant Aai-Nana

would have to make the call from the newly installed telephone in Lele Kaka's house, but I would arrange that. After doing what she had, the least Aai could do was descend one set of stairs to make a phone call.

As it turned out, Aai was . . . if not happy, then not unwilling to walk downstairs to a telephone, because it gave her the opportunity to moon over Lele Kaku's latest acquisition in public, and nag Nana about getting one for us, in private. The plan was made. And the very next day, after Dasraa, the festival that celebrates the triumph of good over evil – Mama-Mami picked me up from home.

'Go carefully,' Nana murmured, as he saw me off. He had been downcast since the day I announced I was going away.

'But you just returned from a trip,' he had said, shaking his head. 'It was nice coming home and seeing you there every day. Now you are off again.'

'Who was it who said that fortitude is the main virtue philosophers need?' I teased.

'Spinoza.' Nana smiled sadly. 'But it's not easy to have it when you are a father.'

Aai's farewell was a marked contrast to Nana's. She merely nodded at me and wished Mami a happy journey. Let alone admitting that what she had done was wrong, the woman hadn't spoken two straight words to me since our fight. So I nodded back at her, as if we were mere acquaintances, and stepped out of the door.

Malu waved goodbye from the window and Juee helped me carry my bag downstairs. 'I'll keep an eye out for letters for you,' she promised, patting my back. 'I'm sure you'll get a yes from one of them.'

246

I smiled at her and walked to the bus stop with Mama and Mami. From there we would take a BEST bus to Dadar Terminus, from where we would catch the train to Matheran.

TWENTY-THREE

We arrived in Matheran around lunchtime, having finished the last few miles of the journey in the adorable toy-train from Neral. It was my first time there and the drop in temperature was both startling and refreshing. Nestled in the Western Ghats, Matheran is a hill-station full of woods, with absolutely no automobiles whatsoever. So we travelled from the train station to our hotel not in a taxi but in two hand-cart-like rickshaws, pulled by two sturdy-looking men.

To my surprise, Padmakar Mama had booked us a deluxe room in the swanky new Divadkar Hotel. I had fully expected to stay at some cheap and simple dharmashala,*

---

* A rest-house for travellers or pilgrims, a dharmashala used to offer cheap accommodation to people who wanted to see India, but had a shoe-string budget. Not to be confused with the town in Himachal Pradesh, where people can get their mind altered in various ways, also on a shoe-string budget.

the way we usually did when we travelled with Nana. The Divadkar Hotel was a class apart from that. Each room had a double bed made by the simple expedient of pushing two old-fashioned four-poster single beds together. The rooms were spacious enough to accommodate an extra mattress on the floor, which is where Padmakar Mama – despite my protests – volunteered to sleep.

'My niece, sleeping on the floor?' he exclaimed in mock outrage. 'How will I live with myself?'

After dropping our bags in our room, we hurried to the hotel restaurant, where Mama ordered us a feast. Our last snack had been hours ago, at Karjat station – possibly the best vada-pav I had ever eaten. As Mami and I tucked in, Mama took us through our itinerary. After lunch, we would rest till evening, then maybe stroll to the nearby market. Tomorrow, early in the morning, we would leave for some sight-seeing and have lunch out.

'You can try horse-riding, if you like, Ila.' Mama winked at Mami as he said this.

'No, thank you. My own two legs will do just fine,' I told him, and he laughed.

As promised, the next morning we left to see Matheran's natural beauty. There was mist all around and the air was bitingly cold. We started with Sunrise Point, which was a few minutes' walk from our hotel. We were the first ones there. Mami had packed a thermos for us and we took turns eating Parle G biscuits dipped in tea, which she poured into the lid of the thermos, as we watched the horizon lighten. The skies turned from pink to orange then, suddenly, the sun was up, casting its light over the valley below us, illuminating

249

everything it touched. What a wonder the sight was: a planet slowly turned its face to a giant sphere of fire and instead of being burned, was blessed with life. Every tendril of grass, the humblest creature alive . . . we owed everything to the sun, which was unaware of our very existence. Perhaps that's why the ancients worshipped it as a God. And this miracle, this sunrise, happened every single day, without us noticing. We just took it in our stride. What other marvels do we take for granted? I wondered.

'You're very quiet.' Mami placed a hand on my shoulder.

'It's a sight that invites silence,' I said softly.

At that moment, the hills rang out with an unearthly cry. 'OOOOOaaaaaaaoooooooOOOOOOO!'

A group of other tourists had come up behind us and one of them, a young man in his mid-twenties, had joyfully screamed his lungs out.

We gave him a disgusted look, which the man didn't notice.

'What Echo Point?' he laughed derisively at his friends. 'No echo only is coming!'

'Arre, Mukesh,' his friend muttered. 'This is Sunrise Point. Echo Point is afterwards.'

'Oh.' Mukesh deflated, then brightened up. 'Are you sure? I can shout again and check.'

'Okay, time to leave, I think,' Mama said, rolling his eyes heavenward.

Our next stop was King George Point, which we reached after a long, yet invigorating walk. The bitter cold of the night had receded and I unwrapped the woollen scarf from around my head as we reached the point. More silence greeted us as we stood at the edge of the cliff, taking in the deep valley below.

'It's better in the rains, all green,' someone said behind us. It was a man holding the reins to a horse. 'Saheb, you want to do sight-seeing? I can take you everywhere on a horse. Baisaheb, also, will find it comfortable. The points are not all close to each other. Lots of walking. Come, I'll take you?'

Padmakar Mama waved him away politely, and after a few more minutes, we moved on from there. Navigating with the help of a map he had obtained, Mama led us down a road that would take us to Echo Point.

'Aho, when are we having breakfast?' Mami asked, as we trudged down a quiet, woody path. 'Ila must be hungry.'

'I can wait, Mami,' I said, although my stomach was rumbling. The cold air was clearly making me hungry, but I didn't want to sound like a child.

'See? Ujoo, you also, na. She's not a little girl,' Mama called out jovially.

We reached the point just around ten o'clock and I fervently hoped those idiots from Sunrise Point wouldn't be there. The sun had literally been rising in front of that twerp – why would you mistake that point for Echo Point? And then scream like Tarzan to test your theory! The fool. These, these were the specimens Aai hoped would take pity on me and marry me! God forbid.

Luckily, there were only two other people there: a couple, clearly on their honeymoon judging from the mehendi on the girl's palms. We reached them just as the man cupped his hands around his mouth and called out. 'Sonaliiiiii, Aaaiiiiii looooveeee yooooooou!'

'Liaaivouuu!' the echo came back, and Sonali hid her face in her hands with terminal coyness.

We stood awkwardly a few feet away from them for some

time, then Mami and Mama exchanged a meaningful glance and we unanimously decided to leave.

'Mama, you don't want to shout Mami's name?' I teased as we left.

'How could I possibly dare?' he joked. 'I leave all the shouting to her.'

Ujoo Mami laughed at that and turned to look at the couple, who were gazing deeply into each other's eyes now.

'Oh, stop your nonsense!' she said good-naturedly to her husband. 'That poor young couple will think all married couples yell at each other after a few years of marriage.'

'They have no reason to complain,' Mama said, loosening the muffler around his neck with one hand and wiping sweat off his forehead with the other. 'Aren't' – he took a breath – 'aren't we leaving so they can have some privacy, then?'

'It's the decent thing to do,' Mami replied. 'Nobody needs random gawkers when you're trying to romance.'

'No . . .' Mama sounded a little out of breath. 'Of course not, you're . . . you're right.'

'Arre?' Ujoo Mami looked him up and down with a mischievous look. 'Huffing already? What is this, aho? Old you have become!'

'No . . . I . . .' Mama stopped walking and grimaced. 'I . . . I think I . . . need to . . .'

And then, to my horror, his legs buckled and he fell to his knees right there, on the dirt path.

Ujoo Mami was immediately beside him, her face contorted with worry. 'Aho? Aho, what is happening to you?' She rubbed his back, even as he sank to the ground, breathing heavily. 'Say something, aho!'

'Mama?' I crouched next to him, feeling his forehead.

It was clammy. His eyes had rolled inside his head and his breath was coming too slowly.

Ujoo Mami had pulled out a bottle of water from her large cloth bag and she sprinkled some water on his face. His eyes opened, but his lids began to close again. 'Aho!' Her voice shook. 'Can you hear me? Come, have some water, you will feel better!' She trickled some water into his mouth and he swallowed as if it was an effort. She tried to give him water again, but her hands were shaking and when she looked at me, I could see bone-chilling terror in her eyes.

'You wait here, Mami,' I said, leaping to my feet. 'I'll go and get help!'

Ignoring her cries of 'Ila! Ila, don't go! Wait!' I ran down the path as fast as I could. We had passed a couple of bungalows on our way there. They weren't very far.

Ignoring the fear rising in my chest, I ran up to the closest one, only to find the gate locked with a big padlock. There was no one home.

Panic gripped me. Padmakar Mama's unconscious face rose before my eyes and I ran again. The next bungalow was about a hundred feet away, and I raced in that direction. To my relief, I found the gate open. I rushed up the few stone steps leading to the main house and knocked furiously on the front door.

'Please open the door!' I called out. 'Someone needs a doctor urgently!'

It took only a few seconds, but it felt like an eternity. At last the door opened – and I found myself staring into the drowsy face of Aniruddha Darshetkar.

He stared at me as if he was still dreaming. To say *I* was surprised would be a massive understatement and so, for a few seconds, we simply gaped at each other in utter shock, my mouth opening and closing without a single syllable leaving it.

'I . . . you . . .' I blinked in confusion. 'You're not . . . in Pune?'

Which, it has to be admitted, is by far the stupidest set of words I have ever uttered, given that he was standing right in front of me, and so was, very clearly, *not* in Pune.

'My sister wanted a change of weather, so I drove down yesterday to have the house opened. She's joining me tomorrow. This is our holiday home,' he explained. 'What are *you* doing here?'

'I . . . my uncle has collapsed not very far from here!' I blurted. 'I need help!'

He nodded immediately, then turned inside the house and called, 'Vishwas!'

A stocky man came bounding towards us from somewhere within the house.

'Come with me,' Aniruddha said to him, and gestured to me to lead the way.

The three of us ran to where I had left Ujoo Mami. When we arrived, we found her cradling my uncle's head, slapping his cheeks gently to keep him awake. She heard us coming and as she looked up, I could see she had been crying.

Aniruddha and Vishwas pulled Mama to his feet and, throwing his arms around their shoulders, half led, half carried him, to the bungalow. I put my arm around Ujoo Mami and we followed them.

Twenty minutes later, Mama was fully conscious, although still a little weak. He was reclining against a pillow on a comfortable four-poster bed and Mami was making him drink electrolyte water that Aniruddha had prepared. I found my own hands were shaking and making an excuse, I left the two of them in the bedroom and came out into the hall.

Aniruddha was waiting there, an anxious look on his face. 'Is he okay?' he asked.

'He is better . . . I . . .' I said, sniffing. 'I don't know what happened . . . he just suddenly . . . he started sweating and then he just seemed to get dizzy . . .'

'Sounds like low blood pressure,' Aniruddha said. 'My mother suffered from it. The symptoms match.'

'That . . . it can happen if you don't eat for a long time, right?' I asked. He nodded. 'That would explain it then. We didn't have any breakfast before leaving for sight-seeing.'

He nodded again. An awkward pause reigned for some time. I couldn't help but recollect the last time we had met and under what circumstances. How harsh my words had been. With that background, he would have been if not justified, then excused, had he refused to help me today. But he hadn't. And now, with every passing second, my embarrassment was growing by leaps and bounds.

'I wanted to thank you,' I said, looking at my feet. 'If you hadn't come so quickly—'

'Chhe-chhe.' He waved his hands in a dismissive gesture. 'Don't even think of it.'

I exhaled and, all at once, my knees seemed to lose their strength and I sank onto the sofa just behind me.

'Shall I call for some tea?' Aniruddha asked, concerned. 'You don't look so well yourself.'

'No, I'm fine, I—' I stopped and pursed my lips. When you're strong, people get used to seeing you like that. They forget that sometimes strength can fail even you. That the burden of strength is too heavy to carry all the time.

'I know what you mean,' he said softly, and I realised I had just said all that out loud.

'I'm sorry, I didn't mean to blurt that out,' I said, thoroughly embarrassed.

'It's alright, you've just had a shock,' he said. 'Vishwas!' he called out. 'Could we have some tea and some breakfast?'

'No, please don't go to any trouble,' I protested. 'As soon as Mama is able to walk, we'll take our leave.'

'Of course,' he said, a small smile on his lips. 'But you'll have some breakfast before that. We don't want to risk another BP drop, do we?'

I couldn't argue with his logic, so I let the matter drop. We sat in silence for a few more moments before Ujoo Mami came out of the bedroom. She thanked Aniruddha, who again waved away her words and insisted we stay for breakfast, in his usual imposing manner. Poor Ujoo Mami, already cowed by the grand house and the awkward situation we found ourselves in, could only nod in agreement.

Breakfast was served in a dining room the size of our entire house in Mumbai. Padmakar Mama, who looked much better than before, joined us.

'Thank you, Aniruddharao,' he said formally. 'You came like a God to us, in our time of need.'

'It was really nothing.' Aniruddha looked embarrassed. 'I'm glad you are feeling better.'

'Much better,' Mama said, digging into his upma. 'And thank you for breakfast. You must allow us to repay your kindness when we are back in Pune. Please come over for lunch sometime. We live in Sadashiv Peth.'

'Thank you.' Aniruddha nodded. 'I would be delighted.'

They talked a little about Pune, some acquaintances they had in common and Padmakar Mama's law practice in the city.

'Where are you staying in Matheran?' Aniruddha asked eventually. 'At the MTDC resort?'

'The Divadkar Hotel,' Mama corrected. 'We had planned to do some sight-seeing for a couple of days, maybe walk around in this fresh air but . . .' He smiled sheepishly.

'What spots did you see?'

'Sunset Point, King George Point and Echo Point,' Ujoo Mami said.

'So you haven't seen Charlotte Lake yet?'

'It was on the agenda before my health betrayed me like this.' Mama shook his head.

Aniruddha began talking about other sights worth visiting in Matheran – and it took every inch of control I had to stop my jaw from hanging open. This man, usually so taciturn and arrogant . . . just look at him now! Making polite conversation with my relatives as if he'd known them forever. How come he had changed overnight? What had happened to all the haughtiness, the superiority complex?

'That sounds like an excellent plan.' Mama beamed. 'Doesn't it, Ila?'

'I—sorry, what plan?' I blinked, startled.

'Aniruddharao was saying that he could take us all sight-seeing tomorrow, if we liked.'

I stared. Why was Aniruddha being so *nice* to us? His help this morning might be explained as a humanitarian act, but this . . . this was beyond courtesy. This was . . .

'That's . . . that's very . . .' I glanced at Aniruddha, trying to find a word. Strange? Unlikely? Unexpected? '. . . kind.' I gave him a hesitant smile. 'But we would hate to be a bother.'

'It's no bother at all,' he said a little breathlessly, then cleared his throat. 'Actually, some friends of mine are coming from the city this evening, and I'm sure they would love to join us tomorrow.'

'The more the merrier!' Mama said, with an expansive gesture.

'Sadanand and Kalyani, of course, you know already,' Aniruddha said, looking intently at me. 'But I would love to introduce you to my sister, Gauri.'

I nodded politely but, truth be told, I was completely confused. I caught Ujoo Mami's eye. She was giving me an appraising look, with an odd smile, which I couldn't interpret at all, so I simply kept my eyes on my upma till I finished it.

We took our leave after breakfast, promising to be ready the next morning for our little tour. Despite Mama's protests, Aniruddha called for three horses to take us to our hotel, saying we had a long day tomorrow so Mama should rest today in preparation. He helped Mama-Mami onto their horses, then gave me a hand as I gingerly mounted mine: a brown filly who seemed a little frisky.

Our eyes met for a moment. His had the most curious expression – one that was almost yearning.

'We'll meet tomorrow, then,' he said softly, as he let go of my hand.

The horse-drivers made a series of sounds that spurred the horses into motion, and we began our slow ride back to the hotel.

TWENTY-FOUR

Morning arrived, and I found myself full of misgivings while getting dressed after breakfast. How had we agreed to spend a whole day with Aniruddha Darshetkar and his merry men? Merry man, actually, and I wasn't at all sure how I felt about seeing Sadanand again. He had left Juee high and dry on his friend's advice and, if Kalyani was to be believed, had moved on swiftly to wooing Gauri Darshetkar. *Stop it*, I told myself. *Am I really considering believing Kalyani?* Oh, God, she would be there too. I made a face in the mirror as I applied kajal.

'What happened?' Ujoo Mami asked from behind me. She was tying her hair into a neat plait. 'Why the face?'

'Oh, nothing,' I said, stepping back to see my full reflection in the mirror. I had worn a Punjabi dress with a long cardigan, my odhni thrown over both shoulders. My hair I had left down – something I could never manage to do in Mumbai's humid weather.

'You look pretty.' Ujoo Mami grinned. 'I'm sure he'll think so too.'

'He?' I asked, startled. 'Who he?'

'The receptionist!' Ujoo Mami answered sarcastically. 'Who do you think?'

'I don't know what you're talking about.'

'Don't you? You think Aniruddharao was so good to us because of your Mama's charm, is it?'

'No, I mean, I don't know why . . .'

'You're not stupid, Ila,' Ujoo Mami said, tossing her plait back from her shoulder. 'Why are you pretending you are?'

When I didn't answer, she pulled me to her and raised my chin. 'Hadn't you told me he was arrogant? That he considered others beneath him?'

'He *was* like that, in Mumbai!' I replied hotly.

'And yet, yesterday, he was the picture of courtesy to us,' she said. 'Not to mention the way he was looking at you.'

'How was he looking at me?' I asked, confused.

Before she could answer, the main door of the room opened.

'Are you ladies ready or not?' Padmakar Mama asked. 'Aniruddharao and his friends have already arrived.'

Giving me a meaningful look, Ujoo Mami picked up her shawl and her purse and headed out of the room.

I followed, wondering what I was supposed to do with all her implications. She seemed to think Aniruddha liked me. But that was impossible. Any man who had been turned down as violently as he had would have no reason to have any lingering affection towards the woman who had rejected him. He had been insulted, misjudged and shouted at. No, there was simply no way on earth he still had any feelings towards me. Yesterday was probably just a fluke, perhaps some residual embarrassment at having to meet me out of the blue like this.

As we stepped out of the hotel, we saw Aniruddha wave to us from across the road. With him were Sadanand, Kalyani and a fair, pretty girl with delicate features.

'Good morning.' Aniruddha smiled at me. 'You know Sadanand and Kalyani . . . and this is my sister, Gauri.'

Gauri Darshetkar bowed her head and softly said, 'Namaskar.'

She was tall for her age and graceful in her movements. And there was an innocence to her that reminded me of Juee. I found myself feeling protective towards her, although we had only just met. I introduced the others to Mama and Mami, then Aniruddha gestured to two horses that had been waiting at the side of the road with their handlers.

'These are for you,' Aniruddha told Mama-Mami. 'We have hired them for the day.'

'Oh, you needn't have!' Mama protested. 'I am perfectly fine now.'

'Of course.' Aniruddha nodded. 'But they will be handy, in case any of the ladies feel tired at any point.'

'How thoughtful of you.' Ujoo Mami smiled at him, and then glanced at me. 'Isn't it, Ila?'

I agreed that it was very thoughtful indeed, refusing to let her meaningful look rattle me.

Padmakar Mama and Ujoo Mami sat on their horses and we began our walk. The road was narrow – there was only enough space for two people to walk side by side, or one horse. So Padmakar Mama and Ujoo Mami led the procession on horseback, followed by me. Behind me were Aniruddha and Kalyani, and they were followed by Sadanand and Gauri.

'We will start with Charlotte Lake,' Aniruddha told us all. 'Then proceed to Louisa Point, where we can have lunch – we have brought some along with us. Then we'll walk to Lord's Point and finally, if everyone isn't too tired, we'll end with Sunset Point, where we can watch the sunset, obviously. Then we will drop our guests at their hotel and go back home. How does that sound?'

'Like a long, tiring day,' Kalyani muttered under her breath.

'You could've stayed behind,' Sadanand told her.

'And be bored by myself all day?' she snapped. 'Really, Dada, you don't understand anything only.'

I felt something my shoe poking at my foot. As I stopped to remove my shoe, Kalyani overtook me. Aniruddha waited, as Sadanand and Gauri, too, walked by.

'Everything okay?' he asked.

'Fine,' I said, fishing out a stray pebble from my shoe and putting it on again. Ahead, Kalyani had turned around and was giving me a look that was pure poison. 'Just a pebble.'

We walked side by side in silence for some time. The only sounds I could hear were the chirruping of birds in the trees, the crunch of dried leaves underfoot and, now and then, a soft snort from Mama-Mami's horses or a jingle from their harnesses.

'So . . .' Aniruddha cleared his throat. 'Have you made any progress in your job search?'

My eyebrows shot up in surprise.

'In Mumbai you had mentioned you were interested in getting a job,' he explained. 'I just wondered if you had taken any steps towards that.'

'I had applied to a few places.' I sighed. 'But I missed their interviews . . . due to some unforeseen events. I've written to them again but . . .' I shrugged.

'It'll be fine,' Aniruddha said bracingly. 'There is every chance that you will be called back. And if not, my advice would be to physically go to the offices. It's more difficult to turn down someone in person.'

'That . . . is a good suggestion, actually. Thank you.'

'Don't mention it,' he said, looking at me for a moment. 'And don't . . . give up. You have chosen a path that's not . . .'

'Easy?'

'Common,' he corrected. 'But if anyone can do this, it's you.'

I was touched, to say the least. Based on what little he knew of me, Aniruddha had concluded that I was capable of pursuing my ambition, when my family, who had known me all my life, had second thoughts about it. Truly strange that I should get support from such unexpected quarters. I thanked him and we walked some distance in silence again before Kalyani's voice rang out in the stillness.

'Aniruddha!' she called out. 'I need some water. Can you help me please?'

Aniruddha walked ahead to help her retrieve a water bottle from one of the bags slung over the back of Padmakar Mama's horse, and Sadanand took the opportunity to fall back.

'Hello,' he said, as I caught up with him.

'Hello.' I gave him a polite smile.

'How is everyone at home?' he enquired, as we walked together. 'Your parents . . . your . . . sisters?'

'Everyone is fine,' I replied, looking straight ahead.

263

'Latika has gone to Goa with our neighbours. And Juee is back from Pune.'

Sadanand stopped dead in his tracks. 'Sorry, when you say she has *returned* from Pune . . .' he said.

'She was there a few weeks ago.' My forehead creased. 'Didn't Kalyani tell you?'

Sadanand looked at his sister, who was sipping water while staring adoringly at Aniruddha. His jaw was working as if he was grinding his teeth, but he remained silent.

'Mama-Mami live in Pune.' I gestured to my uncle and aunt, who had also stopped to drink water. 'She was visiting them.'

'I see.' He looked at his feet. 'And she is . . . she is well?'

I didn't know what to say. What could I have said? No, she isn't well, she is pining for you but putting up a brave front—? She hasn't smiled properly since you left—? She cries herself to sleep every night because you decided to trust your friend's opinion instead of your own feelings—? Fortunately, by this point, we had caught up with the rest.

'Matheran is so lovely,' I said, changing the subject. 'Do you come here often?'

'Whenever Aniruddha calls us over,' Sadanand said. 'Which isn't as often as I'd like.'

'You're more than welcome to visit even while I'm not here, as I'm sure I've told you before,' Aniruddha replied.

'But what would we do without you?' Kalyani said plaintively. 'Your company just makes everything better, doesn't it, Gauri?'

'Yes, it does.' Gauri smiled.

'You say that now,' Aniruddha said to his sister, 'but when I ask you to come to a museum with me . . .'

Gauri's eyes widened and she gave him an embarrassed smile. He laughed and began walking again. Padmakar Mama got on his horse and he and Mami followed Aniruddha. Kalyani bounded ahead to walk next to him, leaving me and Gauri walking side by side, with Sadanand behind us.

'Do you not enjoy museums?' I asked her.

'They're okay.' She gave a small uncomfortable laugh. 'I like natural history more than actual history so . . .'

'Ah,' I said. Then, remembering our conversation about college education at Kaveribai's home, I glanced at Aniruddha's figure ahead and asked, 'And, are you planning to study natural history . . . further?'

'I was considering a BSc in botany,' she replied. 'To start with.'

'Interesting,' I told her. 'And how does your brother feel about that?'

'Oh, he is all for it,' she said happily. 'He said the world is changing and higher education will open up more possibilities for me.'

'Really.' I smiled to myself. 'How progressive of him.'

A few minutes later, we reached Charlotte Lake, a small lake surrounded by trees, with a railing behind which visitors could stand and take in the sight. I wasn't very impressed, to tell the truth. Our high school picnic had gone to Powai Lake and that had seemed much vaster and more imposing than this. Still, it was pleasant to stand by the railing and enjoy the cool breeze coming from the lake, such as it was.

Matheran was idyllic, I decided as we left, but I wouldn't want to live there permanently.

Another quarter of an hour's walk later, we reached Louisa Point. I nearly gasped in delight. The 'point' was at the edge of a cliff and, standing there, you could see an almost panoramic view of the valley below. The day was overcast, and a few white clouds had descended low in the skies, so low I imagined I could touch one if only I jumped high enough. Everything was green and quiet and my city lungs revelled in the fresh air of the mountains.

Aniruddha and Sadanand spread out a cotton sheet they had brought along and we all sat down as Gauri unpacked the lunch. It was methi theplas and dahi boondi, followed by a large thermos of hot tea.

I found my eyes wandering to the lovely scenery.

Aniruddha noticed. 'Beautiful, isn't it?' he asked.

'Very,' I agreed, not taking my eyes off the landscape. 'You are very lucky you get to enjoy this whenever you like.'

'Dada loves bringing people up here,' Gauri said, holding out a cup of tea to me.

'I can see why.' I smiled as I took it. It smelled of ginger and was pleasantly hot.

'I'm sure you would also want to bring people up here, wouldn't you?' Kalyani asked, shooting me a nonchalant look, although there was unmistakable malice in her voice. 'Or should I say . . . person?'

'I don't understand your meaning,' I told her, my forehead creasing.

'No? I just thought, given your . . . high regard . . . for him, you wouldn't mind bringing Jayant Waknis here.'

I saw Gauri give Aniruddha an uncomfortable glance. Her brother's face, so warm and polite a moment ago, had gone stony. Kalyani obviously had no idea of the effect Jayant's name would have on the Darshetkars; she was probably just reminding Aniruddha that I had favoured someone he obviously didn't like. But she had blurted out this nonsense in front of Mama-Mami, and I saw them give me a confused look.

'I think you rather overestimate my regard for him.' I forced a laugh, shaking my head at them, as if to dismiss whatever thoughts were flying through their minds.

'Really?' Kalyani's lips twisted into a smile. 'How odd. The way your sister forced us to invite him over to our house, I thought—'

'Nobody *forced* anyone—' Sadanand began, but I could see Gauri growing more and more upset.

'You thought wrong,' I interrupted. Latika's antics were going to be a constant source of embarrassment for me, clearly. 'Allow me to correct the misunderstanding. I have high regard for one man and one man alone . . .' I paused dramatically, watching Kalyani hang on my every word: 'Chhatrapati Shivaji Maharaj.'

Ujoo Mami chuckled and Sadanand joined in, and soon the conversation turned to forts and palaces, with Padmakar Mama describing his trip to Pratapgad in great detail. Sadanand proposed we go to nearby Prabalgad and Irshalgad the following day, but Kalyani shot down the suggestion by saying we would all be tired after today's sight-seeing and anyway, what was the point trudging up to some musty old forts when there would be nothing left there to see in the first place?

As she bickered with her brother, Aniruddha caught my eye and gave me a grave nod, as if thanking me. But Gauri sat silently, looking at her lap for the rest of the meal, and I felt sorry for the girl.

After lunch, we walked to Lord's Point, but the spark had

267

gone from the day. Gauri's spirits were low, Aniruddha had fallen silent and Kalyani kept complaining about how tiring it was to walk everywhere. We sat on the banks of a nearly dry river for some time, looking out into the vast valley below. The silence was broken by the sound of temple bells in the distance. Aniruddha explained that the Pisarnath Mahadev temple was nearby and at Ujoo Mami's request, agreed to take us all there.

By the time we had taken the God's darshan, the afternoon had passed and there was a slight chill in the air. I pulled my cardigan tighter around me as we stood outside the temple, debating whether to return to the hotel or carry on to Sunset Point. Mama-Mami and Sadanand were all for watching the sunset but Kalyani was complaining about her aching feet. Gauri still looked downcast and I could tell that whatever she had felt about the trip in the morning, her heart wasn't in it anymore.

Aniruddha gave me a questioning look and, glancing at Gauri, I said, 'Actually, I am also a little tired. Maybe we can go tomorrow, Mama?'

Mama looked as if he was going to protest, maybe tease me for being such a weakling, but Ujoo Mami put a diplomatic hand on his shoulder and said, 'Of course, bala. Whatever you say.'

Padmakar Mama offered Kalyani his horse, and she rode in the front with Ujoo Mami on her horse behind her. Mama walked with Aniruddha, discussing Prabalgad and how to get there. Gauri and I walked behind them in silence, followed by Sadanand.

The Darshetkars and the Pingleys saw us to the entrance of the Divadkar Hotel, where we said our goodbyes. Mama and Mami hurried to our room and I was following them, when I heard Kalyani's voice at its usual loudspeaker volume.

'I don't know what *some people* see in her,' she was saying petulantly. 'Ila Bendre is just plain . . . plain.'

And then, Aniruddha's voice, with a shade of annoyance replied, 'No. She is beautiful. In more ways than you could possibly know.'

I felt my breath catch. Had I misheard? Maybe Aniruddha was just contradicting Kalyani because she had annoyed him with all her talk about Jayant? But I refused to analyse his words any further than that. There was no point in reading any more into them, despite what Ujoo Mami would have me believe.

TWENTY-FIVE

The next day, the general consensus between Mama-Mami and me was that we could do with some lazing around.

'It's a holiday after all.' Ujoo Mami gave a humongous yawn as she spoke. 'Let's act like it!'

So we did. After a late breakfast in the hotel's open air dining area, we played cards in our room. After a few games of Badam Saat and Challenge, Mami confessed she was still feeling a little tired after the previous day's exertion and said she'd like to have a nap. Mama, ever of one mind with his wife, decided to do the same.

I glanced out of the window. It was a fine day, with the dining area, bathed in soft, golden sunlight, just a few feet away from our room. It seemed a shame to waste such excellent weather by staying indoors.

'I think I'll sit outside and read,' I declared and, picking up my shawl and the book I had carried with me in my bag, I stepped out of the room.

I found a spot where the sun wasn't directly in my eyes, and settled down to read. Nana had lent me his copy of V. S. Khandekar's *Yayati*. It is a reimagination of the story of King Yayati from the Mahabharat and had won a Sahitya Akademi Award as well as the Jnanpith Award. Nana had recommended it to me.

The weather was pleasant, a cool breeze rustling the leaves above now and then. I immersed myself in the story, page after page revealing Yayati's battle with disillusionment as he grappled with love in its myriad forms. Love, which is both the symptom and the cure of life's many challenges.

So lost was I in the world of the book that I had nearly forgotten where I was when a shadow fell on my page. I looked up.

'Hello.' Aniruddha nodded. 'May we join you?' Behind him stood Gauri.

'Uh . . .' To say I was caught off-guard would be an understatement. 'Yes, of course.'

They pulled two chairs from a nearby table and sat down. I cleared my throat, wondering what to say. Aniruddha's parting words from the previous evening were fresh in my mind.

'Where are your uncle and aunt?' Aniruddha asked.

'They're . . . resting,' I replied. 'Were you passing by, or something?'

'Yes. We thought we'd look in and ask if you all would be interested in visiting Sunset Point this evening.'

'Oh.'

'Gauri, in particular, wanted to take you there.'

I looked at the girl, who smiled shyly.

'The sunset . . . it's really pretty from there,' she said quietly.

'I would hate to bother you,' I began.

'It would be my—our pleasure,' Aniruddha replied, without missing a beat.

'I'll ask Mama-Mami when they get up,' I promised.

'You can call us on this number and tell us what you decide.' Aniruddha pulled out a small notebook and a fountain pen from his pocket and wrote something on it. 'We should leave around 5.30 so we can have a nice, leisurely walk there. It's not far.' He handed me the note and gave Gauri a coaxing look.

'Yes, please come,' she said, and then with a mischievous smile at Aniruddha added, 'Dada will love it if you do.'

Aniruddha glared at her, then looked at me and cleared his throat, as if to cover his embarrassment.

He was *embarrassed*? Oh, God. This was becoming harder and harder to ignore.

'So . . . are you enjoying the book?' he asked, pointing at my copy of *Yayati*.

'I've only just started,' I said. 'But it's quite gripping.'

'Isn't it?' He smiled. 'One of Khandekar's finest works, I'd say.'

'I haven't read much of him,' I confessed.

'Really? *Kanchan Mruga* is good. You should also read *Amrutvel*. I could lend them to you . . .' Our eyes met and he stopped suddenly.

'Do you like reading as well?' I asked Gauri, to cover the awkward moment.

'Sometimes.' She smiled. 'I like music more. I'm learning to play the harmonium.'

'Arre, waah!' I smiled. 'I would love to hear you play sometime.'

272

'Oh, yes, that would be nice,' she said warmly. 'But only if you sing. Dada says you sing very well.'

Taken aback momentarily, I remembered the time Aniruddha and Kalyani had walked in on me teasing Juee through song, and I looked down at my lap in embarrassment. 'He is being too generous,' I assured her. 'I only sing to myself.'

'He *is* very generous,' she agreed. 'But not in this case maybe.'

Before I could respond, I heard a polite cough behind me. The hotel receptionist stood there with an apologetic look on his face.

'Room number seven, right?' he asked and when I nodded, he handed me a slip of paper. 'Telegram for you. We tried calling the room, but nobody answered.'

I frowned. How deeply asleep were Mama-Mami that they didn't hear the telephone? I wondered.

I opened the telegram – and my spine turned cold with fear.

LATIKA RAN AWAY WITH JAYANT. NANA GOING
TO GOA. COME HOME. JUEE

A pit opened in my stomach. Latika and Jayant! How . . . ? Why . . . ? Questions clamoured in my mind but above them all rose a single thought: I had to get back to Mumbai right away. God only knew how Aai was taking this news and with Nana about to head to Goa, I hated the thought of Juee having to handle it all on her own. I clenched my fists, willing my thoughts to come to the present. I needed to tell Mama and Mami. We needed to get on a train as soon as possible.

I sprang to my feet. 'Sorry . . . something has come up,' I told the bewildered Darshetkars, before rushing away.

I had barely reached the door to our room when my knees seemed to buckle. I stood still, feeling the enormity of the situation suck away the strength from my legs. I took deep breaths, struggling for control.

An instant later, Aniruddha was by my side. He saw my face and frowned. 'Is everything okay?' he asked.

'I . . .' I gasped for breath. My vision blurred with tears. 'Latika.' I covered my face with my hand and sank down on the steps outside the room.

'What happened?' His voice was urgent as he crouched next to me.

'Latika . . .' I took a deep breath and looked at him. 'She has run away . . . with Jayant.'

In halting sentences, I told him everything – how Latika had gone to Goa with the Kelkars, how Jayant had mentioned he was leaving town, how Nana was leaving for Goa, presumably to look for the pair of them.

Aniruddha's expression became graver and graver as I spoke. I couldn't bear to look at him. How right Latika had proven him! No character. No culture. Ashamed, I closed my eyes, willing myself not to cry.

It was difficult.

With one single, thoughtless act, my sister had condemned us all. We would forever be known as that family whose girl ran away. Aai thought I didn't know how the real world worked. But I did. I had seen its stares, faced its judgments. Now, it didn't matter what we looked like, what our achievements were, what our ambitions were – from this moment, Juee, Malu and I would be 'those girls'. The ones whose sister ran away. That would be our identity, as far as the world was concerned.

'You know what Jayant is.' I sniffed. 'And Latika . . . she has no money! If he leaves her there and runs . . .' I stood up. 'I need to tell Mama-Mami,' I told him. 'We need to leave right away for Mumbai.'

'Okay.' Aniruddha's expression was unreadable. 'I will make your excuses to Gauri.' And with that, he turned on his heel and walked away.

I hammered on the door to the room. A drowsy-looking Mami opened the door and I barged in. As shortly as possible, I explained the whole situation to her and Mama, who had to be woken up. Mami was shocked into silence, but Mama simply pursed his lips in disapproval before cursing both Latika and Jayant to high heavens. But his face fell when I told him the truth about Jayant – how he had already tried twice to lure respectable girls into marriage for their family's money. Twice he had failed. Would he succeed the third time? With a girl who had no money in the first place?

'I will go to Goa and join Nana,' he said, looking grim. Running a reassuring hand over my head, he added, 'Don't you worry, we will find that —' He uttered a colourful epithet for Jayant and was immediately admonished with an 'Aho!' from Ujoo Mami.

He gave her a *What did I do?* look,* but agreed when I said that we needed to leave right away. Which was how, fifteen

---

* The idea that men should not use foul language in the presence of women is an alien concept in Maharashtra, where women of all classes are privy to the choicest swear words. Indeed, many use them too, with great enthusiasm, usually aiming them at men.

minutes later, we were standing at the reception, checking out of the hotel – a full two days before our planned departure.

'Aho, Godbole!'

Padmakar Mama turned around to find Aniruddha waiting patiently outside the reception. 'Could I have a word?' he asked.

Mama hurried to him and the two men talked for some time. I saw Mama's forehead wrinkle, then his expression cleared and he took Aniruddha's hand in both of his and shook it furiously.

Aniruddha looked composed during this entire exchange, then nodded and left.

'That man.' Mama shook his head as he re-joined us. 'Thank God for the day you met him, Ila. I never imagined someone could help people he barely knew like this.'

'What happened? What has he done?' I asked.

'He has put his car and his driver at our disposal,' Mama informed us. 'We just have to get to the car park at Dasturi. His driver will be waiting. He'll take us to Karjat station, where we can pick up our tickets to Mumbai in the station master's office.'

Ujoo Mami looked at me in surprise and I imagine her expression must have been identical to mine. I couldn't understand it, either.

Using the hotel phone, Mama made a quick call to the Kelkars and left a message, informing Juee that we'd be leaving right away. Then we lugged our bags to the hotel gate, where two rickshaw pullers instantly ran to us.

'Godbole?' one of them asked. 'We've been told to take you to Dasturi.'

TWENTY-SIX

The journey home seemed to take forever. We sat in silence as Aniruddha's driver manoeuvred his white Premier Padmini down the serpentine roads that led from Matheran to Karjat. Outside the car, the sun disappeared behind a few clouds, covering the valley in a hazy gloom. My mind was a storm of emotions. I remembered all the times Latika had called Jayant handsome and dashing, how delighted she seemed that he wasn't going to marry Damayanti. I had dismissed her interest in him as a teenage infatuation, like her inane obsession with Rajesh Khanna. Stupid, stupid, stupid! And, to top it all, I hadn't told anyone about Jayant! Juee, yes, but apart from her, nobody. Nobody who could have seen the danger of Latika's affection towards such a man. I sighed and put my head on Ujoo Mami's shoulder. She patted it absently.

The car pulled up outside Karjat station and, a few minutes later, tickets in hand, we made our way to the platform. The next train was at 4 o'clock. We had skipped lunch in our rush to leave so Mama brought us some vada-pavs from a nearby stall. We ate in silence, Latika's fate playing on all our minds. The train arrived, we boarded and two minutes later, we were off for Mumbai. Luckily, we found two seats in the general compartment. I tried to get Mama and Mami to take them, but Padmakar Mama waved at me to sit.

Back down on the plains, the heat was stifling. The fans in the compartment spun briskly, but the breeze blowing in through the open windows was warm and humid. Sweat trickled down my forehead, but I was too consumed with anxiety to wipe it away.

By the time we reached home, it was evening. Aai opened the door, and my heart sank.

For Aai, looking presentable – neat and tidy or neetnetkaa, as she put it – had always been of paramount importance. She would oil and comb her hair twice a day – once after her morning bath, once in the evening, before Nana came home. Then, she would dab creamy white Afghan Snow on her face, smooth it with Pond's talcum powder from a small pink metal tin, then run her ring finger over the kajal in the little circular green box, before applying it. A dot of kunku between her eyebrows would be the finishing touch.

The woman who opened the door bore no relation to the lady who was usually such a stickler about her appearance. Aai's hair was frizzy, escaping from her plait in wispy tendrils, as if it had seen neither oil nor comb in days. There were puffy, dark circles under her bloodshot eyes and her mouth seemed to have been carved into a downturn.

As soon as she saw us, her eyes welled up. 'Dada!' she said, covering her mouth to stifle her sob.

It felt as if someone had pulled away the ground from

beneath my feet. I was used to seeing Aai impatient, irritated – angry even. But strong, always strong in her many moods. Seeing her distressed like this was disorienting. Like turning the corner on a familiar street and suddenly finding yourself lost, in a strange, terrifying new world.

Ujoo Mami put an arm around Aai and led her into the house. Mama and I followed with the bags.

'Good you came so soon,' I heard Juee say, as I stepped into the living room. She took my bag from me, her face drawn and serious.

'Malu?' I asked, looking around.

Before she could answer, Malu came out of the kitchen, bearing a tray with glasses of water. She held out the tray to me and I took a glass, observing her face. Malu was technically the youngest of us, but she had never really been the baby of the family. Latika's immaturity had ensured that the title belonged to her and her alone. Instead of the childish frolic that should have come naturally to her, Malu had always been studying. And now, as I watched her offer water to Mama-Mami, I realised that she had been forced to grow up much before her time. She hadn't even needed telling that we would need water after our long journey, something Latika would definitely not have sensed so intuitively.

We took turns freshening up, then sat in the kitchen as Juee served us fodnichi poli* and tea. We were a tight fit, so I

---

* Rebirth isn't just a Hindu thing, it's a deeply Maharashtrian one. For instance, leftover polis in a Marathi household are reincarnated as fodnichi poli – poli scraps fried with onions and spices, garnished with coconut and coriander and typically served as breakfast. Because what better way to start today, than by reflecting upon what Life – and Aai – blessed you with yesterday.

offered my chair to Mama and took my plate and cup to the living room, Juee following close behind. We were barely out of the kitchen when I heard Aai sob: 'Dada, how? How, re, how my girl ate dung* like this!'

'Any news from Nana?' I asked Juee, as I picked at my food.

'Nothing yet,' Juee said. 'He called this evening to say he reached Goa safely.'

'Mama said he'd go and help Nana look for Latika,' I said.

Juee sighed and looked at her hands. Then, bit by bit, she told me the whole story. Apparently, the Kelkars had arrived in Goa safe and sound, the day before Dasraa, with Latika in tow. They were staying in a dharmashala near the Shantadurga Kunkalikarin temple in Fatorpa. The rituals they were to perform were scheduled for two days later, as there were festivities taking place at the temple on Dasraa day and a wedding set to happen on the temple premises the day after. The plan was for the family to go and visit the temple on the prescribed morning at an auspicious time and perform the necessary rituals to appease the Goddess. The entire exercise was to take a few hours. But on the morning of the ritual, Latika confided in Sudha that she had her period and that obviously it was out of the question for her to visit

---

*   1970s Maharashtra was nothing if not organised, when it came to romantic relationships. Oh, you're seeing somebody inappropriate romantically? Are you posh? Then you're having an 'affair'. Are you middle-class? Then you're having a lafda. Will your immoral relationship ruin your family's reputation? Then, you are 'eating dung'.

280

the temple with them, in such a condition.* She had urged the family to carry on without her, saying she'd wait for them till they came back. But when the Kelkars had returned around lunchtime, Latika was nowhere to be found. Her bag was also missing. All that remained was a letter addressed to Sudha.

Juee showed it to me. It was classic Latika.

My dear Sudha, it said. *I can't believe this day has finally come! I should have said something to you before, but I am sure you will forgive me when I tell you why I have left. Love has struck, Sudha, love like I never imagined! When I think of my foolish obsession with Hindi film stars now, I laugh at my own silliness. Because I see now that it was only infatuation. But this – this is love! I am in love! With the most dreamy man ever! He is handsome and clever and thinks I am the smartest, loveliest girl in the whole world! Can you guess who it is? I bet you can't! I have been very naughty in keeping it from you, but I had to, you understand. Still, no matter. Soon, there will be no reason for secrecy or hiding things, because we will be married! It won't be a boring old ceremony like usual – it'll be exciting and one-of-a-kind. Like our love! Anyway, I will write to you once it's all done and visit you all in Mumbai soon.*

Your friend,
the soon-to-be Mrs. Latika Jayant Waknis

---

* Women are like Goddesses because they create life. But the bodily function that helps them do that is, um . . . not okay by the Gods. Who created women. Who are like Goddesses. Because they create life. Yup, gotta love that logic.

That was all. Not one word about her family. No acknowledgment of how worried we would be when we found out, leave alone any trace of an apology.

From the kitchen, I heard Aai's sobs. Juee and I exchanged glances. She had pursed her lips, as if she was trying hard not to say something.

'What is it?' I asked. 'Has Aai been . . . difficult?'

'She . . .' Juee sighed. 'She is refusing to blame Latika for what has happened.'

'What?'

'She keeps saying that it would never occur to Latika to break her mother's heart like this and that Jayant must have done some jaadu-tona on her . . .'

'Jaadu—? Has Aai gone mad?' I shook my head in disbelief. The very suggestion that Jayant had practised black magic on my sister to make her act this way was utterly preposterous.

'I don't know,' Juee said miserably. 'Nana told her when our own coin is bad, what's the point in blaming someone else, and she lost her temper. They had a big fight. The way they spoke to each other . . . I've never seen them like this, Ila.' There were tears in her eyes. 'Nana said we should contact the police, but Aai was adamant. She said once we told the police everyone would find out, it would be a big scandal and nobody would want to marry the rest of us.'

I rubbed her arm, feeling sorry for her. I knew what it must have cost Juee to say what she did, to accept that our parents were not perfect. It was not in her nature to question their actions or decisions, and the disapproval in her voice now told me that cracks were forming in her perfect picture of them.

'Sounds bad,' I said softly.

'I haven't even told you the worst part.' Juee sniffed.

'There's something even worse?'

'Ila . . . I didn't notice it at first.' She closed her eyes and shook her head. 'But Latika . . .'

'She did seem drawn towards Jayant, in hindsight.' I nodded. 'We should've seen it sooner.'

'No, it's not that.' My sister sighed. 'After Latika left, I heard Aai say that she couldn't find my gold earrings. The ones that Latika had borrowed, remember? Aai had told me I could have them when I' – she sniffed again – 'when I got married. She can't find them anywhere. She searched from top to bottom.' She looked at me, fear in her eyes. 'I . . . I think Latika might've taken them before she left.'

I stared at her. I'd thought Latika was just stupid, but this . . . this was treachery of the worst sort. And now I found myself believing Aai. If Latika had taken the earrings, then it wasn't her idea. My younger sister was self-centred and brainless; this kind of machination was beyond her intelligence. But then, a part of me asked if I was underestimating her. After all, that trick with the period – and it had to have been a trick; I mean, the sheer convenience of the timing – that was pretty sneaky. And somehow, I doubted that that particular pretext would've struck any man, even one as wily as Jayant.

Either way, this brought up the question that had played on my mind since the moment I'd read Juee's telegram: why had Jayant eloped with Latika, of all people? He was clearly a fortune-hunter and nobody who saw our family could believe we had money. So how had Latika charmed him then? By promising that she could get her hands on some gold? Juee's earrings were not much, but they were made of gold. Weighed some two-three grams or so, which was worth a sizeable sum of money, at least for us. Maybe . . . and here my heart skipped a beat . . . maybe his plan was to take them off Latika and then dump her? After all, once he had the gold, what use would she be to him?

I remembered what Aniruddha had said in his letter. *We live in a world where a girl's reputation is more fragile than a man's.* Latika believed she was in love. If Jayant had promised to marry her, Latika would not stop herself from expressing her love physically. Was that the answer then? Had Jayant merely intended to . . . have his way with her? And if, after that, he took the gold and ran . . . Latika had no job, she had no money, and now, she would have no reputation either. Nowhere to go. She didn't know a soul in Goa, we had no family there, no friends. Yes, Nana had gone there to look for her, but Goa was big. An entire state. She could be anywhere, untethered, at the mercy of the worst kind of people.

Latika wasn't in love. She was in danger. And, in a sudden flash of clarity, I realised that this was the very fate Aai had been dreading for all of us: she lived in constant fear that her daughters would be at the mercy of the world one day. And she was convinced marriage would save us from that. How ironic then, that Latika's attempt at marriage was precisely what had thrown her, and by extension us, into the eye of this storm.

Some believe that there are thirty-three hundred thousand Gods in the Hindu pantheon. Some say there are thirty-three prime deities. Every village has a face of divinity attached to it, every family a reigning God or Goddess.

I closed my eyes and said a silent prayer to them all: *Keep my sister safe, Gods. Against all odds, for all our sakes, keep that selfish, stupid girl safe.*

TWENTY-SEVEN

After Padmakar Mama had left for Goa, we lived in a kind of suspended reality.

We woke up, did our chores, Malu went to school, and Juee and I helped Ujoo Mami and Aai around the house. We pretended life was normal. But all the time, every single moment, we were all waiting. Waiting for Nana's call or Mama's letter saying they had found Latika. Whether she was safe and sound or ruined and sorry, all that would come later. The interminable wait for news was what occupied all our thoughts.

Ordinarily around this time we'd all be busy with Diwali preparations. The whole house would be dusted and cleaned. The kandil would be brought down from the attic, along with the strings of colourful lights we usually put up. Nana would check them all, replace the bulbs that weren't working, then install them, a full week before Diwali began. Aai would be busy making faraal – Diwali snacks – and one by one all of us sisters (except Latika) would be roped in to make chakli, anarse, shankarpaali, karanji, chivda and besan laadoos. Malu would offer to take all the old newspapers to the raddiwala to make some extra pocket money. Juee would plan new rangoli patterns for each day of Diwali, and I would . . . I would sleep peacefully through the night.

None of that was happening this year. The last call from Padmakar Mama had been two days ago, saying he had met Nana and they were scouring South Goa for Latika and Jayant. Nana had begun his search in Fatorpa, showing people a picture of Latika, and by the time Mama had joined him, had given up hope of her being in the area. Together, my father and uncle had covered a few neighbouring districts, with no luck. They had decided to try for a day or two more, then go to the police.

Aai had descended into a fit of despair when she had heard this, but I could see the logic in Nana and Mama's decision. The police would cover more ground, they had more people, they were familiar with the territory and had a better chance of finding Latika than two middle-aged men who were strangers to the region. It had been a spectacularly stupid idea of Aai's not to involve them till now, but I didn't tell her that. *Perhaps she thinks a daughter's safety is not such a big sacrifice to make at the altar of respectability*, I thought bitterly. *One less liability to marry off, after all.*

As if things weren't terrible to start with, the following afternoon we received an inland letter from Vishnubhat. I handed it to Aai with misgivings, and my doubts were proven true, when Aai read it quickly and then crumpled it and flung it on the floor before storming into the kitchen.

287

'Lokasaange bramhadnyaan!'* she huffed.

Juee smoothed out the blue inland and read it out to me in a low voice.

Respected Mama, Saa. Na. Vi. Vee. We are writing because we have just received news of a most shocking nature. It has been brought to our attention that our young cousin, Kumari Latika, has been absconding from home, in the company of a young man of a questionable reputation. Our better half joins us in extending our sympathies to you at this most trying time. It is a truly horrifying scenario for certain and the esteemed Kaveribai Bhagwat agreed with our judgment of these circumstances when we divulged these details to her.

'Who the hell told you to do that?' I asked the letter angrily. 'Gossip-monger!'

Juee continued reading.

She also agreed that, despite the relationship between our two families, this reckless, nay, immoral act of our young cousin has not besmirched the Chhatre name in her esteem, for which, of course, we are eternally grateful. Since Wai is so far away from Mumbai, we are confident that the heat of this wildfire kindled by your daughter will not reach our wife and ourselves. And we must say, when we think of how close we came to forging a closer, more direct bond with your family, we shudder to the depths of our soul and we give

---

*   The saying goes 'Lokasaange bramhadnyaan, swatah korde paashan', meaning someone who goes around handing out free advice to people, while not knowing a thing themselves. You know, like YouTube influencers.

thanks to our namesake, Vishnu, the Protector, who has shielded us from this tragedy.

'Of course!' I exclaimed. 'Only think of yourself, you self-centred little beetle!'

'Ssh, let me read,' Juee said irritably, and I fell silent.

But there are more serious matters at hand. It behooves me, Mama, to offer you some advice in the matter of your daughters. Kumari Latika is but one extreme case of too much freedom leading to downfall. Your upbringing of your daughters — from allowing them to pursue higher education, to leaving them unmarried for so long — has been misthought. When Kumari Ila came to visit, her manner of speaking to Kaveribai reeked strongly of an over-independent mind, a dangerous quality in the gentle sex. Your eldest daughter, while being the model of propriety, has been indiscreet enough to have had an unfortunately public heartbreak. The youngest still has hope, but I fear, if you continue to coax her down the corridors of education, she too will prove difficult to control. Curb the girls, Mama, before another tragedy strikes. Heed our words for they are given in kinship, with the noblest of intentions.

Apart from this, all is well with us. The weather continues fine. We will end this missive with a namaskar to the elders in the family and blessings for the young.

Your most dutiful nephew,
Vishnu Chhatre

Juee stared at me in disbelief.

'Can I scream *now*?' I asked, outraged. I didn't get the chance to, however, because at that moment the doorbell rang.

It was our father. He was alone.

'Nana!' I exclaimed. 'Where is Padmakar Mama?'

'Where is Latika?' Ujoo Mami asked.

'You found her?' Aai asked, bursting out of the kitchen, glancing behind Nana as if he was hiding an entire teenager there.

'No . . .' Nana replied heavily, sinking into the armchair. 'We went to the police also, but they said we had wasted too much time.' He glared at Aai. 'They said they'd keep on looking, but we have gone to them a week after she went missing. They said, after so many days, it was difficult.'

'So . . . so now?' Aai asked. She sounded like a small child that had let go of a balloon and couldn't understand that the balloon couldn't return.

'Now, nothing.' Nana closed his eyes and leaned back in the chair.

'You're . . . you're just going to give up?' Aai demanded, hands on hips. 'She's our daughter! We can't just—'

'What do you want me to do?' Nana opened his eyes again and sat up. He asked calmly, but his eyes were bright with anger. With each word, his voice was rising. 'I went to Goa, I didn't involve the police like you said, I hunted around for days! Like a madman! For a girl whom *you* allowed a free hand—'

'Me?' Aai recoiled. '*I* allowed her to go to Goa, is it?'

'You allowed her to do whatever she liked!'

'And you didn't want to be bothered with her, so you let me!'

'Yes! And now she's left me in no state to show my face in public!' Nana took a deep breath and said in a steadier voice. 'So, I'll ask you again. What more do you want me to do?'

Aai shook her head in disgust and marched off to the bedroom in a way that reminded me exactly of Latika. They had so much in common, it was hardly surprising that Latika was Aai's favourite. Had Aai been more like Latika when she was younger? Had her marriage to Nana tempered her in some ways? Had Nana's rational, logical company pruned the excessively emotional, more dangerous traits of her personality? *If that is true*, I thought, *what will happen to Latika's personality if she marries a man like Jayant?* Nothing good, I was willing to bet.

But I couldn't believe that Nana would just . . . stop looking for Latika. However she was, whatever she had done, she was his daughter. Would he just . . . cast her off? Stop thinking about her and pretend like she wasn't out there somewhere in the world, in need of our help? He wouldn't.

Would he?

Long after the others had gone to bed, I lay awake on my mattress asking myself this question over and over. If Nana did something like this, it would change the way I saw my father forever. A part of me refused to believe this was even possible. But then I remembered his words: *If I don't allow her to go, she'll just stay here and eat all our heads the entire time.* I sighed.

My last thought before sleep claimed me was, *And where on earth is Padmakar Mama in all this?*

Late next morning, the answer arrived in the form of a phone call. Sudha Kelkar came running to our door saying there was a trunk call from Goa for us. It was Padmakar Mama. Nana's conversation with him was quiet and short – trunk calls were expensive and even if Mama was paying, there was no need to disregard the cost. Aai, Juee, Ujoo Mami and I, who had followed him to the Kelkar home – not to mention the Kelkars themselves, who were anxiously waiting for news of the girl who had disappeared on their watch – all strained our ears to listen, but could only make out monosyllabic answers.

'Latika has been found,' Nana announced after he hung up.

A wave of relief passed through us all. Nana, ignoring the curious looks of the Kelkars, thanked them and left.

Once in the privacy of our own home, however, he revealed all.

Apparently, Mama and Nana had been staying with an old law college friend of Mama's in Goa. After Nana left, the friend had told Padmakar Mama that he knew some 'higher-ups', as he called them, in the police, and had convinced Mama to meet them. Through these people, Mama had received word that Latika and Jayant were in North Goa. Mama had travelled there that morning and found them in some village called Anjuna.

'Are they married?' Juee asked.

'Not yet,' Nana replied. 'But Padmakar said the boy will marry her if I agree to pay for the wedding.'

'You must agree!' Aai exclaimed.

'It's not like I have a choice,' Nana said dryly. 'But it will have to be a small wedding. I refuse to waste five paise more than necessary on that girl.'

But Aai wasn't listening. A beatific smile had spread across her face, as if she were a parched desert traveller who had stumbled upon a mirage of a freshwater spring only to discover, against all odds, that the mirage was real.

'My little Latika.' She gave a long, contented sigh. 'All

grown up and about to be married!' Then she seemed to snap out of her reverie and said in a horrified tone, 'Agabai, Diwali is just around the corner! Come, come, girls! There is so much to do!'

TWENTY-EIGHT

If I had thought Aai's behaviour had been annoying after Juee was jilted, she was altogether unbearable now. Not a day went by without her bragging to some neighbour or other about her stroke of luck. Never mind that Latika wasn't actually married yet. Padmakar Mama had written to us explaining that Jayant had acquired a job abroad and he and Latika would leave for Kuwait soon. If Latika was going to be settled abroad, she needed proof of her marriage to Jayant that was accepted internationally, which meant that a quick temple wedding was out of the question. They would have to have a court marriage and get a proper marriage registration certificate, which would take at least a fortnight to arrange. Mama was going to take them to Pune and keep an eye on them till the wedding happened. He had asked Ujoo Mami to return home immediately, which she did.

And we settled down to wait for my sister and her husband to show up at our doorstep.

That was another thing: Mama had written that Latika wanted to stay with us a day or two before leaving for Kuwait. Nana was absolutely fuming at the idea as he paced in the living room.

'I don't even want to see her face again!' he snapped at Aai, when she wondered if she should make some extra besan laadoos for Latika to take along with her. 'So stop acting as if she is some prodigal daughter returning home!'

'Tch, let it go now.' Aai shook her head dismissively. 'How long will you stay angry? Our daughter is married to a handsome young man and she is going to be settled in foreign—'*

'And who knows how your brother wrangled *that*, on top of everything else!' Nana said, but Aai just waved his concern away.

'She is his niece, after all,' she said airily. 'So what if he does something for her husband-to-be?

'What do you mean?' I frowned. 'What did Mama do?'

'Convincing that boy to marry Latika.' Nana shook his head. 'That can't have come cheap. My guess is your Mama has paid the fellow a good amount to take her off our hands. And this job . . . wasn't he a photographer? Now suddenly he has a job, that also in Kuwait? Looks like your Mama's handiwork to me. God knows how I will pay him back.'

---

* For Maharashtrians, 'foreign' is not an adjective. It is a noun, an all-encompassing word for every single country outside India. We don't get fancy clothes from America. We get them from foreign. We don't go to study in Australia – we go to foreign. And if we're really lucky, then maybe one day we won't immigrate – we'll get settled in foreign.

I didn't know what to be more horrified about: the fact that Nana now owed Padmakar Mama a substantial amount of money, which we obviously couldn't spare, or the fact that Nana had spoken about Latika as a liability to get rid of.

Suddenly, I felt like I couldn't stay inside the house for another moment. Making a pretext of going downstairs to get some fresh air, I left.

Outside, the sky had begun to change colour as sunset approached. I sat on the katta near the building, watching the boys from the neighbourhood play with their marbles in the dirt. I picked up a stick and traced patterns in the earth at my feet. I hadn't had a moment to myself since we had left Matheran, not even a minute to sit still and think about what had happened up in the hills. I had been so wrapped up in all the anxiety about Latika, in the uncertainty of her fate and ours, that I hadn't stopped to consider how *I* was feeling about anything.

Or, specifically, about the sea-change I had witnessed in Aniruddha.

The man I had met in Matheran was by no means the same man I had met in Wai, and a far cry from the man I had first met, all those months ago, at Arun's wedding. I recalled his courteous behaviour towards Padmakar Mama and Ujoo Mami. The way he had rushed to help Mama. The way he had introduced me to his sister. His enquiries about my job search and his quiet words of encouragement. And, finally, what he had said about me to Kalyani, when he thought I couldn't hear him. He had called me beautiful, but it hadn't sounded like a superficial compliment. There was no flirtatious intent there, like Jayant's compliments so often had. Aniruddha had seemed like he genuinely meant what he said. And if his behaviour the following day was any indication, perhaps Ujoo Mami hadn't been wrong. Perhaps he really did have feelings for me. And . . . and if this new Aniruddha was anything to go by . . . perhaps . . . I too had . . .

I sniffed. *Well*, I told myself, *that's all over now. You aren't just Ila Bendre anymore. You are the sister of a girl who will soon be married to a man he despises, under conditions that would challenge any ordinary man's ideas of propriety.* And Aniruddha wasn't ordinary. He already found my family crass. This latest exploit of Latika's had probably pushed us over the fence, into the territory of vulgarity. Even if Aniruddha had feelings for me, they had probably vanished by the time we had left the Divadkar Hotel. Who could blame him? *Isn't that how any respectable young man would react?* I sniffed again. *Stop it*, I told myself, wiping the corner of my eye. *You always knew you wouldn't have any luck in matters of the heart. You have already decided to be capable and independent and get a job, so these things won't matter.*

Aniruddha Darshetkar was never in the equation. But as I got up to return home, a treacherous voice inside me whispered, *But it would be nice if he was.*

One week passed swiftly and, a few days later, on the second evening of Diwali, there came a knock on our door. Juee hurried to open it and gasped when she did. Nana scowled. Aai's eyes grew as round as saucers. And me, I couldn't utter a single word. Because of course it was Latika and Jayant as expected – but their appearance! Gods above.

'You look so different, Latu!' Malu squealed at Latika. 'I didn't recognise you only!'

Latika beamed. She was dressed in bright red paisley-printed bell bottoms and a tight beige tie-dye blouse, knotted at the waist. A long black thread with rudraksha beads dangled around her neck like a necklace, and there was a thin, ribbon-like strip of cloth tied around her forehead.

Jayant was wearing a short kurta and tight trousers, but he hadn't shaved and had a full beard and large square sunglasses.

Latika saw us stare, then she tossed back her loose hair and was about to step inside, when Aai stopped her.

'Wait, wait,' she said, and hurried into the kitchen.

She came back with a copper tambya full of water. She made Latika and Jayant take off their chappals, then poured water over their feet, dipped her fingers in the tambya and touched them to their eyes.

With monumental effort, I managed not to roll my own eyes. Tradition is all very well, but such a welcome for a girl whose actions had almost made our family the object of neighbourhood gossip and ridicule? I had to hand it to Aai – all this was flagrantly unnecessary, to say the least.

'So then . . .' Latika asked, stepping inside. 'How I surprised everyone, na?'

I saw Nana's scowl deepen and without a word of welcome to his daughter and her husband, my father retired to the bedroom. I heard the door slam.

Jayant looked a little cowed by this unfriendliness, but Latika was too busy preening in her new clothes to notice Nana's displeasure.

'Do you have a headache?' Juee asked her, pointing to the strip of cloth tied around her forehead.

Aai used to tie one around her own forehead sometimes,

usually when, according to her, 'all this worrying about you girls' marriages is giving me a headache!'

But Latika ridiculed the suggestion. 'Uff, Juee!' She rolled her eyes dramatically. 'Don't be such a simpleton! This is fashion!' Then she gave us all a superior look and made a dismissive gesture with her hand. 'Let it be, you won't understand.'

I was about to retort but she continued. 'You all will not *believe* the fun I've had!' she said excitedly. 'The people I have met! Foreigners, you know! The way they talk, the way they live, uff!' She clapped her hands on her cheeks. 'It's so exciting! So . . . so different! So . . . adventurous! Uff!'

'What is this 'uff'?' I asked her. 'Why are you talking like this?'

'Like what?'

'Like an idiot,' I snapped, but Aai glared at me.

Then she smiled at Jayant nervously and said, 'Please sit, Jayantrao.' She indicated the divan. 'I hope your journey was comfortable.'

'What comfortable?' Latika pouted. 'All that rattling around in the ST bus. Uff! Still . . .' She grinned at Jayant. 'Soon, it will be a different life. In foreign! Now *that* will be comfortable.'

Jayant smiled uneasily at this, but his usual swagger came back in full force a second later.

'What is this job you have got?' I asked coolly.

'It's in a logistics company,' he said, running a hand through his hair. 'As a clerk, for now. But there is scope for promotion.'

'And he will definitely get a promotion soon,' Latika added proudly. 'After all, who can say no to that face?'

'Not you, that's for sure,' I muttered. Juee elbowed me in the ribs with a warning glance.

The rest of the day was excruciating. Latika refused to change into what Aai called 'decent clothes', saying that she had left all her old, boring saris and Punjabi dresses back in Goa since they wouldn't fit her new, glamorous foreign life. When Juee offered to lend her some of her own clothes to wear while she was in Mumbai, Latika simply shook her head with an amused expression – as if a month ago she hadn't been begging Juee to borrow these very same clothes.

'It's a different world out there,' she sighed to Sudha Kelkar, who had come to visit. 'We don't realise it here, but there's a big, exciting world full of adventures and possibilities.'

She had insisted they stand in the balcony to talk and she was tossing her hair this way and that and smiling in a very superior manner at all the people she saw below. Since it was evening time, this included a lot of people, not all of whom thought her clothes and manner were as fascinating as she seemed to believe. But, as usual, my younger sister was oblivious to all this.

She was *so* pleased with herself, for the way things had turned out for her, that I began to realise that she honestly didn't see anything wrong with what she had done.

This became crystal clear halfway into dinner.

We were all sitting in a circle on the living room floor and eating, our plates before us, for what Aai called 'our last meal as a whole family'.

Juee had been picking at her food, and I had guessed she had been fighting the impulse to say something all evening. Now, suddenly, she turned to Latika, who was sitting next to her, and asked her in an undertone if she had taken the earrings Aai had kept for Juee's wedding.

'Yes,' Latika replied matter-of-factly, chewing down a mouthful of rice.

'Where are they?' Juee asked.

'Sold them. Can you pass me the aamti?'

'What do you—you *sold* them?' Juee yelped. 'Why?'

'We needed the money,' Latika replied airily. 'You didn't expect me to starve in Goa, did you?'

'Sold what?' Nana asked, and Juee gave me a frightened look.

'The-earrings-Aai-had-made-for-Juee's-wedding,' Latika said, in an exasperated sing-song way that didn't so much get on my nerves as jump up and down on them repeatedly.

I half expected Nana to say something to Latika, but he merely looked away in disgust, before getting up from his place, plate in hand, indicating he was done with the meal. And, possibly, his daughter.

'Be at least a *little* ashamed,' I told Latika.

'For what?' She sounded genuinely surprised at the idea. 'Aai had kept them for her daughter's wedding, na? I am also her daughter. I took them. I got married. What does it matter what I did with them?'

'Aai?' I turned to my mother, who had stood up, hoping she at least would tell off Latika for her audacity. But as usual, I expected too much.

'What's done is done,' Aai said briskly, as she took her plate to the kitchen. 'Juee bala, we'll get you new ones for your wedding, okay? We'll melt one of my bangles, if needed.'

Juee nodded wordlessly and that apparently was that. One by one, we finished our meal and washed our hands.

As Juee and I helped Aai clear away the dinner things, Latika lounged on Nana's armchair, the thought of helping us in the chore not even wandering in the general direction of her mind.

'I don't even know why we bother with all this gold business,' she said after a few minutes, playing with a strand of her hair. 'Nobody in Goa wears gold anymore . . .'

'Nobody?' I asked. 'Really. *Nobody* wears gold in the entire state of Goa?'

'Nobody interesting anyway.' Latika made a face at me. 'They wear beads and sarongs and flowers in their hair. You don't know *anything*, Ila, you've never stepped out of your little comfort zone. You've never met people who are different from you . . .'

'I know about hippies,' I told her. 'Those are the people you're talking about, right? With the long hair and the drugs and the optional bathing.'

'Typical old-fashioned thinking.' Latika gave a derisive snort. 'Just lumping people into one . . . lump together. All of them are different, okay? Our friends John and Pam came from America to protest against the Vietnam War . . .'

'In India?' I asked. 'When the war is in Vietnam?'

'And Rose is British,' Latika continued, ignoring me. 'She came because she was tired of living a . . .' she scrunched her nose, as if trying to remember, 'capital . . . capitali . . . uff! What is the word?'

'Capitalist,' Jayant provided.

'Capitalist! She wanted to give up her capitalist way of life!' Latika announced in triumph.

'Starting with soap?' I asked.

Latika glared at me, then turned her head away

dramatically and said, 'And Charles is . . . he's French, na, Jayu?'

Juee and I exchanged glances. Jayu? God help us. But Jayant seemed to take it in his stride.

'Half Indian, half Vietnamese,' Jayant said. 'But he has French citizenship.' He took out a packet of cigarettes and a lighter from his pocket, then noticed the frowns on Juee's face and mine. 'I'll just step out for some time.' He smiled, before opening the front door and leaving.

Juee took the last of the dinner plates into the kitchen, to help Aai wash up. I stayed back, getting out mattresses and bedsheets from the cupboard in the corner, to make the beds for our guests – Her Royal Highness Latikeshwari and her Consort, Prince Harming.

'I knew Charles had *some* French connection.' Latika sighed. 'Although now that I think about it, I should have known he was Indian in some way. His last name didn't sound *at all* French. Something Shobha . . . Shobhraj,* I think, it was. Very un-French. But he was *such* a sophisticated man, I tell you! All the girls were mad after him! So *handsome*! Uff! Like a film star!'

'Well, we know how you like *those*.' I unfolded a bedsheet to spread it on one mattress.

But Latika hadn't heard the barb. 'You know, he told me I had *exactly* what it takes to be an air hostess.' She was staring

---

*   If you haven't heard of Charles Sobhraj, he's a serial killer responsible for the murders of about twelve people. There is a Netflix series about him called *The Serpent* and a Hindi film called *Main Aur Charles*. If you *have* heard of Sobhraj, then it's a dead giveaway for your age, so how's your back doing these days?

303

dreamily into the distance. 'I could've become one very easily! I wasn't even married – you can't marry if you're an Air India air hostess, you know. They make you quit if you marry. But Jayu said we could get married later, in secret, once I had the job. All I had to do was wait till Charles took me to meet his contacts at Air India. We were making plans and everything. But then stupid Aniruddha Darshetkar had to show up and spoil everything!'

The bedsheet nearly fell from my hands.

'Aniruddha?' I exclaimed. 'What was *he* doing there?'

Latika sucked in air sharply and made an embarrassed face. 'Tch, tch, tch, I shouldn't have said anything,' she said, covering her mouth with her hands. 'Forget I said anything, okay? We promised to stay quiet. Don't tell Jayu I said anything!'

And with that mysterious reply, my sister traipsed outside into the balcony, leaving me utterly confused.

TWENTY-NINE

There are several awful things you can store in your stomach. Acidity, fear, rage. But of them all, curiosity is one of the worst. It is a constantly wriggling worm. An itch you cannot reach. And I had to bear it for two whole days as, deep in my stomach, a single question twisted and turned like a frisky serpent: *Why had Aniruddha met Latika in Goa?* She, of course, refused to tell me, no matter how cleverly I requested or begged. All she would say was that she had promised Padmakar Mama not to breathe a word of it and she would be in big trouble if anybody found out. Which only piqued my curiosity more, of course. There was no asking Jayant – I wouldn't trust him to tell me the day of the week, let alone the truth in this matter. So I suspended my curiosity, promising myself that I'd write to Ujoo Mami at the very first opportunity I got and demand an explanation.

Two days later the newlyweds took their leave. Aai gave them a tearful farewell from the quadrangle under the building while the rest of us stood anxiously next to Nana in the balcony. A faint smile played on Nana's lips as Latika, dressed in a long, brightly printed skirt and a loose blouse, waved us goodbye from the taxi that would take them to Ferry Wharf, from where they would catch the Dwarka steamer to Kuwait. I marvelled at my sister's optimism. She was about to start a new life, in a strange new country, with a man she barely knew, but there wasn't a trace of fear in her, only boundless enthusiasm. She seemed absolutely convinced that her story would turn out well, regardless. I couldn't blame her. Everything had turned out well for her so far, hadn't it? Who was to say her streak of pure dumb luck wouldn't continue for the rest of her life?

The evening before they left, I had found Jayant smoking in the balcony by himself and taken the opportunity to have a chat. Over the past two days, he had endeared himself to Aai by praising her cooking, complimenting her looks and offering to help her in her chores. Only offering, mind you – I didn't see him actually lift a finger to do any work. Even Nana had softened a bit towards him, and once or twice I caught him laughing heartily at some remark Jayant had made.

He might have successfully conned my parents into thinking he wasn't a terrible person, but I understood what he actually was. And it was time he knew that.

'So, are you all packed?' I asked, conversationally.

'Seems like,' he replied, with his trademark smile. 'Will you be sad to see me leave?'

'As much as any sister-in-law would be, to see a brother-in-law go.'

'Waah, waah, what a . . . *proper* reply.' He laughed in a

teasing manner. 'And here I thought you were all bold. It seems I was mistaken.'

'Speaking of being mistaken,' I said brightly, 'I finally met Gauri Darshetkar a few weeks ago.'

It was as if I had pressed a button that cut off his laughter. 'Oh?' he said, warily. 'And . . . and how did you find her?'

'Very sweet,' I replied. 'Very loving towards her brother.'

'Yes. She is.' He swallowed. 'You met him as well?'

'Yes. We all spent a day together. It was quite an experience.'

'Really.'

'Mmm. I learned so many *interesting* things about some of our . . . ah, common acquaintances.'

He watched my face nervously. I let him suffer in suspense for a few moments, then I smirked. 'Still . . . I suppose nobody else needs to know what I know. And they never will, as long as Latika doesn't get into any trouble.' I looked at him intently, to see if he caught my meaning. 'Right?'

He nodded slowly. We left it at that. In Marathi, we have a saying: Shahanyala shabdaancha maar. A wise person doesn't need a beating to learn a lesson. For him or her, words are enough. And whatever else he was, my new brother-in-law was certainly no fool.

With Latika and Jayant gone, the house was finally empty enough for me to find a corner and write to Ujoo Mami. I explained that Latika had shot off her mouth and begged her to tell me the rest of it.

Her reply came a few days later. I carefully peeled off the sides of the inland letter she had sent and read her neat handwriting:

307

My dear Ila,

Where to begin? Your Mama has told me all that has happened since he went with Nana to Goa, and to say that I was incredulous when I first heard it all would be an understatement. You already know that he was to return to Pune the day after Nana left for Mumbai. What you don't know is that on the very day he was to leave, he was contacted by none other than Aniruddha Darshetkar. Apparently, back in Matheran, the young man had assumed that your Mama would be going to Goa and asked him where he could be reached. Your Mama gave the address of the friend in Goa with whom he and Nana would be staying. Aniruddha showed up there that morning and claimed to have found Latika, safe and unharmed, in Jayant's company in Anjuna. Your Mama accompanied him there and, sure enough, your sister was there, as carefree and untroubled as if she were there for a college picnic! As for getting married, Latika said they would get around to doing it at some point! As if she was talking about a tiresome chore!

How much Aniruddha and your Mama tried to convince her to forget that boy and come home, but she just wouldn't listen. Aniruddha tried to talk sense into Jayant, but as it turned out he didn't have to. Jayant would have happily refrained from marrying Latika. It seems he truly believed that with his looks and charms, he could've made a more advantageous marriage. Not in Mumbai, where he apparently owes people money (that's why he left in such a hurry) – but with some foreigner, who would've loved to marry an Indian and take him back to her country. But then Latika apparently told your Mama that she would kill herself if she didn't get to marry Jayant – really, that girl has such a love for melodrama! – and everyone felt it was best if a wedding happened quickly.

This was easier said than done, of course. First, Aniruddha had to get Jayant to agree to the terms, which our wonderful groom-to-be was very much reluctant to do. He only agreed when Aniruddha offered to pay off all his debts, get him a job away from Mumbai and pay for his and Latika's travel abroad. In vain, your Mama tried to convince Aniruddha to let him bear the expenses. Latika is our niece, after all, and it would've been our duty. But that young man just wouldn't listen. Instead, he had your Mama promise not to divulge any details of the arrangement or Aniruddha's part in this entire affair.

Your Mama even asked him why he felt obliged to do so much and he revealed that he had known Jayant for a while, even witnessed another affair in which he came close to ruining a girl's good name. He feels that, had he made Jayant's character public knowledge then, perhaps all of this wouldn't have happened. Which seems a little far-fetched, if you ask me.

I, as you well know, believe the real reason he went to such lengths is his affection for you.

Which is why I was surprised to receive your letter. You see, I was under the impression that you were aware of all Aniruddha did – the possibility that all this was done without your knowledge never struck me. That he should have taken such efforts to help our family and that too without breathing a word of it to you! I remember, Ila, when I came to Mumbai last, before this unfortunate affair, you spoke of him in a manner that suggested he was somewhat self-centred and arrogant but if I were to put my finger on it, I'd say his flaw is his ability to get his own way in matters. And we should be utterly thankful he did in the matter of your sister. Because, all said and done, her story could've had quite a different ending had he not. One that she seemed entirely oblivious to, by the way, despite me trying to explain it to her as baldly as I could.

I know she is your sister, but she is such a different creature from you and Juee as to confound the mind.

309

I will end this letter by saying that I know you plan to work and never marry, but should you change your mind on that front, it would be wonderful if you could find a man like Aniruddha. Indeed, it would be extremely fortunate if it were him – he invited us for lunch to his home in Pune and it is positively breath-taking! I certainly wouldn't mind seeing you there, as the lady of the house.

   Your loving,
   Ujoo Mami

I cannot begin to describe the effect Mami's letter had on me. How could a man be so generous? That Aniruddha helped find Latika was astounding enough, but what he did for her afterwards? What he did for Jayant, a man he despises so deeply? And the money it must've cost! Forget all that travelling from Matheran to Goa to Pune, but paying off Jayant's debts? Getting him a job? Paying for his and Latika's fare to Kuwait? I had no idea how much it must've all come to, but my guess was the bill ran into thousands, if not tens of thousands. So what if Aniruddha was well-off? Paying that kind of money just so my idiot sister's reputation, and the reputation of our family, stays intact? It was too much.

   Aai-Nana didn't know about any of this, but even if they did, I knew Nana would never be able to pay him back. And in the same way, I knew that this debt couldn't stay unpaid. If my family couldn't pay him back, I would have to.

   I took a deep breath and folded the inland letter. All this while, I had intended to get a job so I could get away from Aai and her obsession with getting me married off. But now, that had to come second. First and foremost, I needed a job – any job – to pay back Aniruddha Darshetkar. I had no idea how

I would do it: the starting salary for anyone, even a junior clerk, was quite meagre from what I heard. But bit by bit, rupee by rupee, I'd pay him back. And I'd tell him so the next time we met.

I just hoped I didn't get tongue-tied when we came face to face again.

THIRTY

My chance came sooner than I had expected.

A couple of days after receiving Ujoo Mami's letter, I had gone down to buy onions for Aai, from the Vasaiwala* who would set up his cart in the society compound. On the stairs, I ran into the postman, who handed me our mail and saved himself a trip to the second floor. I glanced through it and found one envelope addressed to me. I tore it open and gasped.

---

*   Like most big cities, Mumbai doesn't produce its own fruit and vegetables. Where is the space for a farm or an orchard, when builders are eyeing every available inch, trying to configure it into a one-room-kitchen or a 3 BHK. So, Mumbai's fresh produce comes from its outskirts, becoming slightly less fresh along the journey. In the 1970s, the outskirts of Mumbai meant Vasai, known for its wholesale agriculture market, its creek and for being really bloody far away. Vegetable vendors from Vasai were called, imaginatively enough, Vasaiwalas.

It was a letter from Indu Enterprises. The company had stood out among the job vacancy ads because there were hardly ever any private companies on that page, as you usually got a job at one of those places because you knew someone who knew someone who was the neighbour of someone who worked there. But I had applied for the post of junior clerk anyway, and now they were asking me to come for a written test next week!

I took a deep breath, trying to curb my excitement. *No point getting all riled up when you haven't even given the interview,* I told myself. But there was definitely a spring in my step as I clattered down the stairs to the Vasaiwala's cart.

Sudha Kelkar was standing there, rattling off a long list of vegetables to the man. 'Three kilo potatoes, two kilo onions, one kilo carrots, one kilo cucumbers, one kilo brinjal.' She nodded amiably to me as she handed him two large cloth bags.

'Having guests over, is it?' I asked.

'Aga, yes. His* friends are coming for lunch tomorrow, na,' she said absently, then gave me a hesitant look. 'Actually . . . it's Sadanand and Aniruddha. I wasn't sure whether to say . . . what with Jueetai and all.'

'Oh, don't worry,' I said in a carefree manner that completely hid the butterflies that had suddenly erupted in my stomach. 'That's all in the past now.'

'How is Latika doing?' she asked, picking up her now full cloth bags. 'Have you had a letter from her?'

---

*   The English language does not have a respectful second or third person pronoun, unlike Marathi and Hindi. Sudha is referring to her husband, her 'aho' in this case.

'No,' I replied. 'But she's like a cat, you know. Always lands on her feet.' *And thinks of absolutely nobody else but herself*, I added in my mind.

But as I lugged my onions up the flight of stairs, Latika was the farthest thing from my mind. Aniruddha was coming tomorrow! And Sadanand too. I would have to tell Juee. She needed to be prepared. But I had forgotten how opaque my elder sister was. Because when I broke the news, Juee merely nodded and said mildly, 'Oh, is it? How interesting.'

Aai, on the other hand, went into paroxyms of joy. 'I have to invite him over for lunch,' she said, her chin firmly set. 'One taste of our Juee's cooking and the man is bound to—'

'You will do no such thing,' Nana pronounced from the armchair, where he was reading a book. 'You have made yourself look like a fool quite enough where that young man is concerned, without a repeat performance being needed.'

Aai ignored him and cupped Juee's face in her hands. 'You just see, my girl,' she said happily. 'This time, I will make sure he falls for you!'

Juee gave her a thin smile and said nothing. Later, however, when we were alone, she confided in me. 'I wish Aai didn't make such a big thing of this. He is simply coming to visit his friend. He may not even meet us. And that would probably be for the best. Not that I would be bothered if I run into him, you understand. We are only acquaintances, after all.'

I didn't know what to say. But I had the feeling that she was saying all this to convince herself, rather than me.

The next day dawned and the butterflies in my stomach seemed to have multiplied. *Stop it*, I admonished myself.

314

As far as Aniruddha is concerned, you are nothing more than his friend's neighbour now.

But then, asked a voice inside me, why had he gone to such lengths to help us?

Charity, I told it. Ujoo Mami is mistaken. These rich people always look for some cause or other to sponsor. Perhaps Latika was this year's cause for him. Let it go.

But I didn't. I took extra care while getting dressed. Applied kajal, although I had absolutely nowhere to go. So did Juee, but I didn't comment. I didn't have to. My sister kept turning her head towards the door at the slightest sound from the corridor, then catching herself and settling down to reading the homework her tuition students had turned in.

But from her blank stare, it seemed like she wasn't actually reading.

And then, there came a knock on the door. Juee sat stock still, looking at the notebook in front of her, transfixed.

I got up to answer it but Aai beat me to it.

'Arre, Sadanandrao?' she cooed. 'What a wonderful surprise! Come in, come in!'

Sadanand entered with a hesitant smile, and behind him came Aniruddha, his usual serious expression on his face. I tried not to stare. Had he always been this handsome? Gods above. I hastened to the kitchen to bring water for them as Juee cleared away the notebooks. When I returned, the two men were seated on the divan with Aai hovering over them like a concerned bee.

'What will you have?' she asked. 'Tea? Coffee? Sarbat?'

'N-no, nothing, thank you,' Sadanand stammered, looking awkwardly from Aai to Juee.

'Nonsense!' Aai said, with a mock-offended smile. 'This

315

is the first time you have come to our home. How can I let you leave without having anything at all?'

'We were just at Arun's so . . . so we thought we would . . .' Sadanand's words died on his lips as he caught Juee's gaze.

'Perhaps later, then.' Aai beamed good-naturedly. 'It is so good to see you after so long.'

Sadanand agreed that it had indeed been a while since he had met her.

'So much has happened in that time, you know,' Aai continued, a touch of pride in her voice. 'Our Latika? Juee's younger sister? She is married now. Nice young man. Very handsome. Perhaps you know him – Jayant Waknis? They are settled in foreign now.'

Sadanand confessed that he had only met the man once but offered his congratulations anyway. I tried not to look in Aniruddha's direction at the mention of Jayant's name, and failed.

His face remained as composed as ever.

'It's such a relief when one's daughters are well-settled.' Aai gave a happy sigh. 'But look at me, just going on and on. You say – what will you have? I could whip up a snack for you.'

'Nothing, thank you,' Sadanand said. 'We just had lunch at Arun's and . . .' A quick glance at Juee, who blushed. 'Um . . . we have . . . another appointment . . .'

'Oh, you young men!' Aai said, with a motherly affection I hadn't seen a single trace of before. 'Always so busy! Do you even have time to eat? See how thin you look! You need someone to fatten you back up, with some good home food, mark my words!' Sadanand laughed awkwardly but Aai continued. 'I'll tell you what. I'll let you go today, but you

316

must promise to come for lunch later this week. Our Juee is an excellent cook. You had said you missed homemade puran polis, no? She'll make some for you . . .'

'That's very kind . . .' Sadanand began.

'Not at all!' Aai waved him away. 'So shall we say Saturday? Around one o'clock? Or do you eat later than that?'

'Oh . . . uh . . . one is fine,' Sadanand said, with the air of someone who had just found himself in a small room with no door or window in sight.

Throughout this exchange, Aniruddha had sat silently. He may have been part of the divan's upholstery for all the attention Aai paid him. This, of course, would have been rude of her anyway, but knowing what I did of how much he had done for her daughter, the slight seemed particularly offensive.

'Aai . . .' I whispered to her, hoping the men couldn't hear. 'What are you doing? Invite his friend also.'

Aai's genial expression waned a bit, but she recovered and, looking at Aniruddha, added in a polite voice, 'You are also invited, by the way.'

Aniruddha thanked her and, a few moments later, the two men left. He had not looked even once in my direction, forget making eye contact.

I sighed. His rejection I could have borne, perhaps. But his indifference had been like an icy knife to the heart.

THIRTY-ONE

Juee and I spent the next couple of days nearly elbow-deep in puran, with Aai swooping in at the last minute to keep aside the best puran polis for Nana and Sadanand. The slightly burned ones – which I liked better anyway – were for the rest of us.

'You may as well get used to compromise,' Aai told Juee, brushing off some flour that had stuck to her cheek. 'You'll be a wife soon.'

The phrase 'many a slip between cup and lip' was entirely unknown to my mother, clearly. But I couldn't help but feel hopeful for Juee. I had seen the way Sadanand had looked at her when he and Aniruddha had dropped in the other day. The man was still besotted with her – it was plainer than the Deccan plateau.

I tried to talk to her about it when Aai had left us alone in the kitchen, but my sister remained as sphinx-like as ever.

'I wish Aai wouldn't bother with all this,' she said, as

she neatly rolled a puran poli on the wooden polpat. 'It won't make a bit of difference where Sadanand's feelings are concerned.'

'Mmm, you're right,' I said, breaking off a piece of a hot poli and popping it in my mouth. 'If weeks of separation didn't affect the way he feels about you, I doubt a home-cooked meal will.'

She turned her face away from me. 'Don't tease,' she said. 'I'm sure he's getting enough home-cooked meals from Gauri Darshetkar.' She sniffed. 'Besides, it's not like *I* feel anything for him anymore . . .'

'Of course, of course,' I nodded sagely, reaching out for another piece of the poli, only to have my hand swatted away. 'And by that, of course, you mean you are still very much in love with him?'

'He just . . . he upped and left, without so much as a goodbye, Ila!' Juee turned around from the kitchen counter to face me. 'Why on earth would I still feel any love for him?'

'You do, though.'

She glared at me for a moment, then sagged. 'Yes.' She sighed. 'But I really don't want to. It's not fair. He can't just . . . I shouldn't . . . I should be able to stay angry at him for the way he behaved, but I just . . .' She threw up her hands helplessly and I gave her a sympathetic grin.

'Tell you what,' I said, feeding her a morsel of puran poli, 'marry him and then get him to make up for what he put you through. He seems pretty smitten, if you ask me. He'll want to make up.'

Juee gave me a sideways look. 'Since when were you such an expert in these things?' She raised her eyebrows meaningfully. 'Or am I missing something?'

319

'You aren't, but *I* may be,' I told her, as my eyes fell on the big clock on the kitchen wall. 'My train!'

I had almost forgotten my interview! I had to arrive on time, come what may. There was no way I was missing it. A company could give a candidate a second chance, but a third one? Hah. Unlikely.

I ran and changed into the cotton sari that I had starched and ironed the night before, all ready for the next day. Ten minutes later, my hair tied into a neat plait, I rushed out of the house.

When I returned three hours later, I found Aai in the living room, surrounded by plates full of cooling puran polis.

'Oh, are you finally home, Baisaheb?' she asked, sarcastically. 'Or would you like to gallivant outdoors for some more time while we slave away at home?'

'Who *wouldn't* love to be out of the house when greeted with so much love?' I said with a wry smile that made her frown.

'Don't be too clever,' she told me. 'Go wash up and help with dinner. Poor Juee has been making these polis all day. She must be tired.'

I did as I was asked, praying that Saturday would come soon so this circus would finally be over.

Miraculously enough, it did. And with it came Sadanand and Aniruddha, the former holding a packet of mawa cakes, which he handed to Aai.

'How thoughtful!' she exclaimed. 'But why you went through so much bother?'

We left them talking to Nana as we busied ourselves setting up lunch, which was served pangat-style, with Nana,

320

Sadanand and Aniruddha sitting cross-legged on striped satranjees, their plates filled with a variety of delicacies. There was carrot-tomato koshimbir, coriander chutney, fried kurdais, steamed rice, plain polis, potato bhaaji, and the star of the show – puran polis with kataachi aamti.

The kurdais had been fried last of all and the unpleasant task of standing in the blazing heat of the kitchen and dunking them in and out of the hot oil had fallen to me, as Aai had insisted Juee freshen up and look presentable before the men arrived.

Which she now did, in a pale pink sari, smelling of Pond's talc, not a hair out of place. I, on the other hand, had sweat patches in the armpits of my blouse; beads of perspiration streaming down my temples; and my hair was limp, with tendrils sticking to my face, despite the fact that I had splashed water on my face after the godforsaken kurdais had been done.

If Aniruddha had found me even vaguely attractive in Wai, today would be the day he would re-examine that opinion, for sure.

I stifled a yawn. We had been up since six in the morning preparing this spread and I wished desperately that I could sneak into the kitchen and make myself some tea. But that was not to be thought of – we were to be at hand, to serve the three men whatever item they needed more of, while Aai engaged in the traditional activity of aagraha.*

---

*   Aagraha is essentially insisting that someone eats more of something. It can take many forms. One involves suggesting that the eater is bashful, too shy to ask for a second (or third) helping and then piling said helping on their plate, despite their protests that they

'Arre, what is this?' She pouted at Sadanand, ignoring the frown of disapproval on Nana's face. 'Only two puran polis? And you such a young man! Juee! Serve him one more, come on!'

Juee gave Sadanand a questioning look, but he only stared at her. At which point, she blushed and came forward, crouching before Sadanand to place another puran poli on his plate.

'Eat your fill,' Aai told him genially. 'Juee's polis are so light, you know, one more won't make much of a difference. But then, she is a wonderful cook anyway. So many things she makes better than me . . .' And to my horror, she began listing them.

I glanced at Aniruddha to see how he was taking my mother's transparent one-woman campaign to get Juee hitched to his friend. To my surprise, he wasn't paying her any attention at all. His gaze seemed to be focused on Juee, and I saw him look intently from her to Sadanand, almost as if assessing them.

No matter how pointedly I looked at him, he didn't meet my eye.

I sighed inwardly. Well, I told myself, he couldn't have made his intentions towards you any clearer than if he'd taken out an ad in the newspaper. Zero interest. In the great book of his life, you and what happened in Wai are barely a

---

aren't shy, just totally full. Another way involves emotional blackmail, as in: 'Eat this for me, won't you eat it? Even for *me*?' A third is just exaggerating the past, as in: 'In our days, we used to eat twenty-twenty puris at a time. You young people these days have no appetite! Have one more, nothing happens!' Whichever form aagraha takes, it only ends in antacids.

footnote. Nobody reads footnotes.* That's why they're at the bottom of the page.

Still, even if he had nothing to say to me, *I* certainly had things I needed to tell him. So after they had eaten, I left the clearing up to Juee and Malu and boldly ventured towards him as he stood in the balcony, looking out. Sadanand was using the washroom and I wouldn't get an opportunity like this again.

'Supari?' I asked, holding out the small steel container with the mixture of roasted aniseed, coriander seed cores, rock sugar and crushed betel nuts in my hands.

He cupped his palm and I spooned a small amount into it.

'Thank you for what you did for Latika,' I blurted out.

He looked startled but didn't say anything.

'I'm sorry for the way my mother has been behaving,' I said quickly. 'If she knew what you had done . . .'

'I didn't want anyone to know,' he said quietly. 'Not even you.'

'Be that as it may,' I was speaking very fast now, 'I can't un-know it. And I'm so grateful. My whole family is in your debt. And I . . . I know you spent a lot of money . . . I will pay you back . . .'

'That's not—'

'It will take . . . some time.' My stomach felt as if there were a thousand bees in it. 'But I am . . .' I took a breath to steady myself. 'I have given interviews, I'll get a job and once I do, I promise . . .'

---

* Present company excluded, obviously.

He opened his mouth to say something, but at that moment, I heard Aai call out to me: 'Ila! What are you doing there? Sadanandrao has finished his meal – come, give him some supari!' And without any change in her volume she turned to Sadanand and said, 'Juee has made the supari too! Really, everything her hands touch she transforms into something wonderful! It's almost as if the Goddess Annapurna herself has blessed her!'

I resisted the urge to smack my forehead and, with an apologetic smile at Aniruddha, I went back inside.

THIRTY-TWO

Over the next few days, Sadanand's visits increased. He'd have very believable reasons for them too: he happened to be in the area and thought he'd drop in; he had work nearby and thought he'd ask after us; he'd had a hankering for Saurashtra's farsan so he had come all the way to buy some and had bought too much, so he had thought he'd bring us some.

Like I said, *very* believable reasons.

Aniruddha accompanied him the first few times. Not that *that* made a difference to my life, because the man didn't speak two full sentences to me the whole time. He obviously was very embarrassed by my offer to pay him. Probably thought I was ruining his charitable gesture. So why was he accompanying his friend every time? Why couldn't he just avoid me? I'm sure he wanted to. The girl who had refused his marriage proposal and insulted him into the bargain. What sane man *wouldn't* avoid me? But no, he just had to come with Sadanand, sit quietly in his chair and observe us like we were a cricket match, without speaking unless spoken to. So . . . so . . . *aggravating*!

And just when I had decided that this behaviour was aggravating, he suddenly stopped coming over. Which, of course, was so much worse. One afternoon, Sadanand came alone and informed us that Aniruddha had returned to Pune. He would be back in Mumbai in a few weeks, depending on his work schedule. I wanted to ask for more details, but Aai jumped in and started telling Sadanand how he must now feel all alone in the city without his friend and insisted that he come over for home-cooked meals more often, because eating too much outside food could ruin his stomach.

Now, at this point, he *could* have mentioned that he had Prabha to cook for him at home, but he didn't. Which was a good sign and gave me hope, and distracted me from the fact that Aniruddha's absence was . . . affecting me.

More than I liked, at that.

Sadanand would join us for dinner every other night, and after dinner he'd stand with Nana in the common corridor and talk. I could tell Nana approved of him, despite having initially forbidden Aai from chasing after him. Sadanand didn't put on the airs his sister did, and he knew how to listen. He put up with Aai's overfamiliarity too – and I couldn't help but notice that she, who had made such a big deal of Vishnu's stay with us meaning more money spent on groceries, didn't utter a single word of complaint in that regard when it came to Sadanand. I suppose she noticed the quiet pleasure on Juee's face during each of his visits and decided that her elder daughter deserved some joy that didn't involve fulfilling the wishes of her parents.

326

One day, Aai invited him over for lunch instead of dinner. It was a weekday, which meant Nana would be at college and Malu in school. It was also the very day I had to appear for an interview at Indu Enterprises, who had sent a letter a few days before saying that I had passed their test. This was the next step and if I cleared it, I could get the job. The interview was at 12 p.m., which meant that I couldn't help Aai and Juee with preparing lunch. This earned me a frown from Aai, but Juee just spooned a bit of curd on my right palm before I left, and as I gulped it down whispered, 'Good luck! I'm sure you'll pass!'

To be honest, I had been nervous – it was my first job interview, after all. But from what I could tell, it went pretty well. The man conducting my interview, a Mr Kadam, was in his mid-forties. He had a kind face and a reassuring manner that made it seem like I was having a conversation with my uncle, rather than being interrogated by a stranger. Who all were at home? What were my interests? Why did I want to work? Why at Indu Enterprises? I answered his questions as honestly as possible. When I said that I wanted the job so I could help my father support our family, Mr Kadam nodded in approval.

He told me I would hear from them in a few days and, as I rose to leave, he held out his hand. I must say, as I shook it, I suddenly felt very grown-up indeed. Not that I felt like a child at home but that gesture – shaking hands with a man, whom I was meeting on a professional basis – somehow, it made everything seem more real: the job search, the possibility of me getting a job and leaving home – just like that, it all seemed possible.

By the time I returned home, the others had finished

lunch. I was ravenous, barely patient enough to wash my hands and feet before eating. I just wanted to flop down in the living room and attack the food.

But Aai had other plans.

As Sadanand and Juee sat together chatting companionably on the divan, Aai told them,

'You two sit and talk. Ila, just come into the kitchen with me.'

As hungry as I was, I understood. She wanted Juee and Sadanand to have some time alone. It wouldn't be untoward as we would be in the very next room. So, ignoring Juee's startled expression, I followed her in. Wordlessly, she served me food and, in a low voice, asked me to eat as slowly as possible.

I tried to obey, but it was difficult. A growling stomach can really make you eat like a Neanderthal. I ignored Aai's disapproving head shake as I wolfed down my lunch. From the living room, we could hear Juee and Sadanand, their voices a low hum.

About half an hour later, Juee called out for Aai.

'I'll take your leave now,' Sadanand said, when we came out of the kitchen. His eyes looked bright, brighter than they had been some time ago.

'Of course.' Aai smiled. 'When will you visit again?'

'Soon,' he said, looking directly at Juee, before smiling at the rest of us. 'Very soon.' And then he was gone.

Aai raised her eyebrows at Juee, who blushed and smiled and nodded. There were tears in her eyes.

'He . . . he asked?' Aai said, her voice shaking, as if she was too scared to believe it.

Juee nodded again. The next moment, Aai hugged her

tightly and mother and daughter were laughing and crying in succession. I couldn't help but join in. The beatific expression on Juee's expression was enough provocation. What a far cry from those silent tears all those months ago!

When Aai finally let her go, wiping her eyes with the corner of her padar, I threw my arms around my sister. 'Congratulations,' I whispered in her ear.

It all made sense to me now – the way Aniruddha had sat and observed Sadanand and Juee. Something in my sister's expressions this time around must have convinced him that she genuinely had feelings for his friend. Whatever objections he had before, he must have withdrawn them now and paved the way for Sadanand to finally express his own feelings to Juee.

I was thrilled for her, as well as me. What a wonderful day this was for both of us. She was one step closer to marrying a decent man whom she loved, and better still, who loved her back. And I was one step closer to . . . getting a job and moving out. On my own. Alone.

Which was fine, of course. No, not fine, it was good. It was *great*. It was exactly what I had wanted all along. So I should be happy. I *was* happy. Of course. Why wouldn't I be? This was the best course for me. Definitely. Yes. Getting a job would mean being away from Aai and her barbs. It would mean independence and dignity and endless cups of tea, should my heart so desire. What else did a girl need in life? *Love?* a small voice in me suggested, but I ignored it. Love is for optimists. And the kind of love that makes you want to marry someone? That is in short supply. Oh, some get lucky. Padmakar Mama and Ujoo Mami, for instance, who hadn't let even a monumental thing like being unable to have children get in the way of their love for each other. I hoped Juee and Sadanand had *that* kind of love. The kind that makes you bring out the best in each other. The kind that helps you stand together in the face of the worst. The kind that grows with time.

But love like that isn't everyone's destiny. Most people have to settle for the cut-rate version. The kind that begins with attraction – to a pretty face or a charming manner – and ends in bickering. With the entire middle portion being spent realising that beauty fades with age, and charm evaporates with circumstance. And that the very thing that made you love a person once upon a time, could make them difficult to tolerate for the rest of your life. You just had to look at my parents to see that.

But I didn't say any of this to anyone. Least of all to Juee, who looked absolutely consumed with happiness. When Malu and Nana returned, they received the news with equal joy. Malu looked bewildered but pleased, and shyly asked if she might have a new dress for the wedding. Nana simply kissed the top of Juee's head and smiled, before retiring to the bedroom with Aai to discuss the details of everything to come.

Their conversation continued through dinner. Aai was in favour of having a small engagement but Nana insisted they have the wedding soon, once he had had a formal talk with Sadanand about it. Then the subject moved to finances, and my parents left us to make up the mattresses for bedtime, once more returning to the bedroom to discuss the matter in private.

How I wished at that moment that I already had a job! I would've gladly handed them my entire salary to plan Juee's wedding. She deserved a decent affair. I said as much to her as we lay side by side on our mattresses that night, Malu snoring gently on hers next to Juee.

Juee simply waved me off. 'None of that matters,' she said happily. 'All that matters is how he feels about me. He told me he has felt this way from the day we met. He thought *I* didn't feel the same way, can you believe it?'

'I don't.'

'He did, though. Apparently, his sister told him that. That I didn't feel that way about him, I mean. She even told him she had asked me and I had said so! The liar!'

'I had told you so . . .'

'I know! But the lengths that girl can go to! She didn't even tell him I was in Pune, let alone that she had met me! Why would she do a thing like that, Ila? And after pretending to be my friend!'

'Well, she probably wanted Sadanand to marry Gauri Darshetkar, so she could better pave the way for marrying Aniruddha,' I replied, staring at the ceiling. 'You didn't feature in that plan. So she took you out of the equation.'

'Worthless creature!' Juee muttered. Then she sighed. 'Still, it doesn't matter anymore. Sadanand knows what she did. And he loves me. That's enough for me.'

'Really?' I teased. 'It's enough? So you don't want a nice wedding, with some fine silk saris and pretty jewellery?'

'I would marry him in the clothes I'm wearing, in a temple, if it came to it.' She sighed again. 'Or have a court marriage. It doesn't matter, as long as I get to marry *him*.'

I smiled to myself, a little wistfully. What must it feel like, to be so happy? To find someone you didn't just not mind marrying, but someone you couldn't wait to marry? My treacherous mind threw up a picture of Aniruddha, but I scolded it till the picture evaporated. I did not want to waste my time on some one-sided love. And anything involving Aniruddha would definitely be one-sided. I had seen neither hide nor hair of the man since he had left for Pune. I was clearly not on his mind. He needed to stop being on mine! I could do this. I could push him out of my mind. I had more important things to think of, after all. I just had to try really hard and I'd forget him. How difficult could it be? All it took was some willpower.

I willed myself to stop thinking of him completely. Of his face. His smile. That serious expression. Those eyes.

It didn't work.

THIRTY-THREE

There is a phrase in Marathi which goes: 'Nakteechya lagnaala satraashe vighna.' Literally, it means that the wedding of a snub-nosed girl has seventeen hundred obstacles in its path. Figuratively, it means having a ton of problems while trying to get something done.

Juee, of course, has a fine, straight, aristocratic sort of a nose, and I am happy to say that the phrase did not hold true either literally or figuratively in her wedding preparations. That being said, there were an awful lot of preparations to be done.

Since Latika's wedding had been a hurried, haphazard and, above all, extremely private affair, Aai insisted that her eldest daughter's wedding, at least, should be 'done properly'. 'God knows when I will have a chance to marry off a daughter next,' she had said with a meaningful glare at me, which I had ignored.

She could snipe all she wanted. I had received an

appointment letter from Indu Enterprises and I was going to join the company on the first of February, come what may. The earliest auspicious muhurta that the pandit had been able to find for Juee and Sadanand's wedding was mid-January and as soon as we had bid her goodbye, I would begin looking for a good working women's hostel to move into. Nana would miss me, but there was nothing for it. As the world was fond of saying, a daughter had to leave her parents' house sooner or later. I was just taking a different route out.

In the meantime, I helped Aai haggle for wedding clothes and gifts, helped Nana proof-read the invitation patrika and oohed and aahed over Juee's beautiful yellow silk sari – as tradition demanded, a gift from Padmakar Mama and Ujoo Mami.

One morning, I was about to go to the post office to send out the invitations to our relatives, when I heard a commotion from the quadrangle below. Kelkar Kaku called out to Aai from her balcony, which was adjacent to ours. Moments later, I heard Aai's voice in the balcony, full of excitement and curiosity.

'Agabai, such a big car!'

'And there's a driver with a cap and everything!' Malu exclaimed, from beside her. 'Is it some film star?'

'Why would a film star come to our building?' I said, whacking her playfully on her head as I stood next to her.

'Why would Latika be settled in foreign?' she shot back. 'Absolutely nothing that's happening these days makes any sense anyway!'

I grinned and leaned out over the balcony railing to look at the car. A deep green Chevrolet Bel Air was indeed standing in the middle of the quadrangle. A white-uniformed driver was speaking politely to a man who looked suspiciously like Arun Kelkar.

Arun nodded vehemently then turned and pointed up at our floor.

Directly at me.

The window of the Chevrolet rolled down and, to my amazement, I saw the surly face of Kaveribai Bhagwat lean out of it slightly. She caught sight of me and gestured to me to come downstairs.

'I'll just go see what she wants,' I told Aai, with a sigh.

'You know that lady?' she asked, dumbfounded.

'It's Kaveribai Bhagwat,' I told her. 'The lady who gave Vishnu the house and everything. We met when I was in Wai.'

'Is it? Agabai! Invite her for tea, will you? I'll just make some. Malu, run to the Irani and get us some kharis! Tell him I'll send the money later.'

I resisted the urge to tell her that Kaveribai would rather eat glass than have tea and maska khari in a middle-class house, and headed downstairs.

When I reached the car, Kaveribai beckoned at me through the window and asked, 'Is there a place where we can talk in private?' I was intrigued to say the least, but I told her there was a public park nearby which was virtually empty at this time of day. She made a face, but gestured to me to get into the car.

I looked up to where Aai was standing and, through a series of complicated hand movements, communicated that I was going somewhere with Kaveribai and would return shortly. With equally complicated gestures, Aai expressed her permission for this trip.

We drove in silence to the park. The driver dropped us at the main gate, then drove off after Kaveribai instructed him to return in twenty minutes. I pointed to a bench a little away from the entrance gate and followed Kaveribai as she marched towards it and seated herself on one end. I sat at a respectful distance and looked at her enquiringly.

She was wearing a rust-brown irkal cotton sari, with gold earrings set with corals and pearls and a matching necklace. Her expression was dour.

'So,' she began. 'I think you know why I am here.'

I frowned and confessed that I didn't.

'Don't lie to me, girl!' she snapped. 'This innocent act might fool the simple-minded, but I am no fool!'

'I have no idea what you are talking about,' I assured her.

'Oh, is that so? So you know of nothing, no ridiculous rumour, that would force me to travel all the way from Wai to this ghastly city in person?'

'I really don't.'

'Have you no shame, lying barefaced like that?' she demanded, her voice rising. 'Alright, then. Let me spell it out for you. A few days ago, a most appalling report reached me, from a person whom I trust. This report suggested that you are going to wed my Aniruddha. Naturally, I laughed at the very idea! Imagine! Someone like you. So . . . so ordinary, from a family of no consequence. Marrying a Darshetkar? That too, someone as distinguished as Aniruddha?'

I took a deep breath to steady myself. I was torn between sheer surprise and undiluted rage. We had all been taught since childhood to respect our elders. We were told to touch their feet and listen to their advice and hold our tongues when they criticised us, because they were our elders after all. They knew more than us. But whatever this 'more' was, it clearly didn't include basic courtesy in Kaveribai's case.

'I have to admire your confidence,' she said, with a sneer. 'Thinking you can trap someone so clearly superior to you in every way, into marriage. Did you think it would be *that* easy? Did you think Aniruddha would just forget the differences between you and him? Did you think we would *allow* him to forget?' Her laugh was short and forceful, like a bark. 'Perhaps you did think all of that. But thinking and happening are two different things. The moment I heard of this . . . this nonsense, I knew it couldn't possibly be true. I just needed to hear you confirm it, because deny it all you will, I know for certain that it was *you* and your family that started this rumour in the first place!' There were flecks of spittle at the corner of her lips. It was a truly disgusting sight. 'Well?' she demanded. 'Go on. Admit it! Tell me to my face that this rumour is completely false!'

Polite behaviour is called shishthachaar in Marathi. But here's the funny thing. Condescension? Acting stuck-up? That's simply called being shishtha. Kaveribai seemed unable to distinguish between the two. Every time she opened her mouth, all that came out was snobbery and, honestly, I was getting pretty irritated by it now.

So, I pursed my lips and countered it with some finely tuned shishthachaar. 'No.' My voice was calm, my gaze steady, my smile sweet. 'I don't have to say anything to you.'

'What?' Kaveribai's face contorted with rage. 'How dare you! Perhaps you are unaware of this, but Aniruddha will not, *cannot* marry you. He is to marry Ashalata. *My* daughter. This was decided when both of them were children, and it is

337

an arrangement I intend to see fulfilled. And he *will* honour it, since it was made between me and Mai, his late mother!'

'Hmm,' I said. 'Well, if all that's settled as you say, why are you here? Does Aniruddha know you're here?'

'He . . .' She hesitated. 'That is to say, it was always understood that he would eventually marry my daughter, after they had both grown up. I just have to remind him of the understanding. And once I do, the wedding will definitely happen, you understand? So answer me once and for all: have you agreed to marry Aniruddha?'

At this point, it would have been fun to say yes, just to rile her further. But that's the trouble with bringing up children to be fundamentally honest: they can't just lie for fun, no matter how much they want to. Mentally cursing Aai-Nana for raising me well, I replied, 'No, I haven't.'

'Good.' Kaveribai gave a regal nod, her expression slightly mollified. 'And do you swear not to accept if ever such a proposal is made?'

I hesitated. Of course there was no chance of Aniruddha ever asking me to marry him again. But . . . just because there wasn't a chance didn't mean I couldn't . . . hope. Although this hope would ultimately be just as painful as the reality of the situation.

'I will swear to no such thing,' I replied, meeting her gaze with a steely one of my own

'What do you think you are, huh?' she shouted. 'You think I will let some slip of a girl from godknowswhere spoil my plans, you fool? Then not only are you unbelievably daft, you are also very much mistaken.'

'As are you,' I said, getting up, 'if you think I am going to quietly sit here and let you go on insulting me like this.'

She rose too, and drew herself to her full height. 'You don't know me, my girl,' she said, her voice a silken threat. 'I am not someone you want as an enemy. Swear you won't marry Aniruddha and crawl back to your wretched one-room-kitchen life. Or else, I promise you, you will wish you had never met me!'

I sighed. 'I *already* wish that, Kaveribai,' I told her. 'And, for your information, it's a one-*bedroom-hall*-kitchen.' And with that, I marched out of the park, leaving the old hag spluttering in indignation.

About time she learned what *that* feels like – she is the cause of it in others often enough.

THIRTY-FOUR

Ai bought the story I made up on my way home. It's a mark of how giddy with joy she was because she did not once wonder why Kaveribai Bhagwat – that patroness of our cousin, in whose veins ran the blood of godknowswhich nobles – had simply stopped by to extend her congratulations on Juee's wedding. In her current state, this was an event that seemed entirely plausible – she didn't even think to ask why, if she had come to congratulate us, had she not actually come into our house. If she had, I would have invented arthritis for the old woman, if not downright osteoporosis.

Still, I was determined to put the whole episode behind me and submerge myself once more in preparations for the wedding. But one's very best intentions can come to nothing if Fate conspires otherwise. In this case, Fate's agent was Vishnubhat.

A letter addressed to Nana from Vishnu arrived at our

door a week later. Nana began reading it with his forehead furrowed, then a few moments later laughed uproariously.

'Stop reading jokes in the newspaper and go for a bath!' Aai called out from inside the kitchen, where she was making Juee's favourite sudha-ras* for lunch.

'It's not a joke . . .' Nana called back. 'Or maybe it is.' He shook his head in amusement at me. 'I think our poor Vishnu has finally taken leave of his senses, Ila. Listen to this.' He began reading from the letter.

Respected Mama . . . Saa.Na.Vi.Vee. . . We are writing to congratulate you on the good fortune of your daughter Chi. Sau. Ka.† Juee. News has reached us of her impending wedding and we await the receipt of the wedding card inviting us and our fairer half for the same. It is a momentous occasion of much joy for your family, a far cry from the recent unfortunate events that it would be best to never mention again.

Nana sighed. 'Then why are you mentioning them, you fool? Anyway. He goes on to say . . .'

---

* A sticky, delicious dessert made from sugar syrup, lemon juice and charoli nuts.

† A bride-to-be is addressed as Chiranjeev Saubhagya Kankshini – a young lady hoping to be blessed with marriage. This is mostly done in wedding invitation cards, possibly to single her out from the fifteen other names that usually make their way into a card, including but not limited to, the parents of the bride and groom, their siblings, siblings-in-law, parents-in-law and assorted nephews, nieces, pets and neighbours.

Although this is not widely known, we believe there is another cause for congratulations. May we offer our compliments, Mama, on the soon-to-occur wedding of our cousin Chi. Sau. Ka. Ila, with none other than Kaveribai's dear relative Aniruddha Darshetkar? We understand Kaveribai is not happy at all with this match and her ire has been deadly to behold. Aware of our links with your family, we, as well as our spouse, have stayed clear of Kaveribai's wada for a few days now, but are sure to be welcomed back there once Baisaheb's anger has cooled down. Indeed, Mama, we wonder if this is the most pragmatic match for our younger cousin, given the seeds of discord it is spreading among her prospective husband's family. However, you are the family elder and we are confident that your decision in this matter will take into regard what is best for the family. We remain,

Your obedient nephew,
Vishnu Chhatre

Nana raised his eyebrows as he folded the letter, snickering to himself. 'Well, Ila,' he asked. 'What do you say? Should we invite your cousin to Mumbai, so he can have his head checked?' He wiped tears of mirth from his eyes. 'Can you imagine?' he asked. 'Aniruddha Darshetkar, of all people! I've never even seen him glance at anyone beneath his social stature – which is *everybody*, from the looks of it. Him! Wanting to marry *you*! I haven't laughed like this in weeks!'

He went into the kitchen to show the letter to Aai, laughing all the way. I laughed with him, but my heart wasn't in it. Who on earth was spreading these rumours? And why was the world in general believing them? I couldn't think of a single person who even knew what had passed between

Aniruddha and me in Wai. Certainly anybody noticing his behaviour to me since then had no reason to suspect that anything at all had happened. Maybe somebody just wanted to make trouble. But for whom? Aniruddha, or me?

Just the thought of him was painful now. It would invariably lead to me imagining the most ridiculous scenarios, up to and including me proposing marriage to him! The very idea of being in such a vulnerable situation was alarming, let alone the impropriety of the whole thing. I imagined how Aniruddha must have felt when he had asked me to marry him. Had he felt vulnerable at all? There had been some hesitation in his manner. But he had seemed confident of being accepted. How aggravating I had found him then! And now, everything was different. So much had happened and somehow, here I was – considering walking up to a good man and saying, 'Excuse me, would you like to marry me?'

But a part of me wondered what was the worst that could happen. He could say no, of course. Wait, 'could'? He would say no, obviously! And as painful as that would be, at least it would put a definitive end to this state of self-enforced uncertainty. See, hope is like a cockroach – notoriously difficult to kill. You have to squish it, decisively and heavily. And until Aniruddha said, 'No, thank you' to my question, to my face, hope would survive in my wretched heart. Just a small, sharp splinter, nestling in the softness and drawing blood. It didn't matter how sternly I told myself that all this was out of my reach. It didn't matter how much I reminded myself that I had a job waiting for me, that I wanted independence and dignity. Couldn't I have all that *and* marry him? a part of me would ask. Such a delightful notion. Such an impossible one.

Nobody got to have *everything*. This wasn't a romance novel after all. No. This was a different kind of story. In this one, Juee got to have her handsome prince. And I got to arrange the rukhwat.

I was sitting in the living room one morning, shortlisting items for precisely that display – Juee being unnecessarily versatile, I had a lot to choose from. So there I was, covered with crocheted pillow covers and surrounded by cross-stitched wall hangings, when there was a knock on the door. Malu had gone downstairs to her friend's house some time ago and had left the front door open, so I yelled, 'It's open!'

Sadanand walked in, took one look at me and grinned in amusement.

'Laugh all you want now, but remember, half these things will be on show at *your* wedding!' I teased, and then the smile completely dropped from my face, because following Sadanand into the house came Aniruddha.

Before either of us could say anything, Juee came out into the living room and spotted the two men.

'Aiyaa!' She beamed with pleasure. 'We weren't expecting you today!'

'Should I go back?' Sadanand teased, and laughed when Juee blushed.

'When did you return from Pune?' I asked Aniruddha, suddenly realising that I had two separate cushion covers draped on each shoulder. I pulled them down in a hurry and saw a shadow of a smile on his face.

'Last evening,' he replied quietly.

'Oh.'

'Yes.'

'I see.'

'Hmm.'

'How nice.'

'Yes.'

Juee gave me the kind of look she would have if I had suddenly started reciting the national anthem, then turned to Sadanand and asked, 'So, will you stop for lunch?'

'No, no,' he said, drawing closer to her. 'I was hoping . . . we could go to Parleshwar together.'

This statement was so distracting that I actually stopped actively not looking at Aniruddha and turned to look at Sadanand and Juee.

I had never had a romantic relationship, but even I knew that going together to a temple and taking darshan was not exactly the most romantic thing you could do with your fiancée.

Juee, however, beamed, as if she had waited all her life for a man to ask her to accompany him to a temple. 'You'll also come along, na, Ila?' she asked.

I didn't need to be asked twice. A walk to Parleshwar would give me time to talk to Aniruddha. I would ask after his sister. I would tell him I had found a job and that soon I could start paying him back. And I would, under no circumstances, ask him if, by any chance, hypothetically even, there was the slimmest sliver of a possibility that he would consider marrying me. I would not do that. No. Absolutely not.

Oh, God.

Juee and I got ready quickly and out we set. Mumbai footpaths had not been built to be social places: you could not expect a group of four people to walk side by side chatting, on a Mumbai footpath. So, naturally, we fell into two pairs,

Aniruddha and I walking in the front, Juee and Sadanand lagging behind.

I was glad of the distance between us. I was just wondering how to broach the subject of the money with him, when he spoke.

'How are your parents doing?' he asked.

'Oh.' I was a little thrown to be frank. 'They're . . . alright. Busy with the wedding preparations. They have gone to see some wedding halls right now.'

'Of course. I hope your Mama-Mami are doing well too?'

'Yes, they are.'

Was he going to enquire about my entire family, one by one? What next, asking how Malu's schooling was coming along? Hah. I wouldn't give him the chance.

'I'm glad to see you in Mumbai,' I said carefully. 'There was something I wanted to say to you.'

'Is it?' He looked at me with a hesitant smile. 'There was something I wanted to say to you as well.'

'What is it?'

'Ladies first.'

'Very well then.' I took a deep breath. 'I have got a job.'

He stopped walking and stared at me. 'Oh.' Shock was written all over his face, but he rallied. 'That is . . . that is excellent news. Congratulations.' He resumed walking by my side.

'Thank you. It's a post as a clerk in a cargo shipping company. Indu Enterprises. They seem like decent people. I start from the first of next month, so I was thinking—'

'Sorry, did you say Indu Enterprises?' he asked, a wary look on his face.

'Yes. I was thinking I could pay you by money order—'

'Is their office in Andheri?'

'Yes. So every month, I'll pay you a little if you—'

'There is really no need for that,' he said. A closed expression had come over his face.

'But I—'

We had reached the temple. We removed our footwear in the temple compound, and Sadanand and Juee led the way in.

The temple has two parts – one dedicated to Shankar, the other to Ganpati. We went to Lord Shankar's shrine first. As Sadanand rang the big brass bell and Juee bowed her head, Aniruddha and I waited in the mandap area. He turned to me.

'You don't have to pay me back, now or ever,' he told me earnestly. 'I didn't . . . do what I did for your sister to put you under some obligation. I did it because she is *your* sister and I . . .' He sighed. 'I wanted to be of help if I could.'

'I understand.' I bowed my head. 'But I can't accept such a big favour. I would feel . . . beholden to you for the rest of my life and—'

'Even if I was . . . a friend?' He was blinking furiously now, as if to keep some nameless emotion at bay. 'Because . . . I would like you to think of me as a friend. I know . . . that may be difficult for you, after all that has passed but . . . do you think you could . . . try?'

'A . . . friend?' My heart sank. So that was all he considered me then.

'In fact, truth be told' – he took a deep breath – 'I would like very much for you to think of me as more than a friend. Because that is . . . how I think of you. That is how I have thought of you for . . . a while now. Nothing has changed

347

in that respect, for me, since Wai. And I know' – he held up his hands – 'I know you have no intention of marrying and I respect that. You have a job now and that is wonderful and . . .' He cleared his throat. 'I would just like it . . . if I could be a part of your life in some way. As a friend, is also fine, if the alternative is not possible.'

'I—' I began, and then hesitated. I was suddenly finding it terribly difficult to look at his face. My gaze dropped to the hem of my sari. 'I . . . also consider you . . . rather more than a friend. I have, for some time now, as well.'

I raised my eyes to his face and found a relieved smile waiting for me.

'Oh,' he said, the smile broadening as our eyes met.

'Yes.'

'I see.'

'Yes.'

'That's good.'

'It is.'

'So . . . about getting married—?'

'I would like that.'

'Great.'

'Yes.'

'Hmm.' He nodded to himself, suddenly serious. 'This isn't because . . . I mean, you're not doing it out of any sense of obligation, right?'

'Of course not!'

'Good.' An impish smile, unlike any I had ever seen, appeared on his face now. 'Because you should probably know—'

'Ila?' Juee was standing before us, looking at me wide-eyed. I realised I had a huge smile pasted all over my face.

Adjusting my expression to a less startling one, I asked, 'Yes?'

'Do you not want to take darshan?' she asked, as if she were speaking to a small child.

'Darshan,' I repeated, stupidly. 'Yes. Of course. What a great idea.'

As I strode ahead and rang the bell, I was very aware of Aniruddha right behind me.

I doubt Lord Shankar has ever received such a jubilant pair of namaskars.

THIRTY-FIVE

The walk back home felt much lighter.

'You know,' Aniruddha said, as we walked down the footpath behind Sadanand and Juee. 'We have Kaveri Maushi to thank, for this turn of events.'

'Really?' I asked with a frown. 'How so?'

'After she spoke with you in Mumbai, she rang me up and complained about what she called your rude behaviour. She told me how you had flat-out refused to promise that you would never accept a proposal from me.' He looked at me sideways and smiled. 'I thought you would never do that if you had definitely decided against it. So I decided to come to Mumbai and find out for myself where you stood on the issue.'

'Then what was all that business about being friends?' I asked.

'Well, you said you had found a job.' He looked at me. 'I had to take that into account.'

'We still do.' I frowned. 'The office is in Mumbai. You live in Pune. How are we . . . I mean, after the wedding? I can't possibly live in Pune and work in Mumbai. How would that even work? Travelling even one way takes five hours at the minimum. I don't think they would agree to me living in another city, in any case. And I should hate to live here and have you live in a different city. It would be like being married to a travelling salesman!' I glared at him. 'I hope you realise I still intend to work after we get married?'

'I do. I think you'll be splendid at it.'

'But what do I tell the company? How are we going to manage it all?'

'I wouldn't be too worried about it.' He smiled and there was more than a trace of mischief in it. 'I'm sure you'll find them *very* accommodating.'

'Why do you say that?'

'Because I own Indu Enterprises.'

I stopped walking and stared at him. 'You . . . you *own* . . . ?'

'I mentioned I run my father's cargo company. It's named after my mother.'

'Your mother's name was Indu? I thought she was called . . .' I stopped. Did I really think the woman's name had been Mai?* That was like thinking Nana's actual name was Nana. Ridiculous.

---

* Among Maharashtrians of a certain generation, first names were reserved for birth certificates or death certificates. You were known by what you were called in your family. In a family with three sisters, for instance, the eldest was called Tai or Akka, the middle one was Mai and the youngest was Baby. These names stuck for the rest of

'Indumati Darshetkar,' he replied. 'I'll show you her picture sometime. Or you can see it when you visit the Pune office.'

'Pune office?' I asked. 'You mean there is more than one branch?'

'Of course.' He shrugged. 'It's a cargo business. We have branches all over the country. Including Pune, of course.'

My eyes grew even wider. Exactly how well off *was* this man? I didn't want to ask. For that matter, I didn't want to know.

'So . . .' I said slowly, 'I could just work in the Pune office then?'

'Like I said, I think you'll find Indu Enterprises very accommodating.'

'But . . .' I frowned as a thought struck me. 'Will it . . . won't it be awkward for the rest of the staff? Knowing I'm your wife, I mean? My immediate superiors . . . what if they treat me differently because I'm married to the owner of the company? I don't want any special treatment! I don't want people to wonder if I have got this job on my own merit or because I—'

'Okay, okay, calm down,' Aniruddha said in a reassuring tone. 'First tell me, what position have you been offered?'

'Junior clerk,' I replied.

---

your life. Boys had more random nicknames: Nana, Appa, Anna, Bapu – you were called these and other nicknames till they became your entire identity. Walk into a village in Maharashtra and ask, for instance, for Gajanan Sarpotdar and you will get blank stares. But ask someone where Appa Sarpotdar lives and they'll take you right to his doorstep.

'Excellent,' he said. 'That was my first post at the company as well.'

'What? You started as a clerk? But your father—'

'Appa insisted,' he said. 'He was a big believer in learning from the ground up. He had explained to all his managers that every raise, every promotion, I needed to earn it, and only then could I advance in the company. I learned so much that way and, later, nobody could question my authority when I took over from Appa. Because I had worked my way to the top. And I have no doubt that it's exactly what you will do, too.' He gave me a warm smile. 'I'll speak to the Pune office manager. He's been around since the time I was a clerk, so he knows how this goes. You have nothing to worry about.'

'And you're sure that will work? Things will be alright once I join?'

'Haven't you noticed?' he said, with that mischievous smile I was beginning to like very much indeed. 'Things just have a way of turning out exactly the way I want them to.'

I laughed as we reached the gates of our building. Sadanand and Aniruddha took their leave, and Juee and I began climbing the stairs.

'Sorry I left you with Aniruddha all this time,' Juee said. 'I know you don't like him.'

'Well . . .' This was as good a time as any to tell her. 'Actually, I do.' I put on a thoughtful expression. 'I think I'll marry him.'

Juee's expression was priceless. 'Good joke,' she said, when she recovered.

'No, I'm serious. He has asked me to marry him, and I have said yes.'

Juee nearly stumbled on the doorstep as she gaped at me. 'Enough already,' she chided. 'Is this something to joke about, honestly?'

'Oh, God!' I laughed. 'I am telling you the truth. Come here.'

I pulled her towards the balcony. There, in a low voice, I told her everything – Aniruddha's first proposal in Wai, our awkward run-in at Matheran, how changed he seemed at the time. When I explained how he had helped find Latika and later got her married to Jayant and found him a job, Juee looked thunderstruck.

'But . . . what are you saying?' She shook her head, as if trying to make sense of what I had just told her. 'Aniruddha did all this? And *that's* why you're marrying him?'

'No, no, it's not like that,' I said desperately. How was I supposed to make her understand? 'He did do a lot for our family, but that's not why . . . don't you see? He is a genuinely good man, who seems to like me. Not *despite* my appearance, or my desire to be independent or my frankness, but *because* of it. Because of who I am. Don't you understand how rare that is?'

Juee nodded hesitantly. She was smiling as if she did understand, but of course she didn't. She has only ever been loved for what she is. Because what she is, what she has always been is . . . perfect. Fair, beautiful, dutiful, obedient – what's not to love? But me? My complexion, my mouthiness, my belief that a woman can work and still have enough brain function left over to run a house – I had heard a million times how these were areas that needed to be changed; that without such a change, I was not worthy of love. And then, along came this man who saw all this and said, 'What's not to love?' What woman could resist something like that?

Juee couldn't possibly understand what that felt like. But she was smiling broadly now and I knew that, understand it or not, my older sister was happy for me, from the very bottom of her heart. She hugged me, grinning from ear to ear. 'As long as you're happy,' she whispered, just as Aai walked into the living room and saw us standing in the balcony, locked in a hug.

'Agabai, what is this?' she frowned. 'Why are you two making an exhibition of yourselves? People below can see. Come inside.'

'Ila has news,' Juee said, with an amused glance at me.

Well, she's not the only one who can tease.

'Yes, I do,' I said seriously. 'Aai, I have got a job and I begin next month.'

Aai shook her head in disgust. 'You and your fate!' she said scornfully. 'Do what you want and bear the consequences!'

'Ila!' Juee exclaimed. 'Tell her the other news!'

'Oh, right,' I said, with a nod. 'I may have to move and work from their Pune branch.'

The disgust on Aai's face turned to rage. 'Is your generation entirely incapable of asking for permission?' she roared. 'You think you can just come and announce such a big decision? Let me guess. You think you can abuse my brother's hospitality and live in his house while you're there? Hasn't he done enough for us?'

'Aai, calm down!' Juee interrupted, before turning to me with a warning look. 'You better tell her, or I will!'

'Okay, fine.' I held up my hands in a gesture of peace. 'Aai, a rather rich young man has asked me to marry him and I have said yes.'

To say Aai was surprised would be to miss an opportunity for embellishment. Because she wasn't just surprised, she was dumbfounded by shock. Rabid disbelief plastered her features. For a few seconds she just looked from Juee's face to mine, as if willing one of us to crack and reveal that all this was a massive prank. But the two of us simply continued to look earnestly back at her and, moments later, a smile of such incredulity appeared on her face that I had to smile myself.

'You . . .' She pointed a finger at me. 'You are ready to get married?'

'Yes, Aai.'

'To a rich young man?'

'Yes, Aai.'

'And what about his family . . . what are they like?'

How to answer this question? Aniruddha had no family except a sister. Their last name ensured that Aai would find them acceptable. But that was secondary to what *he* was: my kind of person. *My* person, really.

'It's Aniruddha Darshetkar!' Juee squealed, clearly unable to keep quiet any longer.

Aai's eyes nearly popped out of their sockets at this point. 'You mean, Sadanand's friend?' she asked. 'That tall one?' She nodded approvingly. 'Very handsome boy, I have always felt. And so quiet! Only a lucky few get a quiet husband. And he is rich, you say?' Another enthusiastic nod, followed by a frown. 'And he asked you to marry him? Just like that?'

'Yes,' I replied.

'And he is okay with you being . . .' She waved a hand vaguely in front of my face.

'Yes!'

'Really? Huh. Surprising. But good, good. Now, tell me

what he likes to eat and ask him to come over for lunch! Whatever he likes! Well done, my girl, well done! Won't your father be surprised!' And with that, she pulled me into a hug and thumped my back fondly.

Aai was wrong. Nana wasn't surprised so much as aghast.

'Why?' he asked, complete bewilderment spread across his face. 'Why did you say yes? Look, your mother might nag you to get married, but there is always a place for you in this house. There always will be, as long as I am alive. You didn't need to rush off and say yes to a man you barely like!'

'It's not like that, Nana . . .'

'Then what is it? Is it because he is rich? Money isn't everything, bala. I thought you wanted to be independent! What happened to that?'

'I will be,' I said gently. 'I have found a job and he thinks me working after marriage is a good idea.'

'Look, all I know is you can't get married if you don't love and respect the person you're marrying. Everything else is negotiable, but not that. Do you love him? Do you respect him as a person? Does he feel the same way about you? Think carefully before you answer, bala. This is the question of your whole life.'

I sighed. Had my contempt for Aniruddha been so obvious all this time that even Nana was aware of it? Nana, who had been completely unaware that Latika was slowly slipping out of his hands?

'I do respect him,' I said quietly. 'And love him too. And when you find out the truth, so will you.'

So I told him.

After he had heard me out, Nana sat back in the armchair,

a thoughtful expression on his face. 'If what you say is true,' he said finally, 'then I owe that boy my thanks. To say nothing of a pile of money.'

'He doesn't want repaying.'

'Just thanks it is, then.' He grinned. 'I will offer the money, of course. Then he can have the pleasure of refusing me to my face and feeling honourable because of it.' He got up from the chair and held me by the shoulders. 'You seem to have chosen well,' he said fondly. Then his eyes brimmed and he patted my head. 'I just wish you hadn't chosen so soon.'

And with a sniff, he left the room.

THIRTY-SIX

As it turned out, both Juee's wedding and mine became quite the talk of the society. First, because both grooms-to-be had stubbornly refused to take anything from their new in-laws, aside from their brides. And, wonder of wonders, both had first offered to, and then forced, their father-in-law to split the wedding expenses with them.

Aai – ever the economical one – had suggested we have a joint wedding to cut costs even further. 'All our guests will already be there for Juee's wedding, why ask them to come a second time? And just think of how much we will save!' she had reasoned.

But Aniruddha had quietly and firmly refused and Aai had been too cowed by the serious expression of her future son-in-law to force her point. So it was that a month after Juee's wedding, at the first available auspicious muhurta, Aniruddha and I were all set to marry at, appropriately enough, the Lokmanya Seva Sangh hall where we had run into each other all those months ago.

Sitting cross-legged on the dais with Aniruddha by my side, and the priest chanting sacred mantras, I cast a glance at the guests gathered in the hall, seated on the rows of plastic chairs and watching the proceedings, like I once had at Arun's wedding. There was Arun himself, with Sudha and his parents, surrounded by others from our society. Behind them sat some of Aniruddha and Sadanand's college friends. And what looked like the entire staff of the Mumbai branch of Indu Enterprises, led by Mr Kadam.

And, right in the front, Sadanand and Kalyani – him with his customary cheerful smile, her looking like she was being forced to swallow a bitter pill, which I suppose she was, in a way. Juee had told me that once it was certain that she would be marrying Sadanand, Kalyani had resumed her initial sweet behaviour with my sister, acting as if nothing at all had happened. She was considerate and friendly, and tried at every opportunity to behave as if Juee were her long-lost sister, rather than her sister-in-law. But Juee was wise to her wiles now and didn't let any of that fakery take her in.

I beamed at Juee now, as she sat a little way away from me, in the position of honour reserved for the karavali. She looked as beautiful as ever in a royal blue Mysore silk sari, but now she also looked happy – happier than I had ever seen. I saw her catch Sadanand's eye and blush sweetly, and my heart sang for my sister.

On Aniruddha's side as karavali sat Gauri, resplendent in a Maheshwari silk sari, the colour of aboli flowers. We had got to know each other a little better over the past couple of months. Like her brother, Gauri didn't confide in everybody and had taken some time to come out of her shell. But once she did, we got along famously. I think she was a little in awe of me, especially once she found out that I intended to work in the family business after the wedding. I hoped that with time, the awe would change to affection.

Behind Gauri, on the right of the dais, sat Malu, looking very grown-up in a new silk Punjabi dress. She would be the last one to leave home. But with three daughters married off, hopefully Aai would ease the pressure on her, poor thing. And I hoped that, with us gone, Malu would come into her own. It couldn't have been easy to be the youngest in a home with sisters like Juee, me and Latika.

Latika! She had been invited, of course, and had written back saying that she and Jayant would absolutely love to come, if only I could convince Aniruddha to send them some money for the steamer fare and some appropriate clothes, because, you know, we don't wear traditional clothes here, they're far too old-fashioned . . .

I think she is slightly intimidated by Aniruddha, though, because she ended her letter by saying that she would understand if I couldn't broach the topic with him.

I was, obviously, only too glad not to and after mourning the fact that even living in foreign hadn't improved my sister for the better, I thought nothing more of the matter.

The only person who actually missed Latika's presence was Aai, who had mentioned several times in the past few weeks how nice it would have been to have her beloved daughter with her for two such happy occasions.

Today, she was bustling about in a traditional nine-yard sari, fiddling with my meagre rukhwat. Despite my protests, she had insisted on passing off a few of Juee's creations as mine because, 'it doesn't look good, an empty rukhwat. You, na, don't understand anything!' I had marvelled at how she had found time in the middle of planning two weddings to make puran polis to include in the rukhwat. But I had let her have her way. After all, this was probably the last thing she'd win at with me.

Would she cry, when it was time to bid me farewell today? Or would she sigh with relief?

I knew what Nana would do, of course. Make a joke, perhaps philosophise and try to cover up his real feelings. There he was now, standing at the end of the dais in his dhotar and kurta, chatting amiably with one of Aniruddha's paternal uncles. How I would miss Nana! How different life would be, without his witticisms, his ability to laugh at what seemed like the gravest problems. But I suppose what I was losing in that respect would be more than made up for in what I was gaining.

I glanced at Aniruddha. He was sitting next to me, his usual sober expression firmly in place. When he caught me looking, he gave me a small smile. The groom's family is supposed to gift the bride the green sari she wears for the wedding rituals. With no parents to look into these things, Aniruddha had simply taken Gauri and me shopping. We had come away with a parrot-green paithani that Aai would never have allowed me to wear. But Aniruddha had nodded in approval when I had held it against me and simply said, 'If you like it, get it.'

And so I had. Now, draped in the soft silk, my face framed with pearl mundaavlya, I waited as the bhatji instructed Aniruddha to tie the mangalsutra around my neck. He reached out, our eyes met and I couldn't help but smile as

I saw his expression soften, the necklace of black and gold beads suspended between his fingers.

And that's when a voice called out, 'Stop! Stop!'

Aniruddha paused stone-faced, glaring at the guests to see what fool had interrupted us in such a crass fashion. To my surprise, it was Vishnubhat. He was sitting in the second row, next to Chitra, my newly pregnant friend sporting the slightest hint of a tummy. He had his trademark oily grin pasted to his face and he kept looking back and forth between us and Kaveribai, who was sitting in the front row, her daughter sniffling by her side.

She had taken news of the wedding with bad grace and written a strongly worded letter to Aniruddha, expressing her displeasure in no uncertain terms. He had nevertheless invited her to the wedding and as she sat there staring at us with a dour expression, I had wondered if she was here today to give her blessing or to make trouble. The latter, from the sounds of it.

'Kaveribai insists . . .' Vishnu began, then saw my raised eyebrows. 'That is . . . she would like it if Ila recites an ukhana* on this occasion.'

---

* An ukhana is a rhyming couplet that includes the name of one's husband woven into the lyrics. In the olden days, these allowed a married woman to show off her creativity and also to actually use her husband's first name, which would otherwise rust from disuse, given that she would usually refer to him as 'aho'. In the average Maharashtrian wedding, married women ranging from the mother of the bride to the karavalis, would be asked to recite ukhanas at every possible opportunity and ritual. Whether this was just gentle ragging or whether there was a point system involved, remains unspecified.

Ah. The ukhana. I was wondering when we'd get to that. I looked Kaveribai right in the eye and nodded gracefully. Then, I looked at my husband-to-be.

'You don't have to, if you don't want to,' he said gently, but I just smiled.

'I'd love to,' I told him.

Immediately, Juee got to her feet and called out to the guests: 'Ila is reciting an ukhana, please listen!' and the hall fell silent. Well, as silent as a wedding hall can possibly fall.

I cleared my throat and recited: 'Life doesn't come easy for some, nor by accident comes love; for finding a love like Aniruddha's, I thank the Gods above.'

And, as the guests applauded and Aniruddha tied the mangalsutra around my neck, I knew in my heart of hearts that I meant every word.

AUTHOR'S NOTE

I've taken a few liberties with history and geography in this book, so I may as well come clean.

Latika's fangirling over Rajesh Khanna is a little after the height of the actual fan hysteria over him, which peaked by 1972 – a full four years before the events in this book.

Wai has no temple to any deity called Bhagwati – that, along with its antecedents and lore, is purely a figment of my imagination.

Oh, and while Charles Sobhraj definitely preyed on tourists in hippie destinations like Goa, his presence there during the time frame of the book is me taking creative licence.

ACKNOWLEDGMENTS

It's one thing to write a book set in a decade you've been alive in; it's quite a different kettle of fish when it's set five years before you were born. Online research only gets you so far. So if I've got anything historically right in this book, it's largely thanks to my family, especially my parents, who enthusiastically answered all my random questions about the 70s without a word of complaint.

Every book needs at least one good champion and I'm so incredibly thankful that I found two. One in my wonderful agent Judith Murray and the folks at Greene & Heaton. And the other, my lovely editor Sarah Hodgson and everybody at Corvus. Their support and faith, and their many words of encouragement, have been instrumental in making this book what it is. Not to mention all the very helpful suggestions by Belinda Jones, which helped make this story more coherent for non-Indian readers.

I'm also blessed in having some wonderful beta readers:

Suhaan, Pavitra and Ishita – thank you for your detailed and very helpful feedback. I love it when you say nice things about my writing, heh, heh.

I also want to thank my friend Ghotge, for the loan of his underused first name. And for not being an Aniruddhat about it.

And lastly, to my daughter Irawati and my husband Arjun, I want to say thank you for being my constant supporters. I am so, so lucky to have you both in my life.